COUPLE ON HOLD

SHANDI BOYES

Edited by

MOUNTAINS WANTED PUBLISHING

ALSO BY SHANDI BOYES

Perception Series:

Saving Noah

Fighting Jacob

Taming Nick

Redeeming Slater

Saving Emily (*Novella*)

Wrapped up with Rise Up (*Novella - should be read after Bound*)

Enigma:

Enigma of Life

Unraveling an Enigma

Enigma: The Mystery Unmasked

Enigma: The Final Chapter

Beneath the Secrets

Beneath the Sheets

Spy Thy Neighbor

The Opposite Effect

I Married a Mob Boss

Second Shot

The Way We Are

The Way We Were

Sugar and Spice

Lady in Waiting

Man in Queue

Couple on Hold

Enigma: The Wedding

Silent Vigilante

Bound Series:

Chains

Links

Bound

Restrained

Psycho

Russian Mob Chronicles:

Nikolai: A Mafia Prince Romance

Nikolai: Taking Back What's Mine

Nikolai: What's Left of Me

Nikolai: Mine to Protect

Asher: My Russian Revenge

Nikolai: Through the Devil's Eyes

RomCom Standalones:

Just Playin'

The Drop Zone

Ain't Happenin'

Christmas Trio

Falling for a Stranger

Coming Soon:

Skitzo

Trey

ONE

ALEX

I wish for the storm on the horizon to roll in as I watch Dane's casket being lowered into the ground. This is it: a folded flag in his wife's trembling hands, a three-gun salute that startles his daughters, and the fucking wheelchair that commenced his demise. His life is now over. Done. Forgotten before half the mourners have left his gravesite.

I'm mad—*I'm downright fucking furious*—but more than anything, I'm sad.

This wasn't him. That chair they placed at his gravesite is a mockery to the man he once was. They should have let him leave this world standing tall and proud. They should have been the rod in his spine when it was wrongly removed from his back. If they had done their job, I could wake up from this nightmare. I could see his smiling face and smell his taco-laced breath. Instead, I bend down to gather his youngest daughter, Addison, in my arms, the complexity of the situation lost on her since she is only two.

She blows raspberries on my cheek before giggling at my beard tickling her chin. It's a beautiful thing to hear on such a dark and dreary day. Her girly squeals and talc-powder bottom pulls me out of the tempestuous place I've been huddled in the past five days. I thought those eight minutes Dane and I spent hunkered down in the field all those years ago would be my darkest time. I had no idea.

I've lost agents before, men above and below me, but this is different. Dane wasn't just an agent. He was my friend. My brother. The mischief-maker who ensured no task was ever mundane. I might not have survived the academy if it wasn't for him. I saw rules and protocol. He saw adventures and opportunities. We were the same, yet so completely different.

I stop reminiscing when a flash of silver catches my eye. Kristin smiles before handing me a tiny shovel. When I remain standing frozen, fucking lost, she jerks her head to the hole in the ground that will now be forever known as Dane's final resting place. I shake my head when she attempts to remove Addison from my arms. *This will be easier if she stays.*

I don't need to tell Addison what to do when we reach her daddy's gravesite. She digs the pointy end of the shovel into the dirt the pastor uncovered ten minutes ago before tossing it into the hole.

I expect her to continue shoveling, but she surprises me by dropping the shovel to her side before launching herself into my arms. *Maybe I didn't give her enough credit? Perhaps she can feel the sentiment in the air?*

"Good girl," I praise her when her big blue eyes seek approval from mine. "You did great."

And now I must do the same.

It takes another twenty minutes for each member of Dane's family to say their final goodbyes. I've never understood the ritual of shoveling dirt into a grave. I get that it's symbolic that man was born of this earth and has returned to this earth upon his death, but shouldn't the person who has passed be forever carried in our hearts? Why must this be it?

Recognizing that standing graveside at my best friend's funeral won't give me the answers I am seeking, I hand Addison to her mother before heading to the procession of funeral cars tucked in the bottom far corner of the graveyard. The further I travel, the more my focus shifts from one heartache to another. It's been five days since I've seen Regan. Five days of unanswered calls, five days of unread messages, and five days of letting my anger fester to the point of being unhealthy.

She is the cause of the fury slicking my veins, the reason I can't numb my feelings. I need her, but instead of standing beside me as I face my darkest day, she stays at his side, protecting him, sheltering him. *Choosing him.*

I understand she's mad that she caught me in a lie, but I can't fix the mistakes I've made if she refuses to talk to me. I guess I should be grateful? Maybe she's staying away to save me more heartache, because she doesn't want to come clean. I'm not the only one at fault here. I did wrong, but so did she.

If she had talked to me instead of running, I could have explained the documents she found on my computer. I could have shown her that I never used our relationship as a means to get to Isaac. Then perhaps, also, I could have proven Isaac isn't who she thinks he is.

Regan sees what she wants to see. I know the truth.

I was trained to see fact through fiction. I was taught the difference between a man clamoring for power, and one who takes it. I know a criminal when I see one. Isaac Holt is a criminal. He is an immorally unlawful man who blinds people's morals with fancy credit cards and apartments above their pay grade.

I thought Regan was smart, that her beauty was her second most valuable asset, but right now, peering up at the ugly gray sky that won't free me from pretending the wetness on my cheeks isn't tears, I'm beginning to wonder if I knew her at all.

I told her I loved her, but she never said it back. So why am I praying for a miracle as I dial her number for the fifth time today?

Another crack adds to my already crumbling heart when Regan's velvety smooth voice jingles down the line: "You've reached Regan. You know what to do."

I hang up.

No message left.
No pleas for understanding.
Nothing.

TWO

ALEX

It's cold today. Winter has been and passed, but Arlington, Virginia, failed to get the memo. The winds are so brisk, I won't be surprised to see Dane's old sedan covered with a thick layer of snow when we make our way back to the parking lot.

"Come here, Addi. You'll freeze if you don't do up your coat."

She jumps down from the climbing frame she's daringly scaling to race my way. Addison got her personality from her father and her looks from her mother. Her blonde hair is extra bright in the dreary conditions, but her bright blue eyes are a little dull compliments of the super rosy cheeks the nippy winds have given her. She's a cute little thing who's quickly wiggled her way into my heart the past four months.

That wouldn't be hard with how much time I've spent with her, her big sister, Isla, and her mom. I promised Dane I'd take care of his girls no matter what. I've kept my promise.

The past four months have been rough, and I'm not solely referring to Dane's passing. There has still been no contact between Regan and me. For the first week, I called her a minimum of ten times a day. By week two, I lowered my nuisances to three to four incidents in a twenty-four hour period. Once week three rolled by without any returned calls or replies to my many text messages, I did what all desperate *can't take a hint* men do: I called her family ranch.

You can imagine how well that went down? From what I could gather in between Hayden's threats of disembowelment, Regan wasn't avoiding my calls because her cell phone service at the ranch was spotty. She was avoiding me.

Week four saw me facing a whole new set of issues. Not only did Regan cancel her cell service, Dane's life insurance provider denied Kristin's policy claim. Their denial left his family with nothing but a house they can't afford to sell because they owe more than it's worth and a whole lot more heartache.

Dane took his life, believing his family would be better off without him, but he failed to read the fine print. When he was brought in as a consultant at the Bureau, he switched insurance companies. With a new policy, came a new clause. Suicide was not paid for the first two years. He left his family with nothing. Not him. Not the money he thought they'd have. *Nothing.*

Can you see my dilemma? My heart was in Ravenshoe, but my integrity was in Arlington. I couldn't chase Rae even if she wanted me to.

In the beginning, I kept tabs on her, more through Isaac's case than a personal tail, but as the weeks went by, my attention to Isaac's daily movement sheet waned. His schedule hadn't altered from when we began investigating him nearly a year earlier; there was just one detrimental change: Regan was never mentioned in his notes—except once.

It tore me to pieces even more than the words Brandon uttered outside of her apartment four months ago.

Someone on Isaac's team had secured a booking at a family planning clinic in Hopeton, Florida. Although it was illegal for me to ask, I requested for Brandon to hack into the clinic's servers. I needed to know who visited their establishment on a late Tuesday afternoon two months ago.

I ended my day wishing I wasn't so inquisitive.

The appointment was for an R. Myers. Her contact details matched the cell phone Regan once owned, and the "operation" was paid for with Isaac's company credit card. Even if I weren't an agent, I'm not stupid enough to misread that evidence.

I gave Regan a part of me I've never given anyone, and she destroyed it.

I'm not referring to my heart, either.

My back molars stop grinding when a pair of tiny hands cup my cheeks. Addison stares into my eyes, hers oddly familiar. "Awright?" She stumbles over the letter she can't pronounce.

"I'm alright," I assure her while doing up the final button on her winter coat. "There you go, nice and toasty." I tug her into my chest so she won't see the deceit in my eyes.

Addison is an old soul who's been here before. She can count to ten, eat three bowls of cereal for breakfast, and thinks she's cupid. I'm proud of her first two qualities, but I wish she'd cut back on her last trait. I understand her game plan. She can see her momma is hurting, and she wants to ease her pain, but she's looking in the wrong direction if she thinks I can replace her dad.

Even if she weren't my best friend's girl, I'll only ever see Kristin as a friend. Nothing will change that. Not the adorable little eyes of a near three-year-old who holds my hand before reaching out to secure her mother's with her other, nor the six-year-old who misses her dad as much as she's angry at him for what he did.

Unlike Addison, Isla isn't an old soul. She can't understand why her dad doesn't pick her up from school each afternoon, or why he isn't sitting in his office when she charges inside after she's finished ballet. All she sees is his empty chair and the man she wrongly believes is trying to fill his place.

Although Kristin hasn't told the girls what happened the day she arrived home to find Dane, they know what occurred. Kristin does a good job of putting on a brave face, but nothing can reignite the light in her daughter's eyes. Their brightness was snuffed the instant

Dane died because, just like me, they lost a part of their soul that day.

"Again!" Addison races a few steps in front of Kristin and me before leaping off the ground. She giggles loudly when her feet swing in the air. When they return to a solid surface, she squeals, "Again."

Kristin and I continue down the sidewalk of Isla's school with a giggling, swinging Addison between us. Just as it did at Dane's funeral, her laughter heals me . . . until she says, "Again, Daddy!"

Hearing her call me "Daddy" doesn't hurt as much as it did the first time. Don't get me wrong, I'm still shocked, and in all honesty, I don't like it, but after speaking with Kristin, I understand Addison's confusion. She didn't know Dane outside of his wheelchair. He couldn't chase her through the house as I have the past three months, or teach her how to swim in her grandparents' heated pool.

He was there for his girls, but Kristin said numerous times that something was off with him long before she discovered him in his office. He started withdrawing by no longer eating dinner with them and not helping Kristin put the girls to bed. He became a recluse, his focus devoted on nothing but work. I thought keeping him occupied was a good thing. Only now am I realizing how terribly wrong I was.

Striving to ease my guilt, I extend my arm out to its full reach, ensuring Addison gets the biggest launch. When she is high in the air, I release my grip on her hand then catch her in my arms. She giggles and squirms when I burrow my chin into her neck to tickle her with my beard. Every tug she makes on my hair, every deep chuckle, they soothe the nicks in my heart, easing its bleed from a body-maiming gush to a slight trickle.

I stop growling like a grizzly bear when a deep voice says, "So it's true. You do have a wife and kids."

My heart does a wild beat when I pop my head above Addison's now messy bed head. Although the Myers standing across from me isn't the one I am hoping for, any Myers is better than none.

"Hayden . . . what are you doing here?"

He balks but remains quiet. It's unfortunate for him I don't need to hear his words to know of his confession. Clearly, I'm not the only one who bends the rules to protect the people he loves. Ayden is as expendable as me, as his position in the Bureau is the only way Hayden could be aware of my location. I only returned to a desk job last week. Prior to that, I was off the radar. Even Isaac's hacker/security personnel wouldn't have been able to find me.

With a swallow, I place Addison onto her feet so I can scan our location. A woman with an aura like Regan could never be missed, but it's been a long time since I've seen her, so maybe my perception isn't as great as it once was.

My eyes return to Hayden when he says, "She's not here; she's not aware I'm here. I don't even know why I'm here! I guess I wanted to see it with my own two eyes. I'll give it to you, boy, you played me *real* good. I thought you truly cared for Regan."

I want to tell him I cared for her more than he'll ever know, but Kristin's determined scowl and Addison's frightened face stops me. This isn't a conversation I want to have in front of them, much less at an elementary school with parents looking on.

Regrettably, Hayden hasn't noticed the attention his tall frame, wide shoulders, and angry snarl has gained. All he sees is red. "You hurt my girl."

I nod, accepting some of the blame for the downfall of my relationship with Regan. "I did."

Hayden's next fist clench isn't as firm. He's shocked by my admission. He thought I'd fight with the same gusto I did the last time we had words. I don't know why. I had someone to fight for then. I don't now.

"Does she know about Rae?" Hayden nudges his head to Kristin, who is frozen at our side. She's not scared, more cautious than anything.

"Yes." I nod. "But things aren't as you're perceiving them."

Hayden scoffs, the anger lining his face returning stronger than ever. "You've lied before, so why would I believe a thing you say now?!"

"Yeah, I did lie. But I'm not now."

Hayden steps closer, not willing to back down from what he came here to do. I've seen his stance many times in my years at the Bureau. He's mad, which is making him hostile, and his protective instincts are in overdrive, causing him to be more unhinged than usual. He's literally seconds away from detonation, but I have no fucking clue how to talk him off the ledge.

"You deceived her."

"In a way, yes." I use a calm, nurturing tone, checking my naturally engrained machoism at the door. Now is not the time to let my ego speak. "But not with Kristin—"

Before all my assurance leaves my mouth, Hayden yells, "You made her the other woman!"

"No, Hayden. Never." My head shakes more furiously than Hayden's body as he struggles to hold in his anger. "I would *never* do that to her. I loved her."

A mere nanosecond after the words leave my mouth, I want to ram them back in there. I'm supposed to be calming him down, not ramping up his anger.

It's too late now; his anger has reached fever-pitch.

Addison lets out a squeak when Hayden storms the four paces between us so he can fist my shirt in a threatening way. His angry eyes, identical to his daughter's in every way, bear down on me as his nostrils flare. "*Loved?* As in past tense? If you truly *loved* her, you'd still *love* her. She's like her mother—incapable of forgetting."

Although I wholeheartedly agree with him, for once, I don't put myself first. The frightened eyes of a little girl are staring up at me as she fights to save me from the monsters I've sheltered her from the past three months.

"It's okay, baby," I assure Addison when she kicks Hayden in the shins. "He's just upset. It's alright. I'm alright."

"No!" Addison screams when Kristin scoops her up to drag her away from the violent scene unfolding in front of a group of parents arriving to collect their children. "Awex! Awex!"

She kicks and wails against Kristin the entire time, her desire to protect me as fierce as Hayden's wish to safeguard his daughter from more pain. I understand both their plights. Hayden thinks I did his daughter wrong. Addison doesn't know me well enough yet to understand I'm not the superhero she thinks I am. I'm just a man trying to forget one failed promise by ensuring he keeps another.

I wait until Addison is snatched from my view by a large tree trunk before returning my focus to Hayden. Not eager to add more pain to his already brimming eyes, I give it one last shot. "I get you're angry, but you need to calm down. This is *not* an appropriate environment to have this conversation."

After scanning the crowd surrounding us, many of them calling in assistance from the authorities, I pull back in an attempt to yank out of Hayden's grasp. It appears as though Regan got her stubbornness from her father. Hayden refuses to let me go.

"This is your last warning, Hayden. Get your hands off me." My once calm voice is a thing of the past. I'm angry, more burned from prior incidents than the one occurring right now, but mad all the same. Our tussle mimics the one we had months ago in the middle of a field, except then, I was fighting to keep his daughter, not let her go.

Hayden is thirty years older than me and a little less fit, but he doesn't back down when looking a bull in the eyes. "You hurt my girl. Now I'll hurt you."

I dip low to miss his swinging fist before leveraging my weight. I need to ensure the twenty pounds of muscle I've lost the past three months don't affect me when I ram my hand into Hayden's throat before raising my knee to his groin.

Guilt surges through me when he falls to his knees, his lungs wheezing from both my jab to his jugular and his balls. Usually, I use the assailant's subdued position to secure cuffs to their wrists, but since this is Hayden, a man I have no intention of arresting, I crouch down in front of him until we come eye to eye.

For a man of his age, Hayden's grit is undogged. He comes at me again, knocking the wind from my lungs as effectively as his daughter's smile did the first time I saw her. My initial thought is to react to his hit with another bout of violence, but a bell ringing stops me. Instead, I pinch the nerve in his neck. I don't squeeze it hard enough he'll pass out, but he's not going anywhere anytime soon.

"If I had my gun. . ."

I cut off his threat by saying, "Regan wasn't the only one hurt; this has been hard on me too, but you're not seeing the entire picture. What you *think* you know, and what you *do* know are two completely different things." I point in the direction Kristin and Addison went. "Kristin is *not* my wife, and Addison is just a little girl who doesn't understand why she can't visit her daddy in heaven." My words choke a bit during my last sentence, but I pretend they didn't.

While watching Isla cautiously approach us on my right, I dig my wallet out of my pocket. The color drains from Hayden's cheeks when I place an invoice on the cracked concrete under his knees. It is tattered and old, as damaged as my heart.

"Since you're so gung-ho on seeking answers, why don't I give you some facts to work with?"

Hayden's hand shakes when he lifts the family planning clinic invoice from the ground. He stares at me, certain I'm lying, but knowing I have no reason to. As far as we're both concerned, I'm entrenched in a hole I'll never get out of, so why would I bother fighting with half-truths?

"You still lied to her." Hayden's voice isn't as deep as usual, more pained than anything.

"Yeah, I did." I work my jaw side to side before forcing out my next set of words, "But we could have worked past that if she had given me the chance." My eyes take in the invoice I carry more to remind me of the promises I made than to cause more heartache. "But that's something I'll never get over."

I wipe the riled expression off my face, force a fake smile in its place, then swivel my torso to face Isla. "Hey, baby girl. How was your day at school?"

She drops her eyes to the ground as her lips furl downwards. "Where's *my* mom? *She's* supposed to pick me up. Not you."

Hayden takes in a sharp breath, hearing what Isla really wants to say as readily as me: *You'll never be my dad.*

"She's just over there." I nudge my head to the tree Kristin and a still wailing Addison are hiding behind. "Give me a sec to say goodbye to my friend, then I'll take you to them. . ."

I stop talking when Isla pushes off her feet and charges in the direction I gestured. In less than a heartbeat, I take off after her, realizing the promise I made to Dane the day before his death must remain at the top of my agenda. I shifted my goals for years, believing one day justice would be served. Now, five and a half years later, I'm still working with the same set of excuses.

One day, I'll get my revenge.

That day just isn't today.

"This isn't Regan. She wouldn't do this," is the last thing I hear Hayden yell before Addison's cries switch to giggles of happiness with nothing but a hairy chin.

THREE

ALEX

"Oh, god. I'm so sorry."

Kristin covers her flaming cheeks with her hand as she spins away from me. I finish the sit-up I'm halfway through completing before standing to my feet. I would put on a shirt to cover my sweaty torso, but I am without adequate clothing.

"I thought you were asleep?" Upon hearing the exhaustion in my voice, my eyes stray to the clock. *Fuck.* I've been working out for nearly three hours straight.

"I was. I was just. . . uh. . . thirsty." Kristin spins back around to face me, her nerves growing the more she twirls. "Do you often work out in the living room at 2 AM?"

"Mainly." I grab a bottle of water off the table and chug down half its contents before slumping onto the sofa. I'm fucking exhausted, but it feels good getting back to the routine I had before. . . I stop short before I say her name. Four months have passed, yet it still hurts when I think about her.

My teeth grit. I need to stop being such a soft cock. Regan moved on months ago, yet I'm still wallowing in self-pity. Thank fuck my dad is on assignment on the other side of the country, or he would have slapped the bitch straight out of me.

When Kristin stares at me, waiting for more than a one-word answer, I say, "I figured late night workouts would save the girls from seeing me like this." I wave my empty hand down my body, doubling the redness on Kristin's cheeks. "The last thing I want to do is scare them again."

Kristin would never say anything, but I know Isla saw me take down Hayden last month. She's been even more hostile with me since that day, but in a scared, timid way I hate.

My focus snaps back to the present when Kristin murmurs under her breath, "I don't see that *ever* being an issue."

Certain I heard her tone in the wrong manner, I ask, "What have you got there?" I nudge my head to the CD-ROM she's clutching for dear life, hoping to get our conversation back in safe waters.

"Footage from my wedding." She smiles in a way I haven't seen in months while moving closer to me. It's not a reminiscing smile. It's more carefree than that. "Do you remember the bridal waltz Dane forced me to do?"

I laugh. "How could I forget it? Although I don't think you should call it a bridal waltz. It was more a corny eighties 'Thriller'/rumba routine."

She kicks me in the foot before sinking into the empty seat next to me. "I found some video footage in a file on Dane's computer. Thought I might show it to the girls in the morning."

My brow cocks. "You know Dane hid that video for a reason, right?"

"Yes!" she squeals with a laugh. "But it will be good for them to see us like that. You know, carefree and happy. *Not fighting.*" She whispers her last two words.

Her comment is hard to hear, but it doesn't stop me from asking, "Were things really that bad between you two before he passed?"

She peers at me with hurt eyes, upset I'm questioning her integrity. It isn't that I don't believe her; I'm just having a hard time picturing Dane in the manner she's depicted him the past few months. Clearly, his cause of death is proof he was depressed, but for the most part, his life was like mine.

I guess that proves why I shouldn't be questioning her. Men like us don't display our pain for the world to see. We hide it away, often fooling everyone around us that we're fine. Even those closest to me are unaware I've been living without my heart the past four months.

I'm drawn from dangerous thoughts when a zesty scent lingers in my nostrils. Kristin has raised her hand to my face to run her fingers through the wiry hair on my chin. This isn't the first time she's done this the past four months, but it is the first time the air has held this much sentiment.

"I can still remember the shock of seeing you for the first time with a beard. In all honesty, I *hated* it." She breathes out heavily before her tongue delves out to replenish her lips with moisture. "It's grown on me now. It really suits you."

When she scoots a little closer, my eyes drift to the entrance of the living room. I don't know who I'm looking for. The girls went to bed hours ago, and Dane is in a place where he can't reprimand me for getting cozy with his girl. *Unfortunately.*

Kristin's recently brushed teeth fan my lips with mint when she murmurs, "It could have been me and you, you know? You did ask me out first."

Her voice is huskier than I've heard before. Deeper—*needy.*

I remove her hands from my face and place them into her lap. "Then Dane blew in and swept you off your feet."

My attempt to stop skating on thin ice is short-lived when Kristin replies, "Yeah, he did." She licks her lips for the second time before asking, "Have you ever wondered what would have happened if he didn't?"

I shrug, truly unsure. I liked Kristin, but that was because she was hot and available. I never saw it becoming a long-term thing like she had with Dane.

Could have had, I correct myself. Ten years is nowhere near a lifetime.

"I think it could have been something." She swallows numerous times in a row before murmuring, "*Could* be something."

For a second, I want to forget that the wavy blonde hair tickling my shoulder belongs to my best friend's girl, that the lust blazing in her eyes doesn't match the flame I saw in them when Dane recited his vows, or that my mind hasn't been clouded with confusion since my run-in with Hayden four weeks ago, but as much as I wish we weren't two people weighed down with grief, I can't. This is the fucked-up world I live in.

"Kristin. . ." My murmur is more in warning than hope from her hands returning to my face. This is the closest I've been to a woman in months, but it still feels wrong.

The tension in my jaw slackens when Kristin murmurs, "You've got cotton candy stuck in your beard."

I smile, recalling fond memories for once instead of bad. Addison has been nagging me to take her to Disney World for weeks. Although I will take her one day, with my desk salary going toward keeping a roof over her head, I don't see that being any time in the near future. Instead, we went to a local fair. The kids had a blast. Even Isla giggled a handful of times. That alone was worth the dent to my bank balance.

"Tonight was the first time Addison has had cotton candy. She got a little excited."

Grinning at the glee in Kristin's voice, I scrub my hand across my bushy jaw. Even with it being more sweaty than sticky, a sugary scent filters in the air from my hearty scrub. I smile even larger. When Addison offered to share her cotton candy, I never thought I'd wear more of it than I ate.

Once I've scrubbed every inch of my beard, I give Kristin a look as if to ask *is it gone?*

She shakes her head, her smile switching from joy to yearning. "May I?"

I should say no. I should shut this down right now. Instead, I nod. *I'm a fucking moron.*

The rise and fall of Kristin's chest doubles as she fills the last bit of air between us. It's not a long expedition considering she's practically sitting in my lap.

"Stop grimacing," she demands a short time later, mistaking my slumped lips as a result of her yanks to my beard. "This can't be the first time you've had sticky stuff in your beard—surely!"

My ego speaks before my head can cite an objection, "It's not the first time it's been coated in a sugary substance, and it's unlikely to be the last."

Kristin freezes at the same time I stiffen. I'm frozen solid from memories holding my emotions captive. Kristin is stiff because she's hoping the friskiness in my tone will help her escape her nightmare for just a minute. For an hour, she wants to forget. I understand her plea. The woman I crave more than anything is 1500 miles away; that's nothing on how far Kristin would have to travel to see her other half again. She's grieving, but she's also a woman—*a woman with needs.*

With flaring eyes and puckered lips, Kristin's mouth arrows toward mine. Time slows to a snail's pace as my mind races. There are more reasons this is a good idea than it is a horrible one. We live under the same roof; I take care of her girls as if they are mine, meaning we're practically a family, but two points—*two lousy motherfucking objections*—as to why this will never work make me pull back with barely a second to spare.

I love Regan, and Kristin loves Dane. I can't put it any simpler than that.

"I'm so sorry," Kristin murmurs while slumping back onto her side of the couch. "I just want to forget, you know?" She locks her eyes with mine; they're brimming with tears. "He left me, Alex. He chose to leave. Do you have any idea how much that hurts?"

I nod. I feel it every day. Every. Motherfucking. Day. I should have seen the signs. Our arguments were proof that he was struggling, but I didn't do anything about it. I left him to suffer. That makes me just as much to blame for his death as I was his injury.

Hearing the sob Kristin can't stifle, I pull her to sit in my lap. "It will be okay," I promise as I draw her into my chest. "I'll make everything right."

Although I'm worried she'll take my comfort the wrong way, my promise to Dane didn't just center around his daughters. He loved Kristin, so I know without a doubt she's part of the pledge I made. I can't give her what she needs, but I can give her closure.

"I swear to you, I'll make things right. Dane's death won't be in vain because I'll ensure the person responsible for it is held accountable."

I thought fulfilling one of Dane's promises would be enough to stop guilt from eating me alive. Only now am I realizing it adds to my grief. If I had done what I had endeavored to do five years ago, the promise I'm upholding now wouldn't have been needed. Dane would be here, holding his wife in his arms. Instead, he's gone. Forgotten. Never to be the man he was destined to be. And the blame for all that lands on one man's shoulders: Isaac Holt.

I twist Kristin around to face me, my thumbs at the ready to remove the tears falling onto her cheeks. Her strength inspires me when I notice her face is dry. I'm glad she held them back. I've seen enough tears fall from her daughters' eyes the past four months to last me a lifetime.

I give her a few seconds to regain her composure before asking, "What do you know about the night Dane was shot?"

She stiffens a mere second before her mouth falls open.

FOUR

ALEX

"Wow, look at you."

Kristin wolf-whistles as she enters the bathroom I've spent the last hour hogging. The last month has been good for her. She's gained some of the weight she lost the weeks following Dane's death, and the bags her eyes carried the past five months have all but vanished.

She still has a long way to go in her grief, but our interaction on her couch four weeks ago was good for both of us. Since we're jointly grieving the loss of a loved one, we naturally fell into being each other's crutch. It was an okay solution for the short term, but unviable as a long-term fix.

My heartache took me the long route to work out what two plus two equals but after a lengthy internal deliberation, I finally realized I can support someone without being with them 24/7. My friendship with Kristin will be living proof of this.

I've often said I am an agent before I'm a man, so it's time for me to get back to who I truly am. I'll miss Isla and Addison like crazy, but I'm excited about the step I'm taking. By accepting the role offered to me last month, I can provide for them better than I have the past five months while also ensuring their dad's legacy will forever live on.

I don't want Dane to be remembered for the way he died. I want his legacy to reflect the man he was before the life he was destined to live was cruelly stripped away from him.

Remaining quiet, Kristin circles me like a shark as she takes in my recently purchased suit, freshly cut hair, and shaved chin. She startles when her eyes land on the last part of her assessment.

Expensive perfume smacks into me when she stops to stand in front of me. "I thought we agreed on a trim?" Her blonde brows sit high on her face.

I laugh, loving the possessiveness in her tone. She isn't getting her panties in a twist over me; she's claiming ownership of the Viking beard I once had. It's gone. Done and dusted. As invisible as the heart I once owned.

My hand scrapes my baby bottom-smooth jawline. "I figured a new start deserved a new shaving routine. I like it. I don't feel so. . ."

"Homeless?" Kristin fills in, unsure why I couldn't finalize my sentence.

I nod, preferring her suggestion over the many running through my head.

"I get it. It'll grow on me."

She straightens my tie before raising her eyes to mine. The reason for the manly scent on her hands comes to light when she shoves a bottle of cologne into my chest. It's the same brand of cologne she gifted me when I was the best man at her wedding.

"They say the scent makes the man." A frisky wink seals her statement.

My smirk sags a little. I used that saying on Regan when she questioned why my expensive cologne didn't match the economical price of my suit. I can picture the cute little crinkle her nose would get if she were watching the exchange between Kristin and me. She never hid her jealousy well. . . *even while playing me for a fool.*

Hoping to block horrid memories, I accept the cologne from Kristin before splashing some on my square jawline. "Gotta play the part, right?"

Nodding, Kristin removes the cologne from my hand before replacing it with a smaller package. It is the size and shape of a jewelry box, just flatter. Curious to discover what's inside, I crack it open before my brain can object.

I'm stunned when I spot a pair of gold cufflinks inside. They look swanky, and if the brand name curled around the edge is anything to go by, I have no doubt they are. They're stamped Bulgari.

"Kristin, I can't accept these. They're too expensive."

With a shush, she snatches the box out of my hand, removes the cufflinks, then places them on the sleeves of my white dress shirt. I stare at her in shock. It's not my birthday, so she has no reason to spoil me with gifts. But even if it were, she doesn't have the means to indulge me. She's in debt so deep, even my shiny new salary will struggle to cover her and the girls' day-to-day expenses.

"Look. They're perfect." Kristin raises her massively dilated eyes to mine. "If you want people to take you seriously, Alex, you have to look the part."

"I can do that without expensive buttons on my sleeves and cologne that costs more than I make a month," I fire back, my anger rising to a peak it hasn't reached in months.

With a laugh, Kristin slaps my chest. "The cuffs weren't expensive. I got them on sale years ago before they were stuffed into the back of my closet to gather dust. Dane never wore a suit, so I had no need for them until now." She licks her lips, her breathing picking up. "Please don't throw them back in my face. I'm trying to help you like you're helping us."

When she gestures to the hanging open bathroom door with two little faces peeking through it, I inwardly curse. I should have realized where her generosity was coming from. She's not lavishing me with gifts because she's rolling in money; she's putting on a brave front for the sake of the girls.

She did the same thing last month to cheer Isla up after a bad few days. The playhouse she found dumped on the side of the road looked brand new after she spruced it up with some paint and curtains she made from the girls' old dresses. The girls are so enamored with their new pad, they've barely slept in their rooms the past two weeks.

After asking Isla and Addison to wash up in the master bathroom before we eat the farewell cake they baked for me this morning, Kristin tugs down the sleeves of my suit, hiding the reason for the concerned crinkle in my brow.

Once the cuffs are concealed, she returns her eyes to my face. "If it makes you feel any better, we'll say they're a loan. You can give them back at any time. Okay?"

Spotting her deceit from a mile out, I should call her a liar, but if I learned anything the past five months, it is that I am as spineless at calling out Kristin's lies as I was Regan's. Even when they straight up tell me something, I'm hesitant to believe it.

It's not a trust issue; it's just a. . .

I've got nothing—sweet fuck all.

I need to return my focus to the task at hand before my mood sours. "Are you sure you're okay with this, Kristin? I'm only a two and a half hour flight away, but—"

She slaps my mouth with her finger. "We're fine. This needs to happen." Her eyes say the words her mouth never will: *it's time to take down the bastard responsible for my husband's death.*

I nod, agreeing with her. Isaac didn't wrap the noose around Dane's neck, but he may as well have. No matter how hard Dane fought, he never recovered from that night in the field five and a half years ago. It made him depressed, which meant his actions five months ago weren't his own. They were Isaac's.

Kristin flutters her eyelashes. "Besides, it's not just Dane's integrity you're fighting to uphold, Alex; it's yours as well."

Her tone dips at the end, mindful that just because she told the girls to leave doesn't mean we don't have two sets of inquisitive ears listening to our conversation. Isla and Addison have been caught spying on us many times the past five months—Isla almost daily.

"This man is the very reason you and Dane joined the Bureau.

He needs to be held accountable for his actions." Her eyes dance between mine before she adds on, "*All* of them."

The anger fueling her tone makes it seem as though it was her partner caught cheating with Isaac instead of mine. It has me thinking back to one of the last conversations I held with Dane, the one where he implied cheating is the norm in our industry. It also has me wondering if Kristin is more clued in than I give her credit for.

Taking down Isaac won't lessen the sting of Dane's infidelities, but it will sure as hell soothe mine. I've waited for this day for years, and the time has finally come. Isaac is about to face his day of reckoning head on. . .

After I've endured a brief stopover in Milan County, Texas.

FIVE

REGAN

Just a little more.

Slightly to the left.

Perhaps another inch?

The thrill tightening my core intensifies when I tilt my hips. Fingers curl around satin sheets as my blood pressure spikes. He's deeper now, thrusting harder, more powerfully.

I feel myself grow wetter as my heartbeat descends to my pussy. The smell of heated skin on sticky sheets lingers in the air as my lungs complain about the lack of oxygen.

Oh god, yes, right there.

As my lips part for much needed air, every muscle in my body tightens in anticipation, preparing for what is about to occur. This is what I've missed. The rush. The mass surge of adrenaline. *Him.*

Using erotic moans as a distraction, I block Alex from my thoughts. He doesn't belong here, with me, happy. Not now. Not ever. Not even in my dreams. For the past five months, only one person has controlled my destiny: me.

In no time at all, my climactic event is back on track. Today will be a good day. It doesn't matter if I present as a professional woman or the wild child I was in my teens, he understands. I don't want oaths of fidelity or to hear three stupid little words. We do this, then we're done. . . until the need grows too strong for me to ignore once more.

Striving to keep my mind in the game, I raise my ass off the bed then rock my hips back and forth. My climax threatens to shatter when a buzzing sensation vibrates my clit. My tongue thickens as my mouth falls open. I'm moaning on repeat, the tingling in my core building and growing until it reaches the point of detonation. . .

Then it's all brutally stripped away.

"Regan, are you home?"

My eyes pop open as I throw down the flare of my skirt. As Weston raps his knuckles on my cabin door, I dump my Mister 5000 vibrator on the table next to my sticky mattress then yank up my panties. I'm equally peeved and grateful. Peeved I didn't get to finish. Grateful Weston wasn't thirty seconds later. If he were, he would have heard me climaxing—*if I was lucky*.

More times than not, the wave in my core builds and builds and builds, but it never travels further than the crest. My body is punishing me. For what, I don't know. It's been this way for months now. Some may say Alex is the cause of my inability to climax. I refuse to give him the satisfaction. Perhaps I cashed in too many climax tickets during my promiscuous teen years, and now I've been rationed to make sure I use them more diligently?

What? It's better than my first excuse.

After checking my face in the mirror to ensure I'm presentable, I fling open my front door. My cabin is small, meaning only four steps were taken between my bed and the entranceway. It's more a studio apartment than a cabin, but it's mine, it's cozy, and it's full to the brim with the latest and greatest satellite internet money can buy. I haven't missed a second of city life while hunkering down from a storm in the middle of nowhere.

The frustration on my face eases when I spot Weston's broad grin. He's a handsome man the same age as me—a very ripe twenty-

COUPLE ON HOLD   27

seven years. He has creamy white skin, dark shaggy locks, and a grin that proves the dimples in his cheeks are the only thing cutesy about him. He's a devil wrapped up in a boy next door package, and the man my mind should have been summoning during my quest for orgasm instead of the one it kept straying to.

After a huff to announce my irritation at my third thought of Alex in less than an hour, I shift my focus to Weston. "Hey. Another stray cow?"

I exchange my sky-high stilettos for gumboots before joining him under the awning. After one of my designer babies was ruined by a runaway calf last week, I should change my clothes. Alas, hungry baby cows are anything but patient.

"Where was he last spotted?"

I stop scanning the rugged landscape of my family ranch when Weston advises, "I'm not here about a cow. You have a visitor."

A lump lodges in my throat from the way he says "visitor." We don't have visitors around these parts. Everyone knows everyone. There are no strangers amongst family.

Smiling to hide my grimace, my eyes drift in the direction Weston nudged his head. It's late in the afternoon, meaning I have to shelter my eyes from the low-hanging sun. I shouldn't, though, because the rays burning my eyes give me the perfect excuse for their sudden moisture when I spot Alex standing next to Weston's truck.

He looks different from the last time I saw him. More refined. Superior. *Traitorous.* His beard is gone. I'd like to act surprised, but I'm not. He only grew facial hair to hide who he was. Once the truth came out, he had no reason to keep it.

Air puffs out of my nose when my eyes drop to the suit he's wearing. It's still cheap and poorly made, but the way it fits his body, it won't have any woman within a five-mile radius taking notice of its quality—except me. I'm stronger than him. Worthier.

I swallow the lump in my throat when my eyes return to his face. He noticed my scan of his body. His chest sits higher now, his smirk more genuine. He thinks I was checking him out. I wasn't. I was just confirming that my mind wasn't playing tricks on me as it has many times the past five months.

I was also verifying if the removal of his beard coincided with the return of his wedding ring. His finger still sits empty, although I no longer accept that as confirmation on a man's marital status. He fooled me once. He fooled me twice. He'll never fool me again.

"Why did you bring him here?" I ask, returning my focus to Weston.

"Because I told him to."

This voice doesn't belong to Weston. It came from my left. Weston is standing on my right. I don't need to turn toward the voice to know who it came from, but I do.

My dad is standing at the foot of my cabin. He's wearing his beloved jeans and wide-brimmed hat. His boots are dirty, and his brows are furled, but it is the caution in his eyes causing my biggest concern.

I've only seen him wear this look twice before. Once was the night I arrived home after Luca's accident, acting oblivious about what had happened. The second was a little over two months ago. He went on a trip—that raised my first alarm. Unless a family member has died, my dad never leaves the farm. He did that week. He left for three whole days. He was different when he returned, more with-drawn and moody. I would have pressed the issue if I had half a grasp on my own problems.

By the time I felt up to confronting him, his moods had righted as well. Since I didn't want to bring up old issues, I swept it under the rug. It's how I operate lately. Forgetting is easier than deciding if the good times truly did outweigh the bad.

"I don't have anything to say to him," I inform my dad, speaking as if Alex isn't present. "So tell him to turn around and go home." *To his wife. To his daughters. To a life that never included me.*

"I wouldn't be here if I wasn't morally obligated to be here."

There's that thick, deep timbre that invades my dreams every night. The one that keeps me awake when I should be sleeping and doesn't fade even after running for two hours straight.

"The Bureau requested I do this to ensure there are no conflicts of interest."

Of course he's here for them. How stupid of me to think otherwise.

I'm about to tell him to go on his merry way, that I don't give a fuck what he or the Bureau wants, but my brain's slow absorption of his admission stops me.

"Conflict of interest? What conflict of interest could we have?"

My shouted words roll down the valley Alex and I once wrestled in. I choke on a sob when I remember all the feelings he hit me with that weekend. I trusted him, and for what? One big fucking lie after another? None of it was real—not his feelings for me or the promises he made.

My insides break when Alex confirms, "Not us," he angles his head to the side, forcing me to look him in the eyes before snarling, "*Him.*"

One word and five months of hurt slam into me all over again. Something inside of me shifts. I don't know if it is desperation or devastation, but it brings out a side of me I haven't seen in years.

"You have no basis for an investigation into Isaac's empire. Not a single fucking thing!" As my anger resurfaces in the most horrific way, I gallop down the three steps of the patio, unsure whether I want to slap the pompousness off Alex's face or kiss it from him.

I'm confident it is the former when he snarls, "I have nothing now, but I'll soon have *everything*." The chances of our exchange turning violent double when he adds on, "Isaac can't hide behind you forever, Regan. One day he'll step out of your shadow, and just like the day we met, I'll be there waiting for him with my gun loaded and my cuffs at the ready."

His threatful tone stuns me but not enough to reel in my anger. "Isaac doesn't stand behind me. He's stands next to me, at my side, fighting with me, not against me."

Alex's eyes meet mine. The speckles of dark blue I once stared at in awe are gone, swamped by massive pupils. "Was he at your side during your appointment at Westminster, Rae? Was he holding your hand then?"

I freeze, equally petrified and angry. *How does he know about that? No one else knows about the afternoon I spent at Westminster Family Clinic.*

Blatant fury overtakes my hurt when the truth smacks into me. His spying expedition didn't end once he got what he needed. It continued months after we broke up.

"You son of a bitch."

My last word comes out in a flurry from my dad banding his arm around my waist to fling me in the opposite direction of Alex. I'm not going to hurt him. I'm just going to kill him a little.

I claw at my dad's arms, fighting to get away from him. When that fails, I resort to words. "You had no right to pry into my private life! None at all! I have rights!"

"Rights?!" Alex storms closer to me, bringing his devastatingly beautiful and tormented face even nearer to me. "Rights? What about my fucking rights?! Where were my rights when you made the decision you made? That was *my* baby, Rae. You killed *my* baby!"

His voice booms with anger, and his eyes shine with heartbreak, but I'm too numb with fury to notice. My chest burns as I fight to face him head on as I should have months ago, but my dad is too strong and determined to keep us apart.

I knew requesting for my cabin to be built here was a stupid idea, I was just too pigheaded to admit it. I thought I could look past my hurt to see the beauty hiding beneath it. I should have listened to both my heart and my head. I'll never be strong enough for this.

With my dad struggling to keep me under control, Weston backs him up. He steps between Alex and me before spreading his hand across Alex's thrusting chest. With a warning glare, his free hand hovers over the gun on his hip.

His silent warning ends Alex's campaign to reach me in under a second, but it does nothing to weaken his verbal tirade. "It was him, wasn't it? Isaac made you pick—*again*. He made you choose him over me, didn't he, Rae? He forced you to take his side like he always does."

"No!" I shake my head as my fight ramps up all over again. "He helped me choose morals over my libido. Right over wrong. Faithfulness over infidelity!" My words grow in volume to ensure Alex can hear me as my dad drags me kicking and screaming toward my cabin.

Just before we break through the wide open door, Alex shouts, "Expecting to learn morals from a man who doesn't have any is fucking pointless. I thought you were smart, Rae!"

"Don't you dare preach morality when you're the one who is married with two daughters!"

Tears roll down my face unchecked, but I don't clear them away. I'm too hurt to control my emotions, much less my tears, and I'm also too overwhelmed to care that I've lost the fight.

I blow out a hot, temperamental breath when my dad tosses me onto my bed. After growling in warning that his patience has stretched thin, he pivots on his heels and heads for the door. I spring to my feet in an instant.

I'm not even halfway through dispelling months of festering anger, so I've got a shit ton left to disperse. I don't even get two steps from my bed when my dad's furious glare pins me in place. "Sit."

I attempt to give him sass as I always do, but the rarity of his roar subdues me in an instant. "I said sit! For once in your goddamn life, do as I ask you to do!"

The veins in his arms pulsate when he points to a high-back sofa chair in my living room/kitchen. I'm not scared of the fury in his eyes that warns I'll be in trouble if I don't follow his order. I'm just . . . *scared*.

The firm line setting his lips slackens when I flop into the chair as instructed. My knee bobs up and down as my fingers circle my temples. The fury racing through my veins is not as eager to surrender as my heart.

After throwing open my cabin door with the force he used to toss me onto my bed, my dad leans his torso outside. "Get him out of here." He slices his hand through the air as he did when he ordered Ayden to remove a drunk Luca from my eighteenth birthday party.

Alex fires something back, but I miss what he says due to my pulse raging through my ears. I'm not left in the dark long when my dad replies to his thunderous comment, "I had one condition: you maintain a rational head. This isn't rational. You're about to tear each other apart, which means it's time for you to leave."

The shuffling of feet overtakes my shrilling pulse before he says, "Don't make me get my gun, boy. We're not in Washington anymore."

After a few more words, the sound of a truck door slamming shut booms into my ears. An engine's loud rumble replaces its crack a short time later. I wait until Weston's noisy engine becomes a buzz in the distance before dropping my face into my hands. There is so much adrenaline coursing through my veins, my entire body is shaking.

That was worse than anything I imagined when I daydreamed about Alex and me crossing paths. I knew from the way things ended that hostility would play a major role in our reunion, I just had no clue he'd be so mad. What does he have to be angry about? I didn't hurt him like he did me. . .

My inner monologue trails off when a segment of our fight replays through my mind: "That was my baby, Rae! You killed my baby!"

Oh Jesus. He has it all wrong. I didn't go to Westminster as a patient. I went there to support my baby sister, Raquel. That was one of the secrets I mentioned to Alex months ago, the one Raquel promised me not to share with anyone. That's why Ayden's betrayal hit me so hard. I had only found out a week earlier that Raquel was pregnant. She had just started her final year of medical school and was panicked out of her mind. She made me promise not to tell anyone. Although it was another secret added to a list of many, I kept my promise.

The hits keep coming when reality breaks through the angry cloud in my head. Alex screamed those words in front of my father —*my dad*—the man who hasn't looked me in the eyes since his impromptu getaway two months ago.

Oh my god. He believes what Alex believes. He thinks I had an abortion.

"Dad, you don't understand. This wasn't—" I stop myself. This isn't my confession to make. When Raquel wants him to know what happened that day, she'll tell him. "I. . ."

Some of the fury in my chest dulls to an ache when my dad twists around to face me. His cheeks are lined with vibrant red streams, his fists firmly balled, but the moisture in his eyes is stabbing my chest with pain. He looks heartbroken, as if the idea of me aborting his grandchild is too much for him to bear.

"Why, Regan?" he asks, stepping closer to me.

I shake my head, denying the hurt in his voice without words.

"I understand you were mad, that he did you wrong, but that baby didn't know any of that. It was never given a chance."

A part inside of me dies when a tear pops out of his eye and rolls down his cheek. I want to hug him and tell him everything will be okay. I want to promise him I would never hurt him this way, but the love I have for my sister stops me. I'd rather him be angry at me than Raquel. She's handling more than her fair share of heartache right now, so anything I can do to lessen it, I will.

I stop twisting my skirt around my fingers when my dad discloses, "That could have been you, Regan. If your mother went through with her parents' wishes, that baby could have been you."

I take in a sharp breath. Now his heartache makes sense. He's not seeing Raquel's baby as a defenseless fetus or his grandchild; past memories have him seeing it as me. I'm one of those statistics parents use to scare their teens into not losing their virginity at prom, but instead of being conceived at the prom, I was born the week following it.

When my dad kneels down to clasp my hands in his, I wipe away the tears sitting high on my cheeks. "I'll never once regret fighting for you as I did, Regan, but you will *always* regret this. You had options. Even if Alex wasn't there for you, your momma and me would have had your back."

He stops talking as the pain in his eyes morphs into disappointment. That hurts even more than his tears. "If I had done my job as a parent, you would have known that."

My lips quiver as I begin to talk. "This isn't your fault, Dad."

He attempts to shake his head, but a little voice stops him. "She's right, Dad. None of this is your fault."

The smell of freshly cut flowers lingers in the air when Raquel steps into my cabin. The wetness on her cheeks reveals she may have overheard our conversation, but the pride on her face confirms it. She's grateful I kept her secret even with it breaking my heart in the process.

While adding to her thanks with a smile, she dumps a bag full of clothes on the floor before undoing the three buttons of her coat. Dad and I gasp in sync when her five months-pregnant belly pops out from beneath her massive trench coat. My gasp is in admiration for how beautiful she looks. Dad's is in utter shock.

"You're. . . uh. . . He . . . Ah." His eyes jump between Raquel and me as the confusion on his face triples. "What the hell did I miss?"

I laugh at his stumbled question. Raquel settles it. "It wasn't Regan who had an appointment at Westminster. It was me." She locks her glistening eyes with mine, the admiration in them quickly drying her tears. "I thought I was doing the right thing, that my studies were more important than this little guy." She exhales loudly before pushing out, "I was wrong. Everything you said that day was true. I can have both my career and my baby, and I don't need a man to do either of those things."

When I nod, she swivels on the spot like she always does when she's in trouble. "Except perhaps one man." Her eyes lower to our dad, who is still kneeling at my side. "What do you say, Dad? Are you up to the task?"

Time stands still as we wait for him to reply. I swear none of us are breathing. I expect him to lecture Raquel on how he raised us not to depend on anyone, or at the very least leave her hanging for a few seconds longer. He does neither of those things. Instead, he stands to his feet, hollers at the top of his lungs, then twirls his youngest daughter around my cabin as if her feet aren't knocking my knees with every spin.

"I knew I raised you girls right," he squeals, enlarging both my heart and the droplets of moisture in my eyes.

SIX

ALEX

"How did it go?"

I hand my suit jacket to the stewardess grinning brightly at me before slipping into the plush leather chair next to Grayson.

"I did what needed to be done."

Grayson's brows furl, but he saves his grilling for a later date. *Thank fuck.* My meeting with Regan was a disaster. First, I had to get through her father—whom I hadn't seen since our last confrontation—her brother, and her mother, then I was chaperoned to her cabin with a three-car escort like I was an Arabian oil prince—or even worse, a criminal. And what's the first thought I have when I see Regan after months of absence? *I'd do it again and again and again if you were at the end waiting for me.*

She ripped my heart out of my chest, threw it on the ground, then fucking stomped on it, but my cock didn't care. He didn't want to hear the facts my brain screamed at him. He wanted to hunt, to claim his prize. He wanted to fuck her so hard and fast she'd never forget he had been inside her.

Do you know what's even more annoying than that? I want to place all the burden for my appalling thoughts on my cock's shoulders, but I can't. She broke me, yet *I* still want her more than anything.

A feeble chuckle rolls up my chest when I scrub my hand across my chin. I never thought I'd regret the day I rediscovered a razor. I hated my beard. I felt like it was hiding me, but I kept it so long because the months I had it were some of the best months of my life.

My reappearance in Regan's life at Ravenshoe started as a lie, but our connection altered it in an instant. We were real. . . until he fucked it all over.

"Did you bring me what I asked?"

Grayson smirks, amused by the superiority in my tone. With a cocky wink, he hands me a manila folder brimming with papers. His response isn't surprising. He's accustomed to the goodie-two-shoes brother, the one who followed the rules to the wire only to discover they don't protect you when you need them the most. He's never seen me like this. Now I'm the rule maker, the man you better not cross unless you're willing to pay your penalty with your freedom. I don't play dirty, but I don't play nice anymore either. It's hard to be kind when you don't have a heart.

"How much time did Jay get?" I ask Grayson upon spotting Jay's details at the top of the file.

Grayson screws up his face. "Not long enough, but they were lenient on him because he assisted in their investigation."

I arch a brow, prompting him to answer my question without skirting. He follows suit rather quickly. "Stripped of his position and three months' probation."

"Three months' probation? He fired his service weapon at a civilian. How can he only get three months' probation?" Fury highlights my tone.

Grayson shrugs. "You're lucky he got that. At one point, he nearly didn't face prosecution." Upon hearing my grinding teeth, he murmurs, "This is what happens when you leave an investigation before its finalized, Alex."

My teeth grit more. My friend died. I had no fucking choice but to leave.

When I say that to Grayson, the edgy grin on his face subsides. "Sorry, I'm not thinking straight. We're all still shocked about Dane. I'm in disbelief."

I can tell he wants to say more, but shock is rendering him speechless. Dane was a confident, take no shit man, so his loss wasn't just devastating, it was utterly blindsiding. No one saw it coming. Not even those closest to him.

"And Theresa? What slap on the wrist did she get?"

A huff parts my lips when I see my answer in Grayson's remorseful eyes.

"Seriously? Nothing? She set up the entire thing. She black-mailed Jay to be her gofer. How could she not get suspended at the very least?"

Grayson's lips tug high. "She's suffering, just not in the way you're hoping."

I wait, completely fucking lost.

Thankfully, Grayson is as in tune with me as I am him. "She was transferred to the equivalent of jail for agents. She's with IA."

A disbelieving chuckle vibrates my chest. "The Bureau's solution for a rogue agent is to put her in a department responsible for sniffing out rogue agents?"

"It's a brilliant move when you sit back and think about it." Grayson laughs. I fail to see the humor in his reply. "Come on, Alex. You know some of the best agents we have are ones we've transferred from the dark side. They know what criminals are thinking because they think like criminals." He leans back in his chair, his shoulder nudging up. "Theresa will sniff out rogue agents because she knows what they smell like. I'm not happy they went down this path, but I understand why they did it. Once you work past your anger, you might as well."

A *pfft* sounds from my mouth. *I don't see that ever happening.*

Needing a distraction before my thoughts wander in a direction they haven't strayed in years, I focus on the mammoth load of documents in my hand.

"Who's this?" I angle an application to join my team from a recent recruit at an academy near San Francisco to Grayson.

He shrugs. "Don't know. I didn't pay her application much attention. I was brought in to ensure the operation didn't fold while you were playing house, not take on new members. If you want to train a rookie, that's your prerogative, but I sure as hell ain't going there."

His "play house" comment pisses me off, but I understand his hesitation about not taking on new recruits. Crew leaders have enough hassles keeping the bureaucrats from meddling in business they don't belong in, let alone training people not up to the task.

With that in mind, I file Isabelle Brahn's application to join my unit into the file Grayson compiled on Isaac the past five months. Taking advantage of the private jet's generous spacing, I sort out the documents according to importance and timeframe. Although Grayson snickers at my eagerness, he assists in configuring a more suitable timeline.

"You need to bring it back a few years. I'm certain Isaac's connections began months, if not years before he moved to Ravenshoe." He shuffles down the papers so Isaac's college portfolio is at the start of my timeline. "He started college with $895.34 in his bank account. He graduated with over eight million dollars."

An impressive wolf whistle leaves my mouth. It annoys me more than Grayson's earlier comment. Isaac doesn't deserve my praise, not even a bigamist old-fashioned one.

Grayson and I put the two-hour flight time from Texas to Florida to good use. I have a better timeframe of Isaac's life to work with, and I've been updated on any events that occurred the five months I was absent from his case. Unfortunately, the last half of my statement only took a few minutes. Unlike me, the past few months have been extremely profitable for Isaac. His latest dance club is one of his biggest moneymakers. He's killing it—figuratively.

I hope he enjoys his last few weeks of freedom, because things are set to change now that I'm in charge of his operation.

Silence falls over the office I once called HQ when Grayson and I enter a little before 6 PM. The standard workers are still here, the same dingy desks, and moldy windows looking out on the alley. Even the bell I placed above the door is in working order. There's just one difference: I know how to run a tight ship.

"No one is to leave this office before the target leaves his. If the target sleeps from 3 AM to 11 AM, you now sleep 3 AM to 11 AM. If he dines at a restaurant that charges $100 for a plate of sauce, you now eat at a restaurant that charges $100 for a plate of sauce. If he's fucking a two-dime whore in a back alley infested with rats. . ."

I pause, certain they've got the picture.

The hum that follows proves they do: "We fuck a two-dime whore in a back alley infested with rats."

"That's right. We've dropped the ball so many times during this operation that a clean-up crew will be called in sooner rather than later, so if you don't want to *lose* your job, I suggest you start *doing* your job."

I point to a six foot one man with a medium build on my right. "I need these desks moved to the top floor of this building. Organize it."

He attempts to seek further information, but my glare cuts him off. I'm not holding his hand. I'm giving him an order. What more information does he need than that?

"On it," he stumbles out with a nod, realizing there's a new sheriff in town.

"You?" I click my fingers two times as I struggle to place a name with a face I've seen before.

"Michelle," the blonde fills in, stepping closer.

I nod in thanks, appreciative of the eagerness on her mid-forties face. "There was a techie who worked with the team before he was relocated five months ago. His name was Brandon James. I want him brought back to my team—no matter what the cost."

She nods, revealing she is aware of whom I am referring to. Her enthusiasm is snatched away when I add on, "I want him transferred as a field agent."

"I. . . ah. . . I don't have the authority to do that."

"You don't, but I do." I dig out my wallet and hand her my business card. "If you have any troubles, refer them to me. Just dropping my name should keep their inquisitiveness on the down low, but if it doesn't, I'm more than happy to convince them to look elsewhere."

"Okay." She scurries off to do as asked, proving she'll fit into my team nicely.

"For the rest of you. . ." I scan the near dozen men and women eyeballing me with stunned astonishment. ". . . I suggest you go home and kiss your family goodbye, because from tomorrow morning, your ass is mine until we bring this case to the courts."

SEVEN

REGAN

"This can't be right?"

I toss the folder Ayden handed to me onto a stack of many before slouching into the sofa in my parents' living room. It's been five hours since Raquel came clean to our parents about her pregnancy, and I'm still living off the high.

Well, I was doing a mighty fine job pretending her news was the reason for my adrenaline-thick blood and jittery stomach, but that all came tumbling down when Ayden and my dad began to slap me with some cold, hard truths.

After taking a generous sip of the fourth glass of wine my mom handed me five minutes ago, I raise my eyes to Ayden. "Isaac wouldn't lie about this. He told me he was sending money to Alex's family."

"Isaac wasn't lying." This isn't coming from Ayden. It's my dad who is speaking. "For the past five years, he's been funding the living expenses for the family of the man shot outside of a strip club—"

"Cabaret club," I correct, glaring at him over the glass of red I'm chugging down more than I'm enjoying.

I'm the only one drinking, but I need something to numb the ache that's been tearing my chest in two since Alex left hours ago. Unfortunately, I don't see wine filling my requirements. A hard liquor that makes me forget everything a good six hours before I started drinking is the cure I need, not a bunch of files Ayden compiled on Isaac, nor the whispered promises from my mom that everything will work out in the long run. I need to forget—permanently.

My dad clearly learned a few lessons from his daughters when his eyes roll skyward at my grumbled comment. "Whatever the club was, the man you *believed* Isaac was referencing *isn't* the agent he's been making payments to." He lowers his tone, which in turn, eases the twisting of my stomach. "Alex wasn't the only agent shot that day, Regan. Another man was wounded—badly."

Saving me from realizing just how stupid I am, Ayden jumps into the conversation. "The oversight is understandable. Even from an agent's standpoint, to this very day, the details on the second agent's injuries are sketchy. Add that to the fact there are no reports of a second shooter noted in *any* files; it is as if the sniper on the rockface and the second agent never existed."

The fog in my head clears for anger. "They were both there, Ayden. If it weren't for Isaac, Alex and his colleague would be dead."

"Because Isaac ordered for the sniper to be killed?"

My teeth grit when it dawns on me the man sitting across from me is no longer my brother. He's an agent. If the way he is sitting all pompous and straight isn't a clear indication, the interrogation in his tone is a sure-fire sign.

"Isaac didn't order for anybody to be killed. He *saved* two agents' lives. How can you not see that?"

When I attempt to stand to my feet, my dad's hand darts out to hold me hostage on the couch. Red wine splashes onto my thighs, but not a soul notices it. Every pair of eyes in the room are too fixated on my flaming-with-anger face to take in a few extra splotches of red.

"Running doesn't solve anything." My dad's tone is lower, filled with understanding.

I don't take a leaf out of his book. "It does when the people who are supposed to believe you don't. Despite what Ayden or any of his colleagues tell you, Isaac is innocent. He's a good man, Dad." I shake my head as my anger builds to the point of detonation. "Perhaps if you stopped siding with ill-informed men on what they *believe* makes a criminal, and listen to the person you raised to seek the truth, you'd know that."

Proof he heard the underlying message in my reply is exposed when he advises, "I let Alex see you today because I thought it would do you some good."

I laugh. It isn't pleasant. "What good could it do me? He lied to me, Dad. He broke both my trust and my heart, yet you thought seeing him would be good for me? What's wrong with you?"

He takes in a sharp breath at the broken heart part of my statement, but his fighting spirit remains strong. "If you had just given him a chance to speak—"

"Are you serious?! You're taking his side?" I push away from him, equally angered and disgusted. "I'm your daughter, for crying out loud. You're not allowed to have his back."

He scoots closer to me to calm me down with his giant teddy bear hands and gentle eyes. "That isn't it at all, baby girl. There are no sides here. I don't pick teams. You are my daughter, so I'll always have your back—"

"Then tell her the truth, Hayden."

My eyes rocket to the entrance of the living room. My mom has her shoulder propped against the doorjamb. Her cheeks are wet with moisture, but her eyes are bright and brimming with determination. When my dad vehemently shakes his head at her suggestion, she pushes off her feet to bridge the gap between them.

"She has the right to know."

My dad shakes his head again, denying her advice with the stubbornness of a mule. It is nothing new for them. They bicker as much as Alex and I once did. But they love even more than that.

My heart does an elongated beat when my mom cups my dad's jaw in her hands, lifting his eyes to hers. He's a goner now. She's got him right where she wants him. "When she finds out, and don't mistake me, she *will* find out, you'll lose her even faster than you're worried about."

Although I hate that my mom is talking about me as if I'm not here, the raw pragmatism in her voice cuts through me like a knife. Everything she is saying is straight-up honest, and my dad knows it.

"I like having her here, Sally. Home—where she belongs. I don't want it to go back to how it was months ago. We hardly saw her. She was practically a ghost."

That hurts to hear, but it doesn't stop me from saying, "Things are different now, Dad. I've healed so much, my grief is basically gone."

I shock myself with how confident my tone is. I shouldn't be surprised. I *have* grown so much the past few months, I truly feel like I've crossed a stage in my grief where I can understand what happened between Luca and me that night without letting guilt eat me alive.

This kills me to admit, but a lot of my newfound knowledge was gathered during my time with Alex. He deceived and used me, but not everything he did was bad. Even if it was all an act, he showed me the woman I could be if I tried harder. That's exactly what I've done the past few months. I concentrated on me: on my healing, on my relationship with my parents, and on the hurt woman inside of me responsible for the ugly way I reacted to Alex's betrayal.

Two wrongs will never make a right, so I don't know why I believed two betrayals would make us even. I had planned to tell Alex the truth about what really happened that afternoon in my apartment when I saw him again, but with anger, hurt, and frustration fueling our exchange today, I never got the chance.

In a way, it was both good and bad that my dad and Weston broke up our argument. Good, because Alex left the ranch breathing, but bad because if we were given a chance to air our dirty laundry, he wouldn't have left believing I had both cheated on him and aborted his baby. Although it would do little to ease my agitation, I'm sure it would have helped Alex. Then maybe, just maybe, guilt wouldn't still be eating me alive hours after he left.

Recalling the conversation I was in the process of having before my thoughts strayed, I say, "I love the little cabin you built me in the meadow, Dad, but I'm twenty-seven years old. You can't keep me locked in a tower forever."

I bump my knee against his, hoping to ease the tension hanging thickly in the air. It works—somewhat. He only grumbles his comment about finding a bigger padlock instead of saying it out loud. It's not the response I was aiming for, but it's better than him continuing with his stubbornness.

"Now what's this secret you're keeping from me? If it is about my recent online shopping delivery going missing, don't bother. Mom already told me you 'borrowed' them."

My mom swings her arm in the air while galloping like a real-life cowgirl, whereas my dad's cheeks burn with color. Ayden and Raquel just stare from a distance, confident they've missed the punchline but somewhat happy about it. They should be, the last thing I want to imagine is my parents getting down and dirty with the latest and greatest sex toys.

I was hoping a change up in equipment would revive the mojo I've been missing the past five months. After seeing Alex today, I realized no amount of expenditure will fix the problem. My libido he stole all those months ago when we wrestled amongst cow dung didn't return. He locked it away for his own personal use, only allowing it to venture out when he's grasping the reins.

Ugh! Just the thought of him having that power over me fills me with blistering anger. I'm independent, fierce, and strong. . . I just can't get myself off anymore.

Pouting, I shift my focus back to the task at hand. From the way my dad scoots to the edge of his chair to grasp my hands in his, I assume he's going to deliver bad news. His brows have the same deep groove they held when he told me my grandmother had passed. It's also the same expression he wore when my beloved pet alpaca went to alpaca heaven. This isn't a good sign. Whatever he is about to tell me can't be good news.

After bracing myself for impact, I give him a look, wordlessly demanding for him to hit me with it. I'm as stiff as a board, my lungs are full of oxygen, and I have tears at the ready, anticipating anything but what he says next: "Alex isn't married."

EIGHT

REGAN

Nerves take flight in my stomach as a heavy buzz drones into my ears. I've sorted the facts, divided up the pros and cons, but not once have I reached an alternative conclusion. It's time for me to finally come clean to Isaac about Alex and his fellow FBI counterparts.

It took a bit of convincing from all members of my family to believe my dad's confession about Alex being as single as me. I could see the truth in his eyes, feel the remorse pumping out of him, but when you've been lied to time and time again, trust is hard to come by.

Surprisingly, the first thing I felt upon discovering Alex is neither a husband nor a father was anger. If he had a wife, he had a legitimate excuse for the months of absence that have stretched between us. Instead, I only felt more strongly that our time together was nothing but a ruse. Then, as I continued absorbing the facts, I realized his marital status didn't modify the evidence. He still spied on me. He took confidential documents stored on my laptop and used them against the supervisor of his department.

Although he didn't immediately take Theresa's place, his visit to my ranch this afternoon proves he has every intention of doing precisely that. He's going after Isaac—my employer, business partner, and friend—and he's not the least bit concerned about how it will impact me. If that doesn't prove he was only with me to advance his career, nothing will.

I exhale sharply when a deep, rugged voice sounds down the line. "Hey there, Ms. Prim and Proper. How's the cow dung smelling today?"

I smile—*inwardly*. I'd never let Hugo think he has one over me.

"Smelling as fresh as ever. Care to take a whiff?"

I giggle for real when he loudly gags. Hugo is one of the city slickers my daddy always warned me about. He was raised in the 'burbs, but ran amuck in New York City. Distance has done wonders for our friendship. We've grown close the past five months.

"Are you still alone?"

I hear him adjust his position before he murmurs in agreement. "What's this about? Your text was *real* cryptic. The only time I've been messaged to check if I am alone is when my phone is about to be bombarded with nudie pics. Are you gonna send me some nudie pics, Ms. Prim and Proper?"

I nearly reply, *Ha! You wish.* But after the beating my ego took earlier today, I need to have it stroked a little. "Are you opposed to the idea?"

Hugo groans. Don't ask me if it is a good groan or a bad one because I won't be able to answer you.

Deciding to test the waters, I say, "I'm more a *you show me yours, I'll show you mine* type of girl. So, what do you say, City Slicker, are you up to the challenge?"

I freeze when I hear a zipper being lowered. I should be shutting this down before it goes too far, but for the life of me, I can't get my mouth to cooperate with the prompts of my brain. Hugo is a handsome man—*a very handsome man*—only an idiot would fake disinterest in seeing what he's packing. And considering I've had my fair share of stupid moments the past six months, I'm not eager for any more.

But this. . . I'm eager for this.

My heart thuds in my ears when the ding of a text message sounds through my cell phone. I pace three steps to gather it in my hands but keep the screen facing the ground as my brain struggles to clear some of its fog.

I don't want to see this.

I don't need to see this.

But my ego sure does.

With that in mind, I flip my phone over to face me.

An exasperated gasp leaves my lips at the same time Hugo's belly-clenching laugh roars down the line. He didn't send me a picture of his cock. He posted a real-life emoji of a dick. It's a giant eggplant sitting in the vegetable crisper of his fridge. How do I know this? He still has my half-empty bottle of wine from eight months ago sitting on the bottom shelf. He's more of a beer and whiskey type of guy.

"You should have heard how hard you were breathing. I was about to call a medic. I thought you were having an asthma attack."

I gag. "Whatever! I wasn't panting. I was wheezing—in disgust!"

"Yeah, right," Hugo fires back. "You want a picture of my cock."

"Only so I can post it on an anonymous medical show to ask if that much shrinkage is normal."

Loving our banter, Hugo laughs even louder. "Stop. Oh, god, please stop. I can't fucking breathe. The fact you think I have a tic-tac for a cock proves what I've always known. Blondes aren't known for their smar—"

"Stop right there if you want to keep your tic-tac. I haven't brought myself to orgasm today, so you'd best not mess with me."

That nips his laughter right in the bud. "Fuckin' hell, Regan. Don't say shit like that to me."

I cock out my hip to ensure my stance matches my attitude. "Why? Worried you'll be out of a job?"

"Nah. More like tempted to send you a real dick pic to see if you'll follow through with your pledge. Are you a *promise them anything they want to hear to get your way* girl? Or the one I've always imagined?"

I'm about to ask how he imagines me, but he saves me from shaming myself. *Thank god.* "Strong and sexy as fuck on the outside, but as soft and gooey as a marshmallow on the inside."

The tension firing between us shifts. It's flightier now, almost flirty.

My throat works hard to swallow before I force out, "You got one half of your statement right. I am as strong as I am sexy."

An agreeing hum vibrates Hugo's lips.

"But I'm just as hard on the inside as I am on the outside."

His murmur comes to a complete stop. Even though I can't see him, I can picture his mouth opening and closing like a fish out of water.

Not wanting to explain myself, I get back to the task at hand. "I was calling about a security issue at Holt Enterprises."

Hugo groans, not liking the swift change in topics, but he's happy to distract himself from tension that we shouldn't have. "If that's the case, you should be calling Hunter. He's head of Isaac's security team."

"I will, after I've spoken to you first. This affects you just as much as it does Isaac, that's why I reached out to give you a heads up."

He remains quiet, giving me his full attention.

I use it to my advantage.

"So this whole time, you've been running your own investigation on the agents investigating Isaac?"

I halfheartedly shrug. "Not really an investigation. I've just been monitoring them as readily as they've been tailing Isaac. They have nothing, Hugo. Not a single shred of evidence."

"Because Isaac isn't a crook."

An average person would mistake Hugo's reply as a question. I'm not an average person. I know he is loyal to Isaac. He is as loyal as me, meaning he's also aware every word I spoke is true. Isaac has connections with notorious men, but that doesn't mean he runs his empire like they do. He has his own ideas, morals, and ethics. He doesn't need to emulate the men surrounding him to achieve greatness; he just trusts himself and his instincts.

I push my phone closer to my ear. "Although we're both confident Isaac will never face prosecution, we need to remain cautious. I don't want this to blow up in our faces, Hugo."

"That won't happen if you sleep with him."

My brows spike as high as my heart rate. "What?"

There is no humor in Hugo's tone when he suggests, "If you think this guy's issues stem from jealousy, sleep with him. Nothing lowers a man's quest for revenge more than believing he's top dog."

"I'm not sleeping with him." *Again.* The hammering of my heart echoes in my tone.

I hear Hugo adjust his position. "Why not? You said he wants revenge for what he *thinks* happened between Isaac and you, that he'll stop at nothing to right a wrong that *never* happened. This is an easy solution."

That's easy for him to say; it isn't his heart being put on the line for Isaac. Not this time, anyway.

I breathe out noisily to gain Hugo's undivided attention. When I have it, I say, "Alright. . . I'll sleep with him."

Hugo waits, knowing there is more.

He's right. "On the same day you go back to Rochdale to face your biggest heartache head on."

Hugo sighs loudly. "That's different—"

"No, it's not," I shriek, shaking my head. "It doesn't matter if it is two hours or two years, time isn't a factor when it comes to love. Sometimes, the faster they are, the more vicious they burn."

"Regan," Hugo stops, exhales, then starts again, "you love him?"

His question is so quiet, I barely hear it.

It's a pity my heart refuses to ignore the pain fracturing it. "No. I loved who I thought he was. *That's* different."

A stretch of silence passes between us. It's more awkward than the seconds I considered sending him a nude pic to avoid this confrontation. Hugo annoys the shit out of me, which isn't hard considering I find the Dalai Lama annoying, but I hate that I'm letting Alex do this to me. He has no right to influence arguments with a man I am or am not friends with. Just like he has no right to place the demise of our relationship on Isaac's shoulders. That solely resides on him and his fucked up acting skills. *And perhaps me and the time I stupidly threw Isaac under the bus with me—not once, but twice.*

Hugo ends the silence by suggesting, "Let me run this by Hunter before you say anything to Isaac."

I shake my head. "No. I've held on to this information for way too long. It's time for me to come clean on. Furthermore, this is my mistake, so it's my responsibility to fix it."

Hugo makes a *pfft* noise. "That's not the way things work. We're a team, Regan. All of us. When one does wrong, we all do wrong. Furthermore. . ." I smile at how he's mimicking my voice. ". . .from what you're saying, he had a tail on Isaac months before you bumped heads. For all you know, Isaac may already be aware that he's being watched. You know how pedantic he is. Nothing slips by him."

I halfheartedly shrug. "Hunter did mention something a few months ago about switching up our servers to ensure they couldn't be infiltrated."

"Exactly. You're sitting all the way over there in bum-fuck Texas, twisted up in knots about something Isaac may already be aware of. Give me an hour; if he doesn't know anything, you're free to spill your guts. If he's aware, keep doing what you've been doing the past five months. Have his back as he's always had ours."

Some may say I'm a coward for agreeing with Hugo's suggestion, but I'd rather be a coward than an idiot.

NINE

ALEX

"There has to be something we're missing."

I throw the documents Brandon handed me on my desk before spinning around to look out my office window. Yes, I actually have an office with a window that faces more than an alley. Although HQ is still in the same building it was when Theresa helmed the operation, the location, equipment, and agents are the best money can buy.

We have the entire top floor of a building that leases for over thirty thousand a month. Every computer in my vicinity has the most advanced software known to man; my team has doubled in size the past four months, and my salary went from mid-range five figures to nearly six figures a year, yet, I've not found a single shred of evidence that will have Isaac doing hard time.

Not. Fucking. One.

"It's impossible. No businessman keeps their hands this clean. Dig deeper, burrow out his fucking root canals if you have to, but get me what I need!"

Brandon scurries out of my office like he does every time I lose my temper. My crew thought I was a hard-ass when I walked into the office with an air of authority and the determination of a fox months ago. They had no idea. As weeks shifted to months, the larger the angry pit in my stomach grew.

In a month, I stopped recognizing the man reflecting back at me in the mirror.

By two months, I stopped looking in the mirror because I hated the weasel of a man staring back at me.

My third month was tied up with bureaucratic shit every interim leader strives their hardest to avoid.

Regrettably, I had to attend a conference in San Francisco last week. I had no choice. I either represented my team, or they'd shut my operation down. Some good did come from their determination, though. I rerouted my flights so I traveled via Washington DC instead of New York.

I couldn't believe how much Addison had grown in four months. Even Isla was more welcoming to my weekend visit than she had been during my five-month stint in the den of her family home.

It was during my two-night stay that Kristin suggested I look outside the box to bring Isaac to justice. Although I never discuss work with anyone out of the Bureau, her suggestions were plausible enough to deserve a second look. What Theresa did to Regan and me was wrong and immoral, but done right, with the agent aware they're being used in a ruse, it could work.

Isaac doesn't let anyone in. He guards his heart even more carefully than he does his empire. From experience, I know it only takes one woman to unravel everything you've ever known. He's a red-blooded man who treats women like commodities, meaning the chances of Kristin's suggestion working is unlikely, but I've grown so desperate, I'm willing to try anything. I want Isaac to pay for the wrongs he's done, then maybe, just maybe, the pain still charring my heart to ash will weaken.

It's been seven months since Regan used Isaac's credit card to remove me from her life. Seven months of wondering what could have been if she had picked me over him. Seven months of wondering if our baby would have had her green eyes or my blue. Seven months of striving to ignore the embittering anger filling the hole where my heart once lived.

I've grown so resentful the past seven months, I hardly recognize myself anymore. I don't look at people and see the good in them like I used to. I point out their flaws and exploit their defects. I'm not doing it to be mean. I'm doing it to save them from living through the hell I've been living the past eight months. They may hate me for it, but their hate will only be one tenth of the pain they'll endure if they don't learn from my heartache.

With that in mind, I swivel around to face my desk. An email I typed an hour ago sits on the monitor, waiting to be sent. It is only a two sentence message, but its importance is unmissable.

I accept Isabelle Brahn's request to join my department.
Details to be forwarded shortly.

I hit send before I can talk myself out of it. I'm not a spineless agent doing anything I can to get my man. I'm ensuring my shrewdness is on par with the man I'm targeting. Isaac has dogged prosecution for years with underhanded, malicious tactics, so it's time for him to be hit with the same methods.

He's about to meet his match—literally.

TEN

ALEX

"Excuse me."

I watch a pretty brunette of medium height and build enter my office a little after 9 AM. Even with her hip missing the gun most agents under my watch carry, I can tell she's an agent. She's timid, but her constant scan of her surroundings proves her observation skills are on point. Although I'm confident she's a rookie, she must have been surrounded by law enforcement officers during her childhood. She holds herself with authority. . . even with her knees clanging together.

When Michelle walks by her, too busy compiling the evidence we gathered on Isaac the past weekend to pay her any attention, the brunette paces to Brandon's desk. I smirk. She chose well. He's the most fearless-looking agent in my crew. He gives you the friendly *I'll never do anything to hurt you* vibe. It's a pity she failed to see the gleam in his eyes I spotted nearly a year ago.

"Hello," she greets Brandon, stopping at his desk.

Her voice matches her attractiveness. It's sweet, yet sultry. It shouldn't piss me off that her husky tone zapped my cock with an energy it hasn't felt in over nine months, but it does.

"I need that document now, Brandon!" My angry roar is more a warning to my cock than announcing my irritation that it's taken Brandon thirty minutes to gather Isaac's movement sheet from this morning.

Isaac rarely changes his routine, but he did this weekend. Not only did he stay at his office from sun up to sundown Saturday through to Sunday, he flew commercial. Along with his best mate/business associate, Cormack McGregor, Isaac owns a fleet of private jets, but his trip from New York to Ravenshoe earlier this week was done via a business class seat in a commercially owned aircraft.

Although we've yet to discover why he flew commercial, we all agreed it was out of character for him. He's leaving us breadcrumbs; we've just got to follow him in the direction he's attempting to deter us from.

With a goofy grin, Brandon snatches a document off his desk before hightailing it my way. The brunette tracks his race around the room. My brows quirk when her eyes land on me. It isn't the fastest creep of color fanning her cheeks that elicits my odd response; it is the giggle spilling from her lips.

What the fuck does she think is funny?

Realizing she's been busted laughing, she settles her giggles before bridging the gap between us. My lips set into a hard line when my cock notices the natural roll of her hips with every step she takes. She doesn't have the same sexy siren walk Regan has, but it gains her the attention of every male agent in the room. She even garnered the glare of a handful of female agents.

A sweet, feminine scent smacks into me when she stops to stand in front of me. "Hi, I'm Isabelle Brahn, your new agent." She holds out her dainty hand for me to shake.

It takes me replaying her greeting three times before my brain comprehends what she said. "Michelle!" I shout, causing Isabelle to jump. "I thought I ordered a blonde?"

Yep, that sounded as bad out loud as it did in my head. I don't mean to be an asshole. . .

Actually, scrap that. Yes, I do.

I agreed for Isabelle to join my crew because she was described as a goddess who would have any man under her spell within thirty seconds of meeting him. Although I'm pleased with what I'm seeing, Isaac doesn't date brunettes. That's the whole reason I asked on numerous occasions if Isabelle was blonde.

My requests were extremely thorough: an attractive blonde with killer long legs, green eyes and no concerns going undercover for the good of the Bureau. Isabelle is not what I ordered.

"Does she look brunette to you?" I ask Michelle when she arrives at my side.

Isabelle's wide eyes bounce between Michelle and me when Michelle answers, "Umm, yes, she does appear to be brunette."

I work my jaw side to side as anger makes itself known with my gut. "In the past two months, have you ever seen him with a brunette?"

Before Michelle can answer, Isabelle asks, "What does my hair color have to do with my placement?"

The attitude in her voice thickens both my veins and my cock, which engulfs me with so much anger, I feel my pupils widening with every ragged breath I take. "Isaac Holt fucks blondes; you're a brunette."

"Excuse me!" Her two words hiss through her clenched teeth. "I wasn't brought here to sleep with Isaac Holt. I was brought here to help with your investigation."

Is she fucking stupid? I specifically noted in transfer documentation the ruse I was planning to run when she arrived. If she didn't agree with my terms, she shouldn't have accepted her placement on my team. I don't have time to train a rookie, much less one glaring at me as if I'm shit stuck under her stiletto.

I need to knock her attitude down a few pegs. "You were brought here as eye candy." My words are so loud, I hear them twice when they bounce off the stark white walls of HQ.

Upon hearing my roar, the room falls into silence. My team hovers close, the spectacle of watching a rookie agent get slaughtered by their superior too intriguing to ignore.

Hoping to ease the tension teeming between Isabelle and me, Brandon suggests, "We could dye her hair."

"Not happening," Isabelle fires back before I can get a word in.

She crosses her arms under her chest, hoisting her medium-sized breasts into the air. The anger blistering my veins grows when my eyes automatically dart down to take in the goods she's flaunting. This is the exact reason I requested she join my team, so Isaac would for once think with his cock instead of his head, but instead of doing as requested, she has me and every male agent surrounding her acting like morons who can't control their dicks.

I return my eyes to Isabelle, the fury in them uncontained. "Once you're in a dress and a pair of stilettos, Isaac won't care you're a brunette."

The bashfulness I saw beaming out of her earlier is nowhere in sight when she replies, "Once you have a personality transplant and a plastic groin inserted, nobody will care you're a Ken doll."

The crowd watching our charade breaks into boisterous laughter. I'm too bombarded with memories to care. Isabelle has a beautiful face like Regan, same tempting body and strong, determined eyes, but it is her sass that's hitting me the hardest. I fucking loved Regan's take-no-shit attitude. It was one of her most endearing assets. . .*until she used it against me.*

I get she could have done what she did because she was scared, but that wasn't my girl. The Regan I loved was so strong, even the prospect of raising a child alone wouldn't have frightened her. She did what she did because Isaac convinced her it was the right thing to do. He didn't just steal my woman all those months ago, he ensured I'd never look at her in the same light again.

I disperse the fury slicking my skin with sweat by darting my narrowed gaze around the room, which returns it to the silence it held when Isabelle entered. Agents dart in all directions, scurrying to return to the tasks I assigned this morning before I add more responsibilities to their already overflowing plates.

Once I am confident I am without additional eyes, I return my slit gaze to Isabelle. "I know who your uncle was; I know his reputation, but you need to learn your place. You were only brought here as a distraction for Isaac. He never lets anyone in, and you're supposed to be our way in."

Her throat works hard to swallow, but I'll give it to her, she's got spirit. With a roll of her shoulders and the sneer of a fighter, she snarls, "I am an agent of the Federal Bureau of Investigation. I am not a prostitute."

Her speech is strong; her poise tight, but her eyes give away her true self. She won't be forced to play the role I'm demanding she fill for the good of the agency. Her heart, on the other hand. . .

If she hasn't already knelt before her maker, I'm sure it won't take much to convince her otherwise.

ELEVEN

REGAN

I laugh so loud, I startle Axel, my adorable two-month-old nephew, who is sleeping peacefully in his crib. He's lucky he's mega cute with his nine-pound, three-ounce chubby cheeks and golden hair, or I may have killed his mother for calling him a name so similar to Alex's. I get it's a grungy, hip name that will serve him well in the future, but the similarity of his name to Alex's gives his aunty the hives.

You'd think as the months moved on, my resentment would fade. It hasn't. Not in the slightest. It's been over nine months since Alex and I called it quits, yet, I still think about him multiple times a day. This can't be healthy. There should be some switch in our brain we can turn off the instant someone hurts us, so we don't have to live with the pain of their betrayal for months, if not years after it occurs.

I honestly don't know if I can survive another six months of this. I'm an aunty; I have a fabulous job that assures me seven years of study is being put to good use, and my family dynamic is the tightest it's ever been, but I'm miserable. Lost. *Utterly alone.*

My last comment is the most frustrating. How can I feel alone when I'm surrounded by more family and friends than I've ever had? When Luca passed, I sheltered myself away for years. I rarely came home, and when I did, my visits were as short as the tripwire that detonated any time Luca's name was mentioned. I seldom went out, and it was always under vast protest, but I was happy.

Well, I thought I was.

Now. . . now I don't know who the fuck I am.

I'm drawn from somber thoughts when Isaac's deep timbre sounds down the line. "You still with me, Regan?"

I adjust my position so my back faces Axel while talking. I'm on babysitting duty, so I shouldn't horrify him with the gory adult talk I plan to scar him with in his teens.

"Yeah, I was just settling Axel. He's a bit bossy, kind of like someone else I know."

Isaac chuckles, hearing my comment as I had intended: playfully.

"That's why he was adamant about arriving when he did. You don't follow the rules when you can make them."

A smile crosses my face. "He scared the shit out of me."

Isaac murmurs in agreement. "You're not the only one. My pilot is still in shock. He didn't think he'd make it back to Texas before Raquel gave birth. It was a close call."

"It was. Twenty minutes after touchdown, he was born." My eyes drift to Axel, still as smitten as a pig in mud. He is the most adorable little boy I've ever seen. "Thank you for doing what you did, Isaac. Raquel would have never made it home if you didn't lend us your private jet."

The slightest sigh sounds down the line, advising me Isaac heard me, but he remains tight-lipped. He's never been good at accepting praise.

"You could have flown with us, you know. Held Raquel's hand and let her call you lots of horrible names instead of me."

Isaac's laughter loosens the heavy sentiment in the air. I've never seen him scared until that day in New York two months ago. He was petrified when Raquel went into labor six weeks early, but thankfully, even with his mind fritzing, he arranged for his jet to fly us back to Texas where my mom and dad were on standby. It meant he had to travel back to Ravenshoe on a commercial aircraft, but from the story he's sharing, it doesn't sound like it went too badly.

Isaac met someone during his flight. Shockingly, she turned down his invitation for a hook up later that week. I say "shocking" as, excluding me, I've not yet met a woman capable of turning Isaac down when he brings out the charm. He has to beat married women off with a stick. We used to keep a tally before. . .

I stop myself before I have my tenth memory of Alex before the clock strikes two.

"So you took her home from the club, then what happened?"

Isaac pauses long enough to gain my utmost devotion before stammering out, "Nothing."

I balk. "Nothing?! What? Please tell me I'm the only one with a broken vagina."

"Regan. . ."

I love the way he drawls my name when angry.

"One, I don't have a vagina. Two, how many times the past six months have I asked you *not* to mention your vagina when we're talking?"

"About half a dozen—not that I'm keeping a tally." *I am, and the total now sits at thirty-two.* "Come on, Isaac. You have to understand my shock. Your fuck pad isn't called that for no reason. If you were there to talk, Dr. Avery would have moved in weeks ago."

Isaac laughs, easing the tension bristling between us. It's closely followed by two words I never thought I'd hear him say, "She's different."

"Different as in?"

I hope he says something stupid like she has a third nipple or a gimpy leg. I don't want him to be miserable, but as they say, misery loves company.

I hang off every word Isaac says when he murmurs, "When she looks at me, I feel like she's sees me, Isaac, not the myth or the legend—"

"Or the guy with an immensely big head?"

COUPLE ON HOLD   65

He laughs again. "Yeah, and that. She doesn't notice any of that."

"So why no sexy time?" This time, my interest is genuine.

I know how wonderful it feels to be looked at as a person instead of a celestial being, and although it hurts remembering Alex was the only person who has looked at me in such a manner, it isn't as burning today. Isaac is a great guy. He deserves to be happy.

I wait with bated breath for Isaac to answer me. When he does, it isn't the response I'm anticipating. "Isabelle has a weird knack for murmuring under her breath. A lot of the stuff she mumbles makes sense, but there was one thing I wasn't too fond of this morning." Three long breaths pass before he adds on, "She said I was lawless."

"Lawless or flawless?" I'm certain I heard him wrong.

"If my ego was talking on my behalf, I'd say flawless, but I'm reasonably sure she said lawless. She mumbled it a good three to four times so I couldn't miss it." For the first time in nearly eight years, his tone isn't brimming with cockiness.

"Oh." I want to say more, but what could I possibly say?

Something pops into my mind at the same time suspicion runs rife through my veins. "Where did you say you met again?"

Over the next twenty minutes, Isaac gives me a rundown on the events that have occurred between him and Isabelle the past two months. Although I get the manly, lacking detail update, I can fill in the gaps.

It could be past burns making me cautious, but some stuff he says doesn't make sense. First and foremost, why would Isabelle dodge his attempts to bed her? Call me crazy, but she's either not single like she's claiming, or she's gay.

I'm one of Isaac's closest friends, and I'm on the verge of begging him to dive between the sheets with me to bring back my mojo. That's how confident I am of his bedroom skills. His aura screams sex, yet Isabelle continually turns him down.

Is she certifiably insane? Or. . .?

"Play hard to get."

"What?" Isaac's high tone reveals he thinks I'm the only crazy lady he's dealing with.

"Men aren't the only ones who like being challenged. Play hard to get. If she wants you, she'll hunt you down. If she doesn't, you're being played."

He laughs, amused by the fret in my tone. I don't care if he thinks my advice is shit; if he follows it for a day or two, I'll have enough time to launch Hunter into action. If Isabelle is who she says she is, I'll eat humble pie and give Isaac two thumbs up on his endeavor to bed her. But if she's a smoke and mirror trick a certain member at the Federal Bureau of Investigation devised to take down Isaac, she's hours away from having her flame extinguished with my four-inch stiletto.

"Didn't Theresa's ruses teach you anything, Isaac?"

My snarky comment steals the wind from Isaac's lungs as quickly as it snatches his laughter. I don't like hitting him below the belt, but it is my job to protect him, so if the occasional whack is needed to ensure I do my job to the best of my ability, that's what I'll do.

"Isabelle is nothing like Theresa."

The protectiveness in his tone shocks me, but not enough to stop me from saying, "You can't say that since you know *nothing* about her."

He growls. "Sometimes you have to take people at face value, Regan. Not everyone is out to destroy you."

His comment stabs my heart, but it also raises my bitch hackles. "Uh-huh, but only a moron wouldn't attempt to connect the dots. Isabelle arrived at Ravenshoe at the exact time you discovered the FBI was tailing you. It could be a coincidence, but that's a bitter pill to swallow when I'm talking to a man who believes coincidences are only claimed by fools and liars."

A stretch of silence passes between us. It is so dense, only Axel sucking on his hand as he announces his hunger is heard.

"Give me a day, Isaac. If I'm wrong, I'll apologize to Isabelle and never speak a bad word about her again, but I need a day."

He remains quiet. I want to pretend it is because he's considering my request, but I know Isaac as well as he knows me. He's not contemplating; he's weighing what his options are if my hunch is true. If that doesn't prove how deep Isabelle has crawled under his skin, nothing will.

Isaac lives, breathes, and sleeps for his empire. He doesn't put it at risk for anyone. . . except perhaps her.

TWELVE

ALEX

"How many agents have seen this?"

Reid, a recently recruited agent to my division, scrubs his hand along his prickly jaw before murmuring. "None but me."

"Are you sure?" I ask, untrusting of the waver in his tone.

He doesn't balk at my sneer like his fellow comrades. He merely smirks. "I'm certain. Isaac lost the surveillance van as he generally does each evening, but I had the means to keep up with him." He taps his black motorcycle boots together like Dorothy from the *Wizard of Oz*. "The house they're sitting in front of is registered to a recently—"

"Retired police officer. Yeah, I'm aware," I cut him off, well versed on all aspects of Isabelle's life.

Reid's dark brows shoot up high on his face, but he remains as quiet as a church mouse.

"Is this all that happened? Just a kiss?"

I dump a surveillance image of Isabelle and Isaac kissing in Isaac's Bugatti before raising my eyes to Reid's. He waits for me to see the disappointment in them before dipping his chin. "Although from the look on Isaac's face when he left, I doubt it was his choice."

I shouldn't smile, but I do. It's nice to see Isaac getting a taste of his own medicine.

"Where did he go after this?"

The shit-eating grin on Reid's face subsides.

"You lost him?" I ask, reading between the lines.

When he nods, I curse. For the first few weeks of my placement, I gave Regan the benefit of the doubt, confident my visit to her ranch would stop her from undermining my investigation, but as Isaac's ability to slip our radar grew, so did my suspicion. He knows we're tailing him; he just has no clue how in-depth my investigation is.

The instant Isabelle bit back at my demand she go undercover in Isaac's empire, I knew the surveillance images my crew acquired of them the weekend they flew to Ravenshoe were accurate. They had an immediate connection. How do I know this? The fireworks sparking between them as they walked down the jet bridge side by side was as blinding as the ones that forever ignited between Regan and me.

Isabelle is forging her way into Isaac's empire as I had planned months ago, except I'm not forcing her to follow my ruse with the underhanded, scheming tricks Theresa used. I'm just sitting back and watching the show unfold. It's quite simple, really. The more I strive to keep Isaac off Isabelle's radar, the harder she fights to keep him in her sights. It's a brilliant ploy, and not a single rule has been broken to make it happen.

I'm so confident Isabelle is the key to unlocking Isaac's years of criminal activities, I'm not afraid of putting all my eggs into the one basket. Isaac's arrest may not happen tomorrow; it may not happen next month, but I know it will happen eventually.

I just need Isabelle to unlock his vault load of secrets first, then I'll be able to use them against him.

Returning my eyes to Reid, I say, "No matter what you have to do, keep on him 24/7."

"You can't lose an entire fucking plane. It's a plane, for crying out loud!" I bang my phone onto my desk three times to replicate what I wish my fists could do to Reid's face before pushing it back against my ear. "They have to log a flight plan; did you check with the airstrip they flew out of?"

"They want a warrant." Reid's low tone reveals he is as frustrated as me.

I throw my hand into the air. "Then give them a fucking warrant."

"I tried. His lawyer is blocking me at every chance."

And there's the real reason my anger is so firm. For months, any move I make in my investigation of Isaac, Regan blocks. Even something as simple as bringing Isaac in for questioning concerning a recent building application lodged under a false alias was denied by his legal team.

My team is already being strangled by bureaucratic bullshit, let alone crap that shouldn't enter the equation. Regan is pissed, for what? I have no fucking clue! I didn't break her heart and leave her a miserable, grumbly bastard who spends more hours cranky than he does happy. She did that to me!

I exhale a big breath to calm my anger before asking more coolly, "Do you have confirmed footage of Isabelle boarding the plane with Isaac?"

"Yes," Reid confirms, his tone confident.

"Can you take those images and add them to the FBI database? If they land at a commercial airstrip, we have a chance of tracking down their location."

Air whizzes through Reid's teeth. "I can do that, but it will take a couple of hours. If they land before I've thrown out my net, I'll miss them."

My ticking jaw is heard in my reply, "It's better than sitting there, twiddling your fucking thumbs, isn't it?"

"True." Reid isn't the slightest bit concerned by my vicious snarl. "I'll get right on it."

When he disconnects our call, I throw down the receiver of my phone before slouching into my chair. While my brain struggles to get my heart on board with its plans, I run my fingers through my recently cut hair. Since I'm still without my beard, my hair has taken its place when I need to let off steam.

Before either my heart or brain can talk my ego out of it, I snatch up my cell phone and dial a number I had Brandon track down nearly six months ago.

Regan answers my call several seconds later. "Regan Myers, how can I help you?"

"Stop blocking my investigation. If your client has nothing to hide, you have no reason to deny my requests."

I hear a chair creak before, "I'm sorry, who is this? I missed your name at the start of our conversation."

My grip on my phone tightens. She knows who I am, she's just twisting in the knife she stabbed into my heart months ago.

"Alex Rogers, leader of the Ravenshoe division of the Federal Bureau of Investigation. I'm calling in regards to your client, Isaac Holt," I grind out through clenched teeth.

"Isaac Holt, did you say?" The shuffling of papers barely drowns out the smart-ass, condescending tone her voice is laced with. "Hmm, are you sure you have the right number? I don't have a client of that name in my records."

"I've sent requests to your office myself, Rae; don't treat me like an idiot," I seethe.

My unplanned use of her favorite nickname halts her retaliation for barely a second. "Clearly, you're mistaken, Mr. Rogers, as there is no one by that name here either!"

She slams down her phone so hard, its brutal bang breaks through my pulse shrilling in my ears. I clutch my cell so hard, the screen is seconds from cracking.

It does when I send it flying across my office.

"If you sign a contract, you're required to fulfill your contract for the set amount of time on said contract."

"But—"

"No buts, Isabelle. You're not getting out of your contract." My angry voice awards me the attention of the agents surrounding my office. "I don't care if your cat gets run over by a truck or your grandmother dies. You signed a contract. You're going to fulfill your moral obligation!"

My irritation centers more around my exchange with Regan Friday afternoon than Isaac and Isabelle's disappearing act the past weekend, but since Isabelle is the closest person I can take my anger out on, she's receiving the brunt of it.

Isabelle jumps to her feet and charges to the door when I growl, "Now go and do the job you're paid to do!"

I should be ashamed of my attitude. I should slap myself in the face and pull my fucking head in before I make a fool out of myself, but I can't. I'm beyond ropeable.

Just like Regan, I thought Isabelle was smart. I thought she'd see through Isaac's tricks to obscure the man he is beneath the mask. I was so far off the mark, none of my darts came close to hitting the bullseye.

Isabelle is no longer seeing Isaac through the eyes of an agent but through the haze of a lover. I should revel in my triumph, be stoked my plan to force them together worked as I had hoped, but I didn't factor love into the equation.

That woman who just raced out of here, she wasn't sitting across from me to defend her position at the Bureau. She was protecting her man.

If this doesn't make my job ten times harder, I don't know what will.

For every week that passes, Isabelle's influence in Isaac's life increases. First, she defended him in my office, using the excuse she wasn't cut out for my team. Then, she was seen dining with him at one of his restaurants. Although she didn't appear to be his date, him carrying her out kicking and screaming after she kissed another man revealed there is more to their relationship than just friendship.

Now, she's blubbering out an excuse as to why she knew intel on Isaac that an agent who wasn't sleeping with him probably wouldn't know.

"How do you know Isaac was a fighter?" I ask Isabelle while shadowing her into a conference room at the back of HQ.

Her big chocolate eyes dilate as she stammers out, "Umm. . . I'm just assuming. It doesn't seem like an industry you'd get into unless you have some prior knowledge about it."

I praise her flourishing investigation skills as I use a trick I was taught at the academy. It's called a compliment sandwich. Hit them with a compliment, then smack them with a hard truth before finalizing your interrogation with another compliment. It usually stuns them enough they'll reveal information without realizing what they're doing.

Unfortunately, Isabelle is more clued in than I gave her credit for. She remains quiet, proving it wasn't just her looks that helped her graduate the academy with honors.

I toss her a bone, hoping she'll toss me one back. "We recently discovered Isaac was indeed a fighter in an underground fight ring during his college years. That fight ring's organizer was Col Petretti."

Isabelle takes in a sharp breath, revealing she's heard of Col before. She also knows every word I spoke is true. Marked bills planted by the Bureau in Col Petretti's operation will be the start of Isaac's downfall. Although the money he banked during his college years wasn't as high as the men surrounding him, it is enough for a search warrant.

That's why I arrived at my office before the sparrows this morning, so I can prepare the documentation. I'll ensure every i is dotted and every t is crossed so Regan has no chance in hell of stopping me from bringing Isaac in for questioning.

It's time for the man to meet his maker.

My conversation with Isabelle takes a path I never saw coming when Brandon reveals an accident that occurred at the same time Isaac's lump sum payments ceased being deposited into his account every Monday morning during his college years.

While Brandon updates Isabelle, I take in the report he's grasping for dear life. There were two occupants in a car when it veered off the road upon hitting a section of black ice: Ophelia and Cj Petretti, only daughter and oldest son of Col Petretti. Ophelia was killed on impact. Cj spent weeks in the hospital recovering from his injuries before he fell off the FBI's radar.

Fuck.

My heart does a weird beat when Isabelle asks Brandon, "Did Ophelia survive the accident?"

I realize my attention is focused in the wrong direction when Isabelle's eyes flood with tears upon spotting the rapid shake of Brandon's head.

My wish to have more money than sense smacks into me for the third time in a year when my old sedan struggles to keep up with Isaac's town car weaving in and out of traffic.

Isabelle did a good job losing my tail when she snuck out of HQ hours after our confrontation, but since she isn't behind the wheel of the car, and she's being controlled by her heart instead of her head, I have no trouble maintaining a safe but close distance.

When the dark BMW pulls into a derelict warehouse on the outskirts of Hopeton to drop Isabelle off, I use one of the many burnt-out cars scattered around my location to hide my piece of shit sedan. When a lack of government funds forced me to purchase my own vehicle, I nearly splurged, but Isla's eight thousand dollar dental bill squashed that idea as quickly as it arrived. She needed braces more than I needed a nice car.

Kristin returned to work three months ago, but she's not close to taking over the financial reins I've been holding since Dane's death. I honestly don't know if she'll ever be ready. I had no clue kids were so expensive. It makes me wonder if that's why Regan made the decision she did nearly a year ago. She knew the financial burden of having a baby. Although it's a piss poor excuse, one I would have happily argued against if given the chance, it makes my anger not as intense as it once was.

My thoughts return to the present when Isabelle and Isaac exit the warehouse from the same partially open door Isabelle entered ten minutes ago. Isaac is carrying Isabelle in his arms, his hold displaying his arrogant dominance. I wait for him to place her into the passenger seat of his flashy sportscar, throw a shirt over his sweat-slicked body, and dart out of the warehouse lot like a madman before firing up my engine.

Isaac annoys the fuck out of me, but I can put aside my disdain long enough to admit he's admirably cunning. I've lost count of the number of times he's absconded from the surveillance team who tail his every movement. I want to say all his fleeing skills are thanks to his expensive ride, but that would be a lie. He hasn't flown under the FBI radar so long for no reason.

He's good at keeping his hands clean.

———————

Have you ever been torn between doing what is morally right and acting ignorant for the greater good? I'm facing that issue right now. Isabelle is in Isaac's apartment, the one opposite Regan's old crash pad. She's been in there long enough I'm confident the murmurs trickling over the state of the art headphones covering my ears aren't sentences, but not long enough for guilt to force me to do the right thing.

She isn't doing anything against her wishes. The instant she refused to go undercover in Isaac's case, I put her on desk duty, so anything happening in his apartment is not on my shoulders. But no matter how many times I've told myself that the past hour, my heart won't listen.

Fuck!

This is too similar to the ruse Theresa pulled on Regan and me. There are too many similarities at play for me to ignore this. I don't need to shut down this operation, but I need to ensure Isabelle is aware of what is at stake here.

I throw my headphones onto the desk, startling Reid. "Shut down surveillance and remove any footage we've obtained the past hour from our servers."

Reid looks like he wants to argue, but he knows better than to question me. It's a pity I don't need to hear his words to see them.

"She was our agent before she was his. . . *whatever.* I have to fix this." I don't know how, and I don't know why, but I know it's the right thing to do.

My campaign to right my wrongs goes to shit when an attractive blonde captures my attention outside of Isaac's apartment building. A woman with remarkably similar features to Regan is sliding out of the back of a cab. Her hair sits the same length as Regan's the last time I saw her; her smile the same, and even the swell of her chest is oddly similar. There is just one difference: she has a bright pink stripe down one side of her hair.

Even knowing the woman climbing back into the taxi to gather something from the back seat isn't Regan, I can't stop myself from moving toward her. "Rae?"

The blonde clambers onto the sidewalk before spinning around to face me. Although the first thing my eyes should lock in on is her face, a squeal of jubilation steals my devotion. The bag I thought she was climbing into the taxi to gather isn't a bag; it's a baby strapped in a car seat. He has spiky blond hair and a cheeky grin that exposes two little teeth in the top of his otherwise gummy mouth. His eyes are as blue as mine, his jaw just as square. He's a cute little thing. . . even with his familiarities sending my heart rate skyrocketing.

After shaking my head to clear some of the confusion, I raise my eyes to the blonde. I take a step back when the face doesn't match the one permanently embedded in my memory. She is beautiful—insanely gorgeous—but she isn't Rae.

"Sorry, I thought you were someone else."

I don't wait for her to respond before pivoting on my heels and darting down the jam-packed sidewalk. I don't know where I'm going, and I have no clue what I'll do when I get there, but I need to get as far away from here as possible, because that blonde and her adorable little baby are taking my fond memories and turning them into horribly bitter ones.

THIRTEEN

REGAN

"What are your thoughts on your apartment?"

Raquel sighs. If I didn't know her as well as I did, I'd assume she's hating her first taste of Ravenshoe. It's a pity I know her better than I've known myself the past twelve months.

"It's good. It's a great size, and it's really beautiful, but I'm reasonably sure it's beyond my means." She sighs for the second time. "Are you sure it's only $500 a month?"

"Yes," I lie. "Someone died in the apartment across from yours, so no one wants to rent any of the apartments on that floor." I wouldn't have lied if I was concerned it would ruffle Raquel's feathers, but unlike me, she loves blood and gore.

"Was that Axel?" I ask when a coo sounds down the line, hoping to use him as a distraction from the deceit in my tone.

Raquel follows along nicely. "Yeah, he's hungry. . . or pooping? I haven't worked out all his expressions yet."

I laugh. Raquel is too hard on herself. She is a damn good mother, one I hope to emulate one day. Pretending my surprised confession was a consequence of the hormones running rampant through my veins, I switch from perusing pretty dresses to overpriced shoes and handbags. With my mood at an all-time low, I've spoiled myself with a weekend shopping expedition in New York City. It is a delayed birthday gift to myself since I'm another year closer to thirty.

Regrettably, splurging is not having the effect I was aiming for. I'll always love my designer babies, but after having a taste of what love can really be like, materialistic things aren't cutting the mustard. Don't get me wrong; I'm not referring to my brief fling with an FBI agent who has caused more stings to my backside the past twelve months than he did when he spanked it raw. It centers solely around Axel and his adorable little face.

Mostly.

Somewhat.

Not even.

Argh! Axel is a big part of my newfound quest for love, but he's not the only reason I'm not looking at four figure dresses with love hearts in my eyes. Occasionally a man with the same letters in his name as Axel makes an appearance.

For the most part, I've spent the last twelve months without my heart in tatters. Isaac's empire and our joint business adventure has kept my mind so occupied, it's rare for me to catch a moment of quiet. I did what all good businesswoman do: I kept my head down and my bum up. My heavy grind was working. I opened a little office in my hometown, settled into my role of aunty without a single hive breaking out on my skin, and I even aided in preparing Luca's memorial.

It was a good day spent with family and friends as I remembered the boy I once loved. . . until a blast from the past forgot the significance of the day.

When Alex's name popped up on the caller ID in my office, I nearly didn't answer his call. I had taken the day off, and was only there to gather the check I was donating in memory of Luca to an LGBT support group for teens founded at our local high school. I should have ignored Alex's call as I have many times the past twelve months, but for just a second, I wanted to pretend our time together wasn't all a lie, that at one stage he did care for me.

How wrong was I?

He wasn't calling to offer his condolences on what he knew was my darkest day. He wanted me to stop petitioning the courts to throw out his badly compiled warrant requests.

I'm not denying his office's requests to speak with Isaac because I'm a vindictive bitch who prefers spending her weekends preparing motions instead of cuddling my nephew, but Alex gives me no choice. Nothing he's brought forward is enough to convince either a judge or myself that Isaac has something to answer for, meaning, my client has no reason to comply with his numerous requests to attend prearranged interviews.

I can't spell it out any simpler than that.

Add Alex's contact with my sister's wish to return to her studies sooner than the original twelve months she had planned when Axel was born, and you have the perfect recipe for a shit four weeks. My mom is stoked Raquel hasn't given up her dreams to be a trauma surgeon even after having a baby. My dad. . . he's also happy, until he realized the return of her studies meant moving away from home for the second time in her life. This time, she would take the apple of his eye right along with her.

It's been a tough four weeks, and I thought a heavy dose of retail therapy would fix it.

Once again, how wrong was I?

I press my phone close to my ear as I pace to the perfume counter. I have enough dresses and shoes to fill a castle, but I'm sure there are a few vacant spots on my vanity for a nice bottle of perfume or two.

While recalling Axel's delicious baby scent, I suggest, "It could be Axel's teeth making him grumpy? I read that babies get grizzly around his age."

Raquel's sigh shifts from one filled with suspicion to one teeming with glee. "I still can't believe you read all those mother-to-be books."

Her words jut out as though she is rocking Axel while talking to me. I wouldn't be surprised. Any time he's in my arms, I naturally rock. It must be an inbuilt mechanism all females have for blood-related children. I never did it before Axel. Just looking at strangers' babies made me want to buy a chastity belt. I don't get that same skin-crawling feeling when I peer at Axel's adorable face. He makes me soft and gooey. I'd fucking hate it if I didn't love him so much.

"Someone had to read them," I say with a laugh, getting back to our conversation. "If I didn't, I would have assumed you peed your pants in the middle of our flight."

Raquel laughs. "God, did you see the pilot's face when you asked him to fly faster? He almost had a coronary."

"I don't blame him. You're nasty when you're in labor."

Raquel scoffs. "Hey! It hurt—*a lot*. I swear I had phantom pains the entire trip to Ravenshoe last month."

I laugh to hide my grimace. Out of all the towns in the world, she chose to finish her studies in Ravenshoe. I know why she picked it. Isaac and his business partner/best friend are building a metropolis that includes one of the most state of art hospitals you'll find on this side of the country. She'll learn a lot, but I wish she had picked a town I wouldn't hesitate visiting. I haven't been back to Ravenshoe since I convinced her abortion wasn't her only option.

"Hey, speaking of Ravenshoe, how many men did you leave hanging here? I'm getting eyeballed, and it's not the usual scrutiny I'm accustomed to."

I love the haughtiness in her tone. Raquel is hot. She knows it. I know it. And within a few days, every resident of Ravenshoe knew it.

"I'm not you, Raquel. My dates barely branched out from my battery operated boyfriends."

She makes a gagging noise.

"Let's see if you're still gagging when you test out the surprises I packed in your overnight bag."

"You didn't." Her breathing picks up as feet padding across carpet sound down the line. "Where did you put them?"

I grin at her eagerness. "Sheesh, for someone not interested in sex toys, you sound rather excited."

"Shut up and tell me where they are. It's been nearly a year since I've. . ." She muffles her phone, worried Axel will remember our conversation for years to come. ". . .had sex. I'm dying over here."

I nearly say, *you're not the only one*, but the sharp gasp she sucks in reveals she found my treasure trove of goodies. "Oh my god. I know I've had a baby, but I still don't think that will fit."

The store clerk shushes me when I throw my head back and laugh.

After giving her a glare that involves a screwed-up nose and a poked-out tongue, I say, "Believe me, with the right amount of lube, and the correct tilt of your hips, that bad boy will fit in any hole you want him to fit."

Some of the tension I was hoping to relieve during my trip expels when the store clerk huffs loudly before pivoting on her heels and darting to the manager. *Good luck, sweetheart, I spend the equivalent of your annual wage in this store every month, so the chances of having me tossed to the curb are slim to none.*

I want to throw myself out when my pivot has me crashing into a wall of hardness. It isn't the man's packed gun smacking into my nose fueling my desire to flee. It's his manly, virile smell. I've only smelled that scent once before. It was on a man who couldn't afford the cologne he was wearing.

With a roll of my shoulders and a stern warning that I'm not a daft wallflower, I raise my eyes to the person I've bumped into. The blond hair, blue eyes, and razor-sharp jaw I'm anticipating reflect back at me, they're just on a slightly more mature face.

"Grayson, hi."

"Who's Grayson?" Raquel whispers down the line. "Is he hot? From the way your tone dipped and your breathing became non-existent, I'm assuming he's hot. Is he?"

I hold my finger in the air to request a minute before shifting my focus back to my cell. "I have to go. I'll call you tonight. Give Axel a kiss for me."

"What. No—"

The rest of Raquel's demand is lost when I disconnect our call before sliding my phone into my clutch purse.

"Sorry about that." I nudge my head to the clerk who is once again stationed at the sales counter she was manning earlier, minus the pompous glare she once had. "I was just—"

"Giving her a taste of her own medicine?" Grayson interrupts.

I nod. "Pretty much so."

"Good. She deserves it. I've been waiting to be served the last ten minutes, but since I'm not wearing a suit and tie, supposedly my money is no good here."

The tick in his jaw is cute. He's a lot like his brother. Down to earth, focused, and confident enough he doesn't need a suit to gain the ladies' attention. Just the thirty seconds we've been interacting, I've been issued four warning glares. The women of New York are on the hunt, and I'm sheltering their prey.

Happy to be on the receiving end of vicious glares from worthy opponents for a change, I lean my hip on the counter Grayson is standing next to before raising my eyes to his. "What are you after? A new Christmas tie? Flip flops? Or sunglasses that will make you look like a speed dealer?"

"I can get those here?" Grayson's lips quirk when I nod. "Damn, and all this time I was subjecting myself to malls overrun with teens and cranky middle-aged women whose husbands can't get them off."

His reply eases the tension boiling between us. He's not going to bring up Alex, and neither am I, so I can help him with his dilemma and not feel guilty.

"Alright, spill the beans. What are you really after?"

A smell I've missed the past twelve months filters into my nose when Grayson waves a business card in front of my face. "I'm trying to identify this scent. Rumor is it's only sold here."

I glare at him, shocked. "What's so important about that smell?" *Besides the fact it's your brother's cologne?*

Grayson taps his index finger on his nose. I want to pretend his quest is more sinister than it is, but for all I know, he could merely be buying his brother a Christmas gift.

Pretending I can't feel bile burning my throat, I signal for assistance. Although disgruntled, the store clerk arrives in front of us two seconds later.

"My friend would like to purchase a bottle of this cologne." I snatch the business card from Grayson's hand before waving it under the clerk's nose, barely catching the name on the card before Grayson secures it back in his hand: Col Petretti.

While the clerk moves to a glass cabinet in the far back, my mind runs wild. Why would Grayson have a card from Col Petretti, much less one with his brother's scent on it? Col Petretti isn't a nice man. He's the mobster who's been striving to get a foothold into Ravenshoe the past three years. It is only Isaac's friendship with a much more revered member of Col's association that has stopped it from happening.

Before I can answer half the questions in my head, the clerk returns to the counter with a large, fancy-looking box of cologne in her hands. She doesn't set it down. The four-figure price tag on the top ensures she won't relinquish it from her grip without a credit card being handed over.

She does exactly that when I slide my platinum no-limit credit card across the glass countertop. With the skip of a woman about to get a big tip, she processes my credit card as I gather the box in my hands.

"Are you sure it's the right one. . .?"

Grayson's words trail off when I pop open the lid of the Clive Christian X cologne I just purchased. There is no denying that smell. It is rich and pungent, and swirls my stomach with so much unease, my heart speaks before my head can stop it. "How can your brother afford such an expensive bottle of cologne?"

Grayson's balk barely ripples the air, but I still notice it. "Alex wears this cologne?"

I shouldn't nod, but I do.

"Are you sure?"

I give Grayson a look. It's my *do I look like a fucking idiot?* glare. Alex and I may have only been together for a week, but I'll never forget his scent.

"Fuck," Grayson growls when he spots the truth in my eyes.

He doesn't say anything more for several seconds, he just scrubs the scruff on his chin as his eyes continually dart between the price on the receipt the clerk placed between us and the groove burrowed between my brows.

I want to say something to ease the turmoil in his eyes, but I'm honestly lost on what to say. I'm as confused as he is.

After a few more minutes of silence, Grayson digs his wallet out of his pocket. "Forward me your receipt, and I'll have you compensated for the bottle." His hand rattles when he slides an FBI business card across to me. "It might take them a few weeks to process, but I'll push it through as fast as I can."

I'm about to tell him not to bother; I'm not hard up for money, but he leaves the store before I get the chance, leaving me and his brother's overpriced bottle of cologne in his wake.

FOURTEEN

ALEX

"You need a warrant."

I follow the receptionist at Westminster Family Clinic when she moves back to the stack of files she was sorting before I stormed into her office with a heart of steel and a face just as stern.

"I don't want any details about the patient; I just need confirmation of whether or not she had the operation she paid for." My hand rattles when I thrust a receipt in her direction. "Please. This information will never leave this room." I stare into her eyes, showing the rawness that's been eating me alive the past four weeks.

That little boy I saw last month, the one I confused his mother for Regan for barely a second, hasn't left my thoughts the past four weeks. I can't eat, sleep, or concentrate on anything not associated with him. Even knowing his mother isn't Regan, his familiar features are too intriguing for me to ignore. He has my jaw and eyes. He even has the same cowlick curling up the front of his identical blond hair.

"Please. I'm begging you."

I'm two seconds from falling to my knees and pleading like a fool, but the quickest flash of remorse in the receptionist's eyes stops me. With a grin revealing she's more worried than happy, she moves to a stack of filing cabinets on her right. She ruffles through the drawer marked L-M for barely a second before she secures a pink-coded file in her trembling hand.

I swear, my heart stops beating when she pries it open. *Here it comes, months of heartache are about to smack into me with one mammoth swing.*

My eyes dart down to the receptionist at the same time her eyes rocket up to mine. The file is empty. Not partially. Not a little. Empty—*empty*.

"Where did it go?"

She shrugs before her hand delves between the files before and after the one she's holding. "I don't know. Everything else appears to be in order."

"Could it have been filed wrong? Placed in another patient's folder?" I stop pacing around her desk when her glare slices my steps in half. I've already forced her to step over one line today; she's not willing to let me do it for the second time.

"Can you check?"

My fingers rake through my hair when she replies, "I am; it's not here." She slams the filing cabinet door shut before spinning around to face me. "I'm sorry. I tried."

I nod, understanding she did her best, but I can't help but curse God. *Why isn't anything ever easy for me?*

After exhaling a deep breath, I put on the agent's cap I lost upon entering and work this case with the years of skills I have under my belt. "If I showed you her picture, do you think you'd remember her?"

"I guess," she replies with a shrug.

Happy she's at least giving it a shot, I smile in thanks before digging my wallet out of my pocket. Don't ask me why I still carry a photo of Regan in my wallet. I've tried many times to take it out, but failed just as many. She is slotted right between the photos of Isla and Addison that Kristin shipped me last month.

"Aww. Aren't they cute? Are they your daughters?" The receptionist is hoping her comment will ease the tension bristling between us. Unfortunately, I'm too worked up to follow suit.

"No. They're. . ." I'm stumped of a reply. Addison and Isla aren't my daughters, but I take care of them as if they are. "They're my goddaughters," I settle on.

The receptionist does a good job not responding to the angst in my tone.

"Here is Regan." I hand her a photo of Regan peering up at the sky in the seconds following the removal of the tear she shed at the same time every night.

I take in the photo as diligently as the receptionist. With everything going on, I forgot about Regan's grief. I've concentrated so hard on keeping my promises to Dane, I haven't had the chance to sit down and work through my own remorse.

The mad beat of my heart doubles when my eyes drop to my clock to check the date. Luca's memorial was last month. I wonder if Regan went this year? And if she did, was it only Luca on her mind that day?

I'm drawn back to the present when the receptionist says, "I'm sorry. She appears familiar, but I'm not confident enough to declare if she was a patient here."

"We already know she was a patient. This proves it." I tap the receipt on her desk. "I'm just trying to determine if she went ahead with her operation."

"I know." The receptionist pats my arm in a soothing manner. "But I'm not confident I've seen her before, much less that I remember what happened *if* she came here."

I want to argue, but years of training reveals it will be no use. She's being honest. She didn't stutter when grilled or lose my eye contact. She truly can't remember.

"Okay. Thank you for trying." I gather the receipt from the counter and the photo from her hand before stuffing them back into my wallet.

My sloth-like steps out of the clinic slow when the receptionist murmurs, "There could be hundreds of R. Myers in the world."

When I pivot around to face her, she's sitting behind her desk, sorting files like she never said anything. I'm about to ask what her riddle refers to, but the quickest flashback of a file from years ago steals my words.

Raquel Myers, younger sister of Regan Myers.

Holy fucking shit. Did I have my sights set on the wrong Myers?

After a quick mumble of thanks, I stumble onto the sidewalk outside of the 24-hour family planning clinic. It is late, but the number of pedestrians is still at an all-time high. My wide shoulders keep me from being bumped and elbowed when I stop halfway down the sidewalk to yank my phone from my pocket.

Because only one member of my team has my private number, it doesn't take me long to locate the number I called in haste last month. I bite out a string of curse words when the date of my call registers as memorable. I blasted Regan for blocking my investigation on the day of Luca's death. *Fuck—can I be any more of an asshole?*

I press my phone close to my ear when Regan's voice sounds down the line. "You've reached Regan Myers. Please leave your name and number, and I'll get back to you."

"Rae. . ." I grimace. *That wasn't a good start.* "Regan, it's Alex. . . Alex Rogers." *The hole just keeps growing.* "I know I'm probably the last person you want to hear from, but can you call me? It's urgent." I rattle off my cell phone number before disconnecting the call.

Wanting to ensure she can't miss the urgency in my tone, I send a text to her old number. I doubt it's still active, but when you're grasping at straws, you use anything you can.

As my eyes lift from the screen of my phone, the quickest flurry of black freezes my steps. Isaac just darted into a restaurant on my left. Although seeing him dine at expensive restaurants is nothing out of the norm, alarms are ringing in my head. I'm in Hopeton, standing outside a row of buildings Isaac doesn't own. That alone is highly suspicious. Isaac refuses to dine in any establishments he doesn't own.

I slide my cell phone into my pocket before crossing the street. The brutish doorman blocking the entrance Isaac just entered holds his hand out, refusing my entrance. The flash of my badge drops his hand from my chest even faster than he steps out of my path. Lucky, or I would have dispelled some of the anger I've been hording the past year on him and his abhorrent face.

I move through the restaurant lithely, my guard up. If the goon on the door wasn't already an indication that this enterprise isn't lawful, the number of suit-clad man huddled around empty tables is a sure-fire sign. All they need is cigars in their hands and a mafia film set would be at the ready.

"Double whiskey, hold the rocks."

The bartender jerks up his chin before serving me my drink as requested. I withheld the ice as the condensation on the glass gives away the fact I never drink my order. I could not order, but then I'd look even more out of place than I already do.

After placing a twenty onto the sticky countertop, I twist in my barstool to face the mainly empty restaurant. It takes me inconspicuously scanning the area three times before I find the mark I'm seeking. Isaac is sitting in the very far corner. He has his back facing me, but I don't need to see his face to know it is him. I can smell his arrogance from here.

I accidentally swallow a mouthful of the whiskey I'm pretending to swig when Isaac moves enough to the right I can see who he is dining with: Alberto Sokolov, righthand man of Vladimir Popov, mob boss of Las Vegas.

My heart beats in an unusual rhythm when excitement overwhelms me. After twelve long fucking months, I've got him.

Isaac's nuts are about to be pinned to the wall. *Finally.*

FIFTEEN

REGAN

"Izzy just arrested Isaac."

I push my phone close to my ear, certain what I'm hearing is wrong. "What? You said we could trust her, Hugo."

Hunter ran the reports I requested months ago. Although they didn't yield many results, Hugo planted some traps to test Isabelle's loyalty to Isaac. She passed every test with flying colors. We thought she was one of the good guys. Clearly, we fucked up.

"I thought we could trust her. *Fuck.* I don't know. Something's off with this, Regan." Hugo thrashes the motor on Isaac's town car as he weaves through the populated streets of Ravenshoe. "Isaac had me sit with Izzy last night—"

"Because he was worried Vladimir would arrive for their meeting?"

"Yeah," Hugo agrees before he honks at a motorist not cooperating with his desire to get to the police station Isaac has been hauled to. "Did he?"

Even though Hugo can't see me, I shake my head. "Vladimir rarely leaves Vegas, but Hunter had a mark on him just in case." I gather my coat and keys from my desk. "This is my fault, Hugo. I guarantee it."

"You don't know that." I wish his voice reflected the confidence of his statement. "Just because Vladimir's men said the premise was secure doesn't mean it was."

I wish what he was saying was true, but a niggle in my gut cautions me not to be stupid. This is Alex; I'm certain of it. That's why he left a message on my voicemail last night. If he thinks giving me a heads up that he's arresting my client will make up for all the wrongs he's done, he's shit out of luck.

"If you see Isaac before me, tell him to keep his mouth shut." My brisk charge out of my office jolts my words.

A smile crosses my face when the revs of Hugo's car slow. "You better have found a genie in a bottle, because even with Ravenshoe's traffic at its worst, there is no chance in hell you'll beat me to Ravenshoe PD."

I throw open my car door and slide into the warm leather seats before fastening my seatbelt. "Scared to boss Isaac around, Hugo?"

He laughs to hide the honesty in his tone when he says, "More like, I'm not stupid enough to fall for another one of your tricks, Ms. Prim and Proper."

His playful comment has the effect he was aiming for, diminishing the weight on my shoulders by reminding me that Isaac has the best group of people surrounding him. We're a unit. You can't take one of us down without taking us all down.

Alex is about to discover that the hard way.

SIXTEEN

ALEX

I've handled many arrogant men in my time, but Isaac takes the cake. He didn't even look at the evidence I presented to him. His confidence is so fucking high, he'd rather face jail time than answer a few simple questions.

Although I'm certain some of his pigheadedness resides from his naturally arrogant nature, a part of me is wondering if he recognized me. The instant his eyes landed on mine when I joined him in the interrogation room at Ravenshoe PD, the conceitedness beaming out of him tripled. He dropped a line about only men with something to hide needing a lawyer. He could have been referencing anyone, but all my ears heard was Regan's name in place of the lawyer's.

Even bringing Isabelle into the interview room didn't make his arrogance falter in the slightest. If anything, it made him more egotistical. When he stood to put on his jacket, I was five seconds from cuffing him to the table. The only reason I didn't was the fastest glance at a face I'd never forget.

Regan was standing outside the interrogation room door, peering my way. Her eyes were narrowed, and her face was as red with anger as mine, but she was still the most beautiful woman I ever laid my eyes on.

Before my brain clicked back into gear, Isaac was halfway out the door, leaving me in the interrogation room with a rogue agent and evidence Regan would have thrown out of court in under ten seconds. I may have witnessed Isaac dining with a high-up member of the Russian Mafia, but without any evidence of what their meeting pertained to, I'm left without a case.

That's why I'm here, in my office at 4 AM, seeking answers.

I'm also doing everything in my power to stop me from reaching out to Regan again. She hasn't returned the call I made yesterday, and in all honesty, I haven't had a chance to process anything not pertaining to Isaac's case.

In my heart, I want to believe it was Regan's sister, Raquel, who was a patient at Westminster Family Clinic all those months ago, but I've never been fond of coincidences. The appointment was paid with Isaac's company credit card almost two months after Regan and I slept together numerous times without protection. Those are either a shit ton of flukes, or Regan isn't the woman I thought she was.

There's an easy solution for my confusion, but since it requires prying into Regan's private life, I'm hesitant to do it. I pledged to myself over a year ago that I would keep my relationship with Regan separate from my job. I can't do that if I conduct a search on her and her sister in the births, deaths and marriages register.

My eyes lift from a stack of paperwork when a firm voice growls, "You're a real piece of work. If it isn't bad enough you arrested a man with no evidence that he committed a crime, you trashed his home."

Regan saunters into my office, freeing my eyes to scan the entrance she walked through without setting off my intruder alarm.

"Looking for this?" She flicks a gold bell into my chest, the firmness of her throw revealing she arrived ready to maim. "You should rethink your security measures after sleeping with the enemy."

I have no reply. This isn't the first time she's sided with a criminal, but it is the first time she's admitted it.

When her eyes drop to the folders on my desk, I flip them over. She laughs, amused by my attempts to conceal confidential documents. It isn't the husky, ball-clenching laugh I grew to love in an extremely short period of time, but a laugh filled with angst.

"Do you truly think you have anything in those folders I haven't already seen?" Although she's asking a question, she continues talking, stealing my chance to reply. "I've seen it all, Alex." She growls my name more than pronouncing it. "Your unjust investigation of my client. Your bogus claims of evidence." Her glassy eyes dance between mine when she mutters, "Your pathetic acting skills."

Acting skills?

Her seductive scent smacks into me when she places an itemized invoice on my desk. "What's this?" I pick up the document, noticing the two items on the top are white leather couches. "A money laundering operation? Who in their right mind would pay $15,000 for a couch?"

Regan acts unaffected by my deep snarl, but the flutter in her neck gives away her true composure. She's struggling just as much as I am to remain civil.

"These are items *your* department is going to purchase for *my* client."

I dump the paper back on her side of the table. "Why would I buy Isaac Holt new couches?"

She twists her lips to stifle her scream. She shouldn't bother as her next set of words are more roars than sentences. "You either replace the items you ruined during your unjust search of my client's property or face prosecution."

I laugh. It adds to the tension suffocating the air, but considering it was either laugh or yell, I went for what I believed more suitable.

She folds her arms under her chest. I really wish she wouldn't. I'm already having a hard time keeping my eyes on her face, and now she's made my battle ten times worse.

"You should be counting your lucky stars my client is more of a man than you are. He could press charges for the shambles you left his house in."

Her first sentence seizes the last shred of my composure and throws it out the window. I'm ropeable—I'm fuming mad—but more than anything, I'm fucking devastated she has once again chosen Isaac over me.

The vein in Regan's neck works overtime when I stand from my chair. Since she's wearing heels, our heights are even, our eyes locked. "Your *client* is more of a man than me?"

I don't know why I'm demanding she reiterate her statement. The smug expression on her face reveals she knows I heard what she said, but I want her to spell it out for me, to make sure I don't miss whose team she's on.

When she nods, I snarl, "Your client is a criminal! He orders for men to be killed before he sits back in a crystal house, smirking down at the poor fuck's life he ruined."

She rolls her eyes. "You're so far left field, you can't even see the hitter. Isaac hasn't done anything wrong—"

"You want proof?" I interrupt as anger overtakes my heartache. "I'll show you fucking proof. You're so blinded by that man, Rae, you're walking around with blinders on."

She steps around my desk so she can poke her finger into my chest. "Don't call me that! Only my family and friends get to call me Rae."

I stop seeking the evidence I'm after to grab her hand and yank her forward. My tug is so brutal, her breasts press against my thrusting chest. "I could arrest you for putting your hands on me."

Her whiskey-scented breath fans my lips when she snarls, "Then step back and let me get in a good hit. At least then your charges won't be bogus."

I tell myself time and time again it is the alcohol heating her veins responsible for her comment, but it does little to weaken my anger. She's only standing before me now because she's defending Isaac. If the fact this is her first visit to Ravenshoe in over a year isn't enough of an indication, the protective fire in her eyes seals the deal.

She's not here for me. She's here for Isaac.

With that in mind, I release her wrist from my grip and take a step back. "If you want to fight me, Rae, fight me. If you want to hit me, hit me. But don't *ever* accuse me of acting when I was with you. I fucking loved you before you let *him* take everything away from me."

She stands still, seemingly torn on whether to flee or fight. She chooses the former when she turns on her heels and races out the door without so much of a backward glance in my direction.

SEVENTEEN

REGAN

While clamping my mouth with my hand, I scream my frustration into the street. I'm confident the music booming out of Isaac's nightclub will stifle my screams, but I use my hand as a backup just in case.

I knew confronting Alex was a stupid idea; that's why I tossed down a few glasses of liquid courage before vowing allegiance to the cause. I should have smacked him when he placed the offer on the table, but his confession of love utterly blindsided me.

Why is he still playing the same hand? It's been twelve months, for crying out loud. He needs to be dealt some new cards.

I guess that's what I was hoping to achieve by visiting his office this evening. The search his department conducted on Isaac's property was excessive. They destroyed everything: his furniture, priceless family heirlooms, and paintings that can never be replaced. They left no surface untouched. Why? Because Alex is angry at Isaac for something he didn't do.

If I had known the consequences of my actions last year, I would have never thrown Isaac under the bus with me. I was a grown woman who had no qualms telling Alex what I did and didn't like, so why didn't I portray that woman that night? If I had just told Alex to leave, a lot of this heartache could have been avoided.

Isaac is devastated. Unlike me, he didn't just discover the person he's falling in love with is an FBI agent—he had his home trashed, his reputation sullied with unfounded lies, and his businesses placed on the line.

And if the woman I've just seen entering is who I think she is, matters are about to get ten times worse for him.

EIGHTEEN

ALEX

"It's a little fancier than the basement office they shoved me in. Anyone would swear you were sleeping with the boss for the upgrades you've secured the past few months."

Theresa walks into my office, her steps as life-sucking as always. Her blonde hair has grown a few inches longer since the last time I saw her, and she's added a few pounds to her tiny frame, but her eyes are as evil as they've ever been.

"Oh, that's right, you can't sleep with your daddy, can you? You just use his position to your advantage at any chance you get."

Usually, I'd bite back at any insinuation my father's high profile in the Bureau is the reason behind my advancements, but since this is Theresa, a woman more corrupt than she is moral, I'll stockpile my reserves for someone worthier of my fight. Perhaps the blonde who just left my office in near tears before screaming obscenities into the street—the one I was five seconds from chasing down before Theresa reappeared.

"What do you want, Theresa?" Nothing but hostility rings in my tone.

She sets down a photo of my family on a side table before spinning around to face me. "Hmm. Where should I start? At my position you wrongly had me removed from? The rogue agent you've let run free on your team the past six months? Or your connection with Col Petretti?"

I laugh off her first two comments, but her last one has me choking on spit. "I'm connected to Col Petretti? Where did you dig that allegation from, Theresa? The vault load of lies you amassed between sleeping with Isaac Holt and failing to pin your son on him."

She scoffs as anger lines her face. "You can't pin a child on his father."

"Oh, yeah, that's right. Isaac is his daddy. I forgot." Even a stranger couldn't miss the sarcasm in my tone. "So why isn't he paying child support or arranged for visitation?"

"I don't know." Theresa's tone is as mocking as mine. "Perhaps he's upset I didn't take the route Regan did when she discovered one of your swimmers had pierced the raincoat."

Knuckles popping bellow through my office when I clench my fists. "How do you know about that?" My words are so hot, they hiss and sizzle in the air.

"The same way you discovered my secret." She props her ass onto my desk. "A little birdie told me." A brazen wink seals her arrogant statement.

I stand from my chair and walk around my desk. I'm not using my size to intimidate her. I'm just hoping it will. . . *intimidate her.* "You have five seconds to tell me why you're here before I have the utmost pleasure of throwing you out of *my* office."

I'll give it to her. She has balls of steel. She doesn't flinch, balk, or swallow excessively when subjected to my furious wrath. She just stands her ground, proving she's more stupid than she is attractive.

I stop trying to grab her arm when she murmurs, "Clive Christian X."

When my eyes bounce between hers, confused, she adds on, "Your aftershave. It's Clive Christian X. Am I right?"

Although confused about where she's going with this, I nod.

Theresa smirks a smug grin. "It's the exact same brand of after-shave Col Petretti wears."

Her grin morphs onto my face. "That's your connection? An aftershave? You're gonna need more than that to convince a jury."

I assist her off my desk and walk her to the door. I'll never put my hands on a woman to hurt them, so you can imagine how hard it is for me not to dig my fingers into Theresa's bony arm. But I do it. I act like a gentleman—barely!

"I don't need a jury to take you down, Alex," Theresa sneers. "I just need to convince a pretty little blonde that her beliefs are true."

Her arm jerks from my grip when I suddenly stop in my tracks. "What are you talking about?"

She spins to face me, her smile picking up. She thinks she has me right where she wants me. It's a pity our last tussle didn't teach her anything. I'm smarter now, more vengeful. . . *and heartbroken*. That's a lethal combination.

"Regan believes you used her to forge an investigation into Isaac. By convincing her you've sided with Isaac's enemy, it gives her theory more credit."

Her comment fills me with dread, but I act coy. "So? Why would that bother me?"

I step back when she lifts her hand to my face. "You should have kept the beard. It hides the tick your jaw gets any time Regan is mentioned."

I fold my arms in front of my chest, wordlessly warning her I'm two seconds from tossing her ass to the curb. She finds my attempts to act superior amusing. Her cheeks rise, exposing her gleaming white teeth.

"I get it, I do. I saw the surveillance pics. You had chemistry. But seriously, how much time do you need to get over a week-long fling? Regan was good within a few days. You. . ." A laugh finalizes her sentence.

Once her laughter settles, she raises her eyes to mine. They're glistening with humor, but it's the devious gleam of revenge I'm paying the most attention to.

"Let me spell it out in layman's terms for you, so that scrawny brain of yours has no trouble keeping up." She glances over her shoulder to ensure we're alone before returning her eyes to mine. They're even more scheming now. "If you don't help me get back the position I deserve, I'll ensure you'll never win back the woman you're *still* in love with."

I nod, acknowledging I finally understand her threat. She thinks I'm so scared of losing Regan that I'll do anything she wants me to do. The thing is, she failed to realize I've already lost Regan, so I've got nothing more to lose, meaning she's shit out of luck.

"I get it, I do," I mimic, nasal voice and all. "Isaac didn't even need a day to get over you, so you're angry and lashing out, but let me spell it out in a way a vindictive two-faced bitch will understand: you fucked with the wrong man. Not once, but twice. There's just one difference this time around. I won't go down without a fight." I lower my eyes to her level to ensure she can see the honesty in them when I say, "I'll also never be stupid enough to side with a woman like you, much less lie in the same bed of fleas."

When she raises her hand to slap my face, I catch her wrist halfway.

"Nice try; do it again and see how far it gets you."

I drop her hand before moving back to my side of the desk. I won't lie; it's the fucking fight of my life to let her walk out of my office. The only reason I do is because of the tidbits of information she dropped during our exchange. She's aware of Isabelle's connection with Isaac. There is only one way she could know that: I have a snitch in my crew.

That's even worse than discovering the woman I'm in love with is siding with the enemy.

NINETEEN

ALEX

"You have your suspicions on who your nark is?"

Although Kristin can't see me, I jerk up my chin. "I have a few hunches I'm running on."

I hear her twist the old battered cord on her landline phone around her finger before she asks, "Anyone I know?"

"Not unless you're hiding a secret life from me?"

Laughter chops up my words. I wish it was my honest chuckle. Unfortunately, it isn't. I should have known the timing of Theresa's visit wasn't a coincidence. She didn't arrive at Ravenshoe to put in a bid to have her title returned; she's the IA agent the Bureau sent to investigate the possibility that Isabelle aided and abetted Isaac with confidential government documents.

Even with my weekend spent schmoozing my father's colleagues in the hope they'd approve my request to have Theresa pulled off the case hasn't stopped her grilling Isabelle at this very moment, and what can I do about it? Sweet fuck all.

Because I couldn't disclose I was aware Isabelle is in a sexual relationship with Isaac, the bureaucrats didn't see any connection between Theresa and Isabelle. They want Theresa to make an example out of Isabelle, to show what happens when agents cross the line they have marked in the sand.

Can anyone say hypocrite?

Theresa was removed from her position because she withheld vital information on the target she was assigned to investigate. Then she blackmailed an up-and-coming techie to do her dirty work to ensure her hands remained clean and she'd never face prosecution. If anyone should be made an example of, it should be Theresa.

"What are you going to do?" Kristin asks, drawing my thoughts back to the present.

I scrub my hand across my recently shaved jaw. Even with my beard gone a year, the smoothness of my chin still feels foreign. "I don't know. They want Isabelle to go on unpaid leave until the case is resolved."

"It's probably for the best."

I sit up straighter in my chair. "What makes you say that?"

Kristin breathes heavily before forcing out, "You're there for a reason, Alex. Do you really want a rookie agent sidetracking your plans? If you have IA breathing down your neck, you'll never achieve what you set out for."

"That's not true." I grit my teeth, stunned at how violently my words came out. I'm angry, but Kristin doesn't deserve the brunt of my wrath. "I'm here to bring Isaac to justice. I can do that and support my team at the same time."

Kristin's sigh reveals she doesn't believe me. "You said Dane's death wouldn't be in vain."

"It won't be—"

"Come on, Alex. It's been twelve fucking months. How much longer do you expect me to wait?" A chair rolling back sounds down the line before, "I have to go. Addi needs me." Her bitchy tone when she snarled Addi's name is more shocking than her brutally slamming the phone down.

I stare at my phone, shocked and confused. Frustrated tension has fueled most of our conversations the past twelve months, but this is the first time she's lashed out like this. I understand her annoyance. If you told me twelve months ago I'd still be sitting in my office, digging through a mammoth load of paperwork seeking a way to bring Isaac to justice, I would have laughed. I thought he'd be doing hard time by now.

This kills me to admit, but Isaac is a lot smarter than I first perceived. It's not hard considering the people he has surrounding him. They're so loyal to him, they're not seeing the entire picture. I'm so desperate for Regan to see the truth, I'm considering breaking protocol to show her. If she would just step back for a minute to see Isaac through my eyes, she would have a better understanding of everything. My case. My dislike. Why I hate him with every fiber of my being.

My thoughts return from dangerous grounds when I witness Brandon darting past the glass wall of my office with his hand clamped around an ashen-faced Isabelle's wrist. In silence, he makes a beeline for the supply closet all the agents hide out in when discussing matters they don't want publicized. The supply closet isn't soundproof, but it is free of the many listening devices I had installed on the main floor my first week on assignment.

Pretending I can't feel Theresa's eyes on me, I travel the steps Brandon and Isabelle just took. Because I'm a few seconds behind them, I only catch a portion of their conversation. It's enough to understand Brandon is more embedded in Isabelle's life than he's let on. They're talking more as friends than agents.

My suspicion piques when Brandon mentions Isabelle's flight to Ravenshoe, but before I can work through my confusion, Theresa joins me in the corridor. I don't want her to catch me snooping on my fellow agents, so I enter the supply closet Isabelle and Brandon are hiding out in.

When Brandon's narrowed eyes lift to mine, the duplicity in them raises my hackles. He's glaring at me in suspicion, yet he's the one hiding out like a coward.

As I step closer to them, my eyelids squint to match Brandon's.

"It is now after 11 AM, and that report I requested to be completed first thing this morning has still not been finalized, but you have time for a friendly chit chat with Isabelle in the supply closet."

Brandon surprises me by remaining quiet, but I don't miss the flash of anger darting through his eyes. I'm not surprised. They often say it is the quiet ones you need to watch the closest. I'm not just watching Brandon, I'm on to him. Before today, he was down the bottom of my list of suspects. Now he sits at the top of the podium.

I shift my eyes to Isabelle. "I need to see you in my office." When her eyes dash to Brandon as if she is seeking his permission to leave, I snap, "Immediately, Isabelle!"

After a look that reveals she's truly stumped by Theresa's interest in her, Isabelle shadows me to my office. She sits in the chair opposite mine when I lower the privacy blind to conceal our conversation from the agents watching me as closely as I'm watching them. Until I discover my snitch, everyone is on my suspect list.

I've been called many things the past twelve months. Heartless. Anal. The biggest fucking douchebag in the world, but despite all of this, there is one name I've never been called, and that's a shit leader. I'm hard on my team because I want them to succeed in their field of expertise. If that means we can't be friends outside of work, I'm fine with that. I'd rather them see me as their supervisor than their friend. If Isaac's investigation has taught me anything, it is that mixing business and pleasure never works. Eventually, one fucks over the other.

Isabelle is about to learn that lesson right now.

I take my seat before raising my eyes to hers. She looks afraid, which I hate yet understand at the same time. "Because of your unwillingness to cooperate with their investigation, the internal affairs department is recommending you go on unpaid leave until they have finalized their investigation."

The color in her cheeks drains as her throat works hard to swallow. While nodding to acknowledge she heard me, her hand shoots down to the hem of her shirt. She fists it tightly, needing to distract her brain from the moisture welling in her eyes.

"Although I don't agree with their investigation, I believe it will be best for my department if you do take a step back," I continue, my tone less harsh. "Running an investigation like ours is already hard enough, let alone having the internal affairs department breathing down our necks."

My teeth gritting together is the only sign I'm annoyed that I've succumbed to both Theresa and Kristin's pressure. This is my team, so shouldn't I run it how I see fit?

The worry in Isabelle's eyes dampens when I add on, "Once we confirm their investigation is unwarranted, I'll accept you back onto my team, Isabelle, but for the time being, you need to gather your belongings and leave the office immediately."

The last time I said words similar to these, I was filled with an immense amount of satisfaction. I'm experiencing nothing like that now.

After plastering a fake smile onto her face, Isabelle stands from her seat. She clasps the stainless-steel handle of my office door in her hand before cranking her neck back to me.

"Isaac isn't the man you think he is."

Denying me the opportunity to rebut, she exits my office.

TWENTY

REGAN

"Just say the word, Isaac, and I'll hit her with every injunction known to man. You have a restraining order against her. I don't care who she is, she can't just waltz into your office and question you for no reason."

"She isn't after me—"

"This time," I interrupt, my tone high enough that Axel startles. After an apologetic grimace to Raquel, I shift my focus back to my phone. "Theresa has never followed the rules. She could have been ghosting you with Isabelle."

"Come on, Regan. Give me some credit. I'm not stupid."

The hard week he's had is reflected in his voice. He's struggling as badly as I did the month following Alex's betrayal. There were so many times I nearly broke. If it weren't for Raquel and Isaac keeping my thoughts busy, I would have.

"I don't trust her, Isaac. She filed another petition for paternity last week. She's not going to vanish like you're hoping."

He exhales deeply before replying, "Maybe we should give it to her."

I shoot up to a standing position. "Are you insane? Give your

DNA to the most corrupt officer you've met? My god, you're lucky you're in your office or I'd smack you up the head."

The quiver in Isaac's breath exposes he doesn't appreciate me questioning him, but for once, I don't back down. He pays me for exactly this: to keep him and his empire in safe hands.

"You have no reason to grant her request. You know Jeremiah isn't your son. Theresa knows Jeremiah isn't your son—"

"Isabelle doesn't."

My heart does an elongated beat when the truth finally smacks into me. He's not calling me to update me on Theresa's visit to his office last night; he wants me to ensure him he's not an idiot.

Tears prick my eyes when I quote what he said to me during one of my darkest days. "Don't be ashamed to lose your pride to someone you love; be ashamed you let your pride lose someone you love."

I move into the kitchen, ensuring my next set of words aren't overheard. "It's okay to forgive, Isaac. It won't make you weak—"

"I'm not worried about that."

Pretending I can't hear the mistruth in his reply, I ask, "Then what are you worried about?"

A stretch of silence teems between us. It is awkward and plagued with tension.

Just when I think Isaac will never answer me, he murmurs, "Callie." An office chair squeaks before he says, "I can't stop thinking about what will happen to her if I don't continue with my plans. I can't just forget she exists."

"Then don't. Feelings don't automatically switch off when someone deceives you. The connection you have with that little girl is real, Isaac, probably the realest you've had. Don't ignore it because you're wary of someone's intentions. Trust them, your gut, and yourself. They've never steered you wrong before, so why would they when you need them the most?"

Another stint of silence passes between us. This one isn't filled with the same awkwardness as earlier, but with mutual respect and understanding.

"Let me see this through, Isaac? Please." I don't know why I'm pleading on behalf of a little girl I've never met; there's just something advising me this is the right thing to do. "Once she's safe and out of harm's way, you'll have a better idea of the next step you want to take."

Isaac murmurs something, but with my pulse ringing in my ears, I miss what he says.

"Yes?" I'm certain I know him well enough to know which path he wants me to travel, but there's no harm in checking.

"Yes," he confirms. "Just keep it on the downlow. After my arrest, I can't be associated with Vladimir in any way. That's one shroud I don't want draped over my empire for the rest of eternity."

Although he can't see me, I nod. "All our negotiations are on behalf of an entity, but I'll ensure your name stays out of it."

After a few more details, I end our call as somberly as I started it, with a promise to do everything in my power to see him through this.

My heart leaps into my chest when I dump my cell phone onto the kitchen counter then spin around. Raquel has her shoulder propped on the doorjamb of her kitchen with a burping cloth in one hand and an empty bottle of formula in the other. The phony smile she has on her face indicates she heard my conversation, but the unease in her eyes leaves no doubt.

"Don't," I warn when her lips twitch as she prepares to speak. "My situation is nothing like Isaac's."

She shakes her head before dumping the bottle in the sink and the dirty washcloth in a basket of milk-soiled clothing she's preparing to take to the laundry room. Her silence is more telling than her words. Raquel is just like me; she has no issues calling it how she sees it. Although I'd like to pretend motherhood has made her soft, I'm confident it's had the opposite effect. Axel didn't squash her determination; it doubled it, as now Raquel not only refuses to fail herself, she refuses to fail her son as well.

"He used me, Raquel." I bite on the inside of my cheek, hating the whine delivered with my words.

"For what, Regan? A sixty-thousand-dollar-a-year paycheck?" She laughs while spinning around to face me. "He would have gotten more out of you if he knocked you up."

When I scoff, acting as immature as her ridiculous statement, her brow arches high. "I saw the bonus check Isaac handed you last Christmas; that would keep an FBI agent warm for decades to come." She pats my arm the way our mother always does when she wants us to listen. "Talk to him. Things may not be as you believe, but you'll never know if you keep your head stuck in the sand."

I'm about to bite back that she should follow her own advice with Axel's daddy, but I leash my retaliation. Her situation is completely different from mine. She's not keeping his birth a secret; she just has no way of reaching out to his dad.

"I'll think about it." I nearly gag, annoyed I'm succumbing to pressure. The only thing I want to surrender to is my libido and the orgasms it's been holding back the past twelve months, not my annoying baby sister glaring at me with remorse in her eyes.

She stops peering at me when Axel's little cry breaks the silence teeming between us.

"Do you want me to get him?" My question comes out more as a plea. *I hate when he cries.* "He sounds like he needs his Aunty Rae-Rae."

Glee dashes down my spine when Raquel answers, "You can cuddle him to sleep."

It flies out the window when she quickly adds on, "After you've made your call."

"What?!" I screech. "You can't use my nephew against me."

She pulls a face as if to say, *yeah, I can.*

When she pushes off her feet, I follow after her. "This is blackmail! And wrong—"

"More wrong than letting a man believe you aborted his baby?"

That stuffs my attitude right down my throat, but it doesn't stop me from saying, "If he didn't pry into my business, he wouldn't have fucked up the facts."

Raquel glares at me. Not because I'm using the same pathetic excuse I've used since Alex left our ranch in a dust of fury, but because I cussed in front of Axel.

"Sorry." My murmured apology is for Axel not my sister, but Raquel accepts my grumble on his behalf.

While gently bouncing Axel on her shoulder, Raquel shifts her eyes to me. "You had unprotected sex—numerous times, and the receipt from the clinic he gave Dad showed the appointment was for an R. Myers. I can understand his error."

"I also told him I was on my period."

Raquel glares at me. "On the same day you made it look like you had sex with your boss."

"I didn't say sex—"

Her *don't mess with me* mask slips over her face. "No, you just implied it."

"I. . . I. . ." *I've got nothing.*

The reason for Axel's grizzles comes to light when he makes the biggest burp I've ever heard. Raquel stiffens, used to his burps also bringing up almost all his bottle. She gets lucky this time around.

Me, on the other hand. . . she's not even halfway done with me yet.

After putting Axel back in his bouncer, she spins around to face me. "What did you tell Isaac? 'It's okay to forgive. It won't make you weak.' It was good advice, Regan. Advice you should listen to." Her eyes glisten with moisture as her son coos in the background. "If you do that, I'll promise to do the same whenever Axel's dad rocks back into my life one day." Her last two words hold no confidence whatsoever.

When I nod, she rubs my arm in a soothing manner. "I'm going to take a shower. Can you watch Axel for me?"

I nod before all the question leaves her mouth. Nine years ago I thought I'd never love again. Tricks and schemes had me considering the possibility, but Axel abundantly proves I'm still capable of loving.

It's not the same all-encompassing love spouses feel for one another, but it is enough. . . *for now.*

As Axel drifts off into a milk coma, my thoughts drift as well. They begin at the exchange I had with Alex three nights ago before they slowly float back to the first time I saw him after months of absence. The look that crossed his face when he screamed at me about his rights. . . god. I can still feel his hurt to this very day.

Although I am mad at how he deceived me, perhaps some of the guilt I've been carrying the past twelve months will lift if I admit my wrongs in the downfall of our relationship. I don't expect my confession to stop Alex's ridiculous campaign to ruin Isaac, but it couldn't hurt it.

My shaking hands impede my effort to dial a number I haven't dialed in over a year. I expect the operator to tell me the number is no longer in service, so you can imagine my surprise when it instantly rings.

It rings, and rings, and rings, until I chicken out and hang up.

TWENTY-ONE

ALEX

"You've given me no choice. I have to replace his things."

Reid's nose screws up as he slips into the chair opposite me. "Why? We conducted a search—a compliant warrant approved by a judge."

"You destroyed his fucking property." I throw the photos Brandon supplied me of Isaac's private residence across the table.

Although pissed Regan showed up at my office last week solely to protect Isaac, her visit held merit. The search my crew conducted on Isaac's premise wasn't a lawful search. They may as well have gutted his house for how badly they damaged his belongings. Not a single item was left untouched.

My eyes float up to Reid when he murmurs, "What the fuck?" His dark eyes lock and hold with mine. "That was not us."

"What do you mean?"

He sits on the edge of his chair, wordlessly building the suspense. "What's the average number of search warrants a special agent conducts per year?"

I shrug. "It varies depending on the agent. Some could be a hundred, others as few as ten."

Reid's lips twist. "So even if we went with the lower end of the scale, I would have conducted over one hundred and fifty searches in my fifteen years on the job, so you could say I know what I'm doing."

I nod in agreement. Reid is a good agent. It's why I brought him onto my team.

"That. . ." He points to the stack of photos. ". . .will get me nothing but my case thrown out of court." He slouches back in his chair. "I don't know about you, but I ain't in this job for the money."

A ghost of a smile cracks onto my lips. Only a moron would join law enforcement if they're chasing a money pot.

My smile falters when Reid digs his phone out of his pocket. Remaining quiet, his finger slides across the screen before he punches in a six digit lock code. Although I'd never ask, I'm confident his security is as lacking as mine. Every agent knows a six-digit code is a birthday of a loved one. MM/DD/YY. That's what mine is. Except the birthday code in my phone isn't my mom, dad or any of my siblings. It's not even mine. It's Rae's.

I stop thinking back to the giddy fuck I was when I placed her birthday as my lock code when Reid tosses his phone into my chest.

"That's how we left Isaac's residence after our search."

My eyes drop to the screen. Drawers are open, a few cushions are tossed around, and almost every cupboard in his kitchen has their contents removed, but there are no torn couches, shredded paintings or cracked ornaments. You can tell every surface was thoroughly inspected, but they weren't close to being destroyed.

I hand Reid back his phone before inspecting the photos Brandon gave me more diligently. They're a stark contradiction to Reid's recollection of events. "Someone is playing tricks on me."

Reid murmurs in agreement. He only knows of my suspicion that I have a nark in my team because I crossed him off the list fairly early in my investigation. He passed the test I gave him with flying colors. Other agents, including the one who supplied me these photos of Isaac's residence, didn't ace the test. Don't get me wrong, they came close, but not enough for me to remove them from my list.

"Do you think it's Theresa?"

Reid halfheartedly shrugs. "Hard call. Before you logged Isaac's arrest warrant, no one knew of his private residence. We all thought his main base was his apartment on Hector. If she jumped straight on a plane, she could have been here in time, but that means she's been watching your investigation for some time."

I jerk up my chin in both suspicion and confirmation. My suspicion is based on Theresa's interests; for how quickly she arrived on scene, I wouldn't be surprised to discover she's never let this case out of her sight. My confirmation centers around his disclosure of Isaac's residence.

I knew Isabelle would unlock Isaac's case, but I had no clue how profoundly her influence was on him until she led me straight to his private residence. Isaac has always kept his business ventures and his personal life as two separate entities. Isabelle is the first person to merge them together.

A line I swore I'd never cross gets crossed when I say, "Put a tail on Theresa. If this is her, I want to know."

Reid looks highly uncomfortable by my request, but he nods his head all the same. "And this?" He hands me the itemized bill Regan dropped off days ago.

I swivel my tongue around my mouth to soothe its sudden dryness before forcing out, "Pay it."

Reid looks like he wants to say more, but he saves his retaliation. Lucky, as the shrill of my cell phone would have cut him off.

The ragged beat of my heart amplifies when my eyes drop to the screen of my phone. Regan is calling me—again. This isn't the first time she's reached out this week, but it is the first time she hasn't hung up after four rings. It rings and rings and rings until it is seconds away from going to voicemail.

I snatch up my phone, slide my finger across the screen, then squash it to my ear. Although confident her contact is in regards to the matter Reid and I are in the process of discussing, my intuition is begging me not to act in haste. It's warning me to be cautious more than anything.

Still, I answer her call with unbridled attitude, my anger not as quick to subdue when I see her name as it did twelve months ago. "The Bureau is processing your client's claim. Payment will take six to eight weeks."

A sharp exhale sounds down the line. "Good. I'm glad you've finally come to your senses."

I smirk. I'm not the only reeking with attitude. Regan's tone has it in abundance.

"I'll update you when I hear anything."

I'm dragging my phone away from my ear to disconnect our call when I hear the quickest, "Wait."

I try to act cool, but the lightning fast return of my phone to my ear undoes my ruse. Even Reid smirks at my pathetic attempt.

"Yeah?"

I don't know if Regan's big breaths are because she's resisting the urge to laugh at the dip in my tone or because she's struggling to compose herself. If I know Regan as well as I once did, I'd say it is a bit of both. Unfortunately, I hardly recognize myself anymore, much less a woman I once knew.

Just when I think Regan will never answer me, she murmurs, "Can we meet?"

My mouth opens and closes, but nothing comes out—not even a fucking squeak.

I'm not the only one silent. Regan hasn't taken a breath the past thirty seconds, and Reid isn't just quiet, he's frozen like a statue.

"You want to meet?" I ask Regan a short time later, my tone higher than my arched brow.

She coughs to clear the nerves from her throat before replying, "Yeah. I think we should do this in person. We're adults, so there's no reason we can't handle this with maturity. . . Unless you don't want to?"

"No, no, we'll meet. When?" I blurt out before she can change her mind, my voice matching the dismal one I used when asking Melissa Belle to the Prom.

My already skyrocketing heart rate triples when Regan suggests, "Now?"

"Now!" My eyes drop to my trousers. They're not an exact replica of the JC Penney suit she despised, but they're pretty fucking close.

As quickly as panic rained down on me, anger takes its place. She's not arranging for us to hook up. This is most likely a meeting on behalf of her client, so why the fuck am I worrying about my outfit like I don't have a cock dangling between my legs?

I cup my hand around my phone to ensure she can't hear my ticking jaw. "I can't meet now; I've got stuff I need to take care of."

That's a lie, but my heart wasn't the only thing she stole from me twelve months ago; she removed my empathy bone as well.

"Okay." I can tell she is pissed, but she holds back her anger— barely. "Then when *will* you have time?"

I raise my eyes to Reid. I thought he'd be amused by our conversation. He seems more sympathetic than anything. Clearly, I'm not doing a good job of pretending I'm no longer affected by this woman. Even more so when I say, "Uh. . . twenty minutes?"

I hear Regan huff. "It will take me longer than twenty minutes to travel from my apartment to downtown, much less get dressed for the occasion."

A grin tugs my lips high, pleased I'm not the only one worried about maintaining appearances.

"I can come to you?" I suggest with a shrug.

"What?!" Finally, the *sweating over the small stuff like a girl* syndrome has been handed to its rightful owner. "You can't come here!"

"Why not? We're adults having an adult conversation. Why can't that occur in your apartment?"

She grumbles something, but the ringing of my heart in my ears has me missing what she says. "What are you worried about, Rae? It's been twelve months; I'm sure you can hold back your desires for another hour or two."

I can't see her, but I can picture her angry stance and screwed-up face when a deep growl sounds down the line. "I'm not worried about holding back my desires." Her voice is extra snarky during the quoted part of her statement. "I'm just not sure if I can be in the same room without killing you."

A chuckle rolls up my chest before I can stop it.

"I'm not joking, Alex!"

I laugh louder. "I know. That's why I'm laughing." I'm glad to discover she didn't lose her feisty temper when she bites out a string of curse words.

Just as quickly as her derogatory names are delivered, an apology follows them. I smile until I realize her pleas for forgiveness aren't directed at me. It is for someone sitting in the same room as her.

That plucks out my peacock feathers and locks them into an extremely dark and angry place. "Are we doing this or not, Regan? I don't have all day."

I grind my teeth together. That came out more offensive than I intended. I am annoyed. It's just not at Regan; it's more at myself. It's been a year; can't I get over my stupid neurosis already?

"Fine. Come here. I don't care." I hear Regan stand to her feet before a weird cooing noise sounds down the line. If I didn't know any better, I'd swear she's snuggling a cat. . .or *a baby.*

I swallow down the bile suddenly scorching my throat before saying, "I'll see you in twenty minutes."

She murmurs in agreement before lowering her phone from her ear, meaning I only catch her whisper, "I can't swaddle Axel to sleep tonight. Alex is coming over."

Axel. . . Who the fuck is Axel?

TWENTY-TWO

REGAN

A knock at the door sets off the butterflies in my stomach. I know who is knocking. It isn't Isaac. He's off on some naughty weekend in a cabin with Isabelle. Well, I really shouldn't say naughty weekend. It's more a healing expedition, similar to the one Alex and I took last year —the one where you shouldn't be having fun, but you most likely are? That's what they're doing.

Isaac's rekindled relationship with Isabelle is the reason I didn't hang up on Alex tonight like I have the prior week. It took a bit of research, and a shit ton of convincing, but it appears as if Hugo's hunch about Isabelle was spot on. She's one of the rare good guys who just happens to work for the Bureau.

If I were to give Alex the same chance Isaac is giving Isabelle, perhaps I could discover the same for him. He didn't fulfill Theresa's position until her seat was vacant for nearly six months. Did he do that for me? Or did the information he handed the Bureau not work out as he had hoped?

I guess there's only one way to find out.

After a shimmy of my shoulders, I swing open my apartment door. Alex's manly scent hits me before anything. It's masculine and virile, although not as strong as when he had a beard. My lips tuck into the corner of my mouth when I notice the suit he is wearing. It's an upgrade compared to the ones he usually donned, but it's far from the cut and quality Isaac wears every day. His hair is a little overdue for a trim, and the bags under his eyes show his sleep has been as restless as mine the past week. His tiredness is more likely from chasing his tail as he strives to put Isaac behind bars; mine is from my endeavor to stop him.

Once I've taken in his stocky thighs and extra broad shoulders, I raise my eyes to his face. His are still raking over my body, his inspection as thorough as the one I just did of him. While he finishes absorbing my bare legs I just dragged a razor over in a hurry and a cute, yet sophisticated slip dress, I stare at a jaw generally hidden from view by wiry blond hair.

I hated Alex's beard when I first saw it because I knew it was hiding a masterfully crafted jaw underneath. I was right. His jawline is strong and sexy. . . *and oddly familiar.*

Alex coughs, breaking me from my trance.

"Sorry. Would you like to come in?" I roll my eyes. *He didn't travel across town to stand in your entranceway, you dimwit.*

Alex smirks as if he heard my inner monologue before crossing the threshold separating the hallway of my apartment building and my foyer. *One step down. Six hundred trillion to go.*

"Can I take your coat?"

He nods before shrugging off the thick wool coat he's wearing over his two-piece suit. Although I could blame the heavy material of his jacket as the reason for the sweat beading on his neck, my intuition is telling me that isn't the case. For how much moisture is there, anyone would swear he climbed the stairs instead of taking the elevator.

Alex quirks his brow when I murmur, "You shouldn't have bothered."

I gesture my head to my still open door. "Isaac removed all surveillance cameras from his private premises over twelve months ago." When Alex glares at me with suspicion, I ease it. "A little birdie whispered in his ear that others may be watching."

I don't try and hide the fact it was me. It's time for us to both be honest.

After storing Alex's coat in the closet, I spin around to face him. "Would you like a drink—"

"What is this about, Regan? If we're here to discuss Isaac, we should be having this conversation—"

"In the office you're only occupying because of me?"

He looks genuinely stumped by my outburst. If I hadn't been played a fool by him twice before, I may believe his crinkled brow is authentic. It's a pity I stepped out of the lust haze he had me shrouded in over a year ago. *Mostly.*

"Do you truly think I'm so stupid I'd never find out? Those documents you used to have Theresa thrown out of *your* office were only ever seen by three people: Theresa, Isaac, and me." I lock my eyes with his, the anger in them unmissable. "Until you used my laptop."

"I *borrowed* your laptop at The Manor, but I didn't go through your stuff." He scoffs, truly offended. "I didn't scheme and lie to get where I am. Ethics and morals guided me here."

I throw my hands into the air. "Are you seriously denying this?! My laptop was the *only* place those forms were filed!"

"So? That doesn't mean I touched them. People hack into computers all the time. Nothing's confidential once its uploaded onto a server. . ."

Alex's words trail off to silence as a deep groove burrows between his brows. I assume it is because he's recalling the time he stabbed me in the back, but it is only when I follow the direction of his gaze do I realize I am wrong. He's staring at the numerous mom-to-be books I have stacked on my coffee table.

The cinch of his brows jumps onto my face when he murmurs under his breath, "Oh my fucking god, he was my son." When he locks his eyes with mine, I can't tell if it's fury or relief sparking through them. "Axel, you named him Axel? Where is he?"

His eyes cease scanning my apartment when I reply, "He's with his mom. At *her* house."

His chest rises and falls three times before he asks, "You put him up for adoption?"

Realizing I am doing a terrible job of explaining myself, I pace to the documents I placed on my coffee table earlier. I honestly believe my darkest day will always be the day Luca passed away, but this day gave it a run for its money. Even producing more dribble than a dirty old man at a strip club, Axel is the most adorable little guy I've ever met. His two-teeth grin and dimpled smile were literally minutes from being non-existent only twelve months ago. I'm so glad Raquel made the decision she did.

Alex's strides into my living room slow when he spots the document I'm holding. He knows what it is even without glancing at it. I watch his throat work hard to swallow before he raises his eyes to mine. The pain, hurt, and frustration in them mimics what my eyes held the day I drove Raquel to her appointment. It was her body, so it was her choice, but it still stung like a thousand bees.

The flutter in Alex's neck stops beating when I explain, "Axel is my nephew. This receipt was for my sister, Raquel. She changed her mind with barely a minute to spare."

Alex's eyes bounce between mine. "She didn't have an abortion?"

I shake my head. "And neither did I."

Even angry that he was spying on me months after we broke up, tears still burn my eyes. You can't see what I'm seeing. The relief in his wide gaze as anger fades from his face is an incredible visual, nearly as enticing as Axel's chubby cheeks. He looks truly relieved, like twelve months of tension has vanished in an instant.

I'm glad he's finally understanding what happened that day, but that doesn't mean I'll let him off scot-free. "If you weren't spying on me, you would have never had the wrong idea."

"I wasn't spying on you, Rae. I just wanted you to talk to me."

When he steps closer to me, I take a step back, the desperation in his voice too great to ignore.

His approach stops as the tick in his jaw ramps up. "You never gave me a chance to explain anything. You still aren't."

"Explain what? That you lied to me?" I ask, my heart hammering in my voice.

He nods, finally admitting to some of the errors he made.

His nods switches to a shake when I add on, "That you were only with me to advance your career?"

"No, Rae. *Never*."

I grit my teeth, more in warning that the stupid tears in my eyes better stay in there than at the honesty shining in his.

His eyes bounce between mine as he bridges the small gap between us. "Everything that happened between us was true. I'd never hurt you like that, Rae. I cared for you too much to hurt you like that."

When I shake my head, denying his claims, he grips the top of my arms to silently coerce my eyes to him. I shouldn't give them to him. I should tell him to go rot in hell. But instead, for the first time the past twelve months, I listen to my heart instead of my head.

Stupid move. His face is sterner than I remember, his jaw tighter. But his eyes. . . my god. They still have that same look, the ones that prove he hasn't inhaled a full breath since I walked out on him, as if he truly can't breathe without me in his life.

"What I said that morning was true, Rae. Every single fucking word." He brushes away a tear gliding down my cheek so fast, I barely register its descent before returning his hand to my arm. "Then you threw it all away. . . *for him*."

My hackles bristle from the sneer of his last two words, but I take it in stride, recognizing the wrongs I also did. "I didn't che—"

Before I can finalize my sentence, my cell phone buzzes on my entranceway table. If it were my standard number every man in the tri-state area knows, I'd ignore it and sock Alex in the stomach like he deserves, but since it is the number very few have and only use in dire situations, I push off my feet to answer it.

"I'll only be a minute."

Alex groans, his annoyance for the interruption all over his face.

Upon spotting the name splashed across the screen, I send Alex an apologetic glance before darting into the hallway separating my bedroom from the main living area. I can feel Alex's eyes on me, but I'm unsure if the heat of his gaze is suspicion or jealousy.

"The IA's case against Isabelle is being quashed as we speak. They had nothing to stand on." I say my comment loud enough Alex can hear. He needs to know whose team I am on, and it isn't about Isaac or him. It is about the innocent people being dragged into a fight they don't belong in, the women like Isabelle and me.

Isaac releases a quick breath before saying, "I need you at Ravenshoe Police Station, now."

I feel like I've been sucker-punched. "What did you do this time?" Although my comment comes out playful, I'm feeling anything but.

"For once, it isn't me," Isaac responds, grateful for my attempt to stifle the tension radiating down the phone. "But I need you to treat this case as if it were me, Regan. I need you at your very best. This case is more important than any case you've worked on for me previously."

"Come on, Isaac, you know me: I always bring my bat to the game." My pompous and conceited tone hides my worry. "I'll be there in twenty minutes."

Not giving him the chance to reply, I disconnect our call and spin around to face Alex, only to discover he is gone.

TWENTY-THREE

ALEX

My feet stomping down the stairwell of Regan's apartment chops up my words when I say, "Isaac knows about the IA's investigation into Isabelle."

"That can't be right," Reid responds down the line. "You kept her investigation in house, meaning only Isabelle, the investigating officers, and us know about it."

"Don't forget the union rep Isabelle had sit in with her during her interview."

My lungs, which are working through a bad case of oxygen deprivation, get jealous from Reid's sharp inhalation of air. "Brandon's your snitch." Since he isn't asking a question, it doesn't sound like one. "It makes sense: expensive clothes, designer shoes, and a car way beyond his means."

"And a position on Theresa's team back in her glory days, right around the time Regan was thrusted into my line of sight."

A chair creaks seconds before Reid curses. "Where was he transferred to when Theresa stood down?"

"Good question, one of many I plan to find out." I break onto the sidewalk outside of Regan's apartment before asking, "Where are you?"

"Wherever you need me to be."

I smirk. "Good answer."

After requesting for Reid to meet me at HQ, I hang up and dial Regan's number. Although I feel bad leaving like I did, when my gut is throwing me this many warnings, I must act on them.

Although, if being totally honest, I also need some time to decipher what she confessed this evening. Don't get me wrong, I believe what she said. I've just been harboring hurt so long that she aborted my baby, I'm having a hard time separating fact from fiction. I'm sure once I've had a few minutes to stop and contemplate, I'll know which step to take next, and you can be assured it will be a step in the right direction. What Regan said earlier is true. We're adults who need to start acting like adults.

That would be a shit ton easier to do if she'd answer my call.

She doesn't answer my first call or the second one. Not even the third.

I don't hear from her again until her name is listed on the opposing side of an arrest warrant.

"It was you, wasn't it?"

Brandon balks before the panicked expression on his face clears away. Stupid move. I'm so fucking angry right now, I'm two seconds from popping a bullet between his brows.

Not only did I discover halfway into my investigation that one of my agents has been arrested for murder, I also haven't had any contact with Regan. None. Not even with over sixty attempts to reach her. My frustration is at an all-time high, meaning Brandon would be best not to double-cross me—*again*.

I stop abruptly at Brandon's side, cautious to avoid other court goers from crashing into me as they scoot by. "I asked you to show me how to work her laptop, not steal information off her computer!"

Brandon shakes his head, futilely trying to deny my claims, but his eyes give away his true self. He's a liar and a manipulator.

"Regan thinks I stole information from her." My hissed words reveal my teetering mood. "That I used her to better my position."

"That was never my intention. I had no plans to use the information I found; I just forgot that anything uploaded to the Bureau's servers remain uploaded no matter how great your hacking skills are."

The anger running through my veins quickly shifts me from Brandon's superior officer to a man destined for revenge. "You forgot?! How can you fucking forget me instructing you to log out of her computer ten minutes before you did?"

I thrust a computer log printout into his chest, the one that proves he was still logged into Regan's laptop when she got out of the shower. "If that isn't enough proof, how about this?"

My nostrils flare when I spin my phone around to show him the photo I have on the screen. It displays Regan in a skimpy white towel with wet hair and a confused wrinkle between her brows. It's from the morning I told her I loved her.

"You were watching her—"

"No." Brandon shakes his head. "I logged out the instant she entered the room."

"The instant she entered the room in nothing but a towel." My voice is so loud, it startles several people galloping down the courthouse stairs we're standing next to. "What if she didn't have a towel on? What if she were naked?"

I don't know what's frustrating me more, the idea of him seeing Regan like that, or that he's the reason we're apart. For how hard my heart is thumping, I'd say it is a combination of them both.

"I brought you onto my team because I thought you were one of us—one of the good guys."

"I am!" Brandon defends.

"No you're fuckin' not. You're just as rogue and corrupt as Theresa."

Brandon's back gets up. "Who are you to talk? You slept with a target while undercover!"

"Regan wasn't a target!" I scream into his face, my anger overtaking every fiber of my being. "She should have never been dragged into this fight. She's an innocent—"

"Just like Izzy?" Brandon's wild eyes dart between mine. "Yet here she is, at your request, being pranced in front of Isaac like a little plaything—just like Theresa forced you to do with Regan. There is only one difference: you stupidly fell in love."

My fist pops into Brandon's eye without a thought crossing my mind. He should thank his lucky stars Reid drove me here, or a black eye would be the least of his problems.

"Step back, Alex," Reid demands, darting between Brandon and me before my fist adds a black rim to his right eye to match his left. "Step back!" he requests again, more sternly this time. "He's not worth it." He looks five seconds from decking Brandon for me before he shifts his dark eyes my way. "And you're not here for him, remember?"

The confirmation in his deep timbre reminds me of the real reason we've arrived at the courthouse a little after 9 AM. Although Isabelle's arrest is out of my jurisdiction, and she is currently on unpaid leave, she is still my agent, which means she's still my responsibility.

Catching my murderous glare as I step back to right my clothing, Brandon musters up a pathetic excuse. "Nothing I did was outside of my role."

Even with his face sporting a new bruise, my glare ramps up. "A role you no longer hold."

His lips firm, but he dips his chin, acknowledging he understands my request. If his resignation isn't on my desk by close of business today, I'll start proceedings to have him removed from his position with a few charges added.

"And don't think this is the end, Brandon. Your resignation from my team is only the beginning of your sentence."

With that, I shrug out of Reid's hold and finalize the last stairs between him and the entrance of the courthouse. I'm here to show my support to Isabelle, but she isn't the sole reason my steps are double their natural stride.

I've come for Regan as well.

TWENTY-FOUR

REGAN

I silence my phone when Alex's fifth call the past fifteen minutes vibrates the desk I am sitting behind. He's been calling non-stop since he left my apartment with nothing but the scent of his expensive cologne lingering in his wake. Although I've been extremely busy representing Isabelle as per Isaac's request, I can't use it as an excuse as to why I'm not answering Alex's calls.

I'm frustrated he dissed me—*again*. And for what? Because a conversation I had with my employer may have involved some words that stung him? I didn't mention the "batter" part of my conversation to hurt him. I was trying to ease Isaac's tension. He cares for Isabelle so much; ten miles didn't diminish my ability to feel his emotions.

If only I could read Alex as intensely.

Although our conversation was interrupted, I thought we had a breakthrough last night. Clearly, twelve months hasn't made me any smarter.

My confusion is pushed to the side for another day when my phone rings again, this time from a number I recognize. After excusing myself from the room, I accept Isaac's call.

"She'll be free to go any minute now," I say down the line while stepping out of the interrogation room Isabelle is being held in. "The bail terms have been signed; we're just waiting for Hugo to make payment."

Isaac sighs in relief. "He should be there any moment now."

Just as his sentence ends, Hugo blasts through the doors I'm standing next to. "He's here now."

I swear I can hear Isaac's pulse raging down the line. "Good. Meet me outside; you can travel with me to Hunter's."

Before I can advise him that it is best for all involved for him to maintain distance from Isabelle until her court case is over, Isaac disconnects our call.

"Was that Isaac?"

Hugo presses a kiss on my cheek. His friendliness makes me happy more than worried. With all the craziness the past few weeks, this is the first time I've seen him in person in nearly a year. I've missed him and his woodsy smell. . . not that he'll ever know that.

I nod. "He's a little stressed."

"Aren't we all?"

Hugo would never say it, but I know his "we" reference was more about me than him. Isaac is in the dark about my previous interactions with the man trying to take him down, but Hugo is well-informed.

It is terrible of me to do, but hating the focus on me, I shift it to Hugo. "Should you be here, Hugo? A courthouse isn't an ideal location to hide a ghost."

He grins at my attempt to badger him. "It's better than haunting a graveyard for real."

"True," I reply through twisted lips.

He curls his thick arm around my shoulders before dragging me toward the room Isabelle is waiting in. "I appreciate your concern, Ms. Prim and Proper, but you don't need to worry about me. I can *handle* myself."

I loudly gag. The sexual innuendo in his voice is way too much for me to handle right now. I'm hormonal and tired, an extremely lethal combination when you add my exchange with Alex last night into the mix.

Even more so when I spot him accosting Isabelle in the interrogation room. "What the hell is he doing here?"

"Who's that?" Hugo asks, revealing I said my comment out loud instead of in my head as I was planning.

I downplay Alex's role in my life. "He's Isabelle's boss."

"Oh." That's all Hugo says, but I hear so much more. Hugo may be handsome, but he's also smart. That's not rare for Isaac's innermost circle.

Hoping to avoid an awkward confrontation, I break away from Hugo's side, spin on my heels, then nudge my head to the front doors of the courthouse. "Bring your car around front." When he attempts to protest, I quickly add on, "The faster we get Isabelle out of here, the better it will be for *all* involved."

He rolls his eyes, but thankfully that is the beginning and end of his gripe.

I wait until Hugo disappears down the hall before entering the interrogation room. My strong strides don't reveal the faint wobble in my thighs I'm ashamed to admit is there. Although the creak of the door I'm entering drowns out what Alex is saying, I get the gist of it from Isabelle's wide gaze. She looks panicked, a little peeved, but mostly panicked.

"Your bail has been paid; you're free to go, Isabelle."

She nods, acknowledging she has heard me before she focuses her attention back on Alex. "Be the agent you say I could be, Alex. Dig deeper, look harder, and unravel the truth instead of running with speculations. I'm not just talking about my case. I'm talking about Isaac's as well."

My heart thumps harder when Isabelle steps closer to Alex. I'm torn. I want to protect Alex from the anger reducing Isabelle's beauty from that of an angel to a mere mortal, but I'm morally obligated to protect my client.

My fears are unfounded when Isabelle maintains her dignity by delivering her scorn to Alex with words instead of her hand. "And do it without the underhanded and illegal activities like tapping your agents' phones and paying exorbitant airfares."

Her admission shocks both Alex and me, but she fails to see that when she darts out of the room. I wait until she is out of earshot before returning my focus to Alex. I'm about to tell him that she's right. If he would just dig a little deeper, he'd see Isaac as Isabelle and I do, but Alex's questions cut me off.

"What is she talking about? What bug?"

His confusion seems genuine, but I've been burned before so I must act cautiously. "Before her arrest, Isabelle located a tracking device in her cell phone. It was the second one uncovered within a matter of days."

Isabelle didn't find the tracking device in her cell, but Isaac's security team did, which is practically the same thing. What Hugo said months ago is true: if it affects one of us, it affects all of us. Isabelle is now one of us.

I can see Alex wants to switch our conversation from business to personal, but the seriousness of Isabelle's charges stops him. "Were the devices logged into evidence?"

I shake my head. After several run-ins with corrupt members of law enforcement, Isaac is hesitant to trust them. I don't blame him.

Alex steps closer to me, engulfing me with his schmexy scent. "Can the devices be logged into evidence?"

My molars grind when I spot his game plan. He thinks a lack of distance and a roughish grin will have me panting at his side, begging for his scraps.

I have news for him.

"When you bring me a credible warrant, I'll have my men hand them over. Until then. . ."

I allow my exit of the room to finalize my dramatic statement.

He chases after me. "Regan, don't be stupid. This—"

I whip around so fast, not only do his words get shoved into the back of his throat, my fists nearly follow them. "Don't be stupid? The only stupid thing I've done is spend time with you!"

"You need to lower your tone." Alex scans our surroundings, wordlessly pointing out the dozen or more people gawking our way. "I know you're angry, but if you'd give me five seconds to explain—"

"I gave you a chance to explain last night. You left. *Again!*" Although my words are whispers, the anger in them reflects the twisting of my heart.

"Because I wanted to bring you proof." He steps closer to me, popping the invisible bubble I'm striving to keep between us. "And keep you safe."

"Safe from who? Yourself? Or the man from *your* agency who broke into *my* apartment to scare me into being with you?"

He balks, shocked I'm aware of Jay's accusations. It proves what I've always known.

"How stupid do you think I am, Alex?"

"You're not stupid, Rae; you're just working with the wrong facts."

I laugh. It isn't a pleasant, happy laugh. "You're right. I am working with the wrong facts." Now I bridge the gap between us. "Because I stupidly thought maybe you weren't the man I thought you were. That maybe you didn't use me to advance in your career. Clearly, I'm reading the facts wrong."

After a final sneer that warns him I am seconds from detonation, I dart down the hallway.

This time he lets me go.

That hurts more than anything.

TWENTY-FIVE

REGAN

My head pops up from a set of reports I've been perusing the past hour when a doorbell sounds through my apartment. With Isabelle and Hugo taking up residence in my penthouse, the number of guests we've had so far today has surpassed the number I had the six months I've lived here—although none have been who I'm secretly hoping for.

It's been two days since my run-in with Alex at the courthouse, which means it has been two days of radio silence. That's not surprising. He knows I'm on to him, so he's lying low.

When Isabelle's fretful eyes dart to mine, I yank my reading glasses off my face. "Go to your room."

Unlike Isaac, Isabelle doesn't take my demand as a suggestion. She jumps to her feet before racing toward the hallway without a protest leaving her mouth.

Halfway there, a deep voice shouts, "Izzy, it's Brandon."

The tightness in Isabelle's shoulders relaxes. Mine does not. After arguing with Isaac that taking Isabelle onto his yacht for one last hoorah before he steps back and lets me do my job, I overheard some of his conversation with Hugo. Brandon has the handsome boy next door look down pat. His blond hair hangs loosely on the top of his head, and his hazel eyes appear wholesome and down to earth. Even his cheeks blush. But it was snippets of conversation he had with Isabelle that raised my suspicion on his true intentions.

He doesn't want to be Isabelle's friend. He wants something much more risqué than friendship.

Although protecting Isaac's personal life isn't in my job description, you can sure as hell be guaranteed I won't sit back and watch another man cozy in on his girl. I also don't take kindly to men purposely avoiding me. The only time I've been avoided by the opposite sex is when they're hiding something from me. More often than not, it's their marital status, but I don't get that vibe from Brandon. He's sneaky, but not in a creepy, adulterous way.

I check my face in the mirror as Isabelle swings open the door. I'm not being vain; I'm just using my assets as they're meant to be used. When the door fully opens, I scan Brandon's frozen frame. X-ray vision isn't required to check if someone is carrying a gun. He's not packing heat. Well, not anywhere he could hide a gun. The cut of his clothes and the way he holds himself conceal assets he should display, not hide. This makes me even more wary of his intentions. *If he has desirable assets, why doesn't he flaunt them?*

When Brandon skirts past me, I do what all good hostesses do. I offer to take his jacket. It's made of wool and bulky, meaning it is the perfect accessory to hide the weapon I was seeking earlier.

"Thank you." Brandon's tone is as apprehensive as his facial expression.

"You're welcome." My voice is nowhere near as friendly because my sneaky hunt came up empty-handed.

While Isabelle greets Brandon in a way I'm sure Isaac will kill him for, I return to the evidence I was compiling before he arrived. My plan is to pretend I'm busy doing attorney stuff, but in reality, I'm going to keep a close eye on them.

My brisk pace slows when I hear Brandon murmur to Isabelle, "She scares me."

"I heard that." My chest swells like the cat who swallowed the canary. "And you should be scared."

When Brandon's forceful swallow bellows around my apartment, I pivot around to face him. I give him a wink, pretending I meant my comment in jest. He doesn't buy my act. His cheeks flame with heat as his pupils dilate. I just don't know him well enough to tell if he's suspicious or aroused. I think it might be a bit of both.

Realizing he won't talk freely in my presence, I take the documents Regina and Ryan presented Isabelle and me earlier and make my way to my office. I'm hidden halfway down the hall when Isabelle initiates their conversation by offering Brandon a drink, which he declines.

"No thanks, this is a quick pop-in visit." I hear him clear his throat before he says, "I hope you don't mind me popping in like this, but I couldn't call you since Hunter smashed your phone, and I don't know any of Regan's contact details."

"I can give them to you. All you have to do is ask." The instant the words escape my mouth, I want to ram them back in there. This is why I could never be an undercover operative like Alex or Ayden.

I stop panicking that I've blown my cover when Isabelle giggles. It is followed closely by Brandon's soft groan.

I pace a little closer to their exchange when he lowers his voice to whisper, "I just wanted to say that I understand you not wanting to come to the gala with me anymore. With everything going on and all." He is a quivering bundle of nerves. "I don't want you to feel obligated to go with me. You need to concentrate on getting your case cleared."

"Is it this weekend?" Isabelle's high tone indicates she forgot about the pledge she made to Brandon.

"Yes, Friday night, but you don't have to come." Brandon aims for his voice to be understanding, but all I hear is manipulation. He's not here to let Isabelle off from their agreement. He's here to guilt trip her into keeping it.

Although Isaac will most likely kill me when he hears this was my idea, I think Isabelle should keep the promise she made to Brandon. Not because I believe Brandon is an upstanding guy and Isabelle should fall on her sword for him, but because it will give Hugo a chance to evaluate Brandon on his home turf. Men are most honest when they're surrounded by familiar things. It is how Alex's ruse came undone, so who's to say it won't be the same for Brandon?

"You should go." Isabelle's eyes drift to me when I reenter the foyer. "Having you out in public with another man will help make the jury believe you have no association with Isaac. It will also make it look like you're not worried about the case because you're innocent. Only people with something to hide need to be concerned about prosecution."

"You don't think it will appear distasteful for me to go to a fancy gala with a death hanging over my head?" Isabelle asks as her brows tack together.

I shake my head. "No. You knew of Megan from an FBI agent perspective, but you have no personal connection to her whatsoever. You wouldn't mourn the death of a stranger."

Worry lines Isabelle's forehead, but I don't give her the chance to voice her concerns.

"And with you being out of Ravenshoe for a few nights, I won't have to keep checking your room every ten minutes to make sure Isaac hasn't snuck in." I hope she takes my comment as cheeky, because it sounded snarky to me.

After several long seconds of contemplation, Isabelle locks her gaze with Brandon. He's nervously shifting from one foot to the other, exposing Isabelle's answer is more important than he's letting on.

A glint in his eyes I've seen many times before appears when Isabelle asks, "What time are you picking me up?"

While Isabelle shows Brandon to the door, I call Hugo.

It's time to discover who Brandon James really is.

A ragged scream wakes me from my sleep a little before 1 AM. My heart pounds against my ribcage when a second cry soon follows the first. I jackknife out of my bed before darting for the door. Although I'm wearing only a satin slip, I don't stop to secure my robe. Those cries were too horrific and oddly familiar for me to worry about modesty. They match the ones I made in silence over nine years ago.

"What is it?" I ask Hugo, who is standing halfway down the hallway.

His wide eyes shift to me, startling me with how dilated they are. "She's having a nightmare." He nudges his head to the room I assigned to Isabelle. "The door is locked."

Hugo looks at me as if I am crazy when I say, "Kick it in."

I nod, assuring him what he heard is correct before dashing into my living room. I haven't needed Xanax in a long time, but I've kept my prescriptions up to date the past twelve months. Don't ask me why. They're more a security blanket than anything. *I hope.*

When I enter Isabelle's room that Hugo has successfully broken into, I hear the last half of Hugo's apology to Isaac, "It took me a little longer to get in here because she had the door locked."

I don't know what Isaac replies to Hugo, but it must not be good because he grimaces before removing Isabelle's cell phone from his ear.

"He's coming?"

Hugo works his jaw side to side before nodding.

"He can't do that. If the DA finds any connection between Isaac, Isabelle, and Megan, I'll have no chance in hell of getting Isabelle off her charges."

Hugo shrugs before his eyes drop to Isabelle. She looks like a fragile little doll since she is swamped by his large frame. I pop open the bottle of Xanax before tapping two tablets into Isabelle's shaking palm. While she takes them in, certain they aren't sleeping tablets, I pour her a generous serving of the wine I consumed instead of dinner.

She appears hesitant when I suggest she take them, but with her eagerness to forget the nightmare slicking her skin with sweat, she quickly follows through with my request.

"Good girl," I reply, accepting the now empty champagne flute from her grasp.

Within minutes, her shaking ceases, and she's back asleep.

"Was what she saw really that bad?" I ask Hugo, shadowing him into the hallway.

He jerks up his chin. "Worst I've seen."

"Have you seen a lot of dead bodies?" I ask, hearing what he didn't mean to disclose.

Hugo pauses for a few seconds before dipping his chin. "I did two tours in Afghanistan before. . . " His big blue eyes dart between mine as he whispers, "You know."

I nod. *I do know—unfortunately.*

I also know what I must do now.

"What's your plan?" Hugo asks, following me to my walk-in closet.

I dig through a pile of hideous clothing I'd never be caught dead in but am too polite to throw out since my mother gave them to me before saying, "I'm going to stop Isaac from making a costly mistake."

"And you need cowgirl getup to do that?"

Hugo's tone is as high as where my stomach contents sit when I drag a hideous peaked beanie and shredded jeans from the bottom of the pile.

"Did you see the pizza van parked on the street when you arrived home this morning with Isabelle?"

Hugo's nose screws up before he nods.

"Was it still parked in the same spot when you went down to get the wings and pizza you and Isabelle had for dinner?"

The groove between Hugo's brows deepens before he nods again. "Fuck—she has her own surveillance team watching her?"

Unsure if he's asking a question or stating a fact, I reply, "I don't know, but we need to remain cautious. If they're not here for Isabelle, they're here for. . ."

"Isaac," we say at the same time.

With a nod, I stand to my feet and yank my jeans up my thighs. Just before I whip my satin shift over my head to replace it with a sweater, I request for Hugo to spin around. We may have grown friendly the past twelve-plus months, but we're not *that* friendly.

"There are too many fucking mirrors in your room, so I'll wait for you in the living area." Hugo's grumble is more pained than playful, making me wonder if I'm the only one being bombarded with bitter memories.

This is conceited for me to say, and I'd never tell Hugo or Isaac, but a teeny part of me is wondering if the surveillance van is here for me. One of the last things Alex said to me was that he was trying to keep me safe. The pizza van arrived at the front of my apartment that very afternoon.

Hugo's eyes lift when I enter the living room a few minutes later. He doesn't burst out laughing from my disguise as I was predicting. I don't need to hear his chuckles to know of their arrival, though; the big shakes hampering his large frame as he strives to hold in his laughter tell me everything I need to know. My outfit is as disastrous as I was hoping.

The humor in his eyes fades when I say, "Call Hunter and have him remove Isaac's fingerprints from the security server."

"What? He'll kill me!"

I roll my eyes. "Scared, Hugo?"

"No," he bites back. "I'm just not an idiot."

At least one of us isn't.

I grow worried I said my statement out loud when the worry on Hugo's face doubles. The reason for his anxious look comes to light when he says, "You're throwing yourself into the fire to save Isaac."

He's not asking a question. He's stating a fact.

I shrug in halfhearted agreement. "I'm doing what I should have done years ago. I'll have Isaac's back as he's always had mine."

Hugo follows me to my front door. "What if he's in the surveillance van?"

He doesn't need to say Alex's name for me to know to whom he is referring.

"He won't be." I cross the threshold of my door, saving Hugo from hearing the last half of my grumbled statement. "That means he'd have to still care for me."

Which we both know he doesn't.

TWENTY-SIX

ALEX

"Are you sure you don't want me to stay?"

After scrubbing my tired eyes, I raise them from a bank of computer monitors to Reid. "There is no use in us both being tired. Go home and get some sleep; then we'll swap places in the morning."

Even knowing I'm lying doesn't stop Reid from jerking his chin up before he exits the surveillance van we've been camped in most of our day. He's tired. Rightfully so. My position means I work more hours than a standard FBI agent, yet I'm still exhausted out of my mind.

Brandon is smart, but even worse than that is how cunning he is. He has everyone fooled. He didn't even need to flash his badge to gain access to Regan's apartment today. He just sauntered up to the security guard, slapped hands with him like they're college roomies, then entered the idling elevator.

If it weren't for Regan's comment about Isaac removing all surveillance devices from his private premises, I'd be none the wiser to his visit. Unfortunately for Brandon, I don't need to piggyback off Isaac's feed to maintain video surveillance. I just needed Reid and his impressive security hacking skills.

Approximately ten minutes later, tires screeching to a stop pummel my ears. I tap on the mouse button three times, bringing up the hidden device Reid installed in the underground parking lot of Hector earlier today.

Isaac must have broken at least ten traffic laws to make it here this fast. The movement sheet indicated he'd left the dungeon ten minutes ago. The trip usually takes thirty.

He's barely switched off the ignition of his Bugatti before he throws open his door and charges for the elevators in the far corner of the garage. Halfway there, he suddenly stops. My heart beats in an unnatural rhythm when a person steps out of the shadow shrouding half of Isaac's face. Although I can't see their features, I know who it is. A thousand years couldn't erase her feverish frame and the generous swell of her breasts from my mind. It's Regan.

I turn up the volume on my monitor when Regan faintly whispers, "You cannot go in there."

Although I have the volume up as loud as it can go, I don't hear what Isaac replies. Lucky, as I'm five seconds from blowing my cover to wipe the arrogant glare off his face with my fists from the way he is glaring at her, much less hearing the words delivered with it. He stares at Regan in warning, as if whatever she is saying is hurting him as much as he hurt me twelve months ago.

When Isaac attempts to skirt past Regan, she steps into his path, causing his jaw muscle to twitch. They engage in a few more words before Isaac bangs his chest with his fist.

This time, when he heads for the elevator, Regan lets him go. He barely makes it three steps away before he freezes, spins, then snarls.

I stand from my chair when he races back toward Regan. His face is lined with anger, and his fists are clenched. His steps are so long and efficient, he reaches her in less than a heartbeat. I flinch as badly as Regan does when he grabs her wrist.

The only thing stopping me from charging out of this surveillance van and pummeling some sense into him is when he drops Regan's wrist as quickly as he snagged it.

I watch him closely, my nostrils flaring less with each apologetic glance he directs at Regan. I don't know what he's more concerned about: the words they shared, or the way she responded to him grabbing her.

I'm furious about both.

After inhaling a big breath that pushes her chest out, Regan tugs Isaac into the darkened corner she was hiding in before he arrived. It conceals them from the general public, but the night vision filter on my camera keeps me in the loop.

I take a mental note to switch my surveillance vehicle first thing tomorrow morning when Regan nudges her head my way, alerting Isaac to my location. Her glance is so accurate, I have no doubt she's on to me.

After a quick scan of the street, Isaac returns to his conversation with Regan. Have you ever felt like a sitting duck? That's exactly what I feel when Regan swings her eyes in my direction for the second time. If I didn't know any better, I'd swear she can see me through the super dark tint covering the van's back window. She appears to be staring straight at me.

The tension fueling their exchange dampens a short time later when a smirk curves Isaac's lips high. He looks lighter than he did when he arrived, as if a weight has been lifted from his shoulders. After running his fingers through his hair, he takes a step closer to Regan. Whatever he says this time around must be more a plea than a demand as it pops a pondering crinkle between Regan's brows. Her eyes return my way for the third time.

I stare at her, willing her to see in Isaac what I see. To look past the wool he pulled over her eyes all those years ago and perceive who he truly is. When she steps closer to Isaac, I think my prayers have been answered. She's not looking at him with admiration and respect. She appears a little ill, as if it's finally dawned on her he isn't the man she believes he is.

My intuition has never been proven more wrong when she fists Isaac's jacket in her hand before aligning their lips. She murmurs something over Isaac's mouth before she gently nibbles on his lips. I freeze, utterly shocked and sickened by what I'm seeing. It is as if my nightmares for the last twelve months are being played out in front of me, one slow motherfucking detail at a time.

My fists clench when Isaac grips Regan's jean-covered backside to curl her legs around his waist. Fury blackens my blood as they move toward the elevator bank, their bodies intertwined as one, like they're too impatient to keep their hands off each other until they've entered the sanctuary of their bedroom.

I suck in breaths like I'm drowning when Regan places her thumb onto the security panel to call the elevator to their floor. She nibbles on Isaac's cropped beard and neck before reacquainting their mouths, and what do I do? I watch and I stare, but I don't move a fucking inch. I'm too gutted to do anything. I'm dead. Wholly fucking broken.

A train wreck of emotions hammers into me the instant the elevator doors snap shut with Regan and Isaac inside. I'm angry and frustrated, but most of all, I'm heartbroken. Even after all this time, I trusted her, and what do I get for it? This. *Him.*

He ruins fucking everything!

Incapable of holding my anger for a second longer, I lift the keyboard I am standing in front of and toss it across the room. My throw is so strong, the cord connecting it to the monitor snaps before darting across my face. The sting of the wires bouncing across my skin isn't registered by my body. Just like that night in the field all those years ago, I'm too angry to feel anything.

I continue trashing the surveillance van like I'm the Hulk on a rampage. Computer monitors, movement sheets, and the food Reid left in case I got hungry in the middle of the night dart in all directions.

Twelve months ago, I would have been ashamed of the man I am behaving like, but right here, right fucking now, I don't give a shit. Take everything from me.

No, scrap that. I'll give it to you, because tonight proves what I've always known: hard work doesn't mean shit. I've given this job everything I have, every piece of me, and what do I get in return for my effort?

Nothing.

Not a single fucking thing.

No glory.

No girl.

Nothing.

I even lost my best friend.

As I suck in ragged breaths, I scan the area I just destroyed during a lapse in judgment. I'm not surprised I've finally succumbed to the anger that's been eating me alive the past twelve months. I'm only half the man I used to be, and on days like today, I'm not even that.

While running my fingers through my sweaty hair, I search for my gun, wallet, and keys on the floor. I right some of the computer equipment during the process, but it's far from looking how it once did.

Deciding I'll fix it in the morning, I push the chairs under the only piece of equipment still together before exiting the van. If I had a few more minutes, I'm fairly certain even the stainless steel desk wouldn't have survived my wrath. That's how I know it's time to call it a night. I'm filled with so much anger, I don't trust myself.

I've always believed you pick which side of the law to stand on. But now I'm torn. I don't only want to see Isaac behind bars for eternity, I want to kill him as slowly and as painfully as Regan's betrayal is gutting me.

The chance of violence doubles when I exit the van. Regan is standing at the foot of the curb. Her hands are spread across her cocked hips, and her eyes are narrowed, but it is her kiss-swollen lips I notice more than anything.

"I knew it was you."

TWENTY-SEVEN

REGAN

Alex chuckles the laugh of a madman. "Is that why you did it, because you knew I was watching?"

The sneer of his words has me recoiling, but not in shock. When my lips first brushed against Isaac's, I predicted Alex's anger because it was the first emotion that smacked into me when the hairs on my nape prickled.

I've been suspicious of the surveillance van on my street all day, but I was giving Alex the benefit of the doubt. I was certain our twelve months of absence would have clued him in that I hate being spied on.

Clearly, I'm not the only one who's failed to grow smarter the past year.

Alex is just as stupid as me.

The scent of a hot, virile man changes some of my anger into lust when Alex moves closer to me. He's sweating profusely, making my sanity even more reckless. This isn't good. This will not end well. I just kissed a man whose smirk alone makes women come, and what did I feel? Nothing. Not a single fucking thing. But one sniff of Alex's sweaty skin, and I'm seconds from falling to my knees and begging for his scraps.

What the fuck? I came down here to confront him, not organize a hook up.

Alex's next words thin my lust with anger. "Do you feel good, Regan? Did you enjoy rubbing it in my face, ensuring I didn't miss any of the details?"

I attempt to talk, to tell him not to be ridiculous, but his threat stops me. "I swear to god, if you defend him, I'll fucking gut him just like your betrayal gutted me."

"I didn't betray you, because you can't cheat on someone you're *not* with! We're not a couple, Alex! We never were."

"We were back then! We were when you fucked him to get back at me!" It's a little before 2 AM, but the roar of his words doesn't stop numerous lights switching on in the buildings surrounding us. "I trusted you, Regan, and what did I get for it? A cheating, two-timing b—"

My palm steals his sentence with the same brutality he used to deliver it. He glares at me, wordlessly daring me to strike him a second time. When I take up his challenge, he catches my wrist midair. I bang my free fist on his thrusting chest three times, my anger too paramount to be subdued.

I'm not usually a violent person, but there's something about Alex that brings out all sides of me. The stupid. The good. The *I'm so fucking twisted up in knots over this guy I don't know who I am anymore.* They're all showcased in the most horrible light, making me appear as if I am the name he was about to call me.

"I hate you!"

His eyes turn almost black when his pupils swamp his corneas. "For what, Regan? For loving you? For trusting you—?"

"For breaking me! For not seeing what your betrayal did to me! For not begging for forgiveness. You just left, Alex. You just fucking left. . . and you took my libido right along with you."

I'm not ashamed about my last comment. He's aware I liked to explore sexually before he walked into my life, so if anything will express how badly he fucked me over, that confession will. I pound his chest some more. "You broke me, Alex. You fucking broke me!"

He snags my thumping fist from his chest then drags it to his side, pulling me forward. When our eyes collide, something switches. The anger, resentment, and hostility are still in abundance, but instead of expressing them with violence, we choose an equally vicious, yet passionate way.

His mouth smashes down on mine before his tongue traces my stunned lips. Catching my lower lip between his teeth, he gives it a hard tug. My mouth falls open to him in a surrendering purr, my earlier anger submitting just as quickly. He draws the air from my lungs with perfectly controlled strokes of his tongue, but there is no tenderness in his kiss. It is violent and ugly, a twisted mess of despair and devotion.

Although I should be shutting this down, I fight for control, for him to share the reins. He doesn't give me an inch. He continues holding my mouth captive with impressive bites, nips, and dominant licks.

As his kiss ramps up, my thirst to touch him grows. I need to feel his skin under my hands as urgently as my lungs need him to relinquish his mouth so I can secure a full breath.

When I wrench against his hands circling my wrists, his grip tightens, tight enough to leave a bruise. His hold should scare me as much as Isaac's fury did earlier, but this is Alex, a man who'd never lose control, no matter how tense the situation.

A metal material cools the heat raring through my body when he splays me on the floor of the van he was exiting when I confronted him. I was so caught up in our embrace, I didn't notice we were moving, much less him kicking aside mangled computer equipment and papers.

After pinning my hands above my head with one hand, Alex's other moves to the zipper of my jeans. In less than three heart beats, he has the clasp undone and my panties and jeans around my ankles.

My chest rises and falls in a steady rhythm when he frees his cock from his trousers. It is as magnificent as I remembered: thick, veiny, and seeping with pre-cum.

I call out when he lines up before unexpectedly driving home. His name leaves my mouth in a grunt, the sensation of being filled by him unlike anything I've ever felt. The angry tension teeming between us should make the situation feel wrong, but for some reason, it doesn't. Something so good could never be seen as anything less than perfect.

Not waiting for me to acclimate to his girth, Alex withdraws to the very tip before slamming back into me. His second thrust holds the same ferocity as his first. He pounds into me on repeat, shifting my senses into high gear. The brutal slams of his pelvis against mine spread my thighs wider with every grind. He takes me deeper and faster. It's the best sex I've ever had.

"Is this what you want, Regan? Am I giving you what you need?" He pounds into me harder with every word he speaks.

I raise my ass off the ground so I can match his grinds. "Yes, oh god, yes!"

My elevated position causes his cock to slam into my cervix. I throw my head back with a grunt, freeing the moans bubbling in my chest. "God, yes. Fuck me, Alex. Fuck me."

I should feel dirty we're fucking in the surveillance van he used to spy on me only minutes after he witnessed me kissing another man, but I don't. I feel what I always feel when I'm with him. I feel desired. Wanted. Cherished. There is just one more thing I need for this to be perfect: the heat of his skin under my hands.

When I attempt to wiggle out of Alex's firm hold, he growls like a wild animal. I nearly protest until he stares at me, a long, penetrating gaze that steamrolls me with as much excitement as it does resentment. He's not fucking me; he's forcing me to submit.

I'm close to giving him what he wants, to handing over all the control, but that isn't the way things work with us. He wants us to be even, an equal unit. That means he needs to share the power as much as he's demanding for me to relinquish it.

I dig my heels into his ass to slow his grinds. All it does is firm his grip on my wrists. "If you want me to stop, Regan, say the word, and I'll stop, but if you came down here to get what *he* can't give you, then sit back and enjoy the ride, baby, because this is the last orgasm I'll ever give you."

His words burn like a thousand bee stings. He mistook what I said. I didn't confront him because I want him to bring me to climax. I want him to admit the mistakes he made, to beg me to forgive him. I want him to fight for me as strongly as I fought my attraction to him.

I command my body to withdraw from his contact, to take back the last shred of dignity I have left by ending this exchange immediately. But no matter what I say, no matter what I do, it doesn't listen. It meets his pumps grind for grind, trusting the words he spoke as if they're gospel. My body knows I can't get this from Isaac. The thrill, the anticipation of what is about to transpire, it knows I'll never get that from anyone who isn't named Alex, so it's not willing to give it up.

Noticing my body's failure to object to his brutal fucking, Alex drives into me deeper. He screws me like a madman, as if he's marking not just my body but my heart as well. It is like I'm in a dream. My body is tingling with euphoria, and a tsunami of excitement is racing through every inch of me. But my mind is numb, too stunned by the turn of events to process what's happening.

When tears threaten to spill down my cheeks, I snap my eyes shut. It amplifies the electricity in the air. Goosebumps prickle my skin as I freefall into the madness. I quiver and shake; I just don't know if it's in euphoria or fear.

I assume it is the former when my pussy clenches around Alex's thick cock. I try to fight his pull, to prove my body is above the weak, pitiful woman I'm acting like, but the crest in my womb grows with every thrust.

He fucks me so well, the worry of losing my marbles is the last thing on my mind. My orgasm builds and builds and builds, but it won't peak. I can feel it, right there, threatening to dive into orgasmic bliss at any moment, but something is holding it back. *Or someone.*

Leaning forward, I try with all my might to pull out of Alex's grip. With our bodies slicked with sweat, my wrist falls from his hold with only the slightest ache. Just before my fingers weave through the damp hairs curling around his ear, he pulls my hand away.

"Let me touch you," I beg with desperation dangling on my vocal cords.

"No."

He only says one word, but it's the words he doesn't speak that I hear the loudest. He's not granting my body's wish to climax. He's punishing it for kissing Isaac, for breaking his trust.

This isn't a beg for forgiveness fuck. It's a farewell one.

"How can you preach morality when all you *ever* do is lie?"

My veins thicken when his eyes lock with mine. The fury narrowing them should blacken my blood with hate, but it has the opposite effect on my fucked up body, giving it the final push my orgasm needs to finally reach fruition.

I still as a ruckus of devastation pinches the air from my lungs. My orgasm rips through me, owning my body as surely as Alex owns my heart. My insides explode as I let go, surrendering to its power with nothing but violent shakes and a breathless moan.

Although my climax is wondrous, it doesn't save me from the cruelty of Alex's words. "That's where I went wrong, wasn't it? You didn't want a man who would stand at your side, supporting you as if you were his equal. You wanted an alpha. A dominant male who fed your ego like he did your bank balance. I thought you were better than that, Regan. I thought you saw through the glitter and shine to see the real person hiding beneath it."

My eyes stray to his, praying my climax will hide the devastation in them. "I do—"

"No, you fucking don't! You see money. Popularity. Anything you want to see to excuse you from cleaning up the carnage you cause!

You trample people, not caring how they're left after you destroy them. First Luca. Now me."

I couldn't be more shocked if he slapped me in the face. I try to retaliate, to ignore the hunger in his eyes mixing with hate, but I'm truly lost for a reply, equally sickened and mad.

Needing to leave before he spots my tears, I dig my feet into his ass for the second time. A broken keyboard digs into me when I drag my back along the van to get away from him, but I'll endure the pain, suffer the torment. *I always do.*

Since Alex's cock is as thick and as angry as his eyes, it takes a mighty effort to dismount him. When I do, my hands are the next thing I free. Moisture burns my eyes when I glance down at the angry red welts circling my wrists. The last time I wore his marks, it was a beautiful, lust-filled exchange. Tonight's wasn't close to that.

After standing, I yank my panties and jeans up my legs. The amount of wetness glistening on my thighs makes me even angrier. He used my attraction to him to exact his revenge, then he threw a whole heap of hurtful words into the mix. *What man does that?*

"How dare you." I try to think of something more appropriate to say, but I'm honestly lost. I understand he's angry; he just witnessed me kissing a man he believes I cheated on him with, but still, this? I didn't use Luca; I loved him. . . just as I did Alex.

When I say that to Alex, he takes a step back, stunned. "You loved me?"

"Yes!" I exhale three times to calm the fury burning my veins before adding on, "You think you were the only one betrayed here, but my god. . . when I discovered what you had done, I never felt more stupid. You stole information that didn't belong to you and used it against me."

His chest thrusts, his anger overtaking his hope. "No, I didn't—"

I continue talking as if he never did. "Then when I tried to give you the benefit of the doubt, I paid for my stupidity not even eight hours later."

"By sleeping with a man you swore you had no interest in!"

I glare at Alex, ensuring he can see the hurt, anger, and disappointment in my eyes. "I never slept with Isaac. I don't know him like that."

The pain, anger, and sadness I felt when Luca died crash into me all over again, and in no time at all, I'm back to the scared, panicked nineteen-year-old girl I once was.

"The only thing I ever did wrong was trust you." My comment is directed at Alex, but it is for both him and Luca.

"I saw you kiss him, Regan." Alex's tone changes, becoming less stern. "What are you saying? That it didn't happen? That I imagined something I saw with my own two eyes? I'm not a fucking idiot."

The anger he's attempting to control rolls back in when I reply, "Yeah, you are. You just lost the best thing that could have ever happened to you because you're too stupid to step back and assess things properly." The panic twisting his features makes my next sentence the hardest of them all to say, "You're so fucking stubborn, Alex, you can't see what is staring you in the face."

My accusation was supposed to disclose the reason I kissed Isaac, but the sentiment in the air changed it. I'm talking about me, and how fiercely I could have loved and protected him if he hadn't done me wrong.

"Don't," I beg when Alex takes a step closer to me, as if the truth is finally smacking into him. "What I said to you last year was wrong. I should have never done it, but I'm not the only one at fault here. You're just as much to blame for our downfall as me."

Some of the heaviness on my chest lightens when Alex dips his chin in agreement. It barely makes an indent in the frustration clouding our conversation, but it's better than him continuing with the inane stubbornness he's shown the past twelve months.

With a smile revealing I appreciate his effort, I make my way to the partially cracked open van door. I make it halfway out before Alex calls my name. He doesn't call me Regan like he did during our exchange; he's reverted back to my infamous nickname, although that's not the sole reason my heart is being brutally gnawed. It's the words following my name causing my stuttering response: "I'm sorry. I'm so fucking sorry."

Although I'd give anything to pretend what just happened didn't, I can't. What Raquel said weeks ago is true: I've spent a majority of the last nine years with my head in the sand. I've lived a full life, but it was nothing close to the one I could have if I let go of my past and embrace my future.

I never thought I would say these words, but they're the most humble ones I've ever said: I deserve to be happy.

At one stage, I thought that meant having Alex in my life.

Now. . . I'm not so sure.

TWENTY-EIGHT

ALEX

My fist indents the steel floor Regan's back quivered against mere minutes ago when she darts away from the van as if her ass is on fire. I know she heard my whispered apology because the vein in her nape worked overtime the instant it escaped my lips, but she didn't speak a single word.

No acceptance of my apology.

No apology of her own.

Nothing.

While raking my fingers through my hair, I take in the scene. My trousers are huddled around my knees, and Regan's arousal is glistening on my cock, but I feel like the biggest fucking asshole in the world.

I honestly don't know what my game plan was tonight. I wanted to bang my chest and act moronic before hurting her as badly as I was hurting, but instead of doing that by manning up and acting like the adult I am, I used her attraction of me against her. I should have relished the fact she couldn't deny me, even while fuming mad, but instead, I gathered it as intel before using it in the ugliest manner.

As if that wasn't bad enough, I threw Luca into the mix for good measure. I didn't mean to drop his name like I did. I was just so caught up recalling Regan's kiss with Isaac again and again and again that it fell from my mouth before I could reel it back in.

I guess in a way it could be seen as both good and bad. Bad because I hurt Regan more than I ever intended. Good because it forced her to be honest about her feelings. I've been dying for the day she'd tell me she loved me back; I just wish she could have said it in a less hostile environment. Seconds after admitting she had once loved me, she looked at me as if she'd never feel that way again. In all honesty, that gutted me more than witnessing her kiss Isaac.

This may be stupid of me to admit, but I believed her when she said she didn't sleep with Isaac, but why kiss him tonight? If they have no connection, and no intention to pursue one, what was tonight's escapade about? Did she do it because she knew I was watching? Or was it a spur-of-the-moment decision to teach me the repercussions of snooping?

Realizing I'll never clear the fog from my head sitting in a sex-scented surveillance van, I tuck away my half-masted cock then exit the van. Regrettably, this time around, there isn't a frustratingly beautiful blonde waiting for me.

Well, there is, just not the one I'm hoping for.

"Your resignation was forwarded to the head of our department this morning. As of 5 PM this evening, you were no longer an agent on my team."

Brandon moves into my path when I attempt to sidestep him. Stupid move. Reid is gone, and my anger is beyond frayed. Now is not the time to mess with me.

"I stepped out of line."

I throw my head back and laugh a hauntingly painstaking chuckle. "You think? You not only risked my unit's investigation, you might even do time. Do you realize that? One word, and your entire fucking career will circle the drain."

He nods, understanding every word I speak is true. He's lucky I've been so tied up gathering the evidence he left scattered throughout my department I haven't had the chance to discuss his deceit with higher counterparts at the Bureau, or he may have spent the Thanksgiving/Christmas holiday period behind bars.

"If you don't want that, I suggest you take a step back." *Or ten before you lose some teeth.*

As stubborn as he is stupid, Brandon maintains his ground. "I wouldn't be here if it wasn't important." His words are stronger than the weak step he takes so he can hand me the printout he's holding.

I shouldn't take it. I should tell him to fuck off, or better yet, use him to defuse the anger still thickening my veins, but the plea in his eyes reveals there's more than just anger at stake here. He's put both his life and his position on the line to confront me, so whatever cards he's holding must be important.

With that in mind, I snatch the paper out of his hand, nearly ripping it in the process. The unnatural rhythm my heart's been beating jumps up when I scan the document so recently printed it smells of fresh ink. It is a flight manifest for a takeoff scheduled at the Ravenshoe private airstrip for early tomorrow morning.

Although none of the names on the manifest seem familiar, there's only one man in Ravenshoe wealthy enough to own a private jet: Isaac Holt.

"Isaac takes trips like this all the time. He has a comped room at Caesar's." I toss the document back Brandon's way before pushing off my feet.

I freeze midstride when Brandon shouts, "Then why would he schedule the transfer of millions of dollars to an off-shore account before his visit?"

I can think of a million reasons why any man visiting Vegas would hide such an exorbitant amount, but none are legitimate for an unmarried man who doesn't need to hide his side dish from the wife he married without a prenup.

When I spin around to face Brandon, he digs a second piece of paper out of his pocket. This one is more tattered than the first. "Over two hundred and fifty transactions verified to be distributed at the same time first thing tomorrow morning." His hands rattle less this time when he passes the document to me. "He kept the transfer amounts under $10,000 so as not to raise suspicion."

"Then how do you know about it?"

I stop scanning the long list of foreign investment accounts when Brandon replies, "Once a device is introduced to the server, it's never forgotten."

"You used the intel you stole off Regan's laptop to unearth this?"

The paper creases when I fist it tightly after Brandon nods. "But only because I'm trying to help you."

"You're helping me?" My tone exposes that I think he's full of shit, but just in case it doesn't, I add on, "Or are you helping yourself?"

He tugs on the collar of his shirt, suddenly overwhelmed with heat. It's not hot today. It's a pleasant late fall evening; he just can't handle my infuriating glare.

The redness on his cheeks doubles when I step closer to him. "I'll hand it to you: you're smart, have a way with computers, and the looks to fly under the radar for as long as you have, but there is one skill you are lacking that will ensure other agents constantly step over you."

I wait for the long descent of his Adam's apple to finish before continuing, "You can't read people. You can't tell the difference between a friendly glance and a lusty one. When a woman is asking you on a second date, or if she's sizing you up to see if you're a serial killer. Even when the painstakingly obvious is staring you in the face, you're too busy evaluating everything around it instead of the picture you should have been looking at the entire time."

My last sentence resonates more with me than Brandon's predicament. What Regan said tonight is true. I'm so dedicated to ensuring Isaac serves time for what happened to Dane, I'm letting it influence every decision in my life—her included.

"You said on the courthouse stairs last week that the only difference between Isabelle and me was that I stupidly fell in love." My eyes bounce between Brandon's, which are staring intently into mine. "You know that isn't true." I'm not denying I am in love with Regan. I am denying that Isabelle hasn't fallen in love with Isaac. "Whether we agree with it or not, Isabelle loves Isaac."

Brandon shakes his head, although I don't think he realizes he is. "She doesn't know him."

"I know," I agree, "but neither do we. Not really. Isaac keeps everyone at arm's length, even those closest to him, so how can we trust anything we've read? We were trained from the get-go to devise our own opinions, but no one has done that in Isaac's case." *No one but me.*

Brandon attempts a rebuttal, but his words fall short. Lucky, as I have no intention of accepting his excuses.

"If you really care for Isabelle, help me help her."

"How?" The confusion in his tone is the first honest thing I've heard come out of his mouth this week.

"The bugs in Isabelle's phone."

I watch him closely to see if he attempts to discount his knowledge of them. He remains on the honesty route by dipping his chin.

"Do you have the serial numbers for them?"

"They're no good. I ran them through our system twice. Nothing popped up."

"That's not what I asked, Brandon." My voice is thicker than his, more determined. "I have access to channels you can't access." Brandon makes a *pfft* noise, but I pretend not to hear it. "The more people looking into Isabelle's case, the better off she'll be. I thought you cared for her, Brandon."

"I do," he replies, briskly nodding. "Very much so."

"Then give me what I need. It might not lessen the severity of your insubordination, but it will do more good to Isabelle's case than harm."

He deliberates for barely a moment before agreeing to my request. His eagerness to assist Isabelle proves what I've been wondering all along. Isaac isn't the only one under Isabelle's spell. Brandon is under it just as deeply.

TWENTY-NINE

ALEX

It took four days for Grayson's team to unravel the massive knot sheltering the culprit responsible for the bugs in Isabelle's phone, then
another four days to convince Regan I had credible, uncorrupt information to assist her client. I went through every route necessary to
assure her my request to visit her apartment was for a legitimate business meeting, and even then, she acquiesced under protest.

It's fortunate she agreed when she did because I was on the verge
of desperation, mere hours from calling Isaac and demanding he
force her to speak to me. I'm sure that would have gone down
well. *Not*.

I've barely crossed the threshold of Regan's apartment when
Isabelle's boots stomp across the wooden floorboards. She looks in a
hurry, like she's unaware of our meeting this morning.

Upon spotting me standing to the right of her hideously dated
handbag, her teeth grit. My lips curl into an amused smirk when she
snatches her bag off the tabletop to rummage through her belongings.
I'm not surprised at her inability to trust me. I screwed her over more
than once; I just had no clue it was happening months after someone
already orchestrated her demise.

Her chocolate eyes lift to glare into mine when I say, "I didn't plant the bugs in your phone, Isabelle."

My comment is loud enough that both she and Regan can hear. I need them to know whose team I'm on. This fight is not about Isaac or myself. It's about an innocent being framed for a murder she didn't commit.

"The first time I heard about your phone being tapped was when you mentioned it at the courthouse last week."

After seeking the truth from my eyes, Isabelle asks, "Then how did you find out about Isaac's private residence?"

I'm about to reply, but the quickest shift of a shadow steals my attention. Recognizing his cover has been blown, Hugo, Isaac's right-hand man/bodyguard breaks away from the dark corner he was attempting to conceal himself in. My chest swells with smugness from the stern gaze he gives me, but the strokes to my ego aren't enough for me to forget why I'm here.

"I followed you there."

Isabelle's eyes snap to mine faster than a fired bullet. "Me?" she asks when she spots the direction of my gaze.

I nod. "You and Isaac. I lost your tail for nearly fifteen minutes when I followed you from his apartment one night. So you can imagine my surprise when I found Isaac's Bugatti pulled over on the side of the highway on my way home." I cough to clear my throat. "I put a tracker on his car when the windows got a little foggy."

Isabelle's face whitens as her pupils dilate. Just as quickly as her shock arrived, it is replaced with curiosity. "Then why did you take so long to get a search warrant?"

My high chest deflates. "Because back then, we had nothing on Isaac."

Isabelle's lips curl. She looks as smug as a cat staring at an empty fishbowl.

"I said *back then*, Isabelle." I keep my tone high, hoping it will conceal my deceit. "The search we conducted on Isaac's residence was a valid search warrant with a very valid reason."

Regan is too smart not to see through my lie. "You were not invited into my home under the pretense of discussing matters pertaining to Isaac Holt."

She moves to stand next to Isabelle, engulfing me with her delicious scent. "You said you had information that would assist my client. If that statement is false, I suggest you leave my premises immediately before I file an injunction against you."

I remind myself time and time again that my visit this morning is not about my relationship with Regan. I am here to help Isabelle, but it still takes a mammoth effort to shift my eyes away from Regan. Regan's beauty is perfect, but she is ten times more attractive when she's riled up. I just wish it was me she had her fists up and ready to fight for.

Getting back to the task at hand, I smile at Isabelle, hoping to ease the lines in her forehead. She's utterly blind to my charm. Regan is nowhere near as lucky. Her strong stance doesn't falter, but her loud gulp gives away her true self. She's still not immune to me, which means I still have a chance. I didn't fuck up everything last week. . . *except perhaps my heart.*

"I do have credible information that will be of benefit to your client," I inform Regan, my tone both professional and friendly.

She doesn't hear it that way. All she hears is a man hoping to slay one dragon before subduing another. Although I wish it were that easy, nothing has ever been simple for me. I work for everything I have—just the mammoth effort it took for Regan to let me speak with Isabelle is proof of this.

"Then let's get this over and done with." Regan gestures for me to enter her living room before grumbling, "I wouldn't want to take up too much of your *valuable* time."

Over the next twenty minutes, I update Regan and Isabelle on the information Grayson's team unearthed. Most of it is mumbo-jumbo technical stuff I'm not overly familiar with, but for the most part, Regan and Isabelle follow, only stopping to ask the occasional question.

Such as, "So the request for me to join your team was filed before I graduated from the academy?" Isabelle's high brow reveals her confusion.

I nod. "Yes. The original paperwork was dated a month before I was assigned to my position."

I hand her the form that proves her request to join my department was dated months before I began my interim leader role at Ravenshoe.

"But that doesn't make any sense," Isabelle murmurs as her eyes dart between mine. "*You* said you brought me in as a piece of eye candy for Isaac."

Regan's eyes snap to Isabelle's so fast, I'm sure she'll feel their strain for weeks to come. She glares at Isabelle so fiercely, the vein in her neck beats as speedily as Isabelle's pulse thrums in her slim wrists. Although I hate that Isabelle is being subjected to her anger, I'm glad it's not directed at me.

"I didn't know that until after I joined Alex's team," Isabelle explains to Regan, her tone low and reserved. "And I also refused to become a commodity for the FBI. My refusal got me on coffee and filing duties for the past seven months."

Now it's my turn to be subjected to Regan's furious glare. Unfortunately for her, it doesn't have the same effect on me as it does Isabelle. I'm more turned on by her anger than scared of it.

Mostly.

"The decision to bring Isabelle onto my team as a decoy for Isaac was decided after attending a conference in San Francisco in April."

I hate the way she is looking at me right now. *I fucking hate it.*

Hoping to do a better job of explaining myself, I say, "Every male agent in the vicinity kept mentioning a hot new rookie agent who was seeking a placement. I was shocked when I discovered it was the same agent I denied a transfer request from during my first week in the Ravenshoe office as the superior officer."

My eyes drift to Isabelle. "I wanted to see for myself if you lived up to the hype. I was also desperate to force Isaac to make a mistake, so I used any tactic I could find. I heard from a very reliable source that a beautiful lady was his eternal weakness."

"A beautiful *blonde* lady," sneers Regan. "And the person you got that information from knew you were squeezing them for confidential facts. That is why she led you down the garden path."

Isabelle's eyes bounce between Regan and me when we undertake an intense stare down. I peer at Regan, begging for her to see the truth in my eyes. *I fucked up. I'm sorry, but I'm here now trying to make it right. Doesn't that give me some credit?*

Not hearing the words I'm unable to speak, Regan sneers, "Either tell me what information you have that will assist my client, or get the hell out of my house."

I watch her closely, praying the tears looming in her eyes don't fall, because every one she sheds will add more cuts into my already gushing heart. When her tears remain at bay, I trail my index finger across my brow to remove a layer of sweat before digging my hand into my leather satchel.

"It took a bit of convincing, but Brandon supplied me with the serial numbers from the tracking devices stored on your phone."

It was more than a bit of convincing, but allowing him access to Isabelle's uncle's old files was worth it. Grayson's crew hit the motherlode with what they uncovered, and although I don't see it helping my relationship with Regan, it will at least fix some of the mistakes I made with Isabelle the prior six months.

Anger can't excuse my appalling behavior the past twelve months, but grief is easily forgiven. Those last words Dane spoke to me were true. His injury did eat me alive; then, upon his death, grief and revenge stole the last part of the man I once was. I mistreated my crew, my family, and my girl all because I acted on the black tar in my heart instead of working out a way to rid myself of it.

You can be assured I won't make the same mistake twice.

"After searching through many hidden channels, I discovered that the devices were placed in your phone by the FBI."

Isabelle's eyes snap to mine in an instant. I'll give credit where credit is due. She has the angry snarl down pat.

"But not by my department," I clarify. "It was the same person who initially requested your transfer to Ravenshoe."

She glances my way for several seconds before her wide-with-distrust eyes lower to scan the document I'm holding. I can tell the exact moment she recognizes the signature scribbled across the bottom as she takes in a sharp breath.

Regan's response is nowhere near as pleasant. "That bitch." I feel more vulnerable than angry when she lifts and locks her eyes with me. "How could you let this happen to an agent on your team? I thought you said nothing like this would ever happen to a member of your crew. That you were more ethical and better than those before you. This shows you aren't any better than your predecessor. You let Theresa slide in right under your nose and hinder your investigation from the very beginning."

Everything she is shouting is true, but it doesn't stop me from saying, "Regan. . . don't. . . This isn't a personal attack."

When she abruptly stands from her seat, I expect my cheek to feel the sting of her slap for the second time this week. She surprises me by using words to deliver her anguish instead of violence. "No, it isn't a personal attack." She folds her arms in front of her chest. "But it was. You *used* me, all to climb the corporate ladder at the FBI, then you let this happen because you became a jealous green-eyed monster."

I want to grab her shoulders and shake the shit out of her. I want to yell at her that I'm not guilty of what she continuously throws at me, but since those are the responses of a man without a heart, I accept her invisible slap with a deep swallow, knowing, just like me, she needs more than a few seconds to sort through the facts.

I glance up at Regan in hope when she says, "Thank you for supplying us with these documents." My deep exhalation is quickly withdrawn when she adds on, "I'll be sure to pass on my commendations your tact to your superior officers." She jerks her head to Hugo, who has been watching our charade with the eye of an eagle the past hour. "Hugo will show you the way out."

My eyes dart between Hugo and Regan as I struggle to absorb the underlying message in her reply. She's giving me clear signals that she doesn't want our relationship exposed to her work colleague and client. That frustrates the shit out of me.

I try to let it go, to remind myself that we still have a long way to go before we can patch the damage we made, but my ego stops me. "I don't need to be shown out. I already know my way."

After gathering my leather satchel and jacket slung over the back of the chair, I head for the door. I only make it two paces before Isabelle's gasp rings in my ears. With my emotions so caught up in trying to appease Regan, I forgot the real reason I came here this afternoon.

After a big breath, I spin around to face Isabelle. "I'm looking further into how this happened to you, Isabelle. You have my word this will be thoroughly investigated by my department."

Although my pledge could mean nothing to her, Isabelle accepts it with a dignity I've come to admire the past month. "Thank you."

I shift my eyes to Regan to issue her the same promise I just gave Isabelle, but this one is without words. Although her stance remains as strong as mine, her face as impassive, I know she hears the words I can't speak because the smallest glimmer of hope dashes through her eyes before she can remove it.

The string tethering us together may have broken months ago, but the vibrations remain the same. They're invisible to anyone but us, meaning we're the only two people who can both see and hear them.

Today wasn't the mammoth step I hoped to take, but it was one in the right direction.

THIRTY

REGAN

A woodsy smell overtakes the sugary palette I'm devouring like I won't need to run six miles to burn off the nasty calories when Hugo saunters into my kitchen, his look more casual than the suit he dons while working.

"Heading out?"

He jerks up his chin before snagging a bottle of water out of the fridge. "Harlow wants to drag Izzy out for a night of dancing." He takes a hefty gulp before running his hand over his wet lips. "Means I'm stuck babysitting intoxicated women all night."

Hearing the jest in his tone, I grin. "It's got to be more entertaining than sitting around here, playing Xbox in nothing but running shorts and socks like you have the past two weeks."

His smile is more blistering than mine. . . and ten times sexier. "Puh-leeze. I tried to put on a shirt Tuesday. You snatched it out of my hands and threw it into the washing machine claiming it was 'filthy.'"

"It *was* filthy," I say around the spoonful of frosting in my mouth. "And you were going to sit on my five thousand dollar couch. I'd rather have your naked ass planted on there than a stinky old gym shirt."

Hugo crowds me against the kitchen counter, making me forget why I'm gorging on buckets of sugar and downing expensive bottles of wine as if they're the steak and three veggies combination I usually consume every Saturday evening.

I'm hoping overdosing on sugar will stop me from calling Alex like a loser. We've had some contact the past week, but it was all based on Isabelle and her case. We're being professional—*for once*—but it hasn't weakened my desire for him in the slightest.

He spied on me—numerous times—yelled at me, then fucked me like a whore in the back of a trashed van. I should have never spoken to him again. I tried—really I did—but with every conversation we had, the more my anger slipped from my grasp.

Add that to the plea his eyes held when he solemnly vowed to make things right between us, and you've got one messy, fucked-up woman. I could blame my desperation on Izzy and Hugo camping out in my living room the past two weeks, but we all know that's a lie. Even if Isaac didn't give me the stern "no guys" rule he always runs with when it comes to Izzy, there is only one man my body wants— the one who annoys the shit out of her as much as it awakens her every sense.

When I step back and take a hard look at myself, I realize Alex wasn't the only one at fault for what happened two weeks ago. By kissing Isaac, I placed his relationship with Isabelle above Alex and his feelings. Although I can defend my decision by saying I wasn't aware it was Alex in the surveillance van, a little part of me knew it was, so that not only makes the name he was about to call me true, it makes me someone I never wanted to be, someone vindictive and bitter.

I'm drawn from my thoughts when Hugo asks, "You still trying to see my pecker, Ms. Prim and Proper?"

It takes me a few seconds to remember what we were talking

about before I spaced out. When I do, I gag. "Not if it's only big enough for you to call it a pecker, Tic Tac Tate."

Hugo laughs. "I don't know what the fuck Tate did to you, but that poor guy will never live it down, will he?"

I nod, wholly agreeing with him. Tate was one of those asshole boyfriends I mentioned from my high school days. He thought the world shone out of his ass and that he was god's gift to women. He could have gotten away with his attitude if he had the cock to back it up. Regrettably, he didn't just need a fancy car to hide his less than stellar attributes. He needed a whole damn city.

Hugo snatches a loaded spoon of icing out of my hand and stuffs it into his mouth without asking. "What did he do? Come within two strokes? Stick it in the wrong hole? Request for you to turn the lights off. . .?"

"More like: he didn't get it out of his pants before he came. Stuffed his jeans with socks like the girls did their bras, and wouldn't turn the lights off even when I begged him to." I steal back the empty spoon, dig it into the container of frosting, then pop it into my mouth. "I had to work extra hard that night to bring myself to climax. My fingers have never flicked the bean so callously before."

Hugo groans. "Fuck me, Regan. Are you trying to kill a man?"

I run my tongue along my teeth to ensure no chocolate frosting is staining them before smiling. "Nah. I just wanted to get off. It was *sooooo* good. One of the hottest and longest climaxes I've ever had."

Hugo groans again, this one sounding more pained than the first.

"What's the matter, big boy?" My words slur as the pleasant buzz of alcohol finally heats my blood. "Got a scratch you can't itch?"

When Hugo and Isabelle first crashed at my apartment, Hugo happily rubbed in the fact Isaac doesn't let any men outside of his staff within two feet of Isabelle. Although Isaac's machoism is stone-aged and—*sorry Isaac*—pathetic, Hugo's taunt proved I had done a good job of hiding my pain the prior twelve months. It's like nine years ago all over again. I roll my shoulders and smile, even though my insides feel two seconds from cracking.

Hating the tears pricking my eyes, I raise them to Hugo. He's watching me intently, certain my insides aren't as shiny as my outer shell. He's right, but I'd rather keep that to myself for the remainder of my life. . . or, at the very least, tonight.

"You gonna share?"

Hugo drops his big blue eyes to the tub of frosting in my hands before licking his lips. Although his voice sounds as it usually does, all my fucked-up brain hears is a whole lot of sexual innuendo.

I hug the frosting container to my chest, amplifying the generous swell of my breasts. "Do I look like the type who shares?"

His lips arch high, making my pulse accelerate. "I don't know, Regan. Do you?"

Even though his tone reveals he's joshing with me, I up the ante. It's time for this boy to be shown how the big kids play.

After cocking my hip, I drag my eyes down his body in a slow and dedicated sweep. When I return them to his face, his eyes are brighter than they were moments ago, hazier. "What are you willing to give me for it?"

When he fails to immediately bite back at my quip, my brain screams at me to shut this down before I travel a road I never wanted to. But with my heart too busy repairing the cuts a bottle and a half of wine can't heal, I continue down the road of deception, one slow pace at a time.

I fist Hugo's shirt before tugging him closer, bringing him and his gloriously large frame within a mere inch of my shuddering body. Just like the time we flirted over the phone, my ego needs this more than I need to breathe. I want to feel loved, cherished, and wanted, and I want to experience it without wondering if I should be peering over my shoulder, waiting for the knives that will inevitably be stabbed in my back.

Hugo is my friend. He's single and as loyal to Isaac as me. This is a perfect solution. . . if I could just get my fucked up heart to agree.

"Regan. . ."

Hugo's warning snarl trails off when I pop a loaded spoon of frosting into my mouth and suck down so hard, the spoon launches into the back of my throat. Apparently, it wasn't just my heart that went bye-bye twelve months ago; so did my ability to flirt. I'd die of embarrassment if my gag didn't increase the temperature bristling between Hugo and me. It's hotter now, as sticky and as out-of-control as my twisted heart.

Not willing to back down without a fight, I say, "Your turn." My words are throatier than usual, the clump of icing gliding down to my gut making them huskier. *Or perhaps it's betrayal?*

When Hugo attempts to remove the spoon from my grasp, I shake my head. "You'll never appreciate the high you get from frosting until you've sampled it off someone's skin."

I scoop a generous serving of chocolate icing onto my finger before raising it to Hugo's mouth. Moisture teems in regions of my body I never anticipated as I wait for him to make his decision. I wish I were referring to the area between my legs that refuses to drum out a tune unless it's in Alex's presence, but I'm not.

The only big blobs of moisture threatening to spill right now are the ones welling in my eyes. I'm on the verge of crying, equally in devastation and annoyance. I hate what Alex did to me, but more than anything, I hate that I can't hate him for it.

With a groan, Hugo snatches the spoon and nearly empty can of frosting out of my hand, dumps them in the sink, then spins me around to face the kitchen entrance. His stomps across the tile mimic the brutal stabs his rejection is causing my ego. It's only one tenth of the hurt I'm feeling, though.

My ego stops being battered senseless when Hugo murmurs, "You should be grateful you played this trick on me, Regan, because if it were any other man, you'd be on your knees by now."

He guides me down the hallway, throws open my bedroom door, then heads for my king-sized bed in the middle of the room. He tosses me onto the mattress as if I'm weightless before stomping to my bedside table. I should be embarrassed when he dumps a drawer full of sex toys next to my quivering thighs, but even with my heart being shattered twice in under a decade, I still haven't learned the word "timid."

Hugo gathers a tube of lube out of the main bathroom and my phone from the kitchen before plunking them on top of an assortment of vibrators, dildos, and butterfly clips. After dipping his chin, pleased with his effort, he pivots on his heels and stalks out of my room.

"Where are you going?" I ask, shocked and somewhat amused from the strain crossing his handsome face.

"Anywhere with enough noise I can pretend you aren't moaning the moans I think you're going to be moaning."

His reply riddles me with confusion, but it also makes me smile. "And my phone? What's that for?"

"So you can call the man you really want licking the frosting from your finger."

My spine snaps straight. "I can't call him!"

Hugo spins around to face me. "Why not?"

A million thoughts trickle through my tipsy brain, but since none of them are appropriate for an attorney to say about the man prosecuting her client, I remain quiet.

With a smug grin, Hugo turns back around and continues with his brisk departure.

His long strides stop when I shout, "Hey, Hugo?"

He takes his time replying, like he's worried he'll succumb to the tension in the air if he doesn't leave this instant. "Yeah?"

I want to say *thanks for being my friend*, but since I'd hate for him to think he has one on me, I settle on, "Why do you have lube in your bathroom?"

He doesn't answer me, unless you count a groan as a reply.

It's been over three hours since Hugo left. I returned my sex toys to their rightful spot—untouched—folded a basket of clean clothes, and flipped through two dozen TV channels. With my request to have Isabelle's preliminary hearing brought forward finally granted, her paperwork was filed late this afternoon, meaning I've got nothing left to do but wait. Even Callie's case is out of my hands. Isaac paid the funds; now we're just waiting for the transfer to be scheduled. It's a lonely and boring Saturday night.

I can't even visit Axel since he and Raquel are testing out a new nanny. With Raquel's first year residency starting in February, she wants to settle Axel into a new routine. I offered to watch him while she worked, but she said my inflexible hours with Isaac made it unfeasible. Even though I agreed with her, it was still a bitter pill to swallow. I hate the idea of Axel being watched by a stranger. His nanny is nice, but nothing can replicate the care he'd get from someone with the same blood as him.

As my mind shifts to a man with the same cut jaw as Axel and equally blue eyes, my eyes stray to my drawer of sex toys. Only eighteen months ago, I thought I'd never need anything but an endless supply of batteries and my very vivid imagination.

How wrong was I?

The sensation, thrill, and quickening of my pulse remain the same, but nothing can replace the scent of a hot, virile man on the hunt. Sweat is sweat; skin is skin, but when it's mixed with an aftershave that inspires images of hard fucks with beastly, Viking-like men... *my god*. Pure heaven.

My pulse speeds up when, in the corner of my eye, I spot a bottle of cologne I dumped on my dresser weeks ago. I don't know why I packed Alex's aftershave when I flew across the country at Isaac's request. It just landed in my bag without a thought crossing my mind.

Mostly.

Somewhat.

Not even.

Ugh! I went out of my way to pack it. I want to say it's to remind me how I triumphed over the bad times and that I'm stronger than I remember, but that's a crock of shit. I keep it with me because Alex's scent conjures up more good memories than bad.

He let me go at Substanz.

He kept my name out of every report, even though I was a stranger to him.

He even went as far as doctoring the files to make it appear as if there was never a second shooter.

And that was before we officially met.

Now his scent reminds me of his roguish grin when I squirmed beneath him, the extra beat his heart gained when I smiled at him, and how he looked at me as though he couldn't breathe without me in his life. Our time together was short, but I amassed enough memories to last me a lifetime.

With my lower lip caught between my teeth, I pad across my room to gather his aftershave in my hands. The lid has never been cracked, but the smell embedded in its black box assures it doesn't need to be opened to fill me with memories both bitter and sweet.

The thick duvet on my bed clouds me when I flop my back onto the mattress, dumping Alex's bottle of cologne next to my head in the process. While my fingers skate across my fluttering stomach, I recall the last time I smelled his scent in person. Although it was from a distance, nothing could impede his manly smell.

My eyes snap shut as my memories jump back to when we bumped heads in the elevator. My recollections of that afternoon are still a little groggy, but nothing can dampen the concern I saw in Alex's eyes when he scooped me into his arms.

That's when my obsession with him started. I'll always maintain that I'm a strong and independent woman, but having a man literally sweep me off my feet was an occurrence I never saw coming but secretly craved.

As my hand lowers to the dampness my sheer panties are struggling to conceal, my mind drifts to our first kiss. It was vicious and fueled with jealousy, and I loved every fucking minute of it. It assured my mind that I wasn't going crazy; I had just gone a little senseless over a man who stole more than just my mojo.

A grin graces my lips. I thought one taste of Alex would be enough. I had no idea. He was so addictive, one contact demanded another and another and another until we finally surrendered to the desires swarming us with hungry, insatiable electricity.

My back arches from my bed in the same manner it did in the field all those months ago when my fingertip rolls over the aching bud between my legs. My clit is throbbing, the movie rolling through my head compelling its aroused state.

After toying with my clit enough times it stirs up jitters in my stomach, I slip two fingers inside myself. I move them in and out of my snug canal at the speed Alex fucked me in the field. It is leisurely and devoted, while also hungry and needy.

The heat between my legs jumps to a scorching level when I recall how his beard always scraped my chest when he sucked my nipples into his mouth. The bedding entangles my feet when I thrust upward, giving myself to him wholly and without restraint as I wish I had done all those months ago. I can see his rugged grin, smell his sweat-slicked skin.

I grow wetter, slicker. "Please. Oh, god, please," I pant through the stars blistering in front of my eyes, not caring who hears my whimpers. "I need more. I'm desperate, so very desperate. . ." *For you.*

My breathing skids to a stop when my memories fast forward to the night Alex slathered me with frosting. I lick my lips, tasting the sweetness of my earlier splurge as my fingers increase their speed. My treat tonight was deliciously sweet, but it didn't come close to how it tasted when mixed with Alex's skin.

A throaty garble rolls up my chest as I recall the glint in his eyes when I climbed up his thick, enticing body to help myself to his stupendous cock. I never understood the saying "morning glory" until that morning. Let me tell you, it is a spectacular way to start your day.

My fingers grind in and out of my pussy more steadily as I take on the pace of that morning, a slower and more cherished speed since it wasn't just my pussy Alex was consuming. He took his time with me, devouring every inch of me, from my slicked sex to my heart.

A familiar wave curls low in my stomach when I recall the emotions he handed me that day. The lazy smiles. The silent promises. *His pledge of love.*

I still as desire races through my veins. My last memory has me achieving something I haven't accomplished on my own in over eighteen months. I've brought myself to climax.

As a blistering smile stretches across my face, my body relents to the glorious sensation roaring through it. Every fine hair on my body bristles as Alex's name quivers from my lips in a breathless moan. My climax soaks my panties with heat as my body fills with desire. It also loosens the rope that's been lassoed around my throat the past twelve months, allowing my lungs to finally rejuvenate with oxygen.

It is sensational and long. . . until I'm interrupted by a giant with a rugged grin and overly tattooed body.

"Regan, are you alright?"

THIRTY-ONE

REGAN

"Hey, you guys came home earlier than I had expected last night," I say to Isabelle as she saunters into the kitchen.

She huffs. "Yeah, our plans were slightly altered."

She gives me a look. Unfortunately, I don't know her well enough to know what it means. With a grumble, she shuffles to the kitchen counter where the coffee pot is. Her movements match the ones I made this morning when I begrudgingly dragged my post-orgasmic body out of bed. I truly forgot how much work goes into self-climaxing. Not only do you need to stimulate several regions of your body at once, you then shred a thousand calories in under twenty seconds—*if you're lucky*. My muscles are aching so much this morning, I'd be tempted to call it quits. . . if it didn't feel so good.

I stop peering into my empty coffee cup when Isabelle asks, "So, what did you get up to last night?" She strives to keep insinuation out of her tone but does a terrible job.

I shrug. "Nothing much." I bite on the inside of my cheek, attempting to hide my smile.

Isabelle spreads her hands across her hips as her glare ramps up.

A grin tugs on my lips when she arches her brow, calling out the deceit in my tone with an attitude I didn't know she held.

Certain I can subdue her as well as I do Isaac, I reply, "Well, it was way more than nothing. It was *huge*." I fan my flushed cheeks, acting like a real harlot. It's appropriate; my mood is certainly elevated compared to yesterday.

Isabelle giggles while placing a dash of milk into her mug of tea. "Anyone I know?"

Her question truly stumps me. If it were Hugo, I'd wave my magic fingers in the air and savor his whitening gills, but this is Isabelle. She's too timid to see my wild side. I don't want to scare her—yet.

Seconds feel like hours as I strive to conjure up a random guy's name. For the life of me, I can't think of one. At this very moment, I can't even recall the name of the man who pays for my apartment, much less the one leering at me as he strolls toward the kitchen.

"Nope," I answer Isabelle with a shake of my head, deciding a non-generic reply is better than throwing another man under the bus like I did Isaac last year.

Deceit clouds Isabelle's eyes, but I'm saved from answering her silent question when Hugo enters the kitchen. "Morning." His voice is as shit-eating as the grin on his face when he barged in on me last night.

After issuing me a frisky wink that Isabelle misses, he heads for the coffee pot to help himself to a large mug of steaming hot brew. He watches me over the rim of his mug for several minutes, certain he'll have me squirming in my chair at any moment. It's a pity the pathetic, woeful Regan he spotted last night up and left town right alongside my inability to pleasure myself.

If he wants me to bow at his feet as I stupidly endeavored to do last night, he'll need to bring more to the game than a cheeky grin and devastatingly blue eyes that conjure thoughts of the man truly responsible for the return of my mojo.

Spotting my determination from a mile out, Hugo shifts his focus to Isabelle. "Are you ready to head out soon? Avery isn't a fan of tardiness."

When Isabelle remains quiet, Hugo waves his hand in front of her face, making me notice how large it is. *Hmm. Maybe he doesn't have a Tic-Tac for a cock?*

"Pardon?" Isabelle asks, clearly confused when she snaps back to the land of the living.

She's been rather spaced out the past two weeks. As her attorney, I want to pretend her lack of focus is due to her energy being zapped by her campaign for freedom, but as a woman, I know that isn't the case. She's not the only female in this room twisted up in knots over a man. She doesn't want to serve time for a crime she didn't commit any more than she wants to live without Isaac in her life.

My hooded gaze strays to Hugo when he chuckles. "I was asking if you'll be ready to leave in ten minutes for your appointment with Avery?"

Isabelle's big brown eyes dart to the clock on the microwave. She mumbles a cuss word under her breath before pivoting on her heels and darting out of the kitchen. "I'll be ready in five."

Hugo waits for her warped bedroom door to slam shut before shifting his eyes my way.

"Don't you dare."

His grin enlarges. "What? I wasn't going to say anything. I was just going to ask if you're okay? You look a little flushed. Aroused even."

His last sentence comes out in a flurry from my fist landing in his stomach. Bad move. His body is as firm as it looks. My knuckles throb as images of him shirtless flash before my eyes. I gobbled them into my memory bank last week with the hope of using them for future explorations, but after last night's endeavor, I'm certain there's still only one man capable of bringing me to climax.

Last night wasn't the first time I've used visuals of Alex while masturbating, but it was the first time it worked. I want to pretend the sprinkling of memories from our romp in his surveillance van two weeks ago was the reason my libido succumbed to the pressure, but I know that isn't true. It was remembering those three little words he said to me, the ones I've sworn time and time again that I never wanted to hear.

Even if it was a lie, my memories of that morning will never be sullied with negativity. Alex took care of me that night; he held me while I cried, then promised everything would be okay, and it has been. I haven't walked the path I wanted to, but it's been okay. My family is safe. I'm safe. Even Alex is safe.

Now all I need to do is the job I am paid to do. I need to protect both Isaac and his assets. If I get my head into game mode, maybe my heart will follow suit?

"Party pooper," Hugo grumbles when I give him a final glare before exiting the kitchen, my steps more spirited than my earlier ones.

A few hours later, while Hugo and Isabelle go on a run, I call Parker, a member of Isaac's team on the West Coast. "Thanks. I'll pass on the information to Isaac, although I don't see him being happy about the delay. We transferred the money as requested; now they need to deliver the goods."

Parker murmurs in agreement, but his reply shows he's on the other side of the fence. "Things may work like that in a normal industry, but it's Isaac's first dabble in this lifestyle. He's not in charge here."

I breathe out heavily, almost drowning out what Parker says next, "His arrest ruffled feathers, and now with news of Isabelle's court case circulating this side of the country, we need to tread cautiously."

"And what happens to Callie while we wait? Who's looking after her?" The protectiveness in my voice shocks me. I've never been maternal.

"The Popov housemaids are the best of the bunch." I wish Parker's tone sounded more confident. "Besides, Vladimir won't let any harm come of her. She's an asset, not his daughter. In this case, that increases her chances of survival."

I grumble about the arrogant, pigheaded man I hope to never meet while rounding my desk. My steps freeze halfway when, in the corner of my eye, I catch sight of my laptop monitor. Everything inside me tenses when the mouse icon moves around the screen as if it is being controlled by a remote.

My intuition is proven spot on when a set of business acquisitions I filed last week pops up on the screen. They're only there for a second before the print box opens and closes, then the screen goes back to its original setting.

I continue my conversation with Parker, mindful the person accessing my computer may have the microphone activated. "That's true. I guess it's best for all involved if we wait."

Parker mumbles a reply, but I don't hear anything he says over my pulse raging in my ears. I sit in my office chair and activate my computer, praying I can type with how hard my hands are shaking.

The person accessing my laptop is smart. The timestamp on the file he just accessed displays it hasn't been opened in over a week. Although the documents they were hacking are accessible to the public, who's to say that's all they were searching for?

After a few seconds of silent contemplation, I devise a plan of attack. "Parker, I have to go. I forgot about an important meeting Isaac is having with Vladimir at Taste. I'm late."

Parker tries to rebut, but I disconnect our call, cutting him off.

My heart hammers into my ribcage when I snag my coat and my purse. I'm out my front door in an instant, my wish to bust the man spying on me stronger than the worry I'm not putting my best foot forward.

After I agree to a payment of one hundred dollars, I arrive at Taste within a record-breaking three minutes. "Keep the meter running, and I'll tip you another $100."

The cab driver's eyes flare before he nods. In good faith, I hand him the first half of my fare before slipping out of his cab. I want to believe he'd stay without the pledge of extra money, but my trust is extremely low today.

The hostess of Taste greets me with a smile before ushering me to the table Isaac and I regularly share. Although I keep my head low, I still gain the inquisitive gaze of numerous men. . . and a handful of women. This isn't unusual.

Halfway to my table, my steps slow, closely followed by the beat of my heart. There's a man seated at the table Alex always dined at. A bulky laptop bag takes up a large chunk of his tabletop, and the three seats surrounding him are empty. A newspaper covers most of his face, and a cap shelters his eyes, but nothing can hide the wisps of blond hair furling around his ears, much less the sweat dotting his cheeks. *He must have rushed here as quickly as me.*

Although I can't one hundred percent testify the man is Alex, I storm across the room before my brain can cite an objection. This isn't the first or second time he's invaded my privacy. This is the third!

"Fool me once, shame on you. Fool me twice, shame on me. But there is no fucking chance you'll fool me a third time," I grind through gritted teeth before ripping the newspaper out of his grasp.

I take a step back, stunned when the eyes peering back at me don't reflect the color of the ocean. They're brown and green and brimming with treachery.

"Regan, what are you doing here? Is Izzy with you?" Brandon scans the restaurant, hoping his eagerness to locate Isabelle will excuse the deep descent of his Adam's apple.

His acting skills are top shelf. It's just a pity my bullshit radar is even more developed. Brandon leaps to his feet when I yank his laptop out of his bag and crack open the screen. "Let's see how you like having your privacy invaded."

The sweat beading on his forehead lessens when his computer requests a lock code. Recalling the ga-ga faces he makes anytime Isabelle is in his presence, I type in the six digits of her birthday. *Bingo.*

A vicious growl vibrates my lips when the first thing I notice is a screenshot of the invoice I saw hacked from my computer mere minutes ago.

"That's not what it looks like." Brandon slams down his laptop screen, startling the elderly couple seated next to him. "I was researching business opportunities. Those files are assessable to anyone with the knowledge of how to find them."

I twist my lips, acting coy. "True, but I wonder what Isabelle's take on it will be?"

Brandon's gasp ceases halfway up his windpipe when I shove his laptop into his chest before hightailing it out of the restaurant.

He snaps at my heels two seconds later. "I'm trying to protect her."

I have a thousand replies, but none I'm willing to waste on him. I know for a fact he no longer works for the Bureau, so any spying he's doing isn't just immoral, it's illegal.

"She has no clue who Isaac really is. He's keeping things from her." He races in front of me, blocking my access to the idling cab. "Look, I'll prove it. He's been making secret payments to a woman in Arlington the past six years."

Even knowing Isaac keeps nothing from me, I snatch the document from Brandon's hand, his galvanized tone too strong to brush off.

"See, one hundred thousand dollars a month for over six years." He points to synchronized transfers on the fifteenth of every month.

My pulse skyrockets when I notice the digits displayed at the end of the transfer match Isaac's personal bank account—the one he's adamant only he can handle. Upon noticing the funds are being deposited, not withdrawn, my eyes absorb the name at the top of the bank statement: *Kristin Lieberman.*

I say her name a few times, certain I've heard it before but unsure when. It's familiar, but not, if that makes any sense?

Realizing I have the means to satisfy my curiosity directly in front of me, I snatch Brandon's laptop from under his arm, toss it onto the taxi's warm hood, then log into his account. I could ask Brandon who she is, but my trust is still low.

Time comes to a standstill when my Google search of Kristin's name returns numerous hits. Most are dated, but they all center around one main event in her life: the death of her husband and much loved agent, Dane Lieberman.

"When was he killed?"

Although I'm speaking to myself, Brandon answers my question. My heart squeezes when he points to Dane's obituary that reveals the date of his death.

Oh god. It was the day Alex and I broke up.

Fighting through the tears burning my eyes, I hit the image tab at the top of the searches. It brings up a few matches, men in their late sixties and a handful of women, but the ones halfway down are responsible for the tear gliding down my cheek. Although he's years younger, youth can't conceal Alex's cut jaw and piercing blue eyes. He's standing next to a dark-haired man. They have lacrosse sticks in their hands and grubby, sweaty faces.

Against Brandon's advice, I click on the photo. It proves what I suspected: Alex's dark-haired friend is Dane. He and Alex attended the same college. They're photographed several times with a petite blonde named Kristin.

My eyes stray to Brandon. "How did he die?"

While rubbing a kink in his neck, he grumbles, "He killed himself."

"Why?" My question is insensitive, but I'm struggling to believe

Brandon's reply. My quick scroll through Dane's photos reveals he lived a wonderful life. "He had a beautiful wife, an illustrious career, and two gorgeous daughters. Why would he leave that?"

Brandon shrugs again. "Maybe he was depressed?"

"But why, Brandon?!" My squeal gains us the eyes of many Ravenshoe locals.

After wordlessly pleading for me to calm down, Brandon takes over the reins of his laptop. Because he keeps the screen in my line of sight, I let him.

Faster than I can snap my fingers, he brings up a string of reports. The giant confidential watermark covering them reveals he's stepped over the line to show them to me, but it has nothing on the emotions slamming into me when I see the signature scribbled on the bottom of them.

A. Rogers.

It takes me breathing in and out four times before my eyes follow the commands of my brain; then it takes me reading the report three times before the information sinks in. Dane was the man Alex carried down the meadow on his back at Substanz. He placed his life on the line trying to save his fellow agent and friend.

Although both their lives were spared that day, Dane's life was irrefutably affected. The bullet that entered his stomach and exited his back drained the cerebrospinal fluid from his spine. When the doctors attempted to repair it, his spinal cord was severed, resulting in paralysis from the waist down.

I take a step back as sickening remorse twists my gut. Now everything makes sense. Alex's dislike of Isaac. His absence the months following our break up. Even the guilt that flared through his eyes when we wrestled in the cow-dung meadow can be excused. Those suffering remorse don't understand that it's okay to enjoy life. The instead of our heart. How do I know this? It's the sick and twisted game I've been playing for over nine years.

After closing Brandon's laptop, I hand it back to him. "Thank you for showing me that."

He dips his chin but remains worried. "Are you going to tell Izzy about today?"

"I won't have anything to tell her if you tell her first."

He seems confused by my reply, but I don't have time to spell it out for him. First, I need to caution Isaac that my laptop has been compromised, then I need to confront Alex. . . or comfort him? I truly don't know.

But there is one thing I do know: nothing will be solved standing here. With that in mind, I slide into the back of the taxi, leaving Brandon stranded on the corner of Tivot and St. Thomas Street.

The ten minutes it takes to travel to Isaac's nightclub passes in a blur. I'm shrouded by so much confusion, I don't stop to savor the building that's helped the digits in my bank account jump from six figures to seven the past eight months.

I'm so entranced by my thoughts, I don't even realize Isaac is on a call until he says, "Regan is here; I'll call him," into his phone.

The haze in my head grows when he shouts, "Brandon."

I swallow several times in a row. *Why is he talking to Brandon?* I suggested for him to reach out to Isabelle, not Isaac. If that blood-sucking scum is ratting me out, he'll regret it for years to come.

My eyes bounce between Isaac's stern gaze when he says, "Thank you for your help; please keep me updated on Hugo." Although his words are strained, they reveal his genuine thanks for Brandon's help.

He lowers his phone from his ear and slides it into his pocket. When his gaze lifts to me, I feel the color in my cheeks drain. I hate the look he's giving me, but it doesn't stop me from saying, "I need to talk to you—"

"Can it wait?" His clipped tone has me recoiling. "They've taken Isabelle." The knocks keep coming when he adds on, "I need you to call Alex and request his assistance. Brandon said you'd be the best person to ask for his help. I don't know what your history is with him, and at the moment, I don't fucking care. My only concern is making sure Isabelle is safe and getting her home, so I need you to do this for me, Regan."

The urgency in his tone dries my lips. After a quick lick to replenish them with moisture, I whimper, "Okay."

He watches me remove my phone from my pocket while he dials a known number into his cell. I feel like I've been cast in a horribly scripted crime show when he tells his caller Hugo has been shot. "The EMTs have been instructed to take him to your hospital. His ETA should be around. . ." He checks the time on his watch. ". . .Ten minutes, maybe fifteen."

While begging for Alex to pick up, I overhear Isaac's conversation. "I told you everything I know." His chest rises and falls in rhythm with Alex's ringing cell before he pleads, "Jae, Hugo is like family to me."

His desolate tone nearly has me coming undone. Hugo can be more frustrating than helpful, but he's an integral part of my dysfunctional family. If he's been hurt or worse. . . I can't say it. He has to be okay. He's strong and highly annoying, so he'll bounce back. Only the good die young. Right? Luca's short life is proof of that.

I pull my phone away from my ear at the same time as Isaac. His contact was more successful than mine. This is the first time the past two weeks that Alex hasn't answered my call in a timely manner. This fills me with dread more than frustration.

"Not now, Regan," Isaac begs upon spotting the shine in my eyes. "We need to keep it together until we bring Isabelle home. Jae will look after Hugo."

I suck in a big breath before nodding. Jae is a gifted surgeon. She's the reason Raquel requested to do her first year internship at Ravenshoe, so I can be assured everything he is saying is true.

Isaac shoves his hands into his pocket to hide their quiver before asking, "Did you get ahold of Alex?"

I shake my head. "He isn't answering his phone." Even knowing I'm digging myself into a hole I'll never get out of, I say, "But I know where to find him."

The suspicion in Isaac's eyes grows for every step we take between his nightclub and the office building next door. I want to explain myself, but with both fear and worry clutching my throat, I can't produce any words.

When we enter the office I confronted Alex in weeks ago, the hum of activity dulls to barely a whisper. The number of agents milling about the space on a weekend is shocking, but it has nothing on the stunned expression their faces hold from seeing Isaac in person. They're so accustomed to viewing him from afar, they stare at him like he's a ghost.

After shimmying my shoulders, I guide Isaac toward Alex's office. The closer we approach, the harder the butterflies in my stomach flutter. This scenario never came up when I pictured ways of confessing my involvement in his case to Isaac. I thought it would occur in Isaac's office, not in the space a man was awarded after he stole confidential documents from my computer.

That changes some of my anguish to anger. Good. I work better when my veins are thickened with fury. That's why I took up boxing during law school, because I wanted to smash boys more than text-books. Isaac assured me punching a bag would give me the same relief. He was right—for the most part.

While approaching Alex's glass office, I scan my surroundings. Alex is standing behind his desk, peering out of a large window that faces the nightclub I cofounded with Isaac. Before my eyes finish absorbing the defined lines of his back, he spins around to face me.

I forget the urgency of my visit when a broad grin spreads across his face. He rakes his eyes down my body, taking it in as he does every time I'm in his presence. His avid stare quickens my pulse; I'm just not sure if it's a good boost or a bad flutter.

I go with the latter when his smile becomes a snarl. He's spotted Isaac and Hunter behind me, and he's not happy. His manly scent intensifies when his hands ball. He's preparing for battle, ready to take down any alpha game enough to enter his realm without an invitation. It's a pity he has his sight set on the wrong target. He should be watching me as closely as he is Isaac.

I don't wait to be invited in. Bad move. Alex's virile scent is even more potent in the confines of his office. It also proves I read his signals wrong. His back isn't up because he's preparing to defend his kingdom. There's only one possession he's striving to keep after our unexpected raid: me.

I swish my tongue around my mouth to soothe the dryness inside before introducing three extremely influential men in my life. "Alex Rogers, this is Isaac Holt and Hunter Kane." I wave my hand between Isaac and Hunter.

My earlier comment is proven truthful when Alex snarls, "I thought you said you didn't know Isaac Holt."

"I said I didn't know him sexually." I glare at him, warning him now is *not* the time to have this conversation. "You, like always, chose only to hear the words you want to hear."

He attempts a rebuttal, but Isaac cuts him off. "You can finish your lovers' quarrel later. We have more important issues to address." His brimming-with-panic eyes shift to Alex. "Isabelle was kidnapped this afternoon."

Alex balks as strongly as I do. Usually, I appreciate Isaac's directness, but today, having it spelled out like that didn't make it any easier to stomach.

"We have an image of the assailant, but we've been unable to identify him using the police facial recognition software."

The urgency in Isaac's tone makes him miss the quick work of Alex's jaw. He's not happy about his underhanded confession that he's using police sources illegally, but he's beginning to understand why I brought Isaac here.

"Brandon advised me to contact you. He said you would have access to better facial recognition software," Isaac continues.

Alex mumbles under his breath while running his hand over his hair. Although I can't see his eyes, I know he's looking at me. I can feel the heat of his gaze boring into my face as he contemplates what to do. I hope for both Isabelle and Isaac's sakes he is the man I once thought he was, because if he refuses to help us, and Isabelle has been taken by the man Isaac believes is holding her captive, we have a matter of hours before she's found floating in the ocean.

I exhale the breath I'm holding in when Alex says, "For Isabelle, I'll call it a truce, but once she is safe, all bets are off."

"Deal." They seal their agreement with a handshake. It pains Alex more than it pleases him.

After gliding his hand down his trousers, Alex nudges his head to the right. "There's a secure port behind the filing cabinet."

With a nod, Hunter places his state-of-the-art laptop onto Alex's desk. He freezes mere seconds from plugging it into the ethernet port Alex gestured to before swinging his eyes to Isaac. "If I connect to the FBI's server, it could leave your security vulnerable to infiltration. If they get in, I may never get them back out."

My heart skips a beat when Isaac replies, "Let them have it. I have nothing to hide."

I knew he cared for Isabelle, but I had no clue it went this far. Although I'm pleased he's found his Achilles heel, his empire isn't the only thing at risk here. "What about Hugo?"

Isaac's face deadpans as reality smacks into him. He can't protect both Isabelle and Hugo. He has to sacrifice one of them. Unless. . .

I square my shoulders before locking my eyes with Alex. "Promise me your department will not access anything on Isaac's servers today, and I'll forgive you for exploiting me."

Alex balks. I don't know if his shock is due to my pledge of forgiveness or the fact I outed myself in front of Isaac. I assume it is the latter when he says, "I didn't exploit you, Regan."

My lips thin as I struggle to repress a scream. This is why we can't get past what he did, because he refuses to acknowledge his part in our downfall.

After a quick exhalation, I stare at him, wordlessly begging him to do the right thing. If he truly wants to repair the damage he has done, this will be a step in the right direction.

After running his hand over his recently trimmed hair for the second time, Alex's eyes stray to Hunter. "Send the photo to the email address on the card." He hands him an embossed business card. "The FBI servers automatically upload all content on any devices plugged into their mainframe, so I'll use my computer to access the image."

While Hunter fires up his laptop, I whisper my thanks to Alex. When he attempts to step around Isaac, I shake my head. Mistaking my denial as me choosing sides, his face lines with anger. That isn't what I'm doing. There are just more important things at stake right now than cleaning up the mess between us.

In the corner of my eye, I watch Alex take a seat in the big leather chair behind his desk. The clench of his fists looks violent, but I know anger isn't fueling his responses. It's remorse.

He drags his chair in close to his keyboard when Hunter says, "Done."

"We need to hurry before it's too late," Isaac urges after taking in the time on the antique clock hanging in Alex's office. For the sleek, clean lines of his office, it's an odd piece for him to have. It doesn't match the décor, much less the man who owns it.

I stop staring at the unique clock when Hunter grunts, "Move." He barges Alex in the shoulder. "Your two-finger typing is too fucking slow. We'll be here all night at this rate."

Alex isn't happy, but vacates his chair as requested. Within seconds, Hunter sweettalks Alex's computer into being his bitch. The photo Isaac and he discovered on the CTV cameras installed throughout Ravenshoe scrolls through thousands of possible matches while he conducts a second manual search on the tattoo one of the perps had on his arm.

"You need to donate some money to the local police department so they can get this software installed."

Before Isaac can reply to Hunter's smug remark, his cell phone rings. My stomach launches into my throat when I recognize his ring tone. It's his phone that only ever rings when there is trouble.

I try to listen in on Isaac's conversation, but the faintest brush of a hand down my cheek steals my devotion. Alex is standing in front of me, removing the faded line an earlier tear caused my cheek.

The chance of a second one following it is highly likely when he asks, "Are you okay, Rae?"

Although I'm feeling anything but, I nod. If there's a time for me to polish my *I'm fine* skills, today is it. With Isaac's panic at an all-time high, I need to stay in the game. He's not thinking straight, so I need to think for the both of us.

That would be a whole lot easier to do without Alex's schmexy scent engulfing me. "Rae—"

"Not yet, Alex. We need to do this first."

I can tell he wants to argue, but thankfully, Hunter darting across the room steals his words. Alex watches Isaac and Hunter's exchange as eagerly as me, equally sickened by the panic whitening Isaac's face.

"Please help him," I beg after returning my eyes to Alex. "I know I have no right to ask you for anything, but he's my friend, and I don't want him to go through what I went through with Luca. He's already suffered enough, Alex. Don't add more grief to his plate."

I'm about to plead some more, but I realize I don't need to when Alex heads to the other side of his desk. With determined eyes, he yanks open the top drawer to retrieve his gun and badge. He holsters his gun on his waist where it sat when we bumped heads before he snags his jacket off a coat rack. After a quick glance my way, he joins Isaac and Hunter's private conversation.

When Isaac eyes him with suspicion, Alex says, "Isabelle is still an FBI agent. We protect our own," His tone is as demanding as Isaac's usually is. It quickens my pulse, and for once, it's a good thing. "I know this man. I know how he operates. I've been working on his case since I was a rookie."

I glare at Alex. I must have missed something. That's not surprising. The most influential men in my life float to the back of my mind when I'm acting on my libido. . . *and perhaps my heart.* This is inappropriate for me to say, even more so because of the situation we're in, but the amount of testosterone in this room is persuading my libido to leave the dark, scary hole she's been hidden in the past eighteen months. If Isabelle's life wasn't on the line, I'd bottle up the scent for future exploration.

My wicked thoughts come to an end when Isaac sneers, "Then you would know that Col orchestrated this because he wants me. So, if anyone but me enters that warehouse, he will kill Isabelle."

"I know that," Alex interrupts, nodding. "But that doesn't mean you can't have backup waiting in the wings in case things don't go according to plan."

My heart painfully squeezes when he glances at me through lowered lashes. He's doing this for me as much as he is Isabelle.

After a few seconds of contemplation, Isaac informs Alex, "He has Isabelle at a warehouse in Harbortown. You can follow me there." He locks his eyes with Hunter. "Get Tallis out and call Ryan. Tell him we're going back to where it all began."

Not waiting for Hunter to reply, Isaac exits Alex's office. Alex briefly squeezes my hand in assurance before taking off after him. Watching him bark orders at the agents milling around the space is a thrilling experience. He's in his element. Tough and commanding, but he has the full respect of his crew because they trust he'd never place them in harm's way. He has everything under control. *Except me.*

Alex balks when Isaac pauses halfway into his Bugatti to say, "Get in. This will be quicker than the piece of shit car you've been tailing me in the past few weeks."

I shouldn't smile at Alex's stiffened state, but I do. Isaac knows everything, and it's about time Alex realizes that.

"Be careful," I mouth when Alex flings open the passenger door of Isaac's car to slide inside.

His grin reveals he appreciates my concern, but his cocky wink exposes it isn't needed. If you remove our relationship from the equation, he's not the least bit worried.

Within seconds of Alex shutting his door, Isaac's Bugatti flies out of the parking lot, leaving me in a cloud of dust and with a heart just as smudged.

THIRTY-TWO

ALEX

I could charge Isaac with numerous offenses as he races his sportscar through the packed streets of Ravenshoe. He pushes his pride and joy to the absolute limit until we reach the isolated streets of Harbortown. I would if I hadn't silently pledged to Regan to help him with this. Isabelle is an agent of my team. She's smart and independent, which means, just like Regan, she doesn't need a man rushing in to save her. But this is different. If the man holding Isabelle hostage is who Isaac believes it is, we could already be too late.

Col Petretti doesn't take prisoners, especially not when it's a woman who belongs on the other side of the team. I'm not referring to Isabelle's relationship with Isaac, either; I'm talking about her birthright—the surname she went to great depths to hide before she joined my team.

Although surprised Isaac was aware I've been tailing him the past few months, I doubt he's aware of Isabelle's family lineage. If he does, the large monetary amount he deposited in her father's account will be a bitter pill for her to swallow. I don't see even the strongest relationship surviving that.

I flatten my palms on the roof of Isaac's car when he takes a corner so quickly, his tires lose traction with the road. I wait for him to correct his oversight before asking, "What's your plan?"

"To get Isabelle out, uninjured and safe."

I'm about to reply, *duh*, before the quickest collision of our eyes steals my words. He has the same mortified look my face held when Jay had Regan captive in my childhood bedroom. He's truly panicked, immersed in his worst nightmare.

I look at him through the eyes of a man instead of an agent. "Col will check you for a weapon the instant you enter, so the only one you have at your disposal is your body. You'll need to use it to shelter Isabelle."

Isaac peers at me then nods. He's surprised I'm helping him but still wary of my intentions. He's not the only one riding the uneasy train. I'm sitting in a car with my arch nemesis, walking him through the process I used to keep Regan safe a year ago. I couldn't be any more shocked.

While Isaac pulls his vehicle down a street with numerous empty warehouses, I continue my instructions, "Get her down as quickly as you can, cover her with your body, then roll her until she is facing away from danger. The likelihood of a bullet traveling through your body then piercing hers in a life-threatening way is highly improbable. You may not come out of the exchange intact, but Isabelle will be safe."

The knot in my chest loosens when Isaac nods again. Just like me, he'll put his life on the line if it guarantees Isabelle's safety. I'd say it's admirable for him to do if I didn't loathe him so much.

When Isaac brakes, I check that the safety on my gun is off. He pulls his dark car down a concealed road at the end of a bank of old textile warehouses before nudging his head to the one he believes Isabelle is in. It's a few spots up from where we're parked.

"How do you know she's in there?"

Isaac shifts his gray eyes to mine. I don't know what he sees through them, but it must be something decent since he feels compelled to open up to me. "This is where my empire started, in a dingy, dusty rundown warehouse. So where better for him to end it?"

Not waiting for me to reply, he slides out of his car. As I follow him, I catch sight of a stream of black SUVs traveling the route we just took. I smile, pleased my team kept up with Isaac. Considering how many times he's slipped from their net the past year, I didn't think they had it in them.

After introducing me to a man I swear I've seen before, Isaac gives us an update on the warehouse layout. "He'll most likely have Isabelle out in the open. Col likes showboating."

Both Ryan and I nod. Col's grandstanding has seen his slice of the mafia pie significantly trimmed the past five years.

"I just need to get close enough to Isabelle to shelter her, then the rest will be up to you two."

Isaac's massively dilated eyes drift between Ryan and me. Although he appears to be staring straight at us, he isn't. He's here, but he's not. He's trapped in a parallax, unsure if he should act on his heart's desires or his head's.

"Work with facts, Isaac, not emotions. Facts are evidential. Emotions are fact-blockers. If you can keep your emotions out of it, Isabelle will come out of this alive." I wait for him to nod before adding on, "You know Col; use your knowledge against him."

Our showdown with Col goes as predicted. He wanted to gut Isaac as efficiently as Isaac has disemboweled his business the past few years. To do that, he needed Isaac within touching distance of Isabelle. He wanted him to have a front row seat when he killed her. With Isaac following the instructions I gave him, Isabelle came out of the incident without being shot. Col wasn't as fortunate. He lost his life this evening.

"Where are they taking her?" I shout to the paramedic loading an unconscious Isabelle into the back of his van.

"Ravenshoe Private." Isaac answers on his behalf, his gruff tone revealing his guilt is still paramount. He shouldn't be so hard on himself. His tackle may have caused Isabelle's head to hit the concrete floor, but when you're outrunning a bullet, you don't have time to stop and assess the situation. If you ask me, a concussion is a good scenario compared to what could have happened.

My eyes flick up from the dust covering my polished shoes when a set of keys smacks into my chest. I assume they're from my crew, but the fancy emblem on the leather-stitched key assures me they're not. They are the keys to Isaac's pride and joy.

"Watch the brake. She's a little touchy since she rarely gets used." A wink finalizes Isaac's cocky pledge.

Before I can reply that I'd rather eat shit than be seen in his ride again, the ambulance doors slam shut, carting both my target and one of my agents away from me.

Once the ambulance is nothing but a blur in the distance, I shift on my feet to face my team. They scurry in all directions, acting busy. I want to pretend it's because they're skilled agents who know the importance of stamping our seal on this case, but the disdain hanging in the air doesn't allow me to believe this. They're wary about what my reaction will be to their snooping. . . and perhaps inquisitive about why I let the man I'm striving to prosecute leave a crime scene without handcuffs around his wrists.

Not having the time nor the interest in easing their curiosity, I head inside the warehouse where Isabelle was held hostage. On the way, I yank my cell phone out of my pocket. Although business should always come first, I pledged a long time ago that this woman would come before anything. Although she's no longer my girl, I plan to keep my promise.

"Hey." Regan only says one word, but the ones she doesn't speak are the loudest of them all.

"They're safe—*both of them.*" I lower the sneer in my voice before adding on, "Isabelle is being transported to Ravenshoe Private. Isaac is with her." When she inhales sharply, I push out, "She's okay. Just a bump to her head. Nothing life-threatening."

"Oh, thank god. We're still waiting on news about Hugo."

"Hugo?" Surprise resonates in my tone.

"Yeah, he was shot." I hear her throat work hard to swallow. "He and Izzy were running when she was snatched. From what I was told by Hunter, he was shot while chasing the assailant."

My eyes stray to the man sitting handcuffed on the dirty concrete floor during her last sentence. I'm already having trouble working out why Enrique Popov would kidnap his sister, and now Regan's confession is making me even more baffled.

I push my phone in close to my ear when I miss what Regan says next. "Sorry?"

"Are you coming to the hospital?" she repeats.

I shouldn't love the hope in her tone, but I do. Although I'd give anything to answer her silent pleas, I can't. Not yet.

"I've got matters to tie up here before I can leave."

I can't see her, but I imagine her nodding when whooshing sounds down the line. That, or she's sighing in disappointment. I hope it's the latter.

"I'll get there as soon as I can. Okay?"

Her breathing quickens before she whispers, "Okay."

An ill-timed smile creeps onto my lips as I drag my phone away from my ear. Halfway down, I hear Regan call my name. My eagerness to return my phone to my ear causes it to smack me upside the head. I rub the sting while asking, "Yeah?"

"Thank you."

Two words and the entire fucking world lifts from my shoulders. I swear I feel a million pounds lighter.

Grinning like a loon, I reply, "You're welcome." Before I can say any of the stupid thoughts running through my head, I bid her farewell then disconnect our call.

"What?" I snarl at Reid a few seconds later, hating the gleaming stare he's giving me.

He shrugs. "I didn't say anything."

"You won't get the chance if you keep looking at me like that."

Taking my threat as a joke, he laughs it off before nudging his head to Enrique. "What's the deal? I thought he was one of us?"

My lips twist. "You're not the only one."

It takes several hours to unravel the massive knot around Isabelle's arrest, kidnapping, and how it relates to a three-year long battle between Isaac, Col Petretti, and Theresa. By the time I've been instructed by the head of my division to hand my findings to the local detective running the case, the sun has set hours ago. I'm not happy I was pulled from Isabelle's case, but my disdain lessened when Ryan offered to keep me in on the case.

"Are you sure you don't want me to follow you to the hospital? I can give you a ride back to your apartment." Ryan's glacier-blue eyes scan Isaac's sportscar. "Or a tow when his piece of shit breaks down."

I laugh. I like Ryan. . . when he's not pissing on my turf.

"Nah, it's good. My apartment isn't far from the hospital, but I'll hang around for a few, check the scene."

Ryan nods, but his eyes reveal he thinks I'm full of shit. I am. I'm clocking out the instant I see Regan. I've been seeking an in to speak to her for weeks, and tonight may be my one and only shot. I'm not giving that up for anything.

I wait for Ryan's unmarked cruiser to disappear into the abyss before sliding into Isaac's car. I've worked undercover many times during my years at the Bureau, but this is the first time I've felt like a fraud. This isn't me. A fancy car that smells of expensive leather and cologne isn't me.

Don't get me wrong, I'd love to update the car I have now, but I'll never own one that costs me a decade's worth of wages. I have Isla and Addison's schooling to pay before I can think about a better means of transport.

Speaking of Dane's girls, one is calling me now.

"Hey, I was just thinking about you guys." My smile radiates in my words. "Are the girls getting ready for bed?"

"They would, if they had a bed to sleep in." Kristin's voice is snarky and brimming with exhaustion. The reason behind her unusual composure comes to light when she says, "We've been knocking the past hour. Did you text me the right address?"

Oh fuck. With everything happening this evening, I forgot they were driving down this week to spend Christmas with me. With Isaac's case picking up steam, I couldn't take time off, so Kristin offered to bring the girls to me.

"I thought you were coming Tuesday?"

Kristin sighs. "The girls were too eager to wait, so we left early. If a couple of extra days inconveniences you, we can stay at a hotel?"

"No!" I shout. "They traveled fourteen hours to see me, so let them see me." My eyes drop to the clock in Isaac's leather dashboard. "I'll be there in ten, fifteen minutes max."

I push Isaac's car to the absolute limit, punishing it like he did on our way to Harbortown. It reveals some very interesting facts, the most significant being that I've zipped past two patrol cars at a speed well above the designated limit, yet they didn't pull me over. If that doesn't show Isaac is corrupt, I don't know what will.

Kristin, Isla, and Addison slide out of a white sedan when they spot Isaac's sportscar gliding down the road. The tint is so dark, I doubt they know it's me inside. His ride is just too impressive; you can't help but stare when it's in your midst.

Addison squeals when I slide out of the driver's seat. A mix of fruity shampoo and candy filters into my nose when she leaps into my arms. She giggles like she did any time my beard tickled her chin, but my two-day-old stubble is more scratchy than soothing.

"Hey, baby girl. I've missed you."

I squeeze her tightly before tugging Isla to my thigh for a one-handed hug. I'd like to greet her as exuberantly as Addison, but we're still working through the walls she built when she thought I was trying to replace her dad.

"What happened to your minivan?" I ask Kristin when she drags an overstuffed suitcase from the back of a brand-spanking new Audi.

"I wasn't sure if she'd make the trip, so we rented a car." She winks, her mood picking up with her smile. "The sales rep kindly offered me a free upgrade." She jiggles her breasts, ensuring I can't miss how the offer was awarded.

"You?" Her eyes stray to Isaac's pride and joy, which outshines her vehicle by a mile. The thought annoys me more than it pleases me.

I return my eyes to Kristin. "I'll explain everything after we get the girls in bed. It's late."

Her lips thin, but she dips her chin, agreeing with my proposal. It might not be late by adult standards, but for two little girls who spent the whole day traveling, it's beyond bedtime.

"It smells in here," Isla grumbles when we enter my apartment. It's the same one I had when Regan slept over, but with most of my time spent at the office, my housekeeping has gone a little awry.

"It does," I agree, smiling. "But it should clear when we open a few windows."

Placing Addison down, I do exactly that. I then gather an old pizza box, an empty frosting container, and a handful of soda cans off the coffee table and dump them into the trash.

"There you go, just like new."

Isla rolls her eyes before asking which room is hers.

"There's only one room."

Three sets of eyes snap to mine in sync, forcing my Adam's apple to bob.

"I've set up my room for you and the girls," I advise Kristin while guiding her to the room that has brand new bedding and a cot made up in the corner. "And I'll sleep on the sofa bed."

"Like camping, Awex?" Addison asks, her voice still stuttering over her L's. When I nod, she asks, "Can we make s'mores?"

Her excited voice has me nodding without a thought. I'll set up a bonfire in the middle of my living room if it keeps her looking at me like she is, like I'm a superhero, not realizing she saved me as much as I saved her the past year.

"No s'mores until tomorrow. It's late, which means it's time to brush your teeth and get into bed." Ignoring the girls' gripe, Kristin ushers them into the bathroom.

While she ensures their teeth are sparkling clean, I move into the kitchen to make a call. Due to the late hour, it takes Regan a little longer to answer than she did the first time around.

"Hey." Her voice is groggy, making me wonder if she's been crying or was asleep.

"Hey, did I wake you?"

I swear I can hear her lips incline down the line. "No, I'm watching Axel. Raquel is helping Isaac, meaning I'm on babysitting duty until my mom arrives tomorrow morning. He's asleep on my chest. It's why I'm so quiet."

"Did his latest nanny not work out?" I ask, recalling her telling me earlier this week that Raquel had been through three nannies in five days.

Regan laughs before it quickly switches to a shush. "He's teething, so he's being a royal pain in the butt."

I smile. Fuck, I love when she talks about her nephew. Regan could never be accused of being soft. . . until it comes to Axel.

"Listen, I need to take a raincheck on our talk."

"We had a talk rain-checked?" Her voice is as sassy as her attitude generally is.

"We do now," I bite back, feeding the ego I fell in love with even faster than her beautiful face.

"Alright. I guess I'll let you off. *This time.*" She pauses, breathes deeply, then adds on, "But when we talk, we've got a *lot* of things to discuss."

I nod in full agreement. "We do." Way more than she realizes. "Have you seen Isabelle?"

I was given an update on Isabelle a few hours ago, so I'm using her more as a way to keep my conversation with Regan flowing. We've only spoken a few times the past two weeks, and it was barely more than a few sentences, so I'm not willing to lose the opportunity.

Regan exhales. "No. Isaac guaranteed us access tomorrow—after he's had his fill."

I laugh to hide my snarl. Regan is too perceptive to buy my deceit. "Seriously, Alex? You saw how panicked he was for Isabelle today, yet you're still harboring ill feelings toward him. Why?"

"He kissed you—"

"For Isabelle! My god."

Her shouted words stir Axel. His tiny cries bellow down the line at the same time I pick up a pair of bare feet padding toward me.

"I have to go." Regan's voice is a cross between stern and soothing. Stern for me; soothing for Axel.

"Rae. . ."

I hear the stutter of her heart when she says, "Save it for the raincheck, Alex. We're both tired and frustrated, which only increases the chance of us saying something we'll regret. We've done that enough the past year; we don't need any more stupid words shared between us."

"Alright." I have a thousand more words to say, but these are more important than any. "I'm not your enemy, Rae. I'll never be on any team that isn't yours."

"Alex . . ." Her words trail off when she can't find an appropriate thing to say. She settles on the best option when she replies, "I've never wanted to pick sides; that's why I didn't play sports. Now is no different." Axel's cries reach a point she can't ignore. "I'm sorry, I really have to go."

"It's okay. I understand." I twist around to unearth the person responsible for the hairs on my nape standing to attention. Kristin is at the entrance of my kitchen. Her arms are folded in front of her chest, and her brow is bowed. "I've got a few things to settle as well. We'll talk more tomorrow?"

After murmuring "okay," Regan disconnects our call.

"I knew it!" Kristin throws her hands up in the air. "You've pushed aside your pledge to Dane—*again!*"

"No, I haven't." I shadow her into my living room.

While she tosses aside the couch cushions to pull out the sofa bed hiding beneath, my eyes stray to my bedroom door. It is shut, and no light is shining beneath it. The girls sleeping routine must have dramatically improved, because any time I put them to bed, it took three stories, numerous trips to the bathroom, and at least two requests for a glass of water—hence the toilet breaks.

"You said you'd get the man responsible for Dane's death. That nothing would stop you from getting justice." Kristin lifts her tear-welling eyes to mine. "You failed to mention *her*. God, Alex! She aborted your child, refused to answer your calls for months, yet you still follow after her like some sick little puppy."

"She didn't abort my baby. It was a misunderstanding."

Kristin glares at me like I'm an idiot. I understand her response. I was so convinced it was Regan who visited that family clinic, my mind still occasionally slips into the negative void her supposed deceit caused.

"She also didn't sleep with Isaac."

Now Kristin's glare really ramps up. "How do you know this?" Although she's asking a question, she continues speaking, foiling my chance to reply. "Because *she* told you it didn't happen."

"Yes—"

"And you believed her? Oh my god. I thought you were smart."

My back molars smash together. "Hey!"

You can't miss the warning in my tone. She's my best friend's wife and the mother of his daughters, but I'm not going to be treated as a leper in my own home. I also refuse to allow her to speak of Regan in such a derogatory manner. She's barely mentioned her name, but the scorn on her face says more than her words ever would.

"Just like Dane, Regan's caught in a fight she doesn't belong in." Kristin's eyeroll stops halfway when I quickly add on, "Furthermore,

Dane had no issues with me dating Regan when he was alive, so why do you have a problem with it?"

My question stumps her. Her mouth opens and closes, but not a syllable escapes her lips. I fill the silence. "If you're worried my relationship with Regan will somehow alter my bond with you and the girls, you have nothing to be worried about. You guys will always have priority in my life."

"We just won't be your first priority, right?"

Stealing my chance to assure her that they'll always have a top spot in my list, she thrusts a blanket and pillow from my linen closet into my chest before ambling to my room.

"I traveled all the way here to see you because the girls missed you, and what do they get? A man who couldn't wait ten minutes before sneaking off to call the woman responsible for their daddy's demise."

"Kristin. . ." My words trail off when she brutally slams the door I replaced my first day back in Ravenshoe.

THIRTY-THREE

ALEX

Between Kristin refusing to speak to me and Addison's tears because I couldn't spend today shopping for a Christmas tree because I have to work, my mood is at the point of snapping. Add that to Isabelle's court hearing yesterday, and her impromptu meeting with her brother, and you've got a dangerous recipe. I'm exhausted, annoyed, and frustrated as fuck.

The more information we amassed from Isabelle's kidnapper, the more Kristin's statement two nights ago rang true. I've either been walking around with blinders on the past eighteen months, or Isaac's feelings for Isabelle have him making careless mistakes.

Either way, the visit I'm making to Isaac's mega mansion with Ryan will create ripples. Unfortunately, they'll most likely affect my relationship with Regan more than anything.

We've been in contact the past two days, but only an occasional message shared between the times I'm not following clues in Isabelle's case and sharing ghost stories with Isla and Addison around the makeshift fireplace in my living room. I'm dying to see her, but I'm not the only one tied up with family business.

Regan is as busy as me. Her family has come down for Christmas, meaning her penthouse is crammed with more visitors than the two she had last week.

"Did you advise them we're coming?"

Ryan shakes his head as he guides his unmarked police car down a pebbled driveway. "Any requests I log are always denied by his legal team, so I figured a sneaky approach would be best."

I shake my head to hide my smirk, grateful my department's requests aren't the only ones Regan shoots down. I doubt Regan could hold back the authorities for long on this case, though. It's not every day your client is accused of kidnapping and assaulting the police officers who arrested your girlfriend.

Although I'll never side with a criminal, I can understand Isaac's quest for revenge. Ryan showed me the evidence the DA failed to log when Isabelle was arrested. The brutality the male officers used when arresting her was excessive. It's lucky Isaac got to them first, because if it were a member of my team, they wouldn't be cuffed to a hospital bed. They'd be doing hard time with some of the criminals they've taken down. You never put your hands on a woman, much less one who's on your team.

Or was. I'm truly unsure on which side of the law Isabelle now resides.

While clambering out of the passenger seat of Ryan's unmarked car, I take in the large stone house with arched windows looking out over a vista of manicured gardens and manly hedges. Compared to Isaac's pad in the middle of Ravenshoe, this property has a more homey feel to it.

"First time here?" I ask upon spotting Ryan's dropped jaw.

"Yeah. You?"

I nod. I was too busy convincing a judge I had the means to detain Isaac to conduct his search warrant last month.

Just before my knuckles rap a large arched door, a mumble rumbles through it. I cock my brow before locking my eyes with Ryan. He hears my silent interrogation. How do I know this since we've only just met? He removes his gun from his hip as rapidly as I do.

When a second mangled groan rolls through the door, Ryan nudges his head to a side entrance. "I'll cover the back."

I nod before ringing the doorbell. I'm not announcing to the suspect that we're on to him; I'm convincing him we're regular visitors. If he believes we're the mailman or a gardener, he'll be less likely to make a costly mistake.

My gun drops from its braced position when a petite lady of approximately sixty opens the door. Her gray hair is pulled back in a bun, and she is holding a carton of juice.

"Is everything okay, ma'am? We heard groans of distress."

Her eyes flutter in apology before she gestures for me to enter the foyer. Since Ryan's attempts to enter Isaac's property from another vantage point were futile, he follows me. We latch the safeties on our guns when we discern the source of the noise. It isn't someone crying out for help. It is a woman in the midst of ecstasy.

Ryan runs his hand along his jaw to hide his smile. I'm glad he can find amusement in our situation. I'm anything but amused. Isaac is a criminal, a man who has more to answer for than a few speeding tickets. He shouldn't be enjoying life. He should be behind bars.

Another ten minutes pass before Isabelle and Isaac gallop down the large curved stairwell, making my anger more paramount. I have very important things I could be doing; instead, I'm stuck waiting around for him.

"Oh my god," Isabelle murmurs loud enough for Ryan and me to hear.

Her cheeks inflame as her eyes shift to Isaac. He looks as smug as a pig in mud, as if he's pleased we witnessed the grandeur of his life. I'm sure I can cut down his attitude a few notches. We called a truce two days ago, but that was only in effect when Isabelle was in danger. All bets are now off, and my patience is stretched thin.

"Sorry to interrupt," Ryan says when Isaac and Isabelle stop to stand in front of us. The humor in his tone can't weaken the sternness of his next set of words. "We have a few questions we need to ask you in regards to the investigation on the police officers who were kidnapped and held in your yacht."

"We?" Isaac's lowered eyes dart between Ryan and me. "Since when did the FBI and the Ravenshoe Police Department become allies?"

Frustrated by the humor in his tone, I snap, "When we found a *subject* we had common ground on."

If my stance doesn't advise Isaac our truce is over, the glare I give Isabelle is a sure-fire indication. I'm disappointed in her. I thought she was smarter than this. She could have been a brilliant agent if she looked at Isaac through the eyes of an agent instead of a woman, but she can't come back from this. She's stepped too far on the wrong side of the law; she just has no clue how far.

I return my eyes to Isaac. "The police officers were found bound and gagged in your yacht. The same yacht you chartered out of the Vela De Keys Marina on the afternoon the police officers were kidnapped."

Isaac grins like the smug prick he is. "Not everything is black and white. There's a whole lot of gray no one pays any attention to."

"I don't believe in coincidences. There is a logical reason for everything."

Air rustles between Isaac's teeth as he struggles to hold back his chuckle. "Now it all makes sense."

The smell of a cologne that forever features in my nightmares smacks into me when Isaac steps closer. My concern that Isabelle can't see through the haze Isaac has engulfed her in fades when she tugs on his arm in an effort to keep us apart. I appreciate her concern, but she doesn't need to fret. I've taken down men much more powerful than Isaac during my time at the Bureau. It just never held the level of anticipation as it does this time around.

"What makes sense?" I ask Isaac, encouraging him to continue with his arrogant, pompous statement.

He follows along nicely. "Why you've been so persistent in investigating me."

"I've been persistently investigating you because you're a criminal," I reply, stating the obvious.

When I return my eyes to Isabelle, Isaac adjusts his position to block her from my view. If that doesn't show he's worried she'll soon see the real him, I don't know what will.

My eyes snap to Isaac when he says, "It has nothing to do with me being a criminal. You're only investigating me because you're jealous."

I laugh. It is as bitter as the sludge that's been sitting in my chest since Dane passed. "Jealous? Of what? Everything you've ever accomplished was achieved illegally from money tainted with blood. I'd rather be poor than live with low morals like you."

My jaw tightens when Isabelle snaps, "Alex, that's enough."

She's defending him. *Him.* A criminal. A man who'll order the death of her fellow agents without a single consideration of the repercussions. She shouldn't be defending him any more eagerly than Regan does. What is it with women not being able to see who he truly is? He's a criminal—plain and fucking simple.

My anger boils over when Isaac snarls, "You're not jealous of my accomplishments, my power, or my wealth. You're jealous because Regan chose me over you."

I suck in furious breaths, doing anything to quell the anger scorching my veins to black ash. I want to beat him, maim him, or better yet, kill him, but I am a man of the law; my personal desires can't enter the equation. I have to take him down the right way, to show I am a better man than him. It might take me a month, a year, or a decade, but the delay won't water down the sweetness when he's finally behind bars. I'll relish it for years to come.

With his gaze not as arrogant and his stance not as strong, Isaac mutters, "If you believe her decision was based on anything but professional obligation and friendship, then it means you're even more foolish than I first thought."

I take a step back, stunned. That is not what I expected him to say. Does it weaken my anger? Yes, somewhat. Does it diminish my desire to arrest him? No, not at all.

But more than anything, it makes me miss a brief conversation he has with Ryan before he instructs Isabelle to enter the living room with a pretty Asian female with an old doctor's bag in her hand.

Once Isabelle jumps to his demand, Isaac returns his focus to Ryan and me. "Did you arrest the second assailant who kidnapped Isabelle?"

Since I am unaware of Ryan's investigation, I leave Isaac's question for him to answer. "Yes, the information supplied by Enrique before Isabelle met with him was extremely accurate. We netted his assailant and another four members of his crew earlier this morning."

"Do you have any leads in the disappearance of Enrique?" Isaac tries to keep his tone impassive. He does a shit job of it.

"No," I rejoin the conversation since the fog in my head is lifting. "But rumors are that Vladimir was grooming him to take over the family business, so I wouldn't be surprised to discover this is the work of Vladimir's crew. We put a ban on all travel, but by the time it was processed through all the appropriate channels, Enrique was long gone."

Isaac's smirk answers the interrogation in my tone. He had something to do with Enrique's disappearance. I'm certain of it.

Spotting my suspicious glance, Isaac tries to shift the direction of our conversation. "Have you questioned the police officers in regards to who framed Isabelle for Megan's murder?"

Ryan grimaces. "No, they were admitted to Mercer Hospital for dehydration, exposure, and for psychiatric evaluation. Until they're given the all clear, the union reps won't let me close to them."

My annoyance returns stronger than ever. Much to the disgust of my ego, I was denied the same opportunity this morning.

"You have your suspicions on who it is?" Isaac asks Ryan, his tone hopeful.

Ryan shocks me by answering, "I have my theories; I just need proof."

We discussed our plan of attack on the way here. He agreed to keep his cards close to his chest until Isaac gave us the information we needed. This was not our plan.

When Ryan peers at me, requesting leniency, I shrug. I'm not happy about the detour, but from the intel I uncovered from Ryan the past two days, he and Isaac have history. If it's history that will help me close my case, I'm open to an occasional curve in the road.

After dipping his chin in thanks, Ryan returns his focus to Isaac. "One of the captives was Rodney Parvok."

The reddening of Isaac's cheeks matches mine, and his stance is just as frustrated.

His anger becomes paramount when Ryan quickly fills in, "The other was Chase Springfield."

"What more proof do you need than that?" Isaac's tone is dangerously low. "Theresa's minion and her cousin were the two men who brutalized Isabelle during her arrest. Enrique said he learned of the plot to kidnap Isabelle from them, and that he only kept them alive because they had useful information on who framed Isabelle. I think it is pretty obvious who set her up for murder."

Although I agree with him, the law doesn't work that way. "Anything Enrique said to Isabelle is hearsay. It will never hold up in a courtroom."

"I don't give a fuck what will hold up in court." His words are so heated, they sizzle in the air. "If you stopped wasting police resources pursuing a spiteful grudge against me, you wouldn't need to worry about hearsay. You could have squeezed the info from the source. Instead, you're walking around with your head stuck up your ass because your ego got bruised by a woman way out of your league to begin with."

I get he's angry, and I'm an easy target for him to lash out at, but that doesn't mean I'll take his shit lying down. I didn't let my best friend's girl disrespect me even when everything she said was true, so you can sure as hell be guaranteed I won't let the fucker responsible for his death speak to me in such a way.

Glaring at him, I bridge the gap between us, warning him to calm down before I assist him in gaining a better attitude.

When he sniffs, purposely baiting me, the thread I mentioned earlier shreds beyond repair. Fuck protocols and rules. Fuck him. It's time for this fucker to get a taste of his own medicine.

I'm two seconds from wiping the cocky grin from Isaac's face with my fists when Ryan steps between us. "You really think coming to blows will help Isabelle?" Although he doesn't mention Regan, he doesn't need to. His eyes reveal his comment was for me as much as it was Isaac.

Isaac stares at me for several long seconds while deciding his next move. I want him to uphold his arrogance, to swing at me like he really wants to, because then I won't need to worry about the law. I'll be well within my rights to protect myself, one bloody fist at a time.

My wish is left unanswered when Isaac shifts his eyes to Ryan. "You have a week. If you don't arrest Theresa by then, I'll take matters into my own hands."

I'm about to interject, to fire off a comment that it won't be the first time he's gotten his hands dirty, but his next set of words cuts me off. "If I'm going to be accused of something, I may as well do it."

With that, he spins on his heels and heads into the living room Isabelle entered ten minutes ago, not bothering to show us the way out.

"He's not who you think he is," Ryan says when my vicious glare locks with his wide eyes.

"He's not? Then what the fuck was that?" I nudge my head in the direction Isaac just walked. "He'll take matters into his own hands? Who says that?"

Stealing his chance to issue one of the many thoughts in his head, I exit Isaac's property as quickly as I entered it. I've barely made it three steps down the pebbled driveway when my fight switches from business to personal.

"You had no right to interview my client without his attorney present." Regan darts out of the back of a taxi. Her face is as red as mine, her fists just as tightly clenched.

Her casual look and messy bun make my cock swell, but not enough to make my anger subside. She couldn't find more than a few twenty-minute slots to talk to me the past two days, but she can jump in a taxi and trek across town to defend Isaac. That's fucked.

When I tell Regan that, the vein in her neck works overtime. "Because he's my client, Alex! Why can't you get that through your thick head?!" Her eyes bounce between mine as the anger lining her face grows. "You won't stop, will you? You'll keep pushing and pushing and pushing until you force me to pick a team."

Tears well in her eyes when I fail to deny her assumption. I do want her to pick. I want her to pick me. Isaac has had her at his side for years; it's my turn.

"I won't do it, Alex." Her voice is lower now, more reserved. I don't know if spotting Ryan's approach from our right is the cause for her dropped tone or what she says next. "I forced someone to pick his team once before, and look how that ended. I won't do it again."

Remorse hits me like a ton of bricks. I forgot about the time she forced Luca to pick. He died the same night. "Rae. . ."

She slices her hand in the air, silently begging for me to give her a minute to gain her composure. When several deep inhalations fail to subdue either her anger or her devastation, she slides into the back of the cab. She throws money at the cab driver, demanding he floor the gas. The reason for her desire to flee quickly comes to light when I spot a bunch of tears splashing down her cheeks. Others may see them as just blobs of moisture, but to me they reveal her heartache, devastation, and disappointment. And unfortunately, she believes I'm to blame for them all.

I try to let her go, to remember I'm not the one in the wrong here, but the further her taxi rolls away from me, the stupider I feel. I'm not letting my personal life affect my work; I'm letting my work interfere with my personal life.

With a grunt, I push off my feet and charge down Isaac's driveway before my brain can cite an objection. I want to keep the promise I made to Dane, but I want Regan more than anything. She's worth more than regret, revenge, or any other fucked up emotion I've been pummeled with the past six years. I won't have a life worth living if she isn't in it.

I chase Regan's taxi out of Isaac's driveway and halfway down his hilly street before my fucked up knee stops me. It buckles beneath me, sending me and my large frame skidding across the asphalt. Gravel digs into my palms as the roadside shreds the flesh on my knees, but it's nothing compared to the pain tearing through my heart when Regan's taxi continues its journey, her heartache too high to stop and check if I'm okay.

THIRTY-FOUR

REGAN

"You smell like puke."

Laughing, Raquel slides into the seat next to me. The milk vomit rolling down my shoulder is the story of my life lately. Dad got a little eager bouncing Axel on his knee while watching his children open the Christmas presents he arrived with five days ago, but instead of him wearing baby puke as if it's a fur coat, I suffered from his lack of judgment.

What did I say? *The story of my life.*

Realizing Christmas Day isn't the day for deep reflection, I ask, "Don't you have a grown man to mother?"

Raquel tucks her legs under her bottom before twisting her torso to face me. "I've been relieved from my duties."

"By whom?" I know it wasn't Isaac, as he mentioned bringing in additional staff to help her with Hugo's rehabilitation only last night.

Raquel shrugs. "Hugo called me early this morning. Said something about taking a trip."

Her casual tone shocks me. Hugo doesn't take trips. He's a ghost. Ghosts don't have family to visit. Unless. . .

"Did he say where he was going?"

Raquel shakes her head. "No, but it can't be local. He called at 3 AM."

I grimace. That's the equivalent of witching hour for Hugo. He's not a fan of early rising.

Raquel's eyes drop to my phone when it vibrates in my hand. It is playing the ringtone I set for Alex: "Consequences" by Camila Cabello. "How many calls is that today?"

My thumb hovers over the decline button as I whisper, "Three."

Raquel grabs ahold of my hand, stopping me from declining Alex's call for the third time today. "Answer him, Regan. He's been calling you non-stop the past four days."

Biting my lower lip to hide its quiver, I shake my head.

Her sigh ruffles my hair. "Why not? It's Christmas. Don't be mean."

"I'm not being mean." *I'm protecting my heart.*

"Regan. . ."

Ignoring the plea in her tone, I stand to my feet and enter her kitchen. With mom busy making her famous Christmas feast, I doubt she'll have time to grill me like Raquel. I could skip their interrogations altogether if I wasn't crashing at Raquel's apartment. I'm not hiding from Alex; I'm just. . . *hiding.*

There is no plausible solution for our predicament. Alex wants to take down the man I'm contracted to protect, and that's not the worst of it. Even if I weren't Isaac's employee, I would still protect him. That's the part Alex can't understand. Isaac is my friend as much as he is my employer. He deserves to have me in his corner when he's fighting the battle of his life, because he stood in mine when I faced the same challenges.

I'd give anything to have both Alex and Isaac in my life, but Alex would never allow that. He wants me to choose. Since that's something I'll never be able to do, I'm left with no choice but to ignore both him and Isaac right now. If I can't have both of them, perhaps I'm better having neither of them?

"Everything okay?" I ask my mom, who's flapping around the

kitchen like Alex did when Pat chased him out of the chook coop all those months ago. The memory awards me my first honest smile of the week. I thought losing someone via death would always trump losing someone via choice, but this week has proved that isn't true. My mood has been so low the past four days, matching the emotions I handled the weeks following Luca's accident.

My mom stops rummaging through Raquel's scarce pantry to lock her eyes with mine. "I forgot to get the sherry for the forager's pie."

Her brimming-with-panic eyes enlarge my smile. She makes the same pie every Christmas because it's my dad's favorite. "I'm sure it will be fine without it."

"No!" my mom shouts as if I suggested she replace the meat with tofu. "Your dad will notice if it's missing the sherry. It gives the dish a nutty flavor."

When she snatches a set of keys off the kitchen counter, I step into her path. "You can't drive. You've been drinking. This isn't Texas. They'll arrest you here."

I step back when her brow arches high in silent question.

"No—"

She drops her lower lip. "Please, you know how much Daddy loves this dish."

I throw my hands into the air. "It's shepherd's pie, Mom, not a Thanksgiving turkey."

She takes on my stealthy stance, showing who I learned my sass from. "How do you know what we eat for Thanksgiving dinner? You haven't been home for one in over nine years."

Now she has me by the throat, and she knows it.

After weakening her glare, she switches tactics, "Please, Aunty Rae-Rae. Don't you want Axel's first Christmas to be the best one ever?"

Stick me with a fork. I'm done. I'll do anything for that little guy.

With a huff, I grind out, "Fine. But I'm adding a bottle of Henri Boillot onto your tab."

"Grab anything you want." She hands me her credit card, having no idea the bottle of wine I'm referencing sells for between $300 and $1300 a bottle.

After smothering Axel's cheek with sloppy kisses, I make my way to my dad's truck. No matter how many times I assured him he and his giant ass would fit in a first-class seat, he was adamant it wouldn't. He'd never admit it, but I'm reasonably sure a fear of flying was the reason he drove here, not the love of his truck.

With the roads isolated, I make it to one of the scarce few convenience stores open today. They have the bottle of sherry my mom needs to make her dish, but no bottle of Henri Boillot. Instead, I settle on a fruity red that will wash down the two Xanax I'm planning to take tonight.

What? They'll help me sleep. . . and hopefully make me forget I have a broken heart.

I won't rely on them like I did after Luca's passing, but they'll numb the ache enough I can function like normal—for the most part.

My quick steps down the cracked sidewalk slow when a familiar voice rings through my ears. "Ready, Addi; run and I'll catch you."

I step past a broad tree trunk in just enough time to see Alex catch a little blonde girl in his arms. He twirls her around and around and around until they collapse onto the dewy grass in a fit of giggles.

"Again, Awex!" My lips part at the cute annunciation of his name. The little girl's voice is as adorable as her tiny face. She has two pigtails sitting high on the top of her head, and her eyes are as vibrant and blue as Alex's.

I pause, waiting for suspicion to make itself known with my gut. It never comes. I've thrown out enough accusations the past decade, I've got none left to issue. Besides, although I'm watching them from afar, Addi's face seems familiar. I'm certain she's the girl Alex was photographed holding at Dane's funeral.

I watch them for the next several minutes, adoring the giggles roaring from Addi's mouth as Alex weaves her between the swings and jungle gym at the park they're playing at. Seeing him so carefree and happy gives me some semblance of peace. I thought our time apart would be as devastating for Alex as it's been for me, but this proves he's doing okay.

Don't misconstrue me. I'm not angry he's enjoying Christmas Day. I'm happy. He works hard, so he deserves to relish the days where nothing but family and friends are on his mind. I'm just disappointed in myself. This is Axel's first Christmas. I doubt he'll remember it because he's only a few months old, but he deserves not to have his sour-faced aunty ruining all his pictures from the day.

After watching Alex and Addi for another few minutes, I continue to my dad's truck. My steps are springier than earlier, less weighed down. On the way, I spot a lady I'd guess to be early thirties and a little girl a few years older than Addi. Her hair is just as blonde as Addi's, and her eyes are just as blue.

My steps falter when reality dawns: she must be Addi's big sister, which means the lady she is with is most likely their mother. Kristin is pretty. Designer glasses hide half her face, and I can barely see her shiny hair since it's tucked under a Burberry cashmere hat, but the portions of her body peeking out of her wool coat reveal she handled motherhood well. I'd be riddled with jealousy at her put-together display if sympathy wasn't the first emotion to hit me upon spotting her.

Noticing my fumbling steps, Kristin shifts her eyes my way. When she sees the bottles of alcohol in my hands, she mistakes my clumsiness as drunkenness. I shouldn't smile when she snarls at me, but I can't help it. Usually women glare at me because I stole their husbands' eyes. I've never had it happen without a male in the vicinity.

Kristin's sunglasses can't hide her glare, much less the vicious furl of her top lip. I don't have the time or the inclination to engage in a verbal altercation with a woman still grieving, so I dip my chin before skirting past her.

Thankfully, my dad's truck is only a few spots up, meaning I'm saved from the heat of her wrath. After jabbing my keys into the ignition, I kick over the old girl's motor. Just as it fires to life, my cell phone rings, scaring the living daylights out of me.

Noticing the call is from Alex, my eyes dart up to the rearview mirror. His shoulder is propped against the tree trunk I used to shelter myself while spying on him, and his phone is pushed against his ear. His brows are housing a groove they didn't have when he was playing with Addi, and his lips are firmer, but he's still the sexiest man I've ever laid my eyes on.

My eyes shift sideways when a commotion captures my attention. Addi's attempt to race toward Alex as she did earlier is being thwarted by Kristin fisting the back of her winter coat. She keeps Addison and Isla contained at the side of the playground as they wait for Alex to finalize his call. The pain crossing Addi's face cuts me raw. She's peering at Alex, begging for him to come back and play, but since his focus is on his phone instead of her, he fails to notice the tears flooding her eyes.

Guilt overwhelms me. I've been so gung-ho on protecting my heart, I didn't check what my actions were doing to those closest to me. I don't know Addi, but I'm aware of what she's been through the past year. That alone makes me want to protect her, to save her the pain of losing her daddy figure for the second time in her life.

For that reason, and solely that reason, I hit decline on Alex's call.

It's the second most painful thing I've done in my life.

This is my third.

"I can't do this, Isaac. Not only as your lawyer, but as your friend."

My eyes drop to the prenup he had me draw up this morning as my arms fold in front of my chest. I reinforce my pose, hoping he'll know I'm not backing down without a fight today. I didn't walk away from the man I love yesterday for nothing. I did it to ensure both Alex and Isaac remain happy, and this ridiculous prenup won't secure

Isaac's happiness like he's hoping. When Isabelle discovers the terms he put in, it may destroy it.

I balk when Isaac snaps, "I don't pay for your opinions. I pay you to do what I ask you to do."

"This could be financial suicide for you." I lean my hip on the big mahogany desk he is sitting behind while taking in a big breath. "If you get divorced, you'll be decimated. Izzy will get everything."

He nods. "That's the point. Everything I have, I want her to have."

I shake his stupid words out of my ears. "You're smarter than this, Isaac. This won't tie her to you. It won't stop her from leaving you. Heck, it may even encourage her to leave, considering she will end up filthy rich and—"

My words halt when Isaac glares at me. It's a stare I've never been subjected to before. It warns I'm skating on extremely thin ice. His temper is as frayed as mine, his mood just as sour.

With a shimmy of my shoulders, I continue with my campaign. He pays me for my stubbornness, so he's about to get his money's worth. "A prenup is supposed to be a contract that protects your assets. It's not designed as a bribery tool."

I startle when he abruptly stands from his chair. Although his fists are clenched at his side, and his jaw is tight, I didn't balk in fear. I'm reinforcing the bricks I stacked around my heart last night, bunkering down for the third fight of my life.

"I'm not bribing Isabelle to stay with me," Isaac snarls through gritted teeth.

I toss the prenup onto his side of the desk. "Then what do you call this?"

My campaign falters when his lips quiver. "It's called showing Isabelle what she means to me." His eyes bounce between mine as he says, "She's been through hell and back because of me, yet she still stands by my side."

His words affect me more than I'll ever let on. Everything he is saying, feeling, and experiencing is precisely what I said, felt, and experienced when I was with Alex. I thought he could complete me, make me feel whole, but all he did was break me more. I don't want Isaac to go through that. I want to save him from the pain.

"You're giving her everything, Isaac. She could financially destroy you. Everything you have worked so hard for will be gone. Years of hard work wasted—"

"That could have been destroyed because of your inability to keep your mouth shut during pillow talk."

The quick change in our conversation is shocking, but it has nothing on the betrayal in Isaac's eyes. He's peering at me in a way I hoped he never would. It's the same gut-wrenching glare Luca gave me when I forced him to pick. He's ashamed of me.

"How long did you know the FBI was investigating me before I worked it out for myself? Days? Weeks? Months? Years?"

I clutch my chest to ensure my heart remains in place before taking a step closer to him. "Isaac. . . I—"

"Answer the question, Regan."

His eyes reveal he already knows my answer, but he wants me to spell it out for him. "I didn't know he was here—"

"Answer the question."

My chest rises and falls three times before I force out, "Five months."

"Five months from the start or five months before me?"

I try to force the words from my mouth, to for once lead with honesty instead of deceit, but the pain in my chest is holding my words captive. In less than twenty-four hours both my worst nightmares are coming true.

My eyes return to Isaac when he growls, "Regan."

It takes a mammoth effort, but I manage to strangle out, "Five months before you."

Isaac nods as the disappointment in his eyes grows. "And when did you share confidential client/lawyer information with him?"

A tear rolls down my cheek when I shake my head. "I didn't."

"Don't lie to me, Regan."

I lock my eyes with his, both angered and sickened he doesn't believe me. I guess I shouldn't be shocked. I did lie to him—for months!

"I made a mistake I regret every day," I suck in several nerve-calming breaths before adding on, "but I never deceived you."

I nearly say *not in the way you're thinking*, until I recall Alex saying a similar thing hours before his true deceit was unveiled.

Spotting the truth in my eyes, the low hang of Isaac's lids widen. "What type of mistake?"

The chance of holding back the tears in my eyes is nearly lost when he paces around his desk to hand me some tissues. I clutch them tightly in my hands, ensuring my eyes understand my stern, unspoken warning. I don't care how bad things seem, I am *not* to cry. I'm stronger than this.

I exhale a deep breath before issuing the excuse I rehearsed numerous times the past twelve months when I predicted how our exchange would go. "My mistake was trusting him."

Isaac remains quiet, waiting for me to continue. I don't keep him waiting for long. "I fought my attraction to him. You know me, Isaac; after everything I've been through, I never let anyone get close." I lock my eyes with his. "Except you."

If only I had kept my guard up, then I wouldn't be suffering as I am now. *God—when did I get so careless?*

My heart beats at an unnatural rhythm as my mouth spills secrets I swore I'd never share. "I have to give it to him, he was very clever. Not only did he break down my walls, but he made me believe he truly cared for me."

A smile tugs on my lips as memories of Alex's concern the day he washed my wound in the emergency bay race back to the forefront of my mind. At the time, I thought we were strangers. Now I know why he seemed so familiar.

"As the weeks went on, I got careless."

Careless? I got soft. I barely went an hour without thinking about Alex. I thought our connection would have us sprinting past the many barricades in front of us. I was an idiot. Attraction isn't enough. Relationships need a lot more than just lusty sparks.

Isaac coerces my eyes to his before asking, "Because you trusted him?"

I nod. "Yes."

I did trust Alex, but that isn't the only reason I got careless. Normally, I don't let anyone in. If a man came close to knocking down my guard, I chopped down his ego just as fast. That had them running for the hills in an instant.

Unfortunately, Alex didn't give in so easily. The way he helped me through my grief with Luca assured him his placement on my list rather quickly, then, as the days went on, my feelings for him flourished right alongside it.

I stop reminiscing about the good times when Isaac asks, "Are you certain it was him who deceived you?"

My lips firm before I nod. "I went to take a shower one morning, and when I came out, my laptop was open and turned on." I breathe deeply, preparing my lungs for the knock Isaac's disappointment will hit them with before confessing, "It was the laptop I had all the Theresa files saved on."

Isaac surprises me for the second time in twenty-four hours when he fails to react to my confession. It is as if he's already aware Alex knows about his ongoing paternity battle with Theresa. I shouldn't be surprised. Isaac knows everything.

I exhale the breath I'm holding before continuing my story. It feels good to finally get it off my chest. "At first I brushed it off. I thought maybe he was checking his emails or googling movie times for a flick we were going to see, but it didn't take long for my suspicion to grow that he had looked through my files."

The sternness on Isaac's face slackens. "What caused your wariness?"

I shrug. "He mentioned numerous times his dislike for his boss. He never said what he did for a living, but he shared stories about how she was underhanded and shady, and how he'd run things differently if he were in her position."

The quiver of my heart is heard in my words when I say, "The day after my laptop was open, he arrived at my apartment, beaming with excitement because she had been removed from her position, and he wanted to celebrate."

I smile to hide my grimace. With revenge, very little sleep, and a few nips of liquid courage fueling my motives that night, my memories are a little hazy, but no matter how clouded they are, I know it wasn't Alex who suggested we celebrate. That was all me and my stupid quest for revenge.

When Isaac peers at me, encouraging me to continue, I say, "Not very often did Alex drink. He's usually more controlled, but since we were celebrating, I encouraged him to loosen up. I soon realized why he doesn't drink. After a few too many spiked drinks, his lips loosened up as well."

Although my plan that night worked, my endeavor to loosen his lips didn't go as I had predicted. My heart thwacks my chest just recalling the words he said that evening. *"I did, Rae. I meant every fucking word. How can you not believe me? I've been acting like a lovesick idiot all week."*

I swallow harshly to eradicate the bitter taste in my throat before confessing, "With the snippets of information he shared earlier, it didn't take long to realize what industry he was in. When he was asleep, I rifled through his belongings. I didn't find anything concrete except a locked cell phone, so I called Hunter."

When Isaac growls, I push out, "Hunter didn't know what my request pertained to. I told him I needed to hack into a guy's phone to send his wife pictures of her cheating husband. You know how much Hunter hates cheaters."

When Isaac nods, aware of Hunter's dislike of cheaters, I breathe a little easier. The last thing I want is to throw another man into the deep end with me.

Some of the anger on Isaac's face jumps to mine when I disclose,

"Hunter explained how I could gain access to Alex's phone without needing the passcode. When it unlocked, not only did I find hidden emails corresponding to you and your empire, but I also found photos of Theresa's files from my laptop."

I peer out the window of Isaac's office before confessing my darkest sin. "You know the stupidest part? The passcode for his phone was my birthday. That is how good he is. He played the devoted boyfriend act very well." *Nearly as well as he'll fill the role of dad and beloved husband on Dane's behalf.*

My hand sweeps my wet cheek before I return my eyes to Isaac. "I tried to lead him astray, steer him in the wrong direction, but I think I made matters worse. Not only does he believe you're the man your FBI file says you are, he thinks we—"

"Had an affair."

When my mouth falls open, Isaac smirks, appreciative of my shock. "I gathered that after my run-in with him. He doesn't hide his jealousy well." I almost nod, but Isaac's next question steals my attention. "Is he the reason you moved back to Texas?"

"Yes. I didn't want to run the risk of bumping into him." I fold my arms across my chest to hide the shake of my hands. "I wanted to tell you. I tried a few times before I left, but I was ashamed I let him play me like a fool. If I honestly thought he had anything significant that was going to hurt you or your empire, I would have told you, Isaac, but he had nothing. He still has nothing." *Except my heart.*

After a few moments of uncomfortable silence, Isaac assures me, "You don't owe me anything, Regan. Me helping you wasn't under the stipulation that you would owe me. I did it because you'd be an asset to my empire, not to gain your moral obligation for the remainder of your life."

My face scrunches up as I struggle to hold in my tears. He didn't help me because he was my friend; he did it because he saw in me what I saw in him: a wounded, broken soul begging for a second chance. He gave me that chance when he chose me over several more suitable candidates to join his empire. I'll be forever grateful for the day he came into my life; I just wish it could have been done without hurting Alex in the process.

Mistaking my tears as heartache, Isaac says, "If he is your Achilles heel—"

"He isn't." My voice jitters as I struggle to conceal my hundredth lie of the week. You'd think I'd be a pro by now since I've denied the same thing to Raquel and my mom numerous times this week.

I do love Alex; I just don't know how I can have both him and Isaac in my life at the same time.

The sternness in Isaac's eyes softens. "*If* he is, your loyalty the past seven years repaid any debt you think you still owe me, so don't feel obligated to choose between your employer and the man you love."

God—who is this man? How can he read me like this? There have only been three men who've been able to read me so efficiently: my dad, Luca, Alex, and now Isaac.

My voice cracks when I murmur, "Even if I do love him, it doesn't make a difference. He lost my trust. He can never get that back."

"Hugo once told me—"

My chuckle cuts Isaac off. "Why is everyone suddenly taking advice from Hugo?"

I love Hugo—*as much as any little sis loves her big brother*—but you can be assured pigs will fly before I take his advice.

Isaac smirks then shrugs. "It was good advice."

The mirth in his tone thins the tension hanging thickly in the air. Thank god, as it's so potent right now, I feel like I'm being strangled by invisible twine.

After bracing myself for impact, I say, "Alright, hit me with it."

Isaac's smirk enlarges to a full smile. "He said, 'not all mistakes are unfixable. If you work hard enough, even the most broken things can be repaired.'"

I twist my lips but remain quiet. Shockingly, that's good advice. I thought I was broken beyond repair, and Alex fixed me, so maybe there is still hope for us.

No! I made the decision I did because I don't want to force Alex to pick sides. Furthermore, Dane's daughters have been through so much in their short lives; they don't deserve more pain. With a man like Alex at their side, defending and honoring them, I'm certain they'll be saved from additional torment. Although my heart is pained, I've made the right decision.

Now I need Isaac to see sense through the madness.

"She won't accept it, Isaac. Isabelle will never agree to sign that prenup when she notices the terms you have put in there." My eyes stray to the document on his desk.

As Hugo has always believed, Isabelle is one of the good guys. Astonishingly, he voiced a similar opinion about Alex numerous times the past few weeks. I thought he was doing it to ease my guilt, but after seeing Alex with Addi yesterday, I realized I was wrong. Alex is a good guy as well, he just goes about some things the wrong way.

My brows furrow when Isaac replies, "I know."

If he knows Isabelle won't accept his terms, why did he have me draft the prenup as it is?

My confusion clears when Isaac says, "I have *persuasive* techniques I can use to my advantage."

I gag, hoping it will ease the last bit of tension hanging in the air. It does—somewhat.

After snickering at my response, Isaac gets our conversation back on track. "Stop deflecting the topic back to me. Do I need to look for a new lawyer?"

His non-threatening tone keeps me free of worry. It also boosts my ego that's been hiding away the past year. Furthermore, if I remain working for him, Alex will never be forced to choose, and I'll have no chance of reneging on my decision.

"You'll never find anyone as good as me."

"I know." Isaac's quick reply awakens my ego even more. It also reminds me of the pledge I made yesterday, the one where I vowed both he and Alex would live a happy and fulfilled live.

"Regan Myers has never officially worked for *the* Isaac Holt. I don't see why that will change any time in the future." I pause as worry riddles my gut. "If I'm still wanted?"

"Are you sure this is what you want? Because while Alex is investigating me, you can't have a relationship with him."

It kills me, but I nod, understanding his objective. "I understand."

Relief sparks through Isaac's eyes as he moves around his desk to take a seat in his leather chair. "Alright, then let's get down to business." His eagerness shocks me, but not as much as what he says next, "How long does it take to get a marriage license issued?"

I swallow the brick in my throat before locking my dilated eyes with his. "You can't be serious?" When he nods, I squeal. "Why?!"

I love Isabelle, truly I do, but this is insane. They've only been together for a few months, and they're young, so they've got plenty of time to tiptoe toward marriage, kids and awkward family brunches. Alex is the only one allowed to skip the standard courtship routine as he has a family at the ready, waiting for him.

I won't give Isaac the same clemency.

Isaac's wish to race Isabelle down the aisle makes sense when he says, "Our petition to adopt Callie will have more chance of being approved if we're married."

His reply is a hard pill for me to swallow. Not because of the agony on his face, but because the concept of Alex marrying Kristin never entered the equation when I made the decision I did yesterday. All I saw was Addison's devastated face; I didn't consider what steps Alex will need to take to alleviate it. Just thinking about him with Kristin burns—it burns really fucking bad.

"In normal circumstances, that may be true, but this isn't a standard adoption, Isaac." I aim for a professional tone, but it sounds more invidious than anything.

The stabbing pain in my chest doubles when I read the words Isaac isn't saying in his eyes. He's afraid his arrest lost him the chance of securing Callie, but even more than that, he's petrified he's failed Isabelle.

The similarities between his relationship with Isabelle and mine with Alex is shockingly crazy. There's just one difference: Isaac always pulls Isabelle toward him. I always push Alex away. I wonder how different my relationship with Alex could have been if I had Isaac's strength. He had a million reasons to walk away from Isabelle, but he stuck it out, and look at them. They're engaged, living together, and he's aiming to get her down the aisle as soon as possible. If I hadn't seen the hard work he put in, I'd be riddled with jealousy. It also has me wondering if Alex and I could achieve the same results if we put in the same effort?

Realizing I'm backpedaling on hours of deliberating, I get our conversation back on track. "There has to be a way around this, Isaac. We just need to dig deeper."

He slouches into his chair as his fingers rake his hair. "I've tried everything, Regan. I offered Vladimir more money. Suggested I collect Callie instead of having her delivered. Nothing worked." He lifts his eyes to mine, revealing his desperation. "If you have any ideas, my ears are open. I'm willing to give anything a shot—anything at all."

My pulse spikes when an idea I hadn't thought about earlier pops into my head. "Anything?"

Hearing the unease in my tone, Isaac's brow arches. I can see a million thoughts streaming through his eyes, but he only says one: "You want to bring in Alex?"

Breathing heavily, I nod.

THIRTY-FIVE

ALEX

"Are you sure he isn't yours? He looks a lot like you."

I scrub my tired eyes. "He's not my son. I think he's Regan's nephew."

Kristin laughs as if I am an idiot. "Come on, Alex. That's the oldest trick in the book." I attempt to interrupt, to tell her Regan wouldn't lie about something like this, but Kristin continues talking. "Is that her in the photo?"

While absorbing a picture of Regan and a baby who looks remarkably similar to the one I saw months ago, I nod.

"Was that a yes?" Kristin asks with laughter in her tone.

"Yes." My tone is nowhere near as joyful.

Christmas was great. Addi and Isla handled this year's celebration a lot better than they did last year, but my mood is still teetering on an extremely dangerous cliff. I want to pretend all my attitude resides around Isaac and his ability to skirt prosecution for so long, but I've never been fond of lying. This anger involves personal matters, not work, and not all of it centers around Regan.

Let me just say, Kristin is easier handled on her home turf, with her own bed, her own walk-in closet, and her own kitchen. I know the past year has been hard on her, but fuck, tossing her mood swings into the numerous high and lows I'm already juggling was a bad idea.

I stop peering at the photo Kristin sent me when the bell above the entrance door of HQ dings. Isabelle slowly makes her way into my office, her strides as soundless as Regan's contact the past five days. Her steps are so light, she crosses the office floor without a single agent paying her any attention.

When she sneakily opens the top drawer of her desk, I say down the line, "I'll call you back."

Stealing Kristin's chance to reply, I hang up the phone. Feeling the heat of my stare, Isabelle shifts her eyes my way and hesitantly smiles. I don't smile back. I know why she is here, and I'm not happy about it. Isaac has already snatched one woman away from me; I won't let him take another.

After snatching a tattered business card out of her desk, she shoves it in her pocket, then saunters my way. I see nerves work up from her stomach to her throat when I gesture for her to close the door behind her. *This isn't a conversation I want overheard.*

She does as requested before spinning around to face me. She's as frozen as a statue, her lungs working as hard as her fists are balled. After gliding her sweaty hands down her jeans, she takes a seat in the chair opposite mine. Following her lead, I also take my seat.

She swallows numerous times when our eyes lock and hold for several long seconds. Once she has built up the courage, she says, "I'm here to advise of my resignation—"

"Shut up, Isabelle."

Her eyes bulge at the crudeness in my tone. She isn't the only one shocked, but I'm done playing nice. I thought surrounding her with her uncle's files that revealed Isaac's empire was funded in a corrupt, illegal manner would help her see past the mask he wears, that she'd see the real him. If the large diamond on her ring finger is anything to go by, I was horribly mistaken.

When Isabelle attempts to fire an objection, I snarl, "For once, shut up and listen."

Some of the spark I saw in her when we met ignites when she narrows her eyes at my snapped tone. *Good. Bring out the big guns, Isabelle, because you're going to need them.*

"Your resignation from my department has been declined. You signed a contract, and you will fulfill your obligation as stated in that contract." This time my tone comes out as I intended: calm and without anger.

"You'll remain on unpaid leave until you've had time to properly evaluate the situation in full detail. Once you have all the *facts* and you've had the chance to accurately formulate a final decision on your position within my department—without Isaac influencing you —I'll consider accepting your resignation."

Finally realizing where my anger stems from, Isabelle covers her engagement ring with her opposite hand. "Isaac isn't influencing my decisions. I've made my own informed choice, but since I've agreed to become his wife, I can't ethically work for the department that is investigating him. It would be highly immoral of me to do so."

"If you're worried about being immoral, then I highly recommend you remove the blinders you're wearing and take a step back. You're letting your *feelings* for Isaac blind your judgment. Lust and love are two very different things."

Isabelle hits me back just as hard. "Like you'd know the difference."

I take her hit like the man I am. "I'm not the enemy, Isabelle." I cross my arms in front of my chest to hide the rattle her assumption caused them. "The man you're sleeping with is."

She mimics my pose, revealing she's up for a fight. "You don't know him, so your opinion doesn't count."

"And you don't know him either."

Her mouth opens and closes several times before she squeaks out, "I know him."

"Prove it."

She balks at my condescending tone, but she maintains her stern composure. "I'm not falling into your trap. I'm not going to unwittingly incriminate Isaac—"

"So you're admitting he undertakes in criminal activities," I interrupt, hearing what I want to hear.

Isabelle's snapped words bounce off the whitewashed walls of my office. "I didn't say that."

Her determination inspires me, but it is too little, too late. "You didn't need to. The truth is all over your face. You know he is a criminal, just as well as I do."

She snarls, baring teeth. "You're a real piece of work."

She has no fucking idea.

She stands to her feet as rapidly as my anger rises. "First you exploited Regan, a woman who loved you, all to get a fancy glass office, and now you're doing the same thing to me. I'm not as stupid as you think I am, Alex."

My anger boils over from her bringing Regan into a fight she doesn't belong in—*again!*

"Sit down, Isabelle." I strive to keep my voice on the downlow, but many agents' eyes swing my way when it bellows through my office door. "Sit down!" I shout again when she snatches her hideous bag off the floor and races for the door.

She locks her eyes with mine; they're teeming with moisture. "This meeting is over. If you wish to speak to me again, you'll need to go through Brandon, the union representative for our division—"

"Brandon doesn't work for this division of the FBI anymore."

Isabelle's eyes snap to mine faster than I can snap my fingers. "What?"

"Foolish mistakes cause statutory consequences." My warning is more for her than Brandon. He made his bed, and now he's lying in it. She still has time to right her wrongs. "You can't side with criminals and not expect repercussions for your actions."

She shakes her head as disbelief taints her face. "You're making a mistake, Alex. You're so blinded by jealousy, you're not seeing things clearly."

"I'm not the one blinded." I move closer to her. "I'm trying to stop you from making a foolhardy mistake. To get you out of his clutches before you get yourself buried so deep you'll never get out."

"It's too late! I'm already in that deep. I love him, Alex, and nothing you can say will change that."

A deep laugh vibrates my lips before I can stop myself. She has no idea how ridiculous she sounds right now. If she knew what I knew, she wouldn't be thinking this way.

I guess I'll have to spell it out for her. "Isaac is working with Vladimir Popov."

Isabelle freezes as her clutch on my door handle turns deadly. She appears lost, as if she's unsure if she is going or staying.

I help her make the right choice by confessing, "He made an illegal transfer to Vladimir's enterprise for the amount of two point four million dollars."

When she pivots around to face me, she trips over her feet. Her face is as white as a ghost, and her eyes are packed with so much moisture, I'm confident she's seconds from cracking. "Isaac doesn't have any dealings with Vladimir. You must be mistaken."

The pain crossing her face matches mine any time Regan sided with the wrong team, but, positive I'm doing the right thing, I yank open the bottom drawer of my desk and secure a file from inside. I hesitate for a mere second before handing Isabelle the folder. Just like Regan, she deserves to know the truth. Her shaking hands are obvious when she flips open the file to take in the photos inside. I can tell the exact moment she recognizes the man Isaac is seated across from.

"That is Albert Sokolov. He is Vladimir Popov's number two man."

Isabelle nods, acknowledging she heard me before she flips through the photos, only stopping when she arrives at the series of money orders Brandon unearthed weeks ago.

"It took a lot of work tracking their payments through the numerous channels they used. They also kept the transfers under ten thousand dollars to not trigger an alert, but I linked the original transfers from business accounts of Isaac's to an associate of Vladimir's."

I wish I were lying, but it took four sixteen-hour days to match up Isaac's payments with funds deposited into Vladimir's accounts. It was how I kept myself occupied during Regan's latest bout of refusing to take my calls. I guess in a way it was a godsend. I may have stormed over to Regan's apartment and demanded she speak to me if I hadn't kept my head in the game. Considering her father is visiting, long days at the office were best for all involved.

Remaining quiet, Isabelle scans the documents. She takes her time assessing the information, her prolonged gaze revealing she's viewing it through both the eyes of an agent and a woman trapped in a lust trance.

After a few more minutes, she snaps the folder shut before handing it to me. "Thank you for sharing this information with me, but I trust Isaac. He would never hurt me. There has to be something more to this story." Her words are strong, but her voice is anything but.

"Isabelle, don't be foolish. You need to get out of his stranglehold and investigate this more thoroughly." I sigh, grateful my voice is more concerned than angry.

"I will. I'm going to." Isabelle waves her hand around my office. "Just not here." She stops when her words croak.

I give her time to settle herself, but it soon becomes apparent nothing she does will soothe her panic.

"I have to go."

She darts for the door, only stopping when I ask her the question I've been dying to ask for weeks, "Did you know Isaac and Regan kissed?"

Her shoulders roll high before she spins around to face me. "Yes," she answers with a nod.

I freeze, stunned as fuck. *Why isn't she angry?*

"And if you stopped and evaluated the facts like you're requesting me to do, you'd realize why they did it."

Her comment oddly mimics ones I've heard earlier, but since it's coming from a person who was as victimized by their exchange as me, it's a little easier to stomach.

"Isaac isn't a threat to your relationship with Regan, Alex. Only you are. And if you wait too long, you'll lose her, and you'll regret it every day of your life."

After a final glance that is equally sorrowful and angry, she pivots on her heels and exits my office. As she breaks through the glass frosted door of HQ, I slump into my chair. My hand shoots up to the chin I wish was still covered in scruff, as a big clump of wiry hair would have hid the massive tick in my jaw. I'm not mad. I'm more confused than anything. Regan said she kissed Isaac for Isabelle, but how does that make any sense? What benefit would Isabelle get from them playing tonsil hockey?

"I thought you were IA."

My eyes snap to my door so fast, my brain tingles. Regan is standing just outside my office wearing her standard work attire: a tight skirt and a shimmery blouse. Although her shoes aren't as sky-high as the ones she usually dons, they'd still have no trouble gouging out the eye of any man brave enough to give her sass.

I better tread carefully, as her narrowed eyes reveal she heard part of my conversation with Isabelle. Come to think of it, she may have heard all of it. She looks two seconds from cutting out my nuts and boiling them. It's a good look for her; she should wear it more often. I've missed seeing the strong, determined woman I fell in love with. Regan's been so reserved the past few weeks, I was beginning to wonder if I had just lost my best friend.

My hope she is here for personal reasons fly out the window when her shuffle exposes a briefcase I didn't realize she was holding until now.

Noticing the direction of my gaze, she murmurs, "Can I come in?"

Humiliated I was too busy checking her out that I lost my

manners, I stand to my feet and gesture for her to enter. She does, albeit hesitantly.

I wait for her to fill the seat Isabelle just vacated before asking, "What do you mean you thought I was IA?"

A beautiful blush colors her cheeks. It's more an annoyed flush than the uncomfortable heat her blushing face causes to my body. Even irrefutably angry, my body can't help but respond to her closeness.

"Before Isabelle was arrested, she was having issues with a certain member of IA—"

"Theresa?" I fill in.

Regan nods, then growls. Usually, I'd join in, but my veins are still thick with euphoria from seeing Theresa's name on an arrest warrant three days ago. It may be a year later than I would have liked, but Theresa is finally answering the questions she should have been asked years ago.

This kills me to admit, but if it weren't for the information Isaac supplied Ryan with, we may still be chasing our tails. "Theresa shouldn't be a problem for Isabelle anymore."

Regan halfheartedly shrugs. "Maybe not for Isabelle, but I don't see her backing away from my client any time soon." She shimmies her shoulders. "Anyway, back to business."

When her wary eyes stray to mine, I dip my chin, showing I understand she isn't here on a personal matter. She smiles, grateful for my understanding. I really wish she wouldn't, as it has me instantly forgetting work.

My composure is quickly gathered when Regan says, "Because we didn't know who was in the surveillance van, I advised Isaac it wouldn't be wise for him to be seen entering his. . ." she coughs to clear her throat, ". . . *fuck pad* without a woman on his arm."

The remorse in her eyes triples when she stammers out, "The instant our lips brushed, I knew it was you, but by then, it was too late." Her eyes dance between mine. "I know that hurt you to see, but I was trying to keep Isabelle off Theresa's radar. She had done enough damage to Isaac's life, so I did everything in my power to stop her from inflicting more. I swear, at the beginning, I truly thought Theresa was there."

Nodding, I gather a document from my desk drawer. Regan's eyes track my hands when I slide a photo across to her. "What's that?" I see the recognition dawn on her face the instant her question leaves her mouth, so I don't answer her. "That fucking bitch. She was there?"

She picks up the photo Reid printed off the restored servers the morning following my rampage. Although I destroyed their outer shells, the hardware was still good.

"We also uncovered images of Theresa at the gala Isabelle and Brandon attended." My nose screws up. "Amongst other things."

Regan's hand freezes midair as her eyes float to mine. "Other things?"

I give her a look. It should tell her everything she needs to know.

It doesn't. "You have images of Isaac and Izzy fucking in the supply room?!"

"What? No!" My eyes bounce between hers. "They fucked in the supply closet?"

Regan shakes her head while grinning like a Cheshire cat. "No."

Some things never change. She's still the worst liar I know.

"I meant the images of Enrique Popov. Isabelle's brother."

I throw out a bone, hoping Regan will catch it. She does before adding meat to my scarcely covered bone. "We were unaware at the time that Enrique was Isabelle's brother. That didn't come to light until Isaac organized his extradition to Russia."

Her reply ends days of speculation, but I act coy. "Why are you sharing this with me now? You must understand that admitting guilt on behalf of your client is still an admission of guilt."

She twists her lips, revealing she isn't buying my threat. She knows I'm full of shit because she is as smart as she is beautiful. "If you want to use the information I told you, go ahead, but I'll forever deny it."

Although I don't like that she is defending Isaac, the gleam in her eyes during our banter helps me see things clearly. She's not choosing Isaac over me. She's doing the job he pays her to do, and she's doing it well.

Regan sits straighter in her chair. "But the real reason I am here is her."

She hands me a recently printed document. My stomach swirls when I take it in. I've seen documents like this before; they were often used in the sex trafficking ring I went undercover in as a rookie. But instead of the photo showing a girl of barely legal age, it has the photo of a child attached. She would be around Addi's age, which is close to four.

"Who is this?"

My eyes lift to Regan when she answers, "Callie Popov. Isabelle's three-year-old sister." She fiddles with the hem of her blouse as she strives to pretend her eyes aren't welling with tears. "Isaac bought her from Vladimir."

My pulse flutters as recognition dawns. "That's what the two—"

"Point four million dollar payment was for? Yes," Regan interrupts.

She hands me a second document. It's an agreement of purchase that shows Isaac was the successful bidder for Callie. The receipt of payment matches the date Isaac's bank account was drained of two point four million dollars. If these documents were handed to me from anyone besides Regan, I would have never believed them. But since they're from her, a woman I know can't lie even when it's for her benefit, I'm more open to their authenticity.

"Isaac isn't who you think he is, Alex."

I want to believe her, but I can't. Isaac killed Dane. He may not have pulled the trigger, but he ordered someone to do it on his behalf.

My brows furrow when Regan slides another document under my nose. It isn't something a woman of her grace would typically possess. It is a photo of a man with a bullet hole between his lifeless eyes.

"That is—"

"Gabriele Francesco," I interrupt. "He was on the FBI hit list for years before he disappeared."

"Did he vanish six years ago?" Regan asks, her tone high. "Right around the time an FBI agent carried his injured partner down a field on his back?"

"You saw that?"

A tear threatens to roll down Regan's cheek when she nods. "Isaac didn't order for Dane to be shot, Alex. He stopped both of you from being killed that night."

I shake my head before I can stop myself. This can't be right. Isaac ordered the hit. He mocked and ridiculed me that night before he tried to end it in the most horrific way.

Ignoring my denial, Regan continues chipping away at my resolve. "You followed the direction our car went; we traveled west. The bullet entered the upper left quadrant of Dane's stomach. That means it was fired from the north."

She waits, giving me time to recall the night I'll never entirely forget. Dane was facing me when he got shot, but that doesn't mean Isaac didn't have a man lying in wait to take us down. He's not stupid. He would never place himself in a predicament he couldn't get out of. That's why he's dodged prosecution for so long. He never stains his hands with the dirt his empire is built upon.

My eyes lift to Regan when she asks, "Why would the shooter stop, Alex? You weren't dead, so he had no reason to back away from his mission."

"Maybe he wasn't after me." My hammering heart echoes in my voice.

Regan's lips tug high, showing I answered the way she hoped I would. "My point exactly. Maybe he was there for Dane."

"Rae. . ." I swallow several times in a row, hoping it will quell my desire to lash out. I don't do well with people accusing Dane of being a rogue agent. He was a good agent, one of the best I had seen.

Before I can tell Regan that, she shares, "Isaac and I escaped

Substanz because an agent helped us. A tall, wide-shouldered, brunette man—"

"Dane wasn't a rogue agent. He wouldn't do that."

Regan continues talking as if I didn't speak. "He told us precisely where to go and what to do when we got there. We had to wave our arms in the air three times. If we did two, he'd shoot us. Four he'd shoot us. We were to only do three."

A horrible taste coats my tongue when my memories jump to Dane approaching me the night Regan fled with Isaac. I waved my hand in the air to request he stand down. I think I did it three times, but I can't testify to that.

A black tunnel swamps me out of nowhere, pushing me into a dark and tormented place. *Am I to blame for Dane's injuries? Am I the reason he is dead?*

"What?" Regan asks upon spotting my bewildered face.

It is the fight of my life to relinquish my words, but I manage— somewhat. "I waved my arm in the air so Dane wouldn't fire at you. I didn't want you to get injured."

"Oh, shit." When I slump into my chair, Regan scoots to the edge of hers. "That's not what I'm saying, Alex. This isn't your fault."

"How can you say that?! I waved my fucking hand in the air. I'm the reason he's dead!"

Regan fiercely shakes her head. "*You* waved *your* hand, so *you* should have been shot."

Too overcome by grief to believe a word she speaks, she races around my desk, plonks her ass in front of me then cups my cheeks.

"Don't you dare," she warns when I try to pull away from her. "This talk is long overdue, and now that it's happening, you're going to listen until I've finished. Do you understand me?" Although she's asking a question, she doesn't wait for me to answer. "You're a good man, Alex Rogers; you're just shit at separating your emotions from the facts. This isn't about blame. It's about stepping back and looking at the evidence how you've been trained. You're an agent—a fucking good one—so start acting like it."

She glares at me, silently daring me to deny her statement. When I don't, she moves back to the briefcase she dumped at my door on the way in. "Henry doesn't like working with the authorities, so it took more than a favor for him to agree to this."

Her words smack me out of my fog. "Henry Gottle? As in, Mob Boss of New York City?"

Regan's spine snaps straight before her eyes stray to me. "How about we just call him Henry?"

My teeth grit. She just admitted she owes a favor to a notorious criminal. I can't let this slide any more than I can let my grief slip away. "Rae—"

"We're not dealing with *that* right now, Alex. We're dealing with *this*."

Blue prints, aerial photos, and evidence that shouldn't be in the hands of a civilian slide across my desk when she dumps a large manila folder on it. Although it's been six years since I've been in the location marked on the maps, I know where it is. The landscape burned into my retina the eight minutes I spent bunkered down in it.

My brows furrow when Regan says, "Perhaps once we've settled your dilemma, you can help me with mine?"

I stare at her, certain she's not asking what I think she is. I can't do this. Even if everything she is saying is true, and Isaac isn't responsible for Dane's death, I can't side with him.

When I tell Regan that, she says, "Why?"

It's one simple question that causes an avalanche of more.

"Because he cares for Isabelle so much, he couldn't sit by and watch her sister be sold into a sex trafficking ring at the age of three? That he was so torn up about Luca's loss in my life, he helped me in a way I'll never be able to repay? Or because he kissed me because his heart would have ripped out of his chest if he didn't comfort Isabelle after a nightmare? Which one is it, Alex?" She toughens her stance by spreading her hands across her hips. "If it is the last, rest assured we're going to have more than words."

I shouldn't laugh. It's a dick move. But you can't see what I'm seeing. Regan is primed and ready to pounce, and although most of her stance is about protecting Isaac, I see the spark that's solely for me, the one that reveals she'll defend me as honorably as she does him. She is so fierce, she's got enough guts to protect us both—if I'm willing to accept that.

After scrubbing the stubble on my chin, I say, "It is my moral obligation to bring criminals to justice."

Regan's lips quirk. "It is, so why aren't you seeking the *real* person responsible for Dane's death?" She lowers her toughened stance, which in turn loosens the tautness on her beautiful face. If only it could do the same thing to the stabbing ache in my chest. "You've spent six years on this case, Alex, so what's a few hours looking at the evidence with a fresh pair of eyes?"

She's right, I'm just fucking scared. What if I discover it was my fault? What if I am the reason Dane got shot? Could I live with that guilt for the rest of my life?

Regan proves she knows me better than anyone when she says, "Your guilt can't get any worse than it already is. You're at the top of the stack, Alex."

She knows this because she too lives her life with guilt. I already take blame for Dane's injury, and nothing will change that, so I have no reason to fear unearthing new evidence.

With that in mind, I lock my eyes with Regan and nod. I'm not siding with a criminal; I'm putting her needs before anyone else's—even my own.

THIRTY-SIX

REGAN

Several pots of coffee later, we've unearthed a lot of new evidence. The rockface Henry's crew removed Gabriele from after he was taken down by the driver of my getaway car was in the direction Alex fired at before he charged down the meadow field. The high caliber weapon had a state-of-the art scope, meaning the shot he fired at Alex's knee was purposeful. He could have killed Alex, but since the head he was hunting was blocked by Alex's broad chest, he maimed him with the hope his fall would make Dane a sitting duck. He failed to factor in Alex's determination, so he had no clue Alex would shelter Dane's body with his own.

Although Gabriele's death was never reported, his "family" held a candlelight vigil at a local parish the week following the incident at Substanz. Isaac has always said Henry is a good man; he just works in the wrong industry. Allowing Gabriele's family to mourn his loss would have put Henry's syndicate at risk, but it was a risk Henry was willing to take so a mother could grieve her son. He's "allegedly" done the same thing many times during his reign.

With numerous cash transactions and a handful of scribbled notes, we discovered the man who directed Isaac and me to the railway tracks was working on behalf of Henry. He appears to have completed many transactions for Henry the prior four years. Much to Alex's dismay, we've yet to unearth his name. I doubt that will hinder Alex long, though. He's determined to bring him to justice. To him, criminals are algae on the bottom of the pond, but rogue agents are even more perverse than that.

My eyes cease scanning bank reports from Substanz when Alex hands me a sheet of paper. "What's this?"

My heart rate triples when I realize it is the document Brandon gave me last week when he tried to convince me Isaac was keeping things from Isabelle. It must have slipped into my briefcase by mistake. "Not a part of this investigation."

When I attempt to snatch the document out of Alex's hand, he lifts it out of my reach. "It has the same figure deposited into an account on the same day every month for six years. If that isn't a pay-off, I don't know what is." The accusation in his tone isn't shocking, but it is annoying.

"It's not a pay-off. Isaac doesn't hire hitmen. It's. . ."

My words trail off when I can't find the appropriate thing to call it. Isaac wasn't funding Dane's living expenses because he was guilty of shooting him. He just can't stand the thought of anyone suffering like he did after Ophelia's death. This isn't proof of a wrongdoing. It's testimony that there are still good people in the world. You've just got to dig through a hole heap of shit to find them.

In an instant, the color drains from Alex's face. He rummages through his desk drawer until he finds a checkbook at the bottom. When he spreads it across the document so he can match up the sequence numbers with the account number the deposits were made into, he handles it so roughly, the top check rips.

"They match," Alex announces at the same time I ask why he has a checkbook for Kristin in his drawer.

He swallows numerous times before explaining, "Things have been tough for her since Dane passed. I've been helping her stay ahead." He chuckles, but it is a pained laugh. "That's why I'm driving that piece of shit you saw in the parking lot. I can't keep the girls fed, clothed, and have a nice car. Kids are expensive."

"Kristin's broke?" When Alex nods, I ask, "Then how can she afford a $180 hat, $2000 stilettos, and a coat with fur that cost $200 an ounce wholesale? With markup, you're looking at a very expensive outfit, one I've envied many times the past twenty-four hours."

Alex peers at me, shocked and confused. At first, I assume his surprise centers around my extensive knowledge of clothing, but it doesn't take long to realize that isn't the cause of his hanging jaw. I'm well known for my love of designer babies. It's his shock that I've met Kristin fueling his bewilderment.

"When?" Alex asks, his tone low.

"Yesterday." I peer down at my watch that reveals it is a little after 3 AM. "Well, technically, two days ago now."

"Christmas day?"

I nod. "I saw you with Addi. She's adorable."

A proud sparkle glimmers in Alex's eyes. "She is adorable. . . and a handful."

My giggle softens to a husky purr when he scoots his chair closer to mine. Because we've spent the last several hours working side by side, we're on the same side of his desk. I won't lie; it's been pure torture not responding to the occasional brush of his thigh against mine, much less his hot, virile scent.

"If you saw us, why didn't you come over and say hello?"

My nose screws up. "I didn't want to interrupt." I try to keep jealousy out of my tone. I do a horrible job.

When I return my focus to the documents in front of me, realizing now is not the time for pathetic, childish responses, Alex slides them across his desk. His abruptness is aggressive, but I'd be a liar if I said I didn't love it.

With his hand under my chin and his eyes locked on mine, Alex coerces my attention back to him. "Interrupt what exactly?"

I shrug. "You know. You just seemed cozy, that's all. She really adores you, Alex."

"She does, but that's no reason for you not to be introduced." His oceanic eyes bounce between mine before he asks, "What's the real reason you didn't come over?"

"It was nothing. You were busy—"

"Rae. . ."

Alex's growl is pulse-quickening and delicious, ending any hope of me lying to him. "I didn't want you to feel as though you have to choose between them and me, so I made the decision for you."

"Rae. . ." This growl is softer than his first, more reserved. . . *or is it pleased?* "As much as I wish it were different, I'm not Addison and Isla's father. I cannot replace Dane in their lives. I can support them and care for them, but I will *never* fill his shoes." He stares straight at me, ensuring I can see the honesty in his eyes. "I don't want to fill his shoes. Dane was my best friend, but I have my own dreams I want to conquer." My heart stops beating when he announces, "Dreams that include you. You should have never made the decision for me, Rae, because there was never a choice to make. You've always come first. You'll *always* come first."

My lips quiver when I begin to speak. "Even when every time you look at me, you feel guilt for the part I played in Dane's injury that night?"

"Yes," Alex answers without pause. "Because I know you feel the same thing when you look at me. You'd give anything to have Luca here with you, but then you realize we would have never met if he didn't have his accident, so you're torn."

It feels as if a thousand knives stab into my chest when I nod. I would give anything to go back and fix the mistakes I made that night nine years ago, but if I did that, I'd have to give up Alex. I couldn't do that any more than I wish Luca hadn't lost his life that night. It truly makes me torn.

Alex hurt and betrayed me, but he also loved me in a way I've never experienced. I can't give that up. Just the thought of not experiencing the wonder he made me feel in that extremely short week makes me ill. I'd rather live the next sixty years alone than give up those memories.

In a quick catch, pluck, slide maneuver, I end up seated in Alex's lap. "Alex, don't. We don't have time—"

"Shut up, Rae." His brutish tone shocks me as much as it did when he said the same thing to Isabelle earlier. It also makes me giddy. "For once, shut up and listen, then I'll do the same."

When our eyes collide, the intensity in his gaze secures my devotion, but it is the words he speaks next that wholly captivates it. "For months, we've put everyone else above us—our friends, our careers, our family—but not once have we put ourselves first." His beautifully intense eyes bounce between mine as he says, "That needs to stop."

I nod without a single thought crossing my mind—except that my conversation with Isaac earlier today proves what he is saying is true. We've been so caught up making sure everyone around us is happy, we've let our own happiness float away.

That's not acceptable.

I said weeks ago that I deserve to be happy. I solemnly believe that. And so does Alex. He deserves it as much as me. I just really fucking hope his happiness includes me in some way.

My fears lessen when Alex murmurs, "We can't change our past. What happened, happened, but it will continually haunt us if we let it dictate our future. I want you, Rae. I want you so fucking bad, I'd suffer through all the hurt and humiliation again if you were at the end, waiting for me."

I should hate his words. They should make my skin clammy and my stomach hurl. Stupidly, they have the opposite effect. The sweat dotting my skin has nothing to do with sickness and everything to do with him and the look he's giving me. And the butterflies in my stomach, they're the same ones that forever flutter when I think of those three little words he spoke to me all those months ago.

"I love you."

I peer up at Alex in confusion when the voice from my memories is thicker and more sentimental than I usually recall. The reason for the alteration comes to light when Alex's brimming-with-emotion eyes lock with mine. I didn't hear them wrong. I'm just hearing them again.

"You love me?"

Alex's fingers flex on my hip, pleased I responded to his declaration of love this time around, but disappointed it wasn't with the words he was hoping for.

Although concerned, he mutters, "Yes."

My pulse beeps in my neck when I childishly ask, "Still?"

His smile changes from worried to genuine as he murmurs, "Yes. It will never die, Rae. It is forever and ever." He saves my lip from being mauled by my teeth. "Does that scare you?"

I try to leave him hanging, but my overflowing heart has my head shaking before my brain can shut down its eagerness. "Not as much as it should."

"Why does that sound like you need convincing?" The quick change of his tone from loving to dominant doubles my heart rate, and don't even get me started on the growth in his pants. "Do you need convincing, Rae?"

My libido screams at me to say "yes," but my heart is taking charge tonight. A fire ignites in Alex's eyes when I shake my head, but the thickness in his pants remains even with me rejecting him. I'm not surprised. I can feel the lust burning in my eyes, so I can imagine what he's seeing. If it's as blinding as it feels, I'm seriously worried I've caused permanent damage to his vision.

I lick my dry lips when Alex asks, "Raincheck?"

With my mouth still dry, I nod.

"Alright." He smiles in a way that makes me regret every single decision I made. "Now tell me what these payments are, and I'll listen instead of assuming." He nudges his head to the document we were discussing before our deep and meaningful.

Although I feel guilty I'm allowing my libido to override the seriousness of my visit, it doesn't stop me from saying, "In a minute."

Alex's brows meet when I tilt my head to align our lips. I can feel his confusion, comprehend his unease, but more than anything concrete, I can sense his desire. He needs this as much as me.

"It's time to put ourselves first," I murmur over Alex's mouth a mere second before delving my tongue between his lips.

Our kiss starts slow at first, but the instant I fist his shirt to bring him closer to me, it gains intensity. His fingers brush through my hair as his tongue strokes the roof of my mouth. I groan at the delicious flavors activating every sensory button in my body. He tastes like pure heaven. Manly and rich, but with a slight tang of the grounded beans we've shared numerous times tonight.

He kisses me for several minutes; the pace, timing, and affection of our exchange wholly controlled by him. I would fight him for my share, but the intimacy of our kiss has my need to reign supreme on the backburner. It's nice to be cherished. . . for a change.

When Alex's mouth moves from my lips to my neck, the reins are loosened even more. I'm certain he can feel my heart hammering in my chest, but for once, I don't care. Its frantic, out-of-control pace is his fault, so why shouldn't he relish his triumph? You can be certain I will when I swivel in his lap and his thickened cock brushes my heated core.

He breaks away from my neck long enough to whisper in my ear, "Don't start something you can't finish."

"Who said I was? It's about time your sparkling clean office got a little dirty, Mister Fancy Pants."

Alex's teeth grazing my earlobe makes quick work of the smile he feels raising my cheeks. "Are you laughing at me, Rae?" His warm breath hits every one of my hot buttons, inspiring even more recklessness. "I don't think my ego can sustain the sting."

My smile widens. From what I feel bracing on my thigh, his ego had no problems accepting my smile, but just in case, I'll lessen its burn. "I'm not laughing. I'm smiling. Those are two entirely different things."

Alex pulls back and locks his eyes with mine. His matching grin shows he remembers the night he said those exact words to me.

While using his thumbs to clear the evidence of our kiss from my mouth, his gorgeous blue irises float between mine. My god, they'll be the death of me. They show his trust, devotion, and love, and they're solely focused on me.

My heart does an elongated beat when he murmurs, "God, I fucking missed you, Rae. I don't think I've inhaled an entire breath in over a year."

His words make it hard for me to breathe, so I can imagine how deprived his lungs have been the past year. I've grown a lot the past twelve months; I've grown and matured, cried and hated, but more than anything, I've learned—a lot. The main thing being: love doesn't happen without tragedy.

For months, I thought our relationship was the catastrophe needed for modern day Romeos and Juliets to achieve their Happily Ever Afters. I was wrong. It's the tragedies we've already been through that have brought us together. Luca's death. Dane's injury. Even Alex's investigation into Isaac. All of these events occurred for this. For us. The universe has severely fucked up ways of bringing people together, but maybe Isaac is right, perhaps there is beauty behind every tragedy.

I guess there is only one way to find out.

"Rae. . ." Alex groans as if he's in pain when I clamber off his lap to secure my cell phone from my briefcase. I'm not surprised to discover several unanswered calls and text messages from Isaac. He is as pedantic about staying in contact with his staff as he is about their safety.

Spinning around to face Alex, I raise my finger in the air, requesting a minute. Although his brows furl, he dips his chin, agreeing with my request. Good—because that was the final step I needed to make the decision I am making.

After dialing a known number, I push my phone to my ear. Isaac answers two rings later. "Any news?"

I scan the hundreds of documents spread across Alex's desk, some askew from the passion of our kiss. "We're doing well; made some very important headway." I breathe out to eradicate the nerves playing havoc with my stomach. "We still have a ways to go, but the instant we have anything, I'll make contact."

"Okay. Good." He sounds disappointed, as if he was hoping Alex was the answer to everything. He is; he just doesn't know it yet.

"Once we've got everything settled, we need to talk."

Isaac inhales a sharp breath but remains quiet. I'm not surprised. He knows me well enough to know what I'm about to say next. "I've changed my mind. I can't give him up."

THIRTY-SEVEN

ALEX

I stare at Regan, certain I'm misreading the signals she's putting out. She didn't just do what I thought she did, did she? She didn't pick me over Isaac, did she? Surely not. Our kiss was intense, the most sensual and devoted we've had, but still. *This.* I must be dreaming.

Months of wishes are granted when Regan's gaze floats up from the floor. I know that look. It's the one she gave me when she had her fists up and ready to attack any woman who dared to get within an inch of me. My girl is preparing to fight, but for once, instead of fighting to keep me away, she's fighting to keep me.

It's about fucking time!

I don't know what Isaac replies, but the longer they talk, the more the worry on Regan's face eases. That weakens my shit-eating grin by an inch.

I don't want her to give up a part of who she is for me. I fell in love with every piece of her—frustratingly annoying position and all. She shouldn't have to pick between Isaac and me because we're on two completely separate ends of the spectrum. He's business. I'm personal.

With that in mind, I rise to my feet and make my way to Regan.

She eyes me cautiously, unsure what has caused my chest to swell with determination.

"Alex. . ?"

Her voice trails off when I snatch her cell from her grasp and raise it to my ear. Hearing Isaac wish her the best, minus the conceited sneer I was anticipating, makes what I'm about to do ten times easier.

"What did you say to Col Petretti at the warehouse?" Although I'm asking a question, I continue speaking, blocking Isaac's chance to reply. "Hasty decisions cause unforgiving mistakes?"

Isaac murmurs in confirmation.

"That's what Regan is doing." My eyes stray to Regan's wide gaze. "I appreciate what she's trying to do, and I'll be sure to thank her appropriately later. . ." Isaac makes a gagging noise at the same time Regan's face flushes with heat. ". . .but for now, nothing needs to change. Not a single fucking thing." My last two sentences are more for Regan than Isaac.

When she nods, acknowledging she understands my objective, I return her cell phone to her, press my lips to her temple, then excuse myself from the room so she can continue her call with her client in private.

Thirty minutes later, Regan and I are back at my desk, working side by side on Dane's case. Let me tell you, it's a fucking hard feat not to answer the numerous sneaky glances she's awarding me. I wouldn't hesitate if I could give her and this case the same level of attention.

What I said to her was true. For months, we placed the concerns of those around us before ourselves. Although we're still continuing on that path right now, it's not the same. This case is personal for both Regan and me, so it will do our relationship more good than bad.

For that reason, and solely that reason, we'll continue burning the candle at both ends. The faster we get the answers we're seeking, the faster we can work on *us* with just as much dedication.

When I shift a stack of photos to my right, the cause of our deep and meaningful makes a reappearance. It is the sheet of paper showing the monetary amounts Isaac has "allegedly" placed into Kristin's account each month for over six years.

"What are these again?" I ask Regan, handing the list of transactions to her.

While she explains, I listen as I promised earlier instead of jumping in. Her recollection of the facts is plausible. I know firsthand how badly guilt eats at you, but that's an extremely friendly gesture to grant a stranger, so why would Isaac do it?

When I ask Regan, she discloses, "Isaac dated Ophelia Petretti in college."

"Is that how he was introduced to the underground fight circuit he's been photographed at?" Shock resonates in my tone. I was unaware Isaac had a personal connection with a member of the Petretti family.

Regan's eyelid twitches, but she does a good job of concealing her anger. "No, he was in the industry months before they began dating. That's how he amassed enough capital to buy his first club."

The pride in her tone would usually piss me off. Fortunately, Regan isn't the only one open to new possibilities tonight. My mind is as open and free as my heart.

Regan's voice is barely a whisper when she murmurs, "Like we all do when a loved one dies, Isaac took the blame for her death."

I stare at her in shock. *Ophelia died in a traffic accident. How could that be Isaac's fault?*

Before I can ask, Regan adds on, "That's why Isaac is so generous. Money won't stop anyone from suffering the pain he went through, but it does give them the opportunity to grieve freely." I'm about to jump in with the fact that Dane didn't die, so he had no reason to pay Dane's family, but Regan beats me to the point.

"Although Dane didn't pass, Isaac knew the guilt I felt that night. I think he paid Dane more for my guilt than his own."

I give her hand a squeeze, understanding her guilt for the part we both played that fateful night.

Once the pain fettering her face settles, I attempt to settle some of my confusion. "*If* generosity is the reason Isaac is paying Kristin, why is she hiding his payments?"

Regan shrugs, barely concealing her snarl at my stammer of the word "if."

"I don't know. Maybe she's unaware Isaac continued making payments after Dane's death? Or perhaps she's in more debt than she's let on? Who knows? They're questions only Kristin can answer." Her eyes drop to my watch. "Although I don't think now is a good time to ask them." The hunger in her eyes dulls when she whispers, "It's very late."

"Do you want to call it a night?"

Regan shakes her head before the whole question leaves my mouth. "The faster we unjumble this mess, the faster our focus will shift to Callie."

Fuck. I've been so immersed in Dane's case, I completely forgot the reason for Regan's visit.

"We can focus on Callie now. I've got some contacts I can use in Vegas to get an update on her location and sale."

Regan looks surprised. "You'd do that?"

I nod without thought.

"Why?" Her tone is as high as her brows.

"Why not?" I scan the documents spread across my desk. "Nothing we discover tonight will change the outcome in Dane's case." I return my eyes to Regan, pretending there's no moisture glistening in them. "Callie's life doesn't need to be like Dane's. We can save her from this."

Regan's smile assures there isn't a single law I wouldn't break to keep it on her face. Although I don't ever see me being friends with Isaac, tonight has shown me a different side of him. I thought his dealing with Vladimir was shady, that he was building his empire by banding together with men as equally corrupt and malicious as him, but discovering he bid to secure Isabelle's sister within days of starting a relationship with her makes me wonder if I was wrong. Perhaps he isn't algae sitting on the bottom of the ocean as I once thought. Maybe he is just a shrewd businessman.

The payments he made to Vladimir's account last month were the first he's made. Unlike his known dislike of Col Petretti, there's no evidence Isaac and Vladimir knew each other before this transfer of assets. Add that to Regan's confession that Isaac was dating Col's daughter before her death, and you've got a lot of coincidences erased by facts.

This kills me to admit, but my moral compass is swinging in favor of Isaac at the moment. Only by a fraction, but it's better than the deep steer it's always had toward the other side of the pendulum.

One phone call, and I'm assured Callie is safe and without harm. Although Vladimir is wary of handing her over because of Isaac's recent arrest, he has no intention of cancelling the sale. Isaac is the highest bidder, and once Vladimir is assured the exchange will occur out of the law's eyes, he'll organize Callie's shipment to Ravenshoe. It feels wrong discussing a child as if she is a commodity, but from what Bennett said, this is a regular occurrence in the Popov compound.

"You should probably have someone come and collect Callie. I doubt they'll send one of their guys."

Even though Bennett can't see me, I nod. "Regan said Isaac is willing to do anything. I'm sure he'll have the means to arrange something."

With her ear attached to my phone so she can hear Bennett's reply, Regan says, "Isaac has a private jet at the ready. As soon as they say the word, he'll put it in the air."

A wolf whistle leaves Bennett's lips. "Okay. Then we've just got to wait for Vladimir."

"How long do you think that will be?" I ask.

Bennett sighs. "He's unpredictable. You don't want to know the shit I've uncovered since I joined his sanction."

My heart begins to hammer in my chest. "I thought you were there for his son?"

Boots stomping on concrete sound down the line. "I am, but I can't get to Nikolai without going through Vladimir." Bennett stops talking at the exact moment glass shattering sounds down the line. It is closely followed by someone calling him by his alias: Dok. "I've got to go. Things are tense here since Rico's arrest."

Not giving me the chance to reply, he disconnects our call. My throat works hard to swallow as I hang up the phone. Bennett has always been a little flighty, but it went to an entirely new level tonight. He's either scared or so deeply undercover, his thoughts aren't his own.

"I don't want you or anyone associated with you to do that pickup. It's not safe." When Regan attempts to argue, I press my finger against her lips. "You either agree with my terms or I call this case in."

I wait for the anger in her eyes to dissipate before removing my finger from her mouth. It's barely an inch away before she asks, "Then what's your solution?"

My eyes trail over the documents on my desk as I strive to unearth a suitable solution. Minutes of deliberation point me in one direction. "I'll do the hand-over."

"No!" When I attempt to shush Regan for the second time, she yanks away from me with the strength I've always seen in her. Her fists are up and ready again, except this time, she's fighting against me instead of with me. "No, Alex! You said it was dangerous. I'm not letting you do this." She points to a photo of Isla and Addison on my desk. "Those little girls already lost their dad; don't put them through that again."

She does a good job deflecting her worry onto Addison and Isla, but I know where her panic really stems from. She's petrified for herself, about what she will do if something happened to me.

I try to ease her worry. "I can take care of myself—"

"I don't give a fuck if you're the best marksman there is, you're not doing this!"

I continue talking as if she never spoke, "But I'll take back up with me."

Regan's watering eyes bounce between mine. "Who? Your team of FBI agents? The same agents who are actively pursuing the man you're helping? If that doesn't get you thrown out of the Bureau, Alex, it will have IA riding your ass like an inmate serving life. You're not doing this! I won't let you do this."

I love her protectiveness; so much so, it's the fight of my life not to smash our lips together. The only reason I don't is because I learned a hard lesson the past twelve months about what happens when I sidestep the truth to keep things in order. It fucks them up entirely.

"What if I take Ayden with me?" I suggest, lost on a better idea.

Regan freezes as her eyes drift to mine. She doesn't like my plan, but she's open to my compromise.

Hoping she'll continue to see our negotiation in a favorable light, I stack more wood onto the fire. "He's an agent, a top-ranked marksman during his time at the academy, and just like me, he'd do anything for you."

Regan's lips twitch, but not a word spills from them.

"I'll keep him safe, Rae. I'll never let anything happen to him."

"It's not him I'm worried about," she admits, her voice quivering.

This time when I move for her, she doesn't pull away. I tug her until she is sitting in my lap and her ashen face is burrowed into my chest.

"Don't make me do this, Alex. Please don't make me pick," she begs a short time later, her worry at an all-time high.

I swipe away a tear falling down her cheek before raising her eyes to mine. "You don't have to pick, baby. There's no picking. Just like you've done for Isaac the past year, I'm doing the job I'm paid to do. Furthermore, Callie deserves to have more than just Isaac on her side. Let me give her that."

Regan is shaking so fiercely, if I didn't have my eyes locked on hers, I may have missed her dipping her chin in agreement.

"Yes?" I double-check.

I never thought relief would be the first emotion I'd feel upon agreeing to undertake an illegal activity, but there is no doubt sweet relief is the first thing I feel when Regan nods for the second time.

THIRTY-EIGHT

ALEX

By the time Regan and I exit HQ, the sun is breaking over the horizon. I'm not surprised to notice the owner lot at the back of the Dungeon nightclub is empty. Isaac's Bugatti has rarely been seen zooming through the streets of Ravenshoe during the twilight hours the past two months. He was too busy messing up the sheets with Isabelle to worry about his business adventures. How do I know this? His capital took a hit of three million dollars the last quarter, and that's excluding the secret payments he transferred to Vladimir. At one stage, I was pleased his personal worth took a hit. Now I feel like an ass.

I pace a few steps in front of Regan to open the passenger side door of my car for her. I'm not just being a gentleman. It's a little sticky.

Yeah, right.

As she slides in to sit on the cracked vinyl, I ask, "You said Isaac saved both Dane and me that night at Substanz. What did you mean by that?"

Regan scans the alley to ensure we're alone before asking, "Off the record?"

Once her eyes return to me, I nod.

"Isaac called Henry. He thought it was one of his guys firing at you. Turns out it wasn't." Her teeth graze her lower lip before she stammers out, "Our driver took care of the mark."

Her reply blindsides me. That's not what I expected her to say. *Isaac saved us? What the fuck?*

While jogging around to the driver's seat, I work through the facts. Regan's confession confirms there were two shooters that night, which means the rogue FBI's statement about them not waving their hands in the air could have been in reference to their driver. That would make sense because an arm signal was his means of identifying the people he was there to collect.

If that is the case, who was Gabriele there for? I was out in the open minutes before Dane. If he was there to take down agents in a law enforcement shoot up, why wouldn't he have targeted me? I was a sitting duck. Unless he wasn't there for just anyone. He was waiting for the right man.

I'm so deep in my thoughts, I don't realize I've put on my seatbelt, backed up my car, and started my trip to my apartment until Regan asks, "Have you always worn cufflinks?"

Her voice isn't as rickety as it was when we reached out to Ayden to ask if he could remain stateside until Callie's sale goes through. He was apprehensive until I told him I'll treat it as a proper operation. That saw him coming around.

I drop my eyes to the hideous gift Kristin gave me yesterday. Clearly, she failed to notice I haven't worn the cufflinks she gifted me since the day she gave them to me. "No. They're more annoying than anything, but since they were a gift, I thought I should wear them."

Regan's blond brows bunch. "Someone bought them for you?"

"Yeah, why? Don't like them?" I wink at her, smoothing the grooves on her forehead.

She smiles, taking my comment as I had intended: playfully. "They're alright. Better than your suit." Her snarky remarks cool the heated tension brimming between us—in a good way. "I'm just surprised they were a gift. They're pretty pricy."

"How pricy?" I ask, aware of her extensive knowledge of all things bling.

She takes a moment to appraise the blue frog cufflink she can see before replying, "David Webb cufflinks can go for anywhere between $1500 to $2000 apiece."

I choke on my spit. "Apiece?! As in, one pair could cost as much as $4000?"

With a shrug, she nods.

"Are you sure?" My skyrocketing pulse makes my words as weak as my head.

Regan gives me a look. It's her *don't you dare judge my knowledge of designer babies* look. Once all the color has drained from my cheeks, she asks, "Who gave them to you?"

Jealousy echoes in her tone, but I'm too confused to respond to anything but her question. "Kristin."

My confusion jumps onto Regan's face. "Kristin *gave* them to you?"

I nod again. "Because they didn't look as expensive as the Bulgari ones she gifted me last year, I threw them on. I wouldn't have if I knew how expensive they were."

Regan's brows become lost in her hairline. "Kristin gave you Bulgari cufflinks?" Spotting my nod, she asks in a flurry, "What do they look like?"

My face screws up. It's been over a year since I've seen them, but they had an ugly design I can't forget. "An old coin stuffed into a circular design."

"And they're stamped Bulgari?"

I can't tell if Regan's high tone is in excitement or panic, but it keeps the nods coming.

After her finger punishes her cell, Regan swivels her screen to face me. "Do they look like this?"

She has a photo of my cufflinks displayed on her phone. When I confirm she's located the right pair, she squeals, "They're Monete Antiche cuffs! They cost over seven thousand dollars!"

Her ear-piercing scream causes me to swerve onto the wrong side of the road. Mercifully, I right my wrong before we crash into a delivery truck traveling on the other side—barely! With my heart in my throat, I pull my sedan to the curb. This will be a conversation best held while I'm not driving.

After settling my high heart rate, I accept Regan's phone she's holding out for me. I don't need to authenticate her claim; it is the symbol in the bottom corner of her screen that has my palms slicking with sweat. I saw the same logo earlier today. It was on the photo Kristin sent me when she tried to say Regan's nephew was my son.

Regan eyes me curiously when I dig my phone out of my pocket and fire it up. "Where was this photo taken?" I hand my phone to her. Her teeth grit when she notices it is a picture of her and the baby I am assuming is her nephew. "I didn't take it; it was forwarded to me, but where were you when this was taken?"

I throw an imaginary fist in the air when she believes my excuse without any hesitation crossing her face. "I was at On Point boutique with Raquel. She was looking for a dress for graduation."

"So it's a fancy store?" Her screwed-up nose stops when I finalize my question, "One filled with clothes more expensive than a widow could afford?"

Regan scoffs, "On Point isn't up to my standards, but you can't buy a scarf for under three hundred dollars."

My jaw muscle tightens. "And these? How much do these cost?" I flick my finger over the screen of my phone three times until it displays a photo Kristin sent me two days ago when she and the girls went on a factory shopping tour in Orlando. My bed is covered head to tail with clothes, shoes, and handbags.

Regan purses her lips. "My knowledge doesn't extend to kids' clothing." My sigh stops halfway up my chest when she quickly adds on, "But Kristin's boots. . . I bought those babies three months ago. Even my budget found that purchase hard to swallow."

"So they're expensive?"

Regan rolls her eyes. "Yes. Very much so. Even factory, you're looking at a few thousand."

When I growl, she quickly adds on, "People handle grief differently, Alex. Maybe this is Kristin's way of coping?" She licks her dry lips before forcing out, "It's how I coped."

At first, I assume she is talking about Luca's death. It is only when our eyes collide do I realize I am wrong. She's talking about our separation.

I cup her jaw in my hand before running my thumb over her top lip. "But that's different. You have the means to grieve any way you see fit. Kristin doesn't. But even if she did, this isn't the first time I've noticed a pattern like this."

Regan's brows scrunch, confused as to what I mean.

I ease her bewilderment. "Kristin has lavished me with gifts for years. The expensive cologne you ribbed me for wearing, that was a gift from Kristin. Their wedding was extravagant, way above Dane's means, and their house was built to her very strict specifications. Anything Kristin wanted, Dane gave her."

"What are you saying, Alex? Do you think Dane was rogue?" Nothing but caution rings in Regan's tone.

I shake my head without pause for thought. I knew Dane. He was the goofball who rarely followed the rules, but he'd never bend them so much they'd risk snapping. Kristin, on the other hand. . . she doesn't back down when she wants something. Just the number of women she took down to secure Dane's attention assures I can't mistake this.

"The month before our raid at Substanz, Dane and I had just entered our second year at the Bureau, meaning our life insurance went from a pittance to an amount that would keep our families well taken care of in the event of our deaths." My pulse spikes as horrid thoughts bombard me. "The sniper had plenty of opportunity to take me down, but he didn't." I lick my dry lips, hoping it will ease out my next set of words. "Because he wouldn't take me down if I wasn't his target."

Regan's pupils widen when she deciphers my cryptic reply. "Greed makes people horrible human beings, but this. . . Jesus, Alex. Do you truly think Kristin is capable of this?"

I want to shake my head, but my gut is warning me to remain cautious, to pay careful attention to everything and everyone around me. I thought that was because Isaac's attorney is sitting across from me. Now I'm not so sure.

I raise my eyes to Regan. "Who gave you the printout?"

Her brows pinch when she answers, "Brandon."

"You've had contact with Brandon?" Anger minces up my words. I told him to stay away from her. He'll pay for his stupidity with more than his job this time around.

Regan nods, shakes her head, then nods again. "Not really. I noticed someone had hacked my laptop—*again*. . ." She gives me a suspicious look before finalizing her statement, ". . . so I set up a ruse. It led me to Brandon."

I growl; it's a warning rumble that advises we're going to have a very in-depth talk about her personal security the instant we've finished swimming through the shit surrounding us.

Regan's throat works hard to swallow before she nods. Confident she's accepted my silent raincheck, I dial Brandon's number. He's hesitant to answer. I don't know if the early hour is to blame or the fact our calls always end with me screaming threats at him. My ego wants to say it is the latter, but just like the number of cautions my gut has given me tonight, it's warning me not to be cocky.

Just when I think Brandon will never answer my call, he does. I fire straight into an interrogation, most likely making him wish he didn't answer. "How did you hack into Dane's bank accounts? He didn't leave his shit open for anyone to see. He was pedantic about security."

Brandon inhales a sharp breath. "Good morning to you too, Alex."

He thinks he's smart. It's a pity he failed to notice he's already met his maker.

Regan's eyes snap to mine when I say, "You hacked in like you did Regan's laptop, didn't you? Hung around until you got what you needed?"

"No! I had a search warrant for a *very* valid reason—"

"Dane wasn't rogue!" I snarl, cutting him off.

I hear Brandon suck in several breaths before he murmurs, "I never said he was."

He only says one sentence, but it is the way he expresses it that reveals so much more.

"The warrant was for Kristin?" Surprise echoes in my tone. . .or *is it confirmation?* I honestly don't know. I know Kristin. She was with Dane for nearly a decade before he passed, but how well do you truly know someone you're not sleeping with? Something was obviously going on in Dane's life before he killed himself, but I've yet to discover what it was. Could it be this?

Brandon's deep exhalation answers my question on his behalf.

I harden my stomach before demanding, "Tell me everything you know, Brandon."

"I don't know anything—"

"Tell me everything you fucking know, Brandon!" I scream at the top of my lungs, my anger fraying as suspicion runs rife through my veins. "Or I'll make sure every agency from New York to Burbank knows the real reason you go by an alias."

Brandon remains quiet as he authenticates my threat. He shouldn't second guess me. Just because my computer knowledge isn't as extensive as his doesn't mean I can't find a wolf hiding in sheep's clothing.

Although I am as quiet as Brandon, he must hear something in my quivering breaths, as he sings like a canary two seconds later. "Kristin made a $30,000 payment to Gabriele Francesco two weeks before the FBI's raid on Substanz. It was refunded in full the day following Dane's accident."

My heart sinks into my stomach. "Because the hitman didn't get his mark."

When Brandon makes an agreeing murmur with his lips, I lose my shit. I pound my cell phone into my steering wheel before replacing the crumbled glass and metal with my fists. For years, Kristin watched guilt eat me alive over Dane's injury, but not once did she attempt to ease my pain—because she was too busy squeezing me of every drop of remorse before her draining efforts moved to my bank account.

That fucking bitch!

After a few big breaths to calm myself, I lean over and latch Regan's seatbelt before securing my own. She peers at me, shocked that even during my darkest hour, she still comes first. She shouldn't be shocked. She'll always come first. I just hope I still have the opportunity after wringing Kristin's neck.

With Ravenshoe residents relishing the holiday season, traffic is light, meaning I make it to my apartment in under four minutes. The trip usually takes me ten. Regan didn't speak the whole time. Well, I'm assuming that's the case. I'm so deeply burrowed in a dark, dangerous hole, I don't hear anything but the last words Dane spoke to me. He was distant and withdrawn the last two times we spoke, but his tone was always high with suspicion. I thought that centered around Regan's stalker case, but maybe it wasn't that. Perhaps he was suspicious of Kristin? He lived with her 24/7, so he'd know her better than anyone.

When I pull into the front of my apartment building, I swing my eyes to Regan. She has her hand curled around the door handle, preparing to exit.

"No." I yank her back into her seat. "I don't know how Kristin will react to me confronting her, so you're not coming in with me."

Any rebuttal Regan is planning to give is pushed aside for a groan when I unlatch my handcuffs from my waist and loop one around her shuddering wrist before securing the other end to my steering wheel.

"Are you kidding me?! You can't detain me! I'm not a criminal!"

Regan's volume intensifies with each word she speaks, ensuring I can hear her as I race through the rickety gate at the front of my apartment building. "Alex! Come back!"

Although I hate degrading her like this, I'm grateful for my stubbornness when I enter my apartment. Dane must have told Kristin about my trick of hiding things inside frosting tins because she doesn't just have Regan's cracked cell phone in her hand, she also has her gun.

THIRTY-NINE

REGAN

"Alex!"

The number of times I've screamed his name the past ten minutes has left my throat raw and scratchy. I can't believe he did this. I'm not some defenseless woman in need of saving. I can take care of myself. *And him.*

God—if Kristin can organize a hit on her husband, who's to say what she'll do to Alex when he confronts her? I know Alex can take care of himself, but he's not from wealth, so he has no clue how insane money makes people. If they think they're losing it, they'll do anything to keep it, anything at all. *They'll even kill for it.*

I scream Alex's name another three times before I slump into my seat, defeated. When tears threaten to spill, I bite the inside of my cheek. *Now is not the time for crying. I'm stronger than this.*

As anger overtakes my panic, a brilliant idea rolls through my mind. I send my thanks to the yoga gods when an awkward stretch helps me secure a piece of the shattered metal Alex left discarded on the floor after demolishing his phone in a fit of rage. It takes me jabbing the metal shard into the handcuffs' hole three times before it submits to my silent pleas. I'm shaking uncontrollably, my body shutting down with both exhaustion and panic.

Considering the circumstances, I should be ashamed to admit this isn't the first time I've broken out of a set of cuffs, but I'm not. If I wasn't someone known for sexual exploration, Alex's cuffs wouldn't be popping off my wrist with a quick jab, jiggle, pop routine.

Yes! Now I need to arm myself.

I search in all the standard holes most uncover cops hide their spare gun: the glove compartment, under the seat, and the sun visor. My search comes up empty. Recalling Alex's comment about hiding valuable items in plain sight, I scan his car for the second time. He has a gym bag full of sweaty clothes dumped in the back seat, some old newspapers under my feet, and an empty box of Belvita sandwich biscuits.

You'd think my first thought would be the gym bag or the newspapers, but they're not obvious enough, so I head straight for the empty biscuit box. *Bingo.*

My heart rate climbs astronomically when a gun similar to the one Alex taught me to fire drops into my lap. Its safety is on, but dread still thickens my veins. I learned a lot that day at the range. My most valuable lesson: I'm not a fan of guns.

With that in mind, I take a few seconds to calm my nerves. *Maybe Kristin will come willingly, and I won't need to rush in and save Alex?*

Not even two seconds after my stupid thought, my bones jump out of my skin when a cell phone ringing zooms into my ears. It takes me searching Alex's car two times before I realize the noise is coming from me. It's my phone. Because the caller's number is unknown, it doesn't have a customized ringtone like I use for family and friends.

Although now is not the time for chit-chat, my intuition demands I take this call. It's never proven me wrong before, so with a slide of my finger, I press my cell against my ear. "Hello."

"Regan?"

Not immediately recognizing the man's voice, I nod.

He must hear my nonverbal reply. "Is Alex with you?"

"No, he's in his apartment—with Kristin." Usually, my weak voice would piss me off, but I'm too filled with panic to let it bother me today. "Is that you, Brandon?"

"He's with Kristin?" he queries, ignoring my question.

I nod again. "I think?"

"You think or you know?"

I shrug. "I don't know. He cuffed me in his car." Suddenly, a bolt of lightning clears some of the fog in my head. "Why does it bother you if he's with Kristin?"

"Because he didn't let me finish." His reply proves he is Brandon. "Kristin didn't just organize the hit on Dane. She killed him, Regan. She was brought in for questioning this afternoon."

Dread floods me, but I'm hopeful. "Is she still under arrest?"

Brandon exhales deeply. "No. She was released two hours ago."

Fear clutches my throat, but it does nothing to slow me down. I race up the stairwell of Alex's apartment before Brandon can demand me not to, and I barge through his doorway even faster than that.

The horrid thoughts that ran through my head during my thirteen-second sprint come to life when my eyes lock on Alex. His shirt has seeped through with blood, and his eyes are closed. He isn't moving, not even the pool of blood around his mouth is quivering.

"No!" I scream at the top of my lungs, alerting the sleeping residents in Alex's building to the crisis occurring around them.

I swing my arm wildly to the left when a flurry of blonde catches my eye. My breathing comes out in shallow pants when the gun trembling in my hands lines up with a pair of bright blue eyes. It isn't Addison or her mother. It's her big sister, Isla.

"Come here, sweetie, quick, come here," I beg when I hear her mother shouting her name.

"Isla, what did I tell you about hiding?! We need to leave, now! Where are you?!"

I lower my gun to the side, making Isla's pupils narrow before I beg her to follow my request without words. She doesn't know me, but she must trust me. With a sob, she races to my side at the exact moment her mother exits the hallway. Kristin is clutching Addison by the scruff of her shirt, her hold not one I've seen any mother do—and I've seen a lot of shit mothers in my time.

I tug a frozen Isla behind my thigh before raising my gun to her mother's head. "Stay where you are. Police have been called, and they're on their way."

That's a total lie. I'm certain Brandon shouted something about authorities before I threw down my phone, but in my panic, I didn't think to call 911 during my charge to Alex's apartment.

Kristin and Addison's eyes lift to mine at the same time. Kristin smirks when she notices how much I'm shaking; Addison screams. Her screams aren't for me. They are for the man she adores as much as me lying lifeless at my feet.

"Awex!" Addison fights with all her might to get out of her mother's grip. Her loose-fitting winter coat is the only thing that aids in her escape. It slips off her shoulders with a whoosh before she sprints across the room. "Wake up, Awex! Wake up!"

She bangs on Alex's chest, praying for him to rouse in response to the sheer terror in her voice. He doesn't. He remains perfectly still, his heart as uncooperative as mine from witnessing her gut-wrenching display of love.

She loves him nearly as much as I do.

Hoping to ease her pain, I clutch Addison's shirt before hoisting her behind the leg Isla isn't clutching for dear life. Although my hold is as horrid as the one her mother had on her earlier, it is the only option I had to remove her out of harm's way, so I used it.

"Don't you dare!" I shout when Kristin steps forward, hoping her daughters crying behind me will catch me off guard.

She's shit out of luck. Now I'm not just protecting the man I love; I'm defending the two little girls he'd go to hell for. I don't know them, but that won't stop me from protecting them with everything I have. I never understood why Alex defended me at

Substanz all those years ago. Now I do, and I'm going to emulate his grit.

Kristin appears to be staring straight at me, but I know her eyes aren't locked on mine. She's not even focused on her daughters. She wants one of the guns dumped on the kitchen counter a few spaces up from where she's standing. I recognize one of them—it's the Christmas gift Hugo gave me years ago. The other one is unidentifiable, but the silencer screwed on the end makes it obvious it's the reason residents of Alex's building weren't alerted to his distress.

I strengthen my stance when Kristin takes another step forward. "They're my daughters, Regan; you can't just take them."

Although surprised she knows my name, I keep my composure cool. "Don't act like you care about them. You killed their father."

She doesn't attempt to deny my claim. "Because he wanted to take them from me. . . like you're trying to. I'll never let that happen."

"I'm not taking them away from you. I'm *protecting* them from you."

My finger curls around the trigger when she takes another step forward. She smirks at me, stupidly mistaking my determination like many women and men have in my life. It will cost her dearly. I'm not some naïve idiot who'll sit by and watch a man I love be injured and not do anything about it. I'll maim. I'll hurt. *I'll even kill if I have to.*

"Go, leave. I'll let you go." I lock my eyes with Kristin, ensuring she can see the determination in them before saying, "But you're not taking the girls with you." Isla's deep exhalation flutters against my thigh during my last sentence.

Kristin shakes her head. "I'm not leaving without them."

Her deep rumble cautions me to slide off the safety of Alex's gun. "Why? Because they're your ticket to easy street? Tokens in the sympathy game you've been playing on Alex the past fifteen months? It has to stop, Kristin. You can't use people's guilt against them!"

Kristin's composure snaps. She races toward me, snagging the pistol from the kitchen counter in the process. Time slows when I line up my target before pulling back the trigger of my gun. Three pops blast my eardrums. *Bang. Bang. Bang.*

I don't feel the recoil Alex warned of, but the noise is near deafening. My breathing stills to barely a wheeze as my wide eyes take in the scene. Kristin is still standing. She has bullet wounds in her stomach, chest, and right rib, but she's still standing. *How?*

When she raises a shaky hand, the one holding a gun, a fourth pop shatters my eardrums. This one wasn't from me. It came from my side, from the man slumped on the ground unconscious in his own pool of blood. Except he's no longer unconscious. His eyes are open and bloodshot, and he has his service pistol in his hand.

"Awex!" Addison squeals at the same time Kristin's lifeless frame slumps to the ground. She skids to a stop next to Alex as FBI agent after FBI agent swarm his apartment.

FORTY

ALEX

"Sir!" squeals the paramedic treating me when I leap off the gurney and bolt out of the medic van. "A bullet collapsed your lung! You need urgent medical treatment!"

The sharp pain charging from my shoulder to my back dulls to barely a pulse when Regan's frantic search of the half dozen patrol cars, three squad vans, and four ambulances ends upon spotting me.

"Alex." Her hands dart up to cover her loud sob when she spots the wound a thick band of gauze can't conceal.

I push off my feet and race to her, reaching her in under a second. She thumps my chest with her fist three times before her tears soothe the sting of her hit. "You just lost any chance you had of introducing handcuffs into our bedroom. We are never doing that. I don't care how much you beg."

I cough up half a lung while laughing. I shouldn't laugh, but when forced between chuckling and jumping into the air, I chose the one less likely to cause me more pain. She said "our" and "we" in the same statement. If that isn't something to celebrate, I don't know what is.

Although I have a thousand better ways we could celebrate

running through my mind, I keep my thoughts focused—barely. "Where are the girls?"

Regan spins me until I'm facing the paramedic glaring at me before replying, "They're okay. They're with Carly." She stops studying every gingerly step I take to raise her watering eyes to mine. "You could have mentioned Carly was gay, then I wouldn't have spent the last year and a half wondering if you two were getting freaky."

I laugh for the second time. It's not a smart move. I'm working with half a lung, and before Regan got here, half a heart. I can barely stand, much less chuckle over the jealousy lining her face.

The instant the life was snuffed from Kristin's eyes, I knew Regan was safe, but with no one giving me an update on how she was doing mentally, I was riddled with panic. She fired at a living target; that's vastly different than a paper silhouette.

Although I'm confident it was my bullet that ultimately killed Kristin, Regan still shot her. She may have even killed her if the loud ricochets of her gun hadn't filled me with enough adrenaline to draw me back to consciousness.

After climbing the stairs at the back of an ambulance, I shift my torso to face Regan. Other than her cheeks being a little pale, and the vein in her neck working overtime, she looks okay. But just in case, I ask her if she is.

She assists me onto the gurney I fled mere seconds ago before answering, "I'm okay." Her shoulders deflate when she exhales deeply. I grow panicked she lied until she asks, "Did they tell you?"

I extract the rest of her question from her eyes before asking one of my own: "About Kristin killing Dane?"

When remorse clouds Regan's beautiful green irises, I nod. In all honesty, I'm still in shock. I guess I shouldn't be. Unlike everyone around him, Dane didn't see his disability as a disability. It frustrated him, and he would have given anything to go back to the way he was, but he barely stayed down for a minute. It was only those who should have been rallying around him instead of mourning the loss of his legs responsible for the negativity surrounding his injury. If I had done that instead of hiding from him because I hated the guilt I felt every time I saw him, I may have caught on sooner to what Kristin was doing.

"Brandon gave me an update while you gave your statement." My last word comes out in a hiss from the paramedic's chubby fingers poking my wound.

The pain in my eyes has nothing on the hurt reflecting in Regan's hooded gaze. If I didn't know her as well as I do, I'd confuse her concern as worry for me. It's a pity for all involved, I know my girl better than anyone.

"What is it?"

Regan waves off my question as if I'm being silly. I'm not willing to back down so easily. Ignoring questions that need answering hasn't gotten me anywhere fast the past six years, so I'm not interested in walking that same worn track.

"Rae. . ."

Growling her name works every damn time, and I fucking love it. Her eyes snap to mine in less than a nanosecond, and her little vein works even harder. She's not scared, though. She's turned on.

I ask again, "What is it?"

Her chest rises three times before she rushes out in a breath, "I think Isla witnessed Dane's death."

"What?" I ask, certain I heard her wrong.

"She trusted a stranger over her mom, Alex. And she didn't freeze or clam up when I accused Kristin of murdering Dane." The moisture in her eyes doubles. "She wouldn't do that unless she already knew. I think that's the reason she's a little funny with you. She thought scaring you away would protect you." Her lips pop into the corner of her mouth. "I once thought the same thing."

"Once?" I seek her gaze. When I get it, I ask, "So you don't anymore?"

She waits long enough I forget the paramedic is jabbing me with a needle—because all I can feel is a knife piercing my heart—before shaking her head.

I exhale loudly, forcefully pushing the invisible knife away from both me and my heart. I fucking knew she wanted *this* as much as me.

After taking a few moments to calm my erratic heart rate from both her confession about Isla and her pledge of not pushing me away, I hold out my hand palm side up. Months of frustrated tension leave me in an instant when Regan accepts it in under a second.

While tracking my thumb over her frantic pulse, I say, "I'll arrange for someone to talk to Isla. She's so strong, she'll get through this, Rae. I have no doubt of that." *Because she's as brave as you.*

Regan locks her eyes with mine, knowing there's more. She's right.

"Perhaps you could talk to someone as well?" When she attempts to flee, I tighten my grip on her hand. "There's no shame seeking help about what happened today. You're an attorney, not a special agent. But even if you were, I'd still order you a psych workup. It doesn't matter who you are in this industry, if you fire your gun, you get time with the shrink."

"Okay."

I balk, stunned at how quickly she submitted. This isn't like Regan at all. She must be more panicked than she's letting on.

The reason for her quick agreement comes to light when she says, "We'll do joint sessions."

"What?! I'm not going to a shrink." I hear my words twice when they bounce off the medic walls before returning to echo in my ears.

Regan leans forward, bringing her nose to within touching distance of mine. "What's good for one is good for all, Mister Fancy Pants."

My shock at her licking the tip of my nose frees her hand from mine. With a grin that shows she'll make me uphold my pledge, she exits the medic truck. "I'll call Dr. Avery en route to the hospital. I hope the Bureau pays well for a bullet wound, Alex, as her services don't come cheap."

"Rae. . ."

I growl when my attempt to chase her down for the second time is foiled by the clinking of steel against steel. She's cuffed me to the gurney like a criminal, leaving the real perp free to smirk at me from behind rapidly closing doors.

"Rae!" I rattle the cuffs three times. "You're going to pay for this!"

The fury slicking my veins dampens when Regan replies, "God, I hope so," a mere second before the ambulance doors snap shut.

EPILOGUE
ALEX

I shake my head when a drink menu is tilted my way.

"One whiskey on the rocks, three cokes, and. . ." Isaac shifts his gray eyes to Callie, Isla, and Addison. "Water?"

My chest swells high when they boo his suggestion before screaming the demand they've voiced many times today: "Mickey Mouse milkshakes!"

With a grin, Isaac returns his eyes to the waiter at his side. "And three milkshakes, please."

The waiter jots down our order before snagging the menus from the table and sauntering away. When Isabelle shifts her eyes to Isaac, shocked by how Callie, Isla, and Addison have been bouncing off the wall the past ten hours, Isaac shrugs.

"I tried. They didn't want water."

I chuckle—*inwardly*. I'd never let Isaac think I like him by laughing for real.

Alright, I'll give credit where credit is due. Things between Isaac and Vladimir were as Regan stated twelve months ago. Their one-time deal had nothing to do with shady operations and everything to do with Callie.

Although I suffered a bullet compliments of Kristin's surprise attack, against doctor's orders, I traveled with Ayden to Las Vegas to secure Callie a little over eleven months ago—although Isaac will never be aware of that. I asked Regan not to mention it to him. I don't know why. Probably because I don't want him to think he owes me anything. I've also never been overly good at admitting I'm wrong.

My disdain for Isaac will always remain—it's a macho, alpha thing I can't explain—but the FBI's investigation into his empire is now closed. Although Regan would have handled my absence with the strength I saw in her the day my eyes landed on her, I'm pleased to say my crew's focus didn't shift far from Ravenshoe. Now instead of being based out of an office building across from Isaac and Regan's nightclub, we're smack dab in the middle of Hopeton—an easy forty miles from Regan's penthouse. Not that commuting matters since we live in a three-bedroom shack in the burbs.

I really shouldn't say shack. Our house might be one fourth the size of Regan's penthouse, but its decked out with the latest and greatest gadgets, TVs, and furniture that make my eyes burn from looking at the price tag. Although my living conditions have had a massive upgrade since Regan joined my life, the portion of my closet not filled by her "designer babies" still house my despised JC Penney suits and five-dollar ties. They say the smell makes a man, not his outfit, so I'm testing a theory—much to Regan's dismay.

I stop watching Isla twirl with Regan when the waiter sets down an ice cold glass of Coca-Cola in front of me. Isla has really come out of her shell the past week. I'd like to take credit for her blossoming personality, but I'm sure Regan has more to do with it than me.

What Regan suspected last year was true. Isla witnessed what her mother had done to her father. Thankfully, it wasn't in person. With Dane's suspicions growing, he started a video journal two months before his death. He talked about everything and anything: the love he had for his girls, his physical therapy, and how Kristin had started excluding him from family events a few months prior to his death. She even went as far as moving the dining table to a room he couldn't access in his wheelchair so he could no longer join them for dinner.

That last part utterly gutted me.

Dane loved his girls, so to have them taken away from him like that while still living under the same roof would have been horrible for him. I wish he would have spoken up. I understand he thought most of Kristin's anger resided around his inability to take care of her as he once did, but I would have assured him that wasn't the case. It is unfortunate Dane's pride stopped him from doing that. It is also what got him killed.

He discovered the bank account Isaac had been depositing funds into. He confronted Kristin about it and demanded an explanation on how she could blow over five million dollars on shoes, dresses, and handbags.

She killed him that afternoon.

It wasn't hard. Even after being told there was no hope, Dane constantly strived to regain the use of his legs, but it was his inability to stand that made it easy for Kristin to murder him. She didn't even need to hoist him from the ground. All she did was push him out of his chair. His frail legs did the rest.

When Brandon went digging for evidence with the hope it would show Isabelle Isaac wasn't who she thought he was, he didn't just unlock secrets Isaac wasn't aware of; he opened a treasure trove of horrible memories, the main one being Dane's video journals. He was in the process of uploading a new entry when Kristin caught him unaware. I struggled to watch his fight for life, so I can imagine how hard it was for Isla.

The only good thing that came from Dane's video evidence was proof he was never rogue. There were many times when Kristin whispered in his ear, encouraging him to take the payments men in our industry are regularly offered, but not once did he. He upheld his dignity even when his wife told him she hated him for it. Not even Theresa's guarantee of unlimited work swayed his moral pendulum.

I am so fucking proud to call him my friend.

I'm drawn from my thoughts when Isaac asks, "Are you on the job?"

I shake my head.

"Then why no alcohol?"

"It's never interested me," I answer with a shrug. "Haven't touched a drop since my college days. I prefer my thoughts uncorrupted."

Isaac's lips lift against his frosty glass. It's not his usual pompous, egotistical grin. It's more arrogant than that.

"What?"

His smirk grows, happy I took his bait hook, line, and sinker.

"Nothing."

Unwilling to back down without a fight, I ask, "Was it the uncorrupted part of my statement? I'm not rogue. I don't care how much money is thrown at me. I'll never be on the Petretti payroll."

"It has nothing to do with that." Isaac's flat tone strengthens the honesty of his statement.

I scoot to the edge of my chair. "Then what is it?"

"Nothing major. . . It was just your statement about not touching alcohol since your college days." The laugh his sentence is delivered with pisses me off more than it entertains me.

I scrub at the twelve months of growth on my chin, my beard the thickest it's ever been. "What's funny about that? It's true."

Isaac sprays the table with malt-colored liquid when his whiskey leaves his mouth along with a chuckle.

"What the fuck are you talking about?"

I lift my glass of coke to my nose and inhale a large whiff to make sure he didn't slip something into my drink when I wasn't looking. Regan's brilliant plan of sharing our family vacation to Disney World with Isaac and Isabelle to settle the dust between us is five seconds from flying out the window when Isaac laughs even louder.

That punch-up I craved last year is about to come true. Except, I'm not on the clock this week, meaning I can hit first. The only reason I haven't is because I don't want to ruin the girls' vacation. I only see them four times a year when Dane's parents relinquish them from their "overly gooey parenting," as Regan likes to call it, so I don't want to waste a second. Especially on a man as undeserving as Isaac.

After smiling at Regan to assure her the strain on my face isn't what she's reading, I slump deeper into my chair. "If I find out you spiked my drink, I'll suffocate you in your sleep."

Isaac laughs, more amused by my threat than worried. *Stupid bastard.*

My eyes rocket to his when he murmurs under his breath, "It's not me you should be worried about." With a cocky wink, his eyes drift to Regan. She's still watching our exchange behind lowered lashes, like she's got something to hide.

I work my jaw side to side. "Can you watch the girls for ten minutes?"

Isaac arches his brow. "I can give you some pointers if you only need ten minutes."

The tick in my jaw slackens. *I walked straight into that one.* "Rest assured, I don't need more than ten minutes. . ." My eyes stray to his. They hold the same egotistical edge they always carry. ". . . not to spank the sass out of my girl."

Isaac's smirk turns into a genuine smile. "Take all the time you need."

After he downs the half a shot of whiskey left in the bottom of his glass, I stand to my feet and head to Regan. She notices my approach in an instant, her senses shifting up as her eyes scan my brooding frame. She does a good job acting disgusted by the casual tee and plain black shorts I'm wearing, but I see the extra flutter in her neck, the one that says she loves my casual look as much as she does when I'm not wearing a stitch of clothing.

Her frantic pulse grows when I stop to stand in front of her. She's as beautiful as the day I first laid my eyes on her—just as stubborn as well—even more so when I ask, "Did you spike my drink?"

Her eyes snap to Isaac, who is watching our exchange with amusement slashed across his features. I have no doubt that, much like me, he never thought we'd vacation together. But that's not the cause of his wary glance; it's Regan asking, "You told him about that?!"

When Isaac answers Regan with a shrug, she whispers, "Which time?"

"There's been more than once?"

Regan returns her eyes to mine faster than I can snap my fingers. She gives me her innocent, puppy dog look. It isn't a look she can pull off. She's as dark and as dangerous as Isaac; and just like him, she's not ashamed to admit it.

"What? It loosens you up." She drags her eyes down my body in a slow and seductive sweep. "In *all* areas." Her needy tone has my cock swelling so fast it hurts.

The gleaming grin on her face falters the instant her eyes land back on mine. Her breathing shifts to a pant as her lips part for much needed breaths. It's been a year, yet she can still read my every thought.

"We're in public," she warns, thinking it will stop me. "You can't do *that* here."

I take a step closer, popping the invisible bubble I never want between us. "Wanna bet?"

My reply pleases her more than it annoys her, but she acts coy. "What about the girls? They're watching us."

I shift my eyes to the left. Regan is right. All three of them are watching our exchange as eagerly as Isaac and Isabelle. I hesitate in my campaign. It lasts for barely a second. When cheers of encouragement leave Addison and Isla's mouths, my crusade rises to an unprecedented level.

Regan stops snickering at the girls' cat-calls and demands for me to "get her" when she notices the direction of my gaze. Her spine straightens as her *don't take shit from no one* mask slips over her face.

"I could have you arrested for brutality," she warns, stepping back, bracing to run.

I lean in close, ensuring my words are only for her ears. "And I could arrest you for being so goddamn motherfucking sexy, but your wrists are still showing welts from the last time I cuffed you, so I must be patient."

Regan smiles. I really wish she wouldn't. I lost myself to this woman years ago, but she never stops taking. For every day we're together, my love for her grows, which means she steals more of my soul.

Willing to compromise, I suggest, "Tell me what I want to hear, and I'll save your spanking for another day."

Regan's lips brush the shell of my ear when she murmurs, "How about I tell you what you want to hear, and you save my spanking for tonight?" She shifts her eyes to Isaac, narrows them, then says, "When we're alone because Isaac is watching the girls as payment for his *snitching* ways."

Isaac's brows furrow as if disgusted by the thought of having three girls under the age of eight in his care, but something Isabelle whispers in his ear quickly changes his mind. I don't care what Isabelle whispered to him, because when Regan's glistening eyes return to mine, I don't have a single fucking care in the world.

Right here, right now, nothing but hearing the six little words she's about to whisper matters.

"I love you, Mister Fancy Pants."

The end!

The Next Book in the Enigma Series is the Enigma Wedding

Love what you've read? Join my facebook page to keep updated.
www.facebook.com/authorshandi

. . .

Join my READER's group to get Nikolai updates:

https://www.facebook.com/groups/1740600836169853/

Hunter, Hugo, Hawke, Ryan, Cormack, Rico & Brax stories have already been released, but Brandon, Regan and all the other great characters of Ravenshoe will be getting their own stories at some point during 2019.

Join my newsletter to remain informed:

subscribepage.com/authorshandi

If you enjoyed this book - please leave a review.

ALSO BY SHANDI BOYES

Perception Series:

Saving Noah

Fighting Jacob

Taming Nick

Redeeming Slater

Saving Emily (*Novella*)

Wrapped up with Rise Up (*Novella - should be read after Bound*)

Enigma:

Enigma of Life

Unraveling an Enigma

Enigma: The Mystery Unmasked

Enigma: The Final Chapter

Beneath the Secrets

Beneath the Sheets

Spy Thy Neighbor

The Opposite Effect

I Married a Mob Boss

Second Shot

The Way We Are

The Way We Were

Sugar and Spice

Lady in Waiting

Man in Queue

Couple on Hold

Enigma: The Wedding

Silent Vigilante

Bound Series:

Chains

Links

Bound

Restrained

Psycho

Russian Mob Chronicles:

Nikolai: A Mafia Prince Romance

Nikolai: Taking Back What's Mine

Nikolai: What's Left of Me

Nikolai: Mine to Protect

Asher: My Russian Revenge

Nikolai: Through the Devil's Eyes

RomCom Standalones:

Just Playin'

The Drop Zone

Ain't Happenin'

Christmas Trio

Falling for a Stranger

Coming Soon:

Skitzo

Trey

Made in United States
Orlando, FL
27 January 2023

29111822R00173